# PRAISE FOR *THE KUDZ*



"A handsome devil pays a call to a community in North Carolina, and in this funny and moving novel by Mimi Herman, we see the result. *The Kudzu Queen* is about beauty, and familial love, and what we may owe to our friends and neighbors. This novel has both sweetness and suspense, and its cast of characters will stay in your memory long after you have closed this wonderful book."

—Charles Baxter, PEN/Malamud Award winner, National Book Award finalist, and author of *The Sun Collective*

"Mimi Herman's novel is absorbing, nuanced, and as layered as the characters who inhabit it. In equal measure of grace and seemingly effortless narration, the beautifully drawn compelling characters of *The Kudzu Queen* are captivating voices reconciling the tensions between belonging, entrapment, grief, self-doubt, forgiveness, and redemption."

–Jaki Shelton Green, North Carolina Poet Laureate

"*The Kudzu Queen*, Mimi Herman's lively novel, chronicles the history of the prolific Southern vine while also introducing the wonderful character, Mattie Watson, and her family and community. People often joke about kudzu climbing and concealing everything, but in Mimi Herman's capable storytelling, it is just the opposite; she uncovers all that divides humans as well as what binds them together."

—Jill McCorkle, *New York Times* bestselling author of *Life After Life*

"Mimi Herman's delightful new novel *The Kudzu Queen* is as entertaining as it is thought-provoking, filled with smart and subtle observations about race, gender, class, and power. And Herman's spunky 15-year-old heroine, Mattie Lee Watson, is irresistible, with a sense of justice as great as her sense of humor."

–Helen Fremont, award-winning author of *The Escape Artist*

# THE KUDZU QUEEN

Mimi Herman

Regal House Publishing

Published by
Regal House Publishing, LLC
Raleigh, NC 27605


ISBN -13 (paperback): 9781646033102
ISBN -13 (epub): 9781646033119
Library of Congress Control Number: 2022935701



Excerpt from *The Tale of Peter Rabbit* by Beatrix Potter
Published by Frederick Warne & Co. Ltd

Regal House Publishing, LLC
https://regalhousepublishing.com



Printed in the United States of America

For John

# 1

You could tell Mr. James T. Cullowee was something from the moment he drove into Pinesboro in his shiny green Chevy truck. He was a man, not like the boys I knew, with their skinny chests and spotty faces.

That morning, the first Saturday of April, 1941, my mother was shopping with the rest of the mothers in Aronson's grocery. Every county needs a seat, a place to settle when it gets tired of expanding in all directions, but from what my mama told me, it only took a decade after Pinesboro was incorporated for the townspeople and farmers of Cooper County to start believing they'd emerged from different species. The town folk saw us as inbred idiots up to our ankles in cow manure, while we thought they were helpless do-nothings with an allergy to work. However, despite our differences, the whole county poured into town like grain from a feed sack every Saturday for groceries and gossip.

My father, as always, couldn't be found where Mama had left him, sitting on the front porch of the feed store, taking a chaw with the other men. He'd wandered into the hardware store next door, where he stalked the cool dark aisles, picking up a handful of fourpenny nails in one aisle, #10 wood screws in the next, letting them sift back into the barrels as he worked out a new project—a fence to keep deer away from Mama's vegetable garden or a pulley system to lower birdfeeders for easier refilling. He was always thinking of a way to solve a hindrance before it became a problem.

Joey, my little brother, played pick-up baseball with his friends in the field behind the drugstore, while our big brother Danny, who was heading off to Ag School in Raleigh come September to learn scientific methods of farming, pitched for both teams. Little girls crowded the sidewalk playing jacks and hopscotch, and bigger girls, country girls like me and town girls from my high school, stood under shop awnings, comparing dresses and discussing boys. I sat with my best friend Lynnette Johnson on the granite high school steps, watching the town swirl around us like the Cooper River in spring flood.

When the Kudzu King parked in front of the feed store and stepped out onto the running board, everything came to a stop. Mothers paused mid-sentence, men's tobacco spit splattered silently in Pepsi-Cola bottles, little girls froze in their reach for scattered jacks, and Danny's next pitch seemed to hang suspended in a long curve to home plate.

The doors on the truck read: "Mr. James T. Cullowee, The Kudzu King," but you had only to look at him to know he was royalty. Imagine that, a man in a suit and tie when it wasn't a Sunday, wedding, or funeral. And such a man, with golden hair like the Greek gods we'd studied in junior high. His suit was the forget-me-not blue of his eyes, his white shirt so bright you had to squint to look at him. As for his tie, you couldn't tell if he'd chosen that green to match his truck or had the truck painted to go with his tie.

He vaulted over the side rail and stood astride a mountain of leafy cuttings. "Ladies and gentlemen of Cooper County, my name is James T. Cullowee, and I've come to bring you the crop of the future. More versatile than cotton, more profitable than tobacco, more nutritious than corn—this crop will feed your family and livestock and fill your bank account with cold hard cash."

Boys abandoned their baseball game. Mothers stepped out from the grocery doorway in small gatherings of curiosity, while girls, little and big, drew closer. Lynnette and I hopped down from the school steps to stand at the back of the crowd.

"Kudzu, the wonder crop!" He picked up a handful of vines and let them flow like a waterfall from his palm. "It'll grow anywhere you plant it! No plowing, no fertilizer, no weeding, it needs barely a drop of water. Excellent forage for your horses, cattle, and mules, and a ground cover like you've never seen."

The men eased off the feed store porch to the street, where they stood, arms crossed, chaws tucked in their cheeks.

Mr. Cullowee crouched down and offered a piece to a little girl. "Here you go, young lady," he said to her, "and for you, and you—" to the children gathered around the truck.

"Kudzu, the perfect plant! You can jam it. You can jelly it. It'll cure headaches and heart attacks. You can grind it into flour or fry it up as a side dish." He looked each mother in the eye as he handed out his sprigs, though between times he glanced over their heads at the men standing silently on the street.

Like Lynnette and me, most of the high school girls held back, except Glynis Carpentier, a junior with pale skin and black sausage curls who wasn't known for holding anything back. "Step right up, ladies," he told the clutch of girls congregated off to one side. "There's plenty for everyone." Glynis sauntered over, catching the eyes of all the boys and a few men on her way.

I eased in closer. When he handed me a twist of kudzu, his fingers touched mine—and lingered. It was like one of those moments you see in the picture show, when the crowd fades out, leaving a spotlight on the two main characters. Even when another girl took my place, I felt his eyes on me. I walked backward until he spoke to her, then turned and rushed away.

I found Lynnette, who had returned to the school steps. "Don't you want one?" I sat beside her, watching the Kudzu King. Did he look at any other girl as long as he'd looked at me?

"What would I do with it?" She drew up her knees and rested her chin on them, smoothing her skirt over her bare legs.

She had a point. Whether her family lived on "the barrenest land east of the Mississippi," as her father claimed, or whether he was just a bad luck farmer a bit on the lazy side, as my father said, nothing much seemed to grow there. Ever since they'd moved to Cooper County, the Johnson farm had kept Lynnette's family in shoes but not socks.

My daddy owned their land, along with most of the tenant farms down by the river. I suspected he helped them out when they needed it, though he never spoke of it.

"Ladies and gentlemen." Mr. Cullowee stood up, his truck bed still bursting with green sprigs. A few men had ambled over, including my daddy, who'd looked at his piece of kudzu as if trying to decipher it. "As you hold in your hands your very own kudzu cutting, I want to tell you about a special gift for you from the United States government. Uncle Sam is prepared to pay every farmer in America five dollars an acre to plant this magnificent crop. That's not what it will cost you. That's what the government wants to put in your pocket, without asking a thing in return. With this crop, no act of nature can diminish that rich soil you've worked to maintain. Not water, not wind, not even the ravages of time. Friends, our government believes so deeply in the future of kudzu that it is willing to pay you to plant it. And I am here to help make that possible."

Lynnette touched my chin. "Close your mouth, Mattie," she said. "You're gawking."

"But I've never seen—"

"I know," she sighed. "You've never seen a man as handsome as Gary Cooper. You've never seen one as suave as Cary Grant. You've never seen one as—"

"That's not fair, and you know it." I couldn't take my eyes off Mr. James T. Cullowee as he perched on the tailgate. "Not one of them has ever come to Cooper County."

He hiked up his trouser legs, revealing yellow argyle socks and black oxfords so shiny I could have done my hair in their reflection. "I'm afraid I can only stay a few minutes more," he said, his voice low and confidential. "The fine people of Monroe County, Alabama, have asked me to reveal the secrets of kudzu farming, so I'm on my way to lend a hand as they plant their first crop. But in two weeks, I'll be back, to help you get in your own kudzu crop and to assist you in organizing Cooper County's first annual Kudzu Festival.

"Picture this." Mr. Cullowee stood, balancing on his chrome bumper, and spread his arms to encompass Main Street. "Grandstands lining the sidewalks, kudzu vines draped from lampposts. Your high school marching band playing 'Stars and Stripes Forever,' followed by your mayor, the town council, and the fine farmers and businessmen of Cooper County. And the centerpiece of it all: a float full of kudzu, graced by a bevy of breathtaking beauties, one of whom will represent Cooper County as your Kudzu Queen, wearing—" he reached into the mass of leaves and pulled out a green velvet case, opening it to reveal a jeweled crown—"this tiara."

I imagined him placing that tiara on my head, me bowing a little, modestly.

"You plant that little sprig of kudzu I gave you, and by the time I return, you'll be well on your way to a cellar of your own kudzu flower jelly. Even your cows will be thanking me, saying, 'Mm-mmm, how soon can I get some of that delicious kudzu?' It's a cash crop, a miracle crop. Everything you touch will turn to green. It'll make every single one of you—man, woman and child—as rich as Croesus."

He leapt to the ground, and climbed into his truck. "Two short weeks," he said, "and I'll be back." Leaning out the window, he added, "And soon after that, one of you pretty girls will be crowned the Kudzu Queen of Cooper County."

We watched him drive down Main Street, the crowd parting to let him pass. As his truck diminished in the distance, even the dust that rose behind him seemed magical, lightly tinged with green and gleaming with hope. We were going to be the richest county in North Carolina, and one of us, one lucky girl, was going to be a queen.

I stood on the steps beside Lynnette, stupefied, twirling my kudzu stem. But when I saw Lynnette's father glaring at us from across the street, I dropped my hand and glanced sideways to make sure she'd seen him. Mr. Johnson didn't much care for me. He didn't particularly care for anyone, including his own children. When he gave his customary irritated tilt of the head, Lynnette scuttled to the far side of the street to fall in step with her family. Mr. Johnson never wasted a word when an aggravated gesture would do.

Lynnette reached a hand to her little sister Aggie, and held out her free arm for Catherine so their mother could get a better grip on the groceries. Catherine was two and a half, but between

Lynnette and her mother, her feet never touched the ground. Before they got to their old gray sedan, Lynnette held up her hand and Aggie's in a wave. "See you soon," she mouthed silently, so as not to set her father off. Then she climbed in, holding Catherine on her lap. We waved goodbye until they disappeared, as mournfully as if I were sending her off to war.

Lynnette and I had three and a half years of history between us. We'd met on the first day of seventh grade, a day that had begun poorly when I was panicked out of bed by my alarm clock at five. Just because I got to go to school didn't mean the chickens didn't need feeding and the cow didn't have to be milked, my mother informed me every September. Got to go to school, like it was a privilege. Then, when I was milking Sassafras, she kicked the bucket—not died, which would have been all right by me, but actually kicked the bucket—spilling fifteen minutes of hard work. When I came into the house three cups of steaming milk short, my mother knew exactly what had happened, and had the gall to say to me, "Now there's a cow who won't stand to have her teats yanked." Which I wasn't doing. Or not much anyway.

So I was not in the best mood when I waited for the bus on my first day at Cooper River Junior High, and matters got worse when my cream-colored first-day-of-school dress—which I didn't much like anyway, since it made me look even bonier than I already was—got coated with red clay dust, thanks to Mickey Davenport's rusty Ford pick-up and our stupid dirt road.

Then I arrived at school and discovered that nothing I'd learned in elementary had prepared me for junior high. Danny and a few of his friends had tried to tell me, but, being smarter than everyone in the known universe, I hadn't bothered to listen.

Not only was the day divided into class periods between which students flocked like geese from classroom to classroom, but all the girls I'd thought were my friends had miraculously acquired both boyfriends and breasts over the summer—though I'm not sure in which order—and couldn't be bothered with an old flat-chest like me any more. So there I was: friendless, confused, irritated, and on top of that, what had they given me for my first class of the day, before I was even fully awake?

Home Economics.

Now if it'd had the slightest thing to do with real economics, I would have been okay. Math and science had always been a breeze for me. They had facts. Even English was all right, especially when we got to debate. But no, Miss Eleanora Dunne expected me to bake soufflés and sew ruffled aprons. Me, who could burn water. Me, in whose hand a needle was an instrument of accidental but inevitable self-torture.

Of course nobody wanted to be my kitchen buddy. The other girls had probably linked up weeks before, in the middle of summer, planning for this moment, and now marched blithely arm in arm down the row of stoves to pick the ones they'd share for the rest of the semester. My future was clear: I was going to turn into Miss Eleanora Dunne, who'd never married, and who'd devoted her life to making home and hearth in room 207 of Cooper River Junior High.

"Miss Mattie Lee Watson," said Miss Dunne, her voice creaking with rust. "Please stand before Stove 19."

"Vesuvius," that stove was called, though I didn't know that at the time, despite the fact that it was common knowledge. Most of the other girls had heard about the infamous stove from their older sisters—a commodity my parents had shortsightedly neglected to provide me with—which might have been the reason Stove Number 19 was, like me, abandoned.

At that moment, three things happened: the oven door on Number 19 fell open, hitting me sharply on the knee; an anonymous boy, rushing past the classroom window, which had been raised in the frail hope that a cool breeze might chance by, paused in his passage and let a huge fart, a Notre Dame of a fart, a Beethoven's Ninth of a fart; and Lynnette Johnson—soft, skinny, with wispy pale brown hair and green eyes, strewing apologies like milkweed—flustered into class, came to a halt beside the only partnerless person in the room, and closed the oven door.

Everything you need to know about teenage girls you can

learn by spending five minutes in a henhouse, if you dare. The hens huddle together, clacking a lot without saying much. But if one lets on she's different, the rest are liable to peck her to death. The other girls' cafeteria tables were always mysteriously full when I looked for a place to sit, and when they gathered in the halls, planning sleepovers and boy-girl parties, their huddles hushed as I passed, then spilled over with mean laughter. If I planned to survive the henhouse of junior high, and eventually high school, I was going to need an ally. And Lynnette, sweet and innocent as she was, needed one too. There may be better reasons for starting a best friendship, but so far I haven't heard any.

After the Kudzu King's departure that fateful Saturday, I noticed a small commotion to my left and found my brother Joey on his hands and knees, scrambling across the sidewalk.

"Stand up, Joey," I said. "You're embarrassing me."

He stood, which surprised me, since he rarely did anything I said. The clean white shirt Mama had made him wear to town was splotched with green, and he bulged at the belly like a pregnant possum. He'd tied his front shirttails into a pocket that held about eighty kudzu cuttings, leaves spilling onto his feet. "I'm going to be rich, Mattie!" he said. "I'm going to raise my own kudzu crop and be the richest man in the county."

We had a daddy who'd gone to college and a mama who could've, but I sometimes wondered whether Joey had inherited one single iota of their intelligence. He was a powerful argument against genetics. "And how do you plan to tend your kudzu crop and go to school?" I asked. "Last I heard, they weren't letting ten-year-old boys quit school to become farmers."

"You heard the man," Joey said. "It don't take no tending. No fertilizer, no weeding. Just plant it and sit down to count your money."

"*Doesn't* take *any* tending," I said. "And where do you plan to plant this bounty?"

That stumped him for a minute. But then he lit up. "Daddy'll let me use part of a field. I'll tell him I want to learn to be responsible."

"Oh?" I asked. "Do you mean his cornfield? Or his experimental cotton field? Or his tobacco field? Maybe you could just take over Mama's garden?"

"Come on, Mattie." He yanked up his shirtful of kudzu. "Don't be like that. This is my chance to get rich and you're trying to ruin it."

Ruin it, nothing. There was no way I was going to let my little brother make a fortune without me—or worse, waste all that kudzu. He'd shown more brains than usual in gathering it, but he clearly had no idea what to do next. I pulled him under the drugstore awning. "You mean this is *our* chance to get rich," I told him. "What you need is a partner."

"Why should I split anything with you?" he asked, gathering up fallen kudzu stems.

"Because I know where we're going to grow our crop. And I'll help tend it."

He stopped gathering. "Where?"

"Fifty-fifty," I said.

He shook his head. "You're bluffing. You don't know where to plant it any more than I do. Eighty-twenty. And that's only if you do most of the work. And you have to swear not to tell. I don't want anybody stealing my idea."

I tucked my own sprig of kudzu behind my ear like a rose and crossed my heart. "I've got the perfect place, and I'll do half the work. Fifty-fifty. Grab it quick before my price goes up."

With his left hand wrapped around his kudzu haul, Joey stuck out his right. "This better be good."

"Aunt Mary's," I told him, and waited for the idea to take root in his mind.

Aunt Mary had died almost a year before, at the end of April, and left Daddy everything, which came as a great surprise. She'd never seemed to like anyone much, Daddy and us least of all. She was my mother's aunt, sister to our granddaddy, though how they'd come from the same family was a mystery to me. He'd been the sweetest man I ever knew, while she'd been too mean to marry—and almost too mean to die. When she finally did pass, Daddy planted the half-acre between her house and the road with cowpeas to fix the soil, and Mama spent a few days closing up the house. None of us had been there since. Mama and Daddy hadn't yet decided what to do with the house and land: work it, lease it, or give it to Danny when he finished Ag School.

"What about her ghost?" Joey asked, hitching up the sagging kudzu.

"I don't believe in ghosts," I said, though I wasn't entirely sure this was true. "And you don't either."

On the drive home from town, Mama kept her window open just enough to let in a breeze, but not enough to swamp us with dust. Through the crack, she trailed her sprig of kudzu, letting the wind snap at it.

"Aren't you going to plant that, Mama?" I asked from my customary position behind her. I always sat on the right, Danny on the left, and Joey over the hump, because his legs were shortest. That year was a race to see which happened first: Danny going to college, or Joey's legs getting longer than mine, at which point I'd have to sacrifice my prime seat.

"Oh, I don't know," Mama mused. The wind nibbled at the wide leaves, shredding the edges before it finally snapped them off. "I don't have a square inch of space in my garden."

"What about you, Daddy?" Joey asked. Daddy had one hand on the wheel, as he usually did. With the other, he and Mama held hands. Sometimes I thought it was sappy that my parents still held hands, but most of the time I thought it was sweet.

"I think I'll stick with the crops I've got," he answered. "They're doing well enough for us at present."

"Then can I have your kudzu?" Joey asked. "I'm starting a collection." He sat with his knees hunched to his chest and his feet resting lightly on a grocery bag full of kudzu. He'd begged the brown bag off of Miss Hudson, the clerk at Aronson's, who believed Joey was a sweet boy. She didn't know him too well.

"Sorry, Joey, I tossed it out." Daddy glanced at him in the rearview. "What are you planning to do with all that kudzu?"

"Oh, I don't know yet. Maybe take up basket weaving." He should have come up with a better lie. Only old ladies did basket weaving.

"Well, you're welcome to add mine to your collection." Mama extracted her kudzu from the window crack. "Though it may be a bit tattered for a basket."

Through all this, Danny gazed out the window, watching fields move past us at twenty-five miles an hour. He'd taken to doing that lately, quietly watching the things he was leaving, as if he were sipping in everything through his eyes so he could swallow it all once he left home.

"Danny?" Daddy asked. And when he didn't answer right away, "Daniel?"

Danny dredged his eyes from the Cooper River, flowing in its wide bed beyond newly plowed fields. "Sir?"

"You sent in those papers for school yet?" Daddy asked.

Danny nodded, then realized Daddy couldn't see him. "Yes, sir," he said. Of the three of us, he had the best manners. They say no two children are born into the same family, and the eldest is born into a family of adults. That must have been true, because Danny had always been mature for his age. "Daddy?" he asked.

Daddy cocked his head to listen.

"What is it you don't like about kudzu?" Danny leaned forward to hear the answer over the whistling from Mama's window.

"Don't know enough to like it or dislike it." Daddy shifted to see Danny in the mirror. He generally made a point of looking at the person he was talking to, even if it was only us kids.

Sometimes, when we drove home on a Saturday, I'd play a game, closing my eyes as we headed up the gravel drive and opening them once we'd stopped. I'd look at our house as if I'd never seen it, big and white and welcoming, with its wide veranda and swaying porch swing, and fall in love with it all over again. The second story, where we all slept, sat neatly on top of the rooms where we did our daily living: the cool, dark hallway, the bright kitchen, and the dining and sitting rooms Mama managed to keep elegant despite the rest of us, who were all—including Daddy—careless about wiping our feet.

After dinner Mama headed for the kitchen to tidy up and start supper, Daddy out to the pigpen to repair a board the pigs had worked loose. Our sow, Stevie, was always on the verge of bolting for the woods, followed by whatever piglets were currently in residence. Danny went up to his room, I suspected to look for the seventeenth time at the course catalog that had arrived in yesterday's mail. With everyone occupied, Joey and I were able to make a clean getaway with our kudzu haul.

To get to Aunt Mary's land, we had to cut through the woods for about three-quarters of a mile. There wasn't a much of a path, since nobody in our family had ever felt inclined to visit Aunt Mary except on official occasions like Thanksgiving and Easter, when we drove. The road to her property was about three miles longer than the shortcut through the woods. When she was alive, my brothers and I had needed every one of those miles to gird ourselves for a day with her.

Aunt Mary had been prone to criticism. She'd criticized everything from our table manners to the fact that we persisted in growing taller between visits. The last time we'd seen her before she died, even Joey had outdone her by a couple inches, and she'd had plenty to say about children who didn't have the courtesy to remain a normal height. If you spoke a word out of turn, she'd send you to sit on the most uncomfortable chair in the parlor, facing her dead stuffed spaniel, Buster. Which was what happened to Joey last Easter when he'd tried to explain to her, "It's not as if I have a choice in the matter, ma'am."

Joey and I bushwhacked through the woods. He'd found a stick to fend off any copperheads we might come across, so I let him go first. I carried our bucket of kudzu cuttings, full of water and heavy as homegrown sin, Mama's trowel stuck into my skirt waistband.

The walk took just short of forever, with every narrow branch in the woods conspiring to whip me across the face, and the mosquitoes competing with spiderwebs and sweat to see which could aggravate me most. Finally, we emerged into the clearing behind Aunt Mary's garden, which was considerably overgrown with spearmint.

"Let's take some to Mama so she can make tea," Joey said.

"I thought you wanted to keep this a secret," I reminded him. "What exactly do you plan to say when she asks, 'Where'd you get that fine-looking mint, children?'"

The house gave off a pugnacious air, like it was daring you to step over the threshold. I'd been scared enough of Aunt Mary when she was alive. I had no intention of messing with her ghost, if they existed and if she had one.

We edged around the house to the field, which spread from her front porch to the road. Fortunately, nobody drove down this road, since it led nowhere but to Aunt Mary's house. So there was no one to tell on us for what we were about to do. The cowpeas Daddy had planted were thriving, spilling over the edges of the field.

The rest of our family would have sat back in amazement to see Joey and me weeding that day. Every living thing that wasn't a cowpea or an earthworm got yanked out of that field, along with a few rocks that had crept in since the last time Aunt Mary had ordered Joey to clean up her property, a task she'd assigned him after Thanksgiving dinner each year, while everyone else slept off the turkey. As we weeded, we dug out small sections to allow room for our kudzu to grow, leaving most of the cowpeas intact in the hope that Daddy wouldn't notice—at least for a while—if he happened by.

It was heading for dusk when we got the last cutting planted and watered from the pump, one bucket at a time. We gazed over our field, pleased at how artistically we'd woven our kudzu in with the cowpeas so they were perfectly camouflaged.

The upstairs windows of Aunt Mary's house glared yellow in the late afternoon sun, like disapproving eyes. Back in the woods, Joey swept his stick from side to side to discourage snakes as we sprinted home. I scraped branches out of my way and wiped off sweat-drowned mosquitoes, the empty bucket clattering against my leg.

We panted into the yard as Mama stepped onto the porch to call us in for supper. "Where have you been to get yourselves so filthy?" she asked.

Joey and I looked down at our town clothes. If there was a clean spot anywhere on either of us, I couldn't find it. Being older and more experienced, I came up with an explanation before he did. "Out in the woods, building a fort," I confessed. It was a good lie, and I'd been looking for a use for it since the drive home.

"Why do I bother to buy you nice clothes?" she said, barring our entry. "To the pump with both of you. Take off your shoes and socks before you come in this house. I can hardly see if you've still got feet for all that mud."

# 2

Once I'd scrubbed off a layer of skin, I changed into a clean skirt and blouse and presented myself in the kitchen for inspection. Without a word, Mama handed me a cut glass dish of potato salad. My mother had a practical habit of forgiving wrongdoing immediately, as long as you made reparations. I put the potato salad on the table and went back for the chicken. The table had been set, which was my job, but she didn't mention it, so I didn't either.

Daddy and Danny came in, laughing about the piglets' interest in Daddy's repairs. "I think they were casing the joint," Daddy said out of the side of his mouth like Jimmy Cagney, "getting ready to make a break for it." As we bowed our heads for grace, Joey slid into his chair wearing a fresh shirt and trousers. His cheeks were pink from washrag burn.

I waited until we'd finished the meal and were rounding the corner into dessert—banana pudding—before asking if I could spend the night at Lynnette's.

"I suppose so," Mama said, "if it's all right with her mother."

"She doesn't mind," I told her, which wasn't entirely the truth. Lynnette's mother liked me well enough, but worried that I might be a bad influence on Lynnette, with my tendency to act before considering the consequences.

"Have you asked her?" Mama asked, raising an eyebrow.

"Not exactly." I hadn't asked Lynnette either, for that matter, but I generally spent Saturday nights with her any time I could get permission.

"Telephone." My mother pointed to the hallway. "Not now," she said, when I pushed back my chair. "After supper."

"Can I go to church with them too?"

"*May* I." My mother gave her "proper grammar" sigh. She had a sigh for every occasion. "Yes, you may."

My parents were firm on the idea of us getting religion, but flexible about whether we got it with them at First Baptist or elsewhere. Unlike Lynnette's family, who attended Mount Sinai Baptist Church every Sunday morning and Wednesday evening—without the benefit of Mr. Johnson's company—my parents believed once a week was enough for anyone. As far as they were concerned, the Lord probably made an appearance at every church in the world on Sundays—being omnipresent and all—not to mention synagogues and mosques and other places on the days when those folks worshipped. So we could get right with the Lord wherever we happened to pray. This came from my father having been raised Lutheran in Delaware while Mama was a homegrown Baptist who liked to decide things for herself. I'd learned the hard way not to discuss religion outside my family when Taylor Wagner knocked me down on the playground in third grade. All I'd done was claim the Lord probably spent more time with Jewish people than he did with us Christians, since he'd known them longer.

The happy result of my parents' open-mindedness was that I could spend Saturday nights at Lynnette's house and go to Mount Sinai with her the next morning. Saturday nights were better at the Johnsons' than Fridays, when Mr. Johnson drank at home, sitting on the front stoop and getting surlier as the bottle emptied. He'd stumble into the house after midnight, cursing the furniture until Mrs. Johnson rushed downstairs in her long nightgown to soothe him.

"He's going through some hard times," Mrs. Johnson would apologize the next morning.

But Mr. Johnson tended to disappear on Saturdays just before supper, a magic trick for which I was grateful. Sometimes, if Lynnette and I were in her room, I'd catch a glimpse of him through her window, heading for the road, his creased face barely visible under his hat in the gathering darkness. Next time I looked, he'd be gone. Swept up by a passing car, not to reappear until Sunday afternoon.

Most parents in the county thought nothing of taking a

palm to their kids in public or private, but Mr. Johnson could be relied upon to use a closed fist. Meekness riled him more than sass, which meant Mrs. Johnson usually got the worst of it. He seemed to have a soft spot for Aggie, but Catherine irritated him just by existing, though she was the most placid child I'd ever seen, a pure butterball of pleasure. At two and a half, she hadn't learned the word "no." Sometimes he'd yell at Mrs. Johnson for producing three worthless girls, as if she'd done it all by herself.

He'd never hit me. I dreaded the day it occurred to him to do so, not only because I was afraid of his fist. While my parents didn't like the way he treated his wife and children, the one thing that would have brought Daddy tearing over in a towering rage would have been for Mr. Johnson to lay hands on me. If Daddy ever got in a fight with him, I didn't know what would happen. Daddy was stronger and smarter and his reflexes weren't thrown off by whiskey, but Mr. Johnson was sneaky and mean to his wiry bones.

Mama had made me swear up and down that I'd never be alone in a room with Mr. Johnson, a promise I had no trouble keeping. Our preacher said that the Lord loved all his creatures, but if He had the slightest sliver of affection for Mr. Johnson, He was a whole lot more forgiving than I'd ever be. I sincerely doubted that Mr. Johnson had a soul.

After I'd scraped my banana pudding bowl with my finger—and gotten a mind-your-manners look from Mama—I helped my brothers clear the table, to make up for not being around to set it. Then I called Lynnette to tell her I was coming over, crammed my necessities into my mother's old train case, and ran for the door, tossing a "See you after church" over my shoulder.

Mama snagged me before I made it through, divesting me of the overnight case and placing it on the hall table, where she snapped open the latch. "Hmm, just as I thought." She drew out the church dress I'd stuffed under my nightgown and Sunday shoes. "This'll keep the worst of the wrinkles out," she said, shaking out the dress and rolling it up loosely. "Just because you act like a heathen doesn't mean you have to dress like one."

To get to Lynnette's I had to cut through Daddy's newly planted cornfield. Though it was coming on dark, I could still see the paths between rows of seedlings. Our corn was healthy as a football team, but Mr. Johnson's looked like ninety-eight-pound weaklings. I ran through the field, swinging my train case and dreaming of kudzu. What if these fields were filled with kudzu instead of corn? Glorious, healthy kudzu, so green it glowed in the dark. Daddy would see our field and say, "Children, you are agricultural geniuses! You must show me how to grow kudzu that pretty!"

I imagined myself ambling through gleaming rows of kudzu in a white dress, hand in hand with Mr. James T. Cullowee. "Mathilda—" he'd say, with love in his voice, though the only person who usually called me Mathilda was my mother when I'd crossed a line. Then it was "Mathilda Lee Watson?" with an ominous upswing on the last syllable. Anyhow, Mr. Cullowee would say, "Mathilda, you are my muse, my inspiration. How did I ever survive without you?"

Lynnette's house rose up forbiddingly in the dusk, gray paint peeling from the clapboard siding in wide curls, exposing wood almost as gray. Where the second story of our house rested neatly on the first, the Johnsons' seemed to lean like an old dog that wanted to lie down and sleep. The front looked bare, with its cracked concrete stoop instead of a porch, but someone had tacked a sleeping porch onto the back years ago, where it hung lopsidedly.

I found Lynnette darting around the yard with Catherine on her hip, scooping fireflies into a Mason jar and clapping a punched-hole lid on it to keep them inside.

"See?" Lynnette told Catherine. "You sneak behind them while they're busy lighting up, so they don't even know you're there." Catherine stretched her chubby fingers to grab for a firefly, but it flitted from her reach. When they moved into the light, I saw a new bruise on Lynnette's cheek. I knew better than to ask.

She'd just go quiet and it would spoil our whole night. She'd long ago given up telling me how clumsy she was with doors.

Aggie had abandoned her jar in the scrub grass. She stood on a stump, holding out her hands, palms up.

"What's she doing?" I asked Lynnette.

"Shh," she said, putting a finger to Catherine's lips. "Wait."

Aggie was wild, though not the way people usually think of wild things, as in dangerous, liable to attack at the slightest provocation. She was wild the way deer are: wary, standing frozen in shadows to blend into trees, apt to wheel away if startled. You didn't look Aggie in the eye. Even Lynnette rarely did, and only if she wanted to be certain she had Aggie's attention.

A firefly landed on Aggie's left palm, then another on the pad of her right index finger. Aggie held perfectly still.

"Why do they do that?" I whispered.

"I don't know," Lynnette whispered back. "They just do."

Lynnette put the girls to bed with a story, as she did most evenings, while her mother rested from making supper. Though she'd been sick as long as I'd known her, Mrs. Johnson never looked so frail as she did on a Saturday night, when the relief of her husband's temporary absence seemed to open a dam, letting the week's weariness flood into her face.

Tonight, Lynnette told Aggie and Catherine the story of Moses and his big sister Miriam, how Miriam watched from the bulrushes until her baby brother was safe with Pharaoh's daughter. "What's a 'rushes, Lynnie?" Catherine asked, as Lynnette slipped a clean cotton nightgown over her upstretched arms.

"It's a big old water weed you can hide in." Lynnette checked Catherine's diaper pins to make sure they weren't poking.

"Do we got them?" Catherine asked.

"Nope," Lynnette said. "But Mattie's got some by her part of the creek."

"Can I see?" Catherine asked.

"Maybe sometime," Lynnette said, tucking Catherine into her crib, and pulling the quilt up to her chin.

Aggie sat cross-legged on her bed, wearing an old white T-shirt instead of a nightgown. She stretched the bottom of the shirt over her knees and examined the long wrinkles it made.

"Let me see those feet, Miss Aggie," Lynnette said.

Aggie lifted her shirt and poked out her feet for examination.

"What are you doing, putting those filthy things on my clean bedclothes?" Lynnette said, though not crossly. Aggie and dirt were usually seen in conjunction with one another, so Lynnette expected them to keep company. "Get them off the bed this minute while I get a rag."

Aggie braced her arms behind her to lift her feet off the covers. Lynnette returned with a wet washrag and sat on Aggie's bed, swinging her sister's feet onto her lap.

"Cold," Aggie said.

"That's what you get, Miss A.," Lynnette scolded lightly. "If you'd wash your own self before you went to bed, you could make the water as warm as you want."

Once the girls were tucked in, Lynnette and I went down to check on her mother, who lay on the sofa, a damp cloth across her face.

"Aren't you going up to bed, Mama?" Lynnette asked.

"In a minute," her mother said, her breath fluttering the cloth. "Did the girls go down all right?"

When I'd first started sleeping over at Lynnette's, her mother was pregnant with Catherine, and used to apologize to Lynnette all the time. "I wish you didn't have to take on so much," she'd say. Most children had family responsibilities, especially by our age, but with Mrs. Johnson sick, Lynnette took on more than usual. Nobody ever talked about what Mrs. Johnson was sick with, but whatever it was, it left her too weak to do much beyond preparing meals.

"They're fine." Lynnette crouched by the sofa. "Come on, Mama, I'll help you up." Without protestation, Mrs. Johnson wrapped her arms around Lynnette's neck. Lynnette pulled her mother to her feet as if she were no bigger than Catherine, and walked her up the stairs. Mrs. Johnson seemed thinner than she had the week before, the bones of her shoulder blades outlined sharply against the back of her thin housedress.

Usually when I slept over, Lynnette and I stayed up late, talking about boys we liked and teachers we didn't. Lynnette could stretch out the subject of Bobby Mason for a good forty minutes. As far as I was concerned, Bobby Mason had about thirty seconds' worth of interestingness about him, though I had to admit he was nicer than most boys. As for me, I hadn't lit on a boy I liked, so my ramblings tended toward whichever movie star took my fancy. Lately I'd graduated from Errol Flynn to Cary Grant. I was definitely becoming more mature.

That night we drifted toward sleep, lying on our backs in her narrow bed as if we were floating in the ocean, our shoulders touching. The quarter moon lit the dried flowers she'd placed in jars on her bureau. It cast shadows among the few dresses that hung on a wooden dowel strung by wire from the ceiling. I thought of the kudzu Joey and I had planted, and wondered if it had grown yet. I wondered about my promise to Joey. Surely he didn't mean I couldn't tell Lynnette.

"He's pretty, isn't he?" Lynnette asked dreamily, as if she might be talking in her sleep.

"Bobby Mason?" I asked, turning on my side to face her.

"Not him." She lifted an arm to trace spirals in the air with her finger. "The kudzu man. He has pretty hair."

I hadn't realized she'd paid much attention to Mr. Cullowee. I considered all the things I could say, how for the first time I might actually be in love, and that it wasn't what she'd believed it was, my usual movie star crush. But then I thought: No, I want to keep this one thing to myself.

"Uh-huh." I lay back until sleep washed over me, bringing dreams of him in its wake.

Unlike me, Lynnette never had to be told to do her chores. We woke in the muddy morning light, and went out to feed the chickens and collect eggs. In truth, Lynnette fed the chickens and collected eggs, while I admired her work. They were one of the farms that supplied Aronson's grocery with eggs. Mr. Johnson took no part in it, chickens being beneath him.

Lynnette had a way of gentling all animals. She slid the eggs out from under the chickens as deftly as a magician pulling silk scarves from a hat, quieting them with a steady murmur of "cooey-cooey-cooey." I helped milk their two nanny goats, which they kept instead of cows. I wasn't fond of goat's milk, with its rotten hay smell, but I liked Lynnette's sweet nannies. Their big teats made them easier to milk than Sassafras, like using training wheels. They were so patient I sometimes dozed off in the middle of milking.

We washed and dressed for church while Mrs. Johnson made breakfast. Lynnette's church was poorer than ours, but people tended to dress up more, as if making up for weekday deficiencies with Sunday splendor. Catherine raised her arms sleepily for Lynnette to lift her out of the crib, while Aggie had to be roused from where she lay sprawled across the bed, tangled in blankets after her nightly battle with sleep.

By the time Lynnette eased the sleep-snarls out of Aggie's thick brown hair and combed Catherine's blond wisps, Mrs. Johnson had pancake batter made. From upstairs I could hear the hot frying pan sizzling with goat butter. Lynnette hustled the girls into their Sunday dresses, straightening Aggie's hem. "Pull up your socks," she told Aggie, who yanked up her sagging white anklets. Lynnette swung Catherine onto her hip, and we all went downstairs.

Sunday breakfast at the Johnsons' always came as an unexpected relief, no matter how often I was privy to it, as if week after week Mrs. Johnson had received a stay of execution. This was the only day I saw her smile all the way, showing her pretty white teeth. Other days, she kept her mouth shut, smiling only at the corners, as if to keep anything from getting in or out.

On that particular Sunday, she was singing as we entered the kitchen, the hymn that was featured in their church program every week, "What a Friend We Have in Jesus." She smiled as if she believed that Jesus was her personal friend as well as her personal savior.

She'd done the pancakes in the shapes of our initials. The syrup pitcher was full to the brim, and she'd given us each a mug of warm coffee milk, a drop of coffee darkening the frothy goat milk.

After breakfast, Lynnette and I slopped the hogs with eggshells from the pancakes and gristle from supper the night before. Those girls wouldn't have dared arouse their father's ire by leaving food on their plates. The Johnson hogs mostly had to rely on weeds and grubs.

When Lynnette and I came in, slop bucket rinsed clean and pigs grumbling and rooting, Mrs. Johnson stood at the door in her dark blue church dress and gray hat, holding the girls' hands. Lynnette and I washed up, pulled on our white gloves and headed for the car. Mrs. Johnson generally drove with the same caution she applied to everything, but that morning she steered with one long-gloved hand loosely holding the wheel, humming about her friend Jesus.

Lynnette's church was better at uplifting than ours, with people sometimes taken by the Holy Spirit and compelled to call out in tongues or faint dramatically. That day the congregation was relatively sedate, but it was nice to see Mrs. Johnson smiling quietly, as if Jesus still kept her company. When the preacher exhorted us to consider the lilies of the field, "Even Solomon in all his glory was not arrayed like one of these!" I thought of Mr. Cullowee. That might have been sacrilegious, but I figured the Lord had made him, too, on a particularly good day.

After church, I found Joey at home on the porch swing, his leg bouncing a million miles a minute. "Come on," he said, jumping up. "We've got to see how it's doing."

"I have to change," I told him. "Mama will skin me if I mess up another outfit."

When I came downstairs in jeans and an old sweatshirt of Danny's, Joey was fidgeting by the chicken coop, bucket in hand. The trip through the woods felt faster without lugging all those cuttings. I barely noticed Aunt Mary's house looming as we ran past it.

I don't know what we expected—maybe giant plants four times the size of the ones we'd put in the ground—but we found a field of sagging kudzu propped up by cowpeas.

"Water," Joey gasped. He ran to the pump to fill the bucket.

"Hold on." I felt the soil around the nearest plant. Damp. When I plunged my fingers down, the dirt felt wet all the way through. "I think it's just transplant shock."

Reluctantly Joey set the bucket down. "They can't die. Not after all this work."

"They're not going to die," I told him.

"But what should we do?" Joey asked. "I could run get some of Daddy's fertilizer."

"I think it needs to rest. Anyhow, Mr. Cullowee said it doesn't need fertilizer."

"Are you sure?"

"Pretty sure. Let's give them a day and see."

Joey overturned the bucket at the edge of the field and sat on it, generously leaving enough room for me to sit beside him. We watched the kudzu a long while, willing it to rally, as if it were a relative confined to a sickbed. Finally, the cirrus clouds made way for stratus clouds. A cool breeze ushered in the late afternoon.

"I think it's looking better, don't you?" Joey asked.

"Definitely," I told him.

We made our way past Aunt Mary's house, already less frightened by it, and walked home through the woods, swinging the bucket between us, as if we might actually like one another and not just be stuck together by blood and circumstances.

# 3

On the Monday after the Kudzu King's appearance, I faced a line-up of unpleasant entertainments: a first period history test I hadn't studied for; a lecture on behavior from my English teacher who'd been out with the flu and wouldn't be pleased at how we'd treated her substitute; a boring biology class with Miss Gladys Lynch, who could suck the blood out of any subject; and a morning sky as dark as Hades.

Generally, Joey dawdled over breakfast, drawing monsters on his plate with egg yolk or building sausage forts to defend the pancakes, until Mama warned him the school bus was about to leave without him. At which point he'd stuff any remaining food into his mouth, flood it with milk and run for the end of our driveway.

But that day, as soon as I'd rinsed the egg tracks off my breakfast plate, he grabbed my arm. "See you later, Mama!" he called, pulling me out the door. She waved absently, already on to the next part of her day, that mysterious stretch of hours that didn't revolve around us.

Daddy and Danny were in the experimental cotton field across the road, getting the ground ready for planting. Around seven-thirty, half of Danny's baseball team would crowd into his truck to drive to school. Joey dragged me to the road, not even glancing at Daddy and Danny. "We'll go straight to the field after school," he said.

"What about homework?" I asked. "And chores?"

"We'll do those first," he said.

"Right," I said. "And that's not going to be a giveaway to Mama?"

"We'll tell her we're turning over a new leaf. She'll like that." As the bus labored up, he thought of something else. "You didn't tell her, did you?"

"Tell who what?" I asked.

The bus kicked up gravel as it slowed. Carla Ann, the driver, cranked open the door.

"Lynnette. About our kudzu." He glanced toward the bus as if an army of spies might be leaning out the windows. "When you slept over."

"No, but I don't see why I shouldn't."

"You can't tell anybody," he said. "You promised."

"Y'all coming or not?" Carla Ann called.

"Just a sec," I called. "I can't keep secrets from Lynnette," I told Joey. "It'll hurt her feelings."

"And if she can't resist telling her mother, and her mother tells Mama?" he asked. "It's not like we've got permission to use that field."

I had to admit it didn't seem unlikely. I followed him up the steps and edged through the crowd to my usual place at the back. The bus boiled in a stew of noise—boys outtalking each other, girls gossiping, and Carla Ann yelling at them all to hush.

Taylor Wagner propped his feet on the seat in front of him until Carla Ann glared at him in the rearview. Any one of those boys would've made two of her, but they all knew better than to mess with her. Taylor dropped his feet and said, "It's a load of bull, that kudzu mess. My mama planted some in her garden and it withered and died."

Nobody pointed out that everything Mrs. Wagner planted in her garden tended to wither and die, except the wooden bench Mr. Wagner had built for her, and even that was starting to mildew. The woman had a black thumb. I suspected her problem was overwatering. She lavished too much attention on everything in her care, including Taylor, which might have explained why neither his brand new blue jeans nor the bus seat could quite contain him.

By the time the bus stopped at the end of Lynnette's driveway, sharp splinters of drizzle were shooting down from the gray sky. The kitchen door was shut and the house was dark.

Carla Ann called from the front, "They gone somewhere?"

"I don't think so," I called back. It was amazing how, with all the noise on that bus, you could pick out what was being said specifically to you. "Can you give them a minute?"

I was preparing for Carla Ann's usual lecture about how she had a schedule to stick to, when the kitchen door burst open and Lynnette and Aggie rushed out, Lynnette holding her book bag over Aggie's head to shield her from the rain. They squeezed their way down the aisle and Lynnette fell into the seat beside me, pulling Aggie onto her lap, so we could all three fit. Lynnette blew a strand of Aggie's hair out of the way. "Electricity's out."

"Again?" Maybe it was the weather, but more likely Mr. Johnson hadn't paid the bill.

"Mama won't open the Frigidaire. She's trying to keep the food from going bad until we get the electric turned on again." She shifted Aggie in her lap. Aggie was a wiry girl, but solid.

"Goat milk and cornflakes again?" I asked.

"It's not so bad," Lynnette said. "But she—" she tilted her head at Aggie—"decided she doesn't drink goat milk. I gave hers to Catherine and put the bottle in the stream so it'll keep."

The girls in front of us were arguing about whether the Kudzu King's hair was blond or light brown. I could have told them it was golden. "But I dropped that nasty plant right into the street," one said. "It was filthy."

Aggie stared out the window, which meant she was in Aggieland, where everything was green and the animals spoke to her. No other human beings lived there, though a limited number of people were allowed occasional entrance. I was not one of them.

"I dreamed about him last night," I whispered to Lynnette. It was true. I had.

"Who?" she asked, still caught up in electricity outages and goats' milk.

"Mr. Cullowee."

"Mr. who?" I couldn't believe she'd forgotten so quickly. In an endless year of deadly dullness, a Greek god had descended on Cooper County and she didn't even remember his name, though it buzzed in the air around us and she'd spoken of him herself two nights earlier.

"The Kudzu King," I said.

She shifted Aggie again. "Mama says when you dream about a person, they're dreaming of you too. It's like they come to visit while you're asleep."

The bus pulled up beside West Cooper Elementary. "Little kids out," Carla Ann hollered.

The elementary kids trooped down the aisle, tripping over book bags that littered the floor. Aggie dropped from Lynnette's lap and started to trudge toward the front.

"Just one minute, you," Lynnette told her. "You haven't kissed me goodbye."

Any other ten-year-old girl would have eaten toads before kissing her sister in public, but since Aggie didn't recognize that other people existed, she had no one to be embarrassed in front of. She gave Lynnette a peck, pulled up her jacket hood, and headed into the rain behind Joey.

You'd have thought emptying the bus of a dozen kids would give the rest of us more room, but it's a proven fact that teenagers expand to fill all available space. Boys arm-wrestled across the aisle, girls crouched on their knees facing backward to talk to friends behind them, and books and belongings spilled everywhere. The humidity from outside mingled with boy sweat. My first period history test was beginning to seem like a welcome reprieve.

"What did you do after church?" Lynnette asked. She was smoothing the wrinkles from her skirt, so I didn't have to meet her eyes. Keeping a secret from Lynnette was one thing, but I didn't want to lie any more than I had to.

"Oh, this and that." I hoped she'd understand when I finally told her.

We sat quietly for the last few miles to town, though I felt fidgety inside. Lynnette was comfortable saying nothing when she had nothing to say. It wasn't a talent I shared. Outside, the raindrops got fatter and more frequent. Carla Ann's wipers swept across the windshield in a steady rhythm all the way to the junior high and finally the high school.

Circles of umbrellas populated the schoolyard when we arrived, like mushroom fairy rings. When the county kids spilled out of the bus, the buzz of voices multiplied. The town girls huddled together, their bright yellow and pink umbrellas spread in a roof that kept them all dry. Lynnette and I stood outside the circle, listening to their voices rising above the rain. The junior and senior girls crowded around Mabel Moore, speculating on who was likely to be chosen as the Kudzu Queen. Mabel was fixing to graduate and had already done professional modeling for the Hudson-Belk department store in Raleigh. She was exceedingly pretty, with porcelain skin, big hazel eyes and long eyelashes that dipped delicately whenever a teacher called on her in school. She had shoulder-length doe-brown hair that she generally wore pinned up, revealing the perfect nape of her perfect neck. She'd managed to grow to the ideal height to lay her head neatly on a football player's shoulder. She was the kind of pretty anyone would recognize, boys and girls both, but it didn't make her stuck up. She was a lot nicer than most of the other town girls.

"Mabel, you're bound to win," said one girl.

"Oh no," Mabel said firmly. "Glynis is much prettier than I am." Technically that was true. But Glynis Carpentier was a different kind of pretty. You know how they sometimes say, "Beauty is only skin-deep"? Well, in biology class we'd learned that skin is made of dead cells sitting on top of live ones. With Glynis, I'd say those dead cells were all the pretty there was to her. Everything from her dermis layer down to her stingy heart was pure-T ugly.

By the time Joey and I got to the field that afternoon, the rain had stopped and the kudzu had revived, with leaves fanning in the breeze as if to say, *What was all that fuss about?*

Each afternoon that week, we did our homework, fed and watered the pigs and chickens, collected eggs, and finished the afternoon milking, then raced through the woods to Aunt Mary's. I'm sure Mama was suspicious over how quickly we finished our work—and how little we complained while doing so. Or maybe she was counting her blessings:

Blessing 1: Chores done

Blessing 2: No whining

Blessing 3: Children out from underfoot

For the first few days, our kudzu grew in baby steps, creeping an inch or two across the ground as it dug in with new roots. We watered it religiously, despite Mr. Cullowee's assurance that it didn't need water, and weeded everything out of its path. We left the cowpeas, but rooted out any other vegetation that threatened our crop: grasses, wisteria, and the ivy that swaggered out from the foundation of Aunt Mary's house to tyrannize other plants.

Gradually, we appropriated tools, with an eye for anything abandoned that might be useful: a chipped hoe, a shovel with a split handle, a dented bucket. If Daddy noticed broken objects disappearing, he never mentioned it.

Most of the week we worked in silence, feeling the sun on our bare arms and the muscles burning across our shoulders, with our backs to the disapproving windows of Aunt Mary's house. She'd been hard on Danny and me, but she'd seemed particularly determined to make sure Joey wasn't spoiled. Whenever we'd gone to her house, she'd singled him out for extra chores, like yanking down the wisteria vines that were strangling her magnolias. Sometimes I caught sight of Joey viciously wrenching up a weed, and wondered if he was thinking of her.

We ended every afternoon by sitting on upturned buckets, watching the kudzu to see if we could catch it growing before our eyes.

After town on Saturday, Mama asked if I wanted to head over to Lynnette's before the storm descended. The weather that April seemed determined to guarantee an abundance of May flowers. All week, I'd seen Lynnette on the bus and in school, but had been too busy to go by her house. Lynnette hadn't complained, but she never complained about much of anything. A twinge of guilt angled under my ribcage. "I'll see her on Monday," I said.

It was a wonder my mother didn't put a hand on my forehead to check for fever. "If you want to spend the afternoon with her, I can spare you early, as long as you're back in time tomorrow for Easter service," she said. "It's been nice of you to spend all this time with your brother, but I'm sure Lynnette misses you."

"Well, me and Joey—" I caught the beginnings of the grammar sigh and made a mid-sentence correction. "I mean, Joey and I, we're sort of…building something."

"Really?" she said. "When can I see it?"

"When it's ready," I said quickly. "Come on, Joey. We've got to work on our fort."

"But the weather—" Mama began.

"That's okay," Joey said. "Mattie's not sweet enough to melt."

Joey and I ran through the dark woods, feeling the pressure of the overhanging clouds. When the clouds started dumping rain, we dashed to Aunt Mary's house and stood under the eaves. Aunt Mary had been too cheap to install gutters, so the rain fell in sheets, trapping us against the house. In our little cave of rain, the air felt warm and sticky.

"I hope the rain doesn't hurt our kudzu," Joey said, wiping sweat off his face with a grubby palm. "I think it may be at a delicate stage."

"I don't think kudzu has a delicate stage," I told him.

As we stood pressed against the house, I became mesmerized. The longer I watched, the more solid the rain became, until it looked like a wall of glass.

"I dare you to go inside," Joey said.

At my back the house felt chilly, whispering icy breath into my spine. "Nope."

"If you go in and stay there for fifteen minutes, I'll do the chickens for a week."

I hated the chickens more than any other chore.

He gave me the innocent look he usually saved for times when he got in trouble, but still hoped to smarm his way out of it. "You don't have to if you don't want to," he said sweetly.

"Just because you're a little brother doesn't mean you're

required to be annoying."

He gave a sad shake of his head, a spot-on imitation of Daddy when he was disappointed in us. "I'm afraid it does, Mattie."

"One week." I held up a finger. "One whole week and no complaining. For fifteen minutes. Just to show you there's nothing to be afraid of."

He crossed his heart. "Deal."

I edged over to the front corner of the house. Most people used their kitchen doors, but no one had ever entered Aunt Mary's except by the front. The foundation was too slick to climb, and red mud gathered in puddles around it. There was no way for it but to make a run into the rain. Straight through the rain, under the elm to rest, then onto the porch, hiking up my skirt to take the steps like a football player running bleachers.

At the top, I looked down at Joey. "Halfway there," he encouraged me. Somewhere in my dash he'd ceased to be my adversary and had become my ally. And going into Aunt Mary's house had stopped being something I was doing to prove I wasn't afraid, or to get out of a week of chicken chores. Now it was a challenge.

The cool brass doorknob refused to turn. The wind shifted, chilling me in my wet clothes. I shook the knob, but it held fast, as obstinate as Aunt Mary. Nobody in the county locked their doors, but Aunt Mary'd had a mortal fear of thieves, who'd ultimately stolen the one thing she couldn't lock up. Mama and Daddy, when they'd put the house to bed, had kept it as she had, as if they were as afraid of her wrath as we were. I think we all hoped that if we left Aunt Mary's house alone long enough, her spirit would get tired of defending it, like a bully who tries to ruin a game, then slinks off when nobody's willing to stick around and play.

"Maybe there's a key," Joey called. Aunt Mary wouldn't have hidden one. She rarely left her house, and hated visitors. On the few occasions when she did cross her own doorstep, for church or the market, she carried her ring of keys—house, woodshed, Buick—zipped into the inside pocket of her black patent leather pocketbook. But Mama or Daddy might have left a key hidden somewhere, so they wouldn't have to bring it home to taint our house with her meanness.

Even something as small as a key can carry someone's spirit, the way my grandfather's pocket watch, which I still wore on a chain around my neck some days, made me feel safe, ticking the time as his heart had done when I'd sat on his lap as a little girl. I'd press my ear to his chest and reassure him, "Your heart's beating, Papa."

"Glad to hear it," he'd reply.

I lifted the doormat, felt in the mailbox, and ran my fingers around the doorframe. Nothing. Finally, I found it under the brass pot to the left of the door. Aunt Mary had planted mums in flower urns on each side of the door. Funeral flowers were the closest she ever got to friendly perennials. The key slid in as if the lock had been oiled, which, knowing Daddy, it probably had, but the door stuck, swollen by humidity. When I put some shoulder into it, the door swung open.

To my left stood a mahogany entry table, empty except for a silver letter tray and a porcelain statue of a man on a rearing horse. A cobweb stretched from the horse's left foreleg to the man's hand.

I closed the door behind me. The room was still, except for the muffled rain and the tick of the anniversary clock on the mantel. I took in a breath, thinking: I'm breathing leftover Aunt Mary air. I listened carefully for a sharp crack from upstairs that might mean, "Go away," but all I heard was the steady rain and the clock. The clock face, an ornate moon and sun, of mother of pearl and gold, read 4:49. Had I been there a minute yet?

I stepped into the sitting room, running my finger along the carved mahogany back of the formal sofa, with its bulging grapes and thin sharp leaves rising like a cockscomb above the striped silk upholstery of blue, yellow, and rose. I sat on the sofa, perching as if I'd been invited to tea but wasn't sure of my welcome. I looked for Buster, Aunt Mary's dead stuffed spaniel. Could he have been buried with her? I traced my finger over a row of small green enamel boxes on the coffee table, lined up like pretty soldiers, leaving a clear swipe in the dust along the top of each one. It looked wrong, so I rubbed the sleeve of my blouse over them to clean them off.

On the mantel beside the clock a cream-colored china plate sat upright in a twisted gold wire frame. A shepherd and a shepherdess danced while lambs frolicked around them. It was the sort of thing Mama might like, and I wondered if she planned on taking it home, once Aunt Mary's meanness had worn off it. I figured Mama deserved it for the sharp criticism she got every Thanksgiving and Easter. "Too much pepper," Aunt Mary would grumble, or "What kind of fool overcooks sweet potatoes?"

The rain outside the front window made the kudzu invisible. Mama always said there was nothing she liked better than a good rain to clear the air. Thunder and lightning storms were her favorite. When Danny and I were little, she'd pop a pot of popcorn and we'd snuggle up beside her to watch the weather through the sitting room window, as if we were at the picture show. She'd smile out at the rain, as pleased as if she had arranged it herself.

I looked at the clock. 4:51.

None of us kids had ever been allowed upstairs. I expected the stairs to creak, warning Aunt Mary's spirit of an intruder, but the red carpet runner absorbed my footsteps. I cleaned the dusty banister with my sleeve as I tiptoed.

An Oriental rug ran the length of the hall, ending at a bathroom with a claw-foot tub. I stood in the middle of the hall, between two closed doors. The one on the right rattled in its frame. Not the room I wanted to start with, in case Aunt Mary's spirit had gotten trapped and was trying to get out. I turned the glass knob across the hall, shielding myself behind the door, like a movie detective, as I opened it and peered in.

Two tall forms stood draped in sheets in the otherwise empty room, their heads almost touching the low ceiling. When I pulled up the hem of the closest sheet, my hand brushed up against a small furry foot. Swallowing my heart, I lifted the sheet higher. A wide-shouldered fur coat hung on a rack, with what I guessed was a mink stole draped over it, claw feet dangling. I yanked the sheet off and found furs hanging from every hook. At first I thought I'd come across a fortune in furs, enough to pay for Danny's schooling, but then I saw bare patches here and there, as if something had been nibbling on them.

On the other rack roosted a small flock of hats: a wide-brimmed red felt hat, an old-fashioned cloche of peacock feathers, a dressy black velveteen with a red satin band, and a straw hat with a blue and white polka-dotted ribbon.

In all the times I'd seen Aunt Mary—every Easter and Thanksgiving and hundreds of Sundays in church, suffering her pinches on my arm when I wriggled in the pew—the only outer garments she'd ever worn had been a shapeless green wool coat, a poorly knitted hat of the same shade for winter and a man's gray fedora in summer. I couldn't imagine why she'd owned all these furs and hats, and why they had a room to themselves.

The door across the hall clattered insistently. Downstairs, the clock struck five. If I didn't open that door while my courage was up, I'd never do it. So I shoved it open and jumped back. A whoosh of wind escaped, but it seemed fresh and cool, not at all what I would have expected from Aunt Mary's outraged spirit.

I peeked around the door. Nothing but a neat bedroom with an open window through which wind and rain blew, while sheer white curtains danced wildly. A high brass bed with a white chenille bedspread. To the left of the bed stood a mahogany step stool. Her own bed had been so tall she couldn't climb into it without help. I closed the window, and the curtains settled into a damp demureness. I smoothed the bedspread where the wind had blown it into wrinkles.

Below the window, a puddle of rainwater had pooled. I wiped it up with my sleeve, which was already dirty and bound to get soaked further when Joey and I ran home.

On the wall to the right of the bed was a tall oval photograph of a woman, covered in domed glass. Was that Aunt Mary's mother, my great-grandmother? I'd never seen a picture of her. She had the same thin lips as Aunt Mary, but hers were quirked in a smile, and her eyes were tinted the warm brown of my mother's. Beside that picture was a matching oval picture of a young man I'd never seen, dressed in a soldier's uniform. A chintz lady's chair stood below the pictures, with an empty bud vase and a music box on a small table beside it. When I pressed the latch of the music box, the lid sprang up, revealing a tiny ballerina who pirouetted to a tinny "Für Elise." It was a sweet room, the room of a lonely woman who had liked pretty things—which made me feel sorry for her. Maybe her meanness had come from some sadness I hadn't known about, instead of springing to life full-blown the minute she was born.

I patted the bedspread one more time, straightened the pictures and slipped out, closing the door. If Aunt Mary needed a place to stay a while longer, I'd make sure she wasn't disturbed.

As I went down the stairs, I heard a creak or two, but they were comfortable creaks, not angry ones. I slid my sleeve down the opposite banister, finishing the polish job I'd begun. The grandfather clock read 5:07.

When I let myself out, Joey was staring at me from the foot of the steps, shivering in the pouring rain, his hair plastered flat to his head. "You were in there forever."

"Just looking." I held up the key. "Want to see?"

He shook his head and spikes of hair flew up. "Uh-uh. Come on, Mattie, let's go home."

I locked the door and slipped the key beneath the pot. I was just as glad he didn't want to go inside. Aunt Mary's sadness was her secret, and now mine.

By the time we reached the woods, we were soaked to the spine, so there wasn't any reason to run. We walked, feeling the rain all around us, as if we were in Mama's favorite kind of movie, a sad one where somebody dies, and someone else is left to mourn all alone.

Most Sundays our preacher was as lively as tapioca pudding, droning on while the congregation dozed and his wife sat upright in the front pew. Mrs. Davenport generally looked sour, as if she believed the feast of life to be limited to a steady diet of green persimmons. Maybe she thought her dour expression pleased the Lord. The only creature that ever made her smile was her cat, Fluffy, who spent Sundays on her lap, sleeping through the sermon. That woman never went anywhere without her cat.

But that Easter Sunday, Pastor Davenport rose to the occasion, waking both the cat and the congregation. He lifted his hands to heaven, wiggling his fingers, and calling out in a voice that filled the church. "And Jesus *said* unto her, *I* am the resurrection, and the life," he proclaimed, hoisting up his voice like a hammer and pounding down on the important words. "He that believeth in me, though he were dead, yet shall he *live*: And whosoever liveth and believeth in me shall *never* die. Believest thou *this*?" He paused and said in his normal voice, "John 11:25-26."

It seemed like everything got born again, or born for the first time, in spring: the fields of cotton and corn and tobacco, the robins in the tree outside my window, the grass, even the river, which swelled up with rainwater. Maybe Cooper County was being reborn, too, thanks to kudzu, I thought. Maybe even I was.

Over the next week we recorded our kudzu's growth religiously, often measuring more than five inches in a day. Danny wasn't the only one who could study scientific methods of farming. On Sunday, after the rain let up, the kudzu had looked chastened, like a boy after a whupping he knows he's deserved. But by Monday, the kudzu had puffed itself up to twice its previous size, bragging about how tough it was. By the day before the Kudzu King was due to return, our crop had grown a good three feet, making even Daddy's corn look paltry.

I couldn't sleep for excitement that night. Moonlight spread through my window, making soft puddles on the floor. I memorized my ceiling—every crack and seam. I wondered if he'd remember looking into my eyes.

# 4

The Saturday of the Kudzu King's return dawned bright and clear.

I thought he'd be well pleased at the impact he'd made. In the two weeks he'd been gone, kudzu fever had taken hold. Those who'd planted their sprigs outdoors discovered that Mr. James T. Cullowee had told them the honest truth. You never saw a healthier looking plant, with its trios of shiny green leaves. It would grow if you turned your back, or if you didn't. Even on kitchen windowsills it spread, a friendly blanket of green that brightened kitchens and spilled luxuriantly into porcelain sinks. But what was one sprig per person, compared to the haul Joey and I had made? I was sure we were the only ones in the county with an entire field of kudzu.

Mr. Cullowee slowed his truck as he drove into town, keeping pace with families walking along the road, chatting with mothers and fathers. Little boys climbed up and rode atop a fresh green crop of kudzu. When the truck headed past us on Main Street, Joey vaulted onto the kudzu, clasping his skinny arms over his head as if he'd won the world prizefighting championship. It was sort of true. Our kudzu was growing like Jack's beanstalk and it had been all Joey's idea.

A new white banner across the tailgate proclaimed "Kudzu! The Crop of the Future!" in large green letters, with "James T. Cullowee, Kudzu Promoter" below.

Mr. Cullowee cut his ignition, rolled to a stop in the middle of the street and stepped onto the running board. He reached under the kudzu behind the cab and pulled out a crate of pint jars. "I have here a gift from the fine ladies of Dawson County, Georgia—now in their second year of kudzu cultivation—to the lovely ladies of Cooper County, North Carolina." From the crate he drew a jar and held it up to the light to admire its red translucence. "For each household represented today by a fine upstanding housewife, one jar of kudzu blossom jelly."

Ladies started trickling from their families toward the front of the crowd. "Go on, Mama." I gave her a gentle push. "Get your jelly."

The Kudzu King handed the first jar to the mayor's wife, who'd taken her place at the head of the line, as she tended to do in most situations. "Mrs. Beulah Sampson, isn't it?" the Kudzu King asked. How he'd figured that out, I had no idea. Mrs. Sampson bore a distinct resemblance to our sow, Stevie, especially when her round cheeks pinked up, as they now did. "I believe it's legal to carry kudzu jelly across state lines," he said to her, "but perhaps you'd best not tell your husband." He winked over the crowd at the mayor, who stood on the steps of the courthouse where he could see and be seen.

Joey jumped down and dragged Mama forward. "This is my mama," he said proudly. "She makes the best pepper jelly you ever tasted."

The Kudzu King smiled at Mama. "Then you'll want the jar of the best kudzu jelly I've got. This jar comes from a lady out by Crystal Falls Lake who made only one batch. I've been saving it for someone special."

Taylor Wagner's mother pushed forward, calling, "Give me a jar of that special jelly!" followed by more mothers, reaching to receive their jelly bounty. The men held back, like tent ropes keeping the crowd from collapsing inward.

"And for you gentlemen," Mr. Cullowee said, as the last lady tucked her jelly jar into her basket. "Perhaps you've noticed that the price of tobacco is getting so high, you can hardly afford to smoke the very crop you grow?" He pulled a pack of store-bought cigarettes from the pocket of his crisp white shirt. "Well, I could hardly believe it myself. But dried properly, kudzu combines with Carolina tobacco to make the finest cigarette I've ever had the privilege of smoking. And I've taken the liberty of having a pack made up for each and every one of you."

He reached under the vines again, and pulled out several cartons of cigarettes, which he flared like a hand of playing cards. With a penknife, he opened one carton, resting the others on the side of the truck. "You can grow your kudzu side by side with your tobacco, so the smells mingle even in the field. One-tenth the investment of tobacco, with a year-round growing season and no natural enemies—you'll find kudzu is the perfect crop to augment what you have in the ground right now."

A few men moved forward, then a few more. One took four packs and tossed them to friends waiting along the sidelines. Lynnette's daddy took two and stuck them in the pocket of his old black jacket. Even some of the high school boys edged up to Mr. Cullowee. He gave them each a pack, same as the men.

"I'll try some if you don't mind," Danny called.

"Plenty to go around, boys." Mr. Cullowee handed a pack to Danny, and looked beyond him to Daddy, who shook his head. I'd never seen Daddy smoke a cigarette, despite the fact that he had a whole field of tobacco, so I didn't think it likely he'd take it up now.

The last few men and boys got their cigarettes, whereupon the Kudzu King reached under the kudzu once more—and paused. That kudzu was like a Christmas tree. I couldn't wait to see what would come out from under it next.

"Well, I don't know if I should." A serious expression passed over his face. "Ladies, I have a special treat for your children, but I need your permission to share it."

"What is it?" shouted several young children, and a few older ones, Joey among them.

"After all," the Kudzu King continued, "it is approaching dinnertime. I wouldn't want to spoil your children's appetites for the excellent midday meals I know you'll be preparing."

"Please!" called the children.

"I don't know," said Mrs. Walker. Her two little boys were dragging her toward the truck, while her daughter Ann Marie stood next to Glynis Carpentier and tried to pretend like she didn't know her own brothers. "It's awful close to—"

"Let them have it," Mrs. Carpentier called out, in a voice as lazy as a cream-fed cat. "What harm can it do?"

With that, the Kudzu King pulled out a Santa bag stuffed full, and raised it high above his head. "Candied kudzu flowers," he cried, tossing paper-wrapped candies into the crowd. Children grabbed for the candy as it fell to the sidewalk. I felt it was beneath me to scrabble on the ground, but I bent down to pick up a few in case Joey and I decided to make some to sell.

When I stood up, a group of town girls and their mothers had gathered around the Kudzu King, chatting with him like they'd bought and paid for him and wanted to get their money's worth. Chief among them was Glynis, her tiny rat-dog Mr. Bubbles straining at the end of a rhinestone-covered pink leather leash.

I edged behind the town girls, who were oohing and aahing over the pages of a photo album that lay on the hood of Mr. Cullowee's truck. One beautiful Kudzu Queen after another, all in flowing white gowns, but otherwise completely different—a tall blond here, a well-developed redhead there, and one girl with hair so dark and straight she had to be part Cherokee.

When I turned back, the crowd had dispersed to go about its business, leaving only the girls and their mothers mooning over the album. Most of those mothers had no idea how to grow corn, much less kudzu, but they knew they wanted their daughters to be queen of it.

I could tell I wasn't going to get one inch closer to Mr. Cullowee, let alone have the chance to say something charming so he'd remember me as the fascinating girl he met on his return. So I went to Aronson's to see if I could be any help to Mama, or maybe beg her to buy some gingersnaps. The store-bought ones were crisper than the ones she made at home. Though I asked every week, she'd yet to give in, but I thought I might be wearing her down.

I truly intended to help my mother, but when I stepped through the doorway into the dark coolness of the store, I saw Lynnette's mother talking earnestly with Mr. Johnson. "You go out there and ask him," she insisted. "It's the Christian thing to do."

He shook his head. "Who knows how long he'll stay? Could be weeks. Months."

"It doesn't matter," she said. "He's a stranger here."

When he said, "Least he can do is throw in something toward rent," her brows clapped together like thunder.

Mrs. Johnson wasn't normally a directive woman, though Lynnette had told me her mother had been a schoolteacher before she'd married. This new side of her interested me enough to follow Mr. Johnson into the sunlight to see what he'd been directed to do. He paused to say a few irritated words to Lynnette, who was crouched on the sidewalk, teaching Catherine to do, "Miss Mary Mack," while Aggie convinced a roly-poly to curl up around a blade of grass.

When he moved on, I stepped up beside Lynnette. "What's your father doing?"

"Mack, mack, mack," Catherine recited.

Lynnette grasped Catherine's hands lightly to halt her patting. "Inviting Mr. Cullowee to come stay with us," she said.

I wondered if having an important guest like Mr. Cullowee might make Mr. Johnson act right, not to mention how it could benefit me for him to stay next door in my best friend's house. "But where will he sleep?" I asked.

Lynnette shrugged. "Wherever Mama puts him, I expect."

Mr. Johnson threaded his way between town girls in their Saturday dresses, his shoulders hunched in his black jacket, a crow among swans. When he reached the Kudzu King, he stuck out his hand. "My wife and I would like to extend you an invitation," he said loudly. "We're hoping you'll do us the honor of staying in our home while you're stopping in the county."

I looked at Lynnette in surprise. She was still paused in her game with Catherine, watching her father. She shrugged. "He can speak well enough when he has a mind to. It doesn't mean he means it."

When I was little, I'd thought "no 'count" meant a person who didn't know his numbers. By the time I'd gotten a grip on counting to a hundred, I'd learned that "no 'count" and "shiftless" were often strung together like dime store pearls. It wasn't until I met Mr. Johnson that I decided "shiftless" was the wrong adjective to apply to someone who was of no account. In fact, he was entirely shift-ful, especially when he was around someone who had something he wanted—money, power, an ounce of happiness—anything he felt the world had deprived him of. When he talked to my daddy, his eyes were continually shifting, never meeting Daddy's except to glance off them. His weight would shift as if he couldn't stand to stay in one place too long. And he'd shifted his family from one hardscrabble tenant farm to the next all Lynnette's life until they'd come to Cooper County.

Lynnette watched her father with a wariness born of experience. Any change in routine could ignite his short fuse. Even Aggie, who didn't appear to be listening, froze, while Catherine, oblivious, folded Lynnette's fingers one by one toward her palm, chanting, "Mack, mack, mack."

"How kind of you," Mr. Cullowee said to Mr. Johnson. "I'd be delighted."

I thought somebody ought to warn him that being a guest in Mr. Johnson's house might not be as delightful as he anticipated, but it wasn't going to be me.

"When you're through with all this—" Mr. Johnson looked at the simpering town girls, who wilted under his glare. "Come over with your things. Anyone can tell you how to get there."

"It'll be all right," Lynnette said quietly, as if she were trying to convince herself.

"Sure," I said. "It might even be a good thing."

Mr. Johnson headed for their car. Lynnette gathered Catherine on her hip, holding out her free hand. Without looking, Aggie reached for Lynnette, pausing as she rose to ensure that her roly-poly was securely coiled around the grass blade. They trailed behind their father, and took their customary places in the car, where Mrs. Johnson waited in the passenger seat, looking for once like a queen who has commanded and been obeyed.

Mama had finished her shopping and stood on the sidewalk

of Aronson's, chatting with some town mothers. From what she'd told me about her days at Consolidated, she'd been the sort of popular high school girl I wished I could be, not snotty, but well-liked by everyone, like Mabel, able to be nice to unpopular kids without being mocked herself. She never described herself like that, of course, but I could see it in the way the town mothers tilted their heads to listen as she spoke, and her easy laugh when they said something clever.

The crowd around Mr. Cullowee diminished as mothers pulled their girls away to go home for dinner. The baseball game ended. While Joey gathered his bat and glove, Danny wandered over and stood beside me. We watched Glynis laugh and push against Mr. Cullowee's shoulder, fluttering her eyelashes over sharp gray eyes, while her dog sniffed at his shoes. "Oh, you!" she teased, as if she'd known him forever. I guessed Glynis's mother expected her to get home on her own. Eventually.

"She's a piece of work, isn't she?" Danny said.

Mr. Cullowee leaned against the driver's door, arms crossed over his chest.

"Do you think he likes girls like that?" I asked.

Glynis reached up to adjust the barrette that held her thick dark hair. Mama would never have let me buy a dress that low-cut. I wondered if Glynis stood in front of the mirror every day to practice arching her back so her bosom would stick out like that.

"That girl's a cobra-in-training," Danny replied. "Let's rescue him." He strode to the truck. I scurried behind him, slowing when I caught up so I wouldn't appear too eager. "Mr. Cullowee?" Danny said.

The Kudzu King looked over Glynis's shoulder with what I hoped was gratitude, though it might have been curiosity.

"Danny Watson." Danny stuck out his hand. "And my sister Mattie."

Mr. Cullowee gave Danny's hand a solid shake. "You a farmer, Watson?"

"Aiming to be," Danny said.

"What's your crop?" Mr. Cullowee asked.

"Mostly corn and tobacco," Danny told him. "And my father and I are working on an experimental strain of cotton, weevil-resistant."

"Interesting," Mr. Cullowee said. "Sounds like you know what you're talking about."

Glynis smiled from Mr. Cullowee to Danny, as if deciding which was the tastier treat.

"He's going to Ag School in Raleigh this fall," I blurted, my voice squeaky. I instantly regretted having spoken. I'd been aiming for Greta Garbo, not Laurel and Hardy.

Glynis gave me a look, which clearly said: *I got here first. Back off.*

Mr. Cullowee put his hand on my shoulder. "You must be proud of your brother, Mattie."

"Yes, sir, I am." I resisted sending a look of triumph in Glynis's direction.

"You wouldn't know the Johnson family, would you, Danny?" Mr. Cullowee asked.

"Sure," Danny said. "They're on the next farm over from us. Lynnette Johnson is Mattie's best friend."

Mr. Cullowee shifted to Danny and me, as if Glynis had turned invisible. "They've invited me to stay with them a while. I don't suppose you'd consider riding with me to provide directions?" Glynis gave me an evil glare, which I nobly ignored.

"Don't see why not," Danny said. "Mattie, run over and ask Mama if you can come too."

Whatever Danny wanted for the next month—breakfast in bed every day, his Sunday shoes polished, his room cleaned to Mama's satisfaction—as far as I was concerned, he could have it. I dashed across the street, slowing to a sedate walk as I approached the knot of mothers passing around snippets of gossip like chocolates in a candy dish.

"Mama?" I panted. "Mr. Kudzu—I mean Mr. Cullowee—he wants Danny and me to ride with him to the Johnsons' house. Can we?"

She looked across the street. Mr. Cullowee had tilted back his hat to reveal his noble brow. Glynis appeared to be modeling as a pin-up girl, leaning against the Kudzu King's truck with her tight skirt rucked up to mid-thigh and a look that said, *I'm innocently taking some sun here while I wait for these men to finish their business and realize how sultry I am.*

"Mattie, we don't know anything about this man," Mama said.

"But Mr. Johnson invited him to stay with them," I pleaded.

"That, oddly enough, is not an argument likely to persuade me to allow my only daughter to get in a truck with a strange man."

"Danny will be with us," I said. "Don't you trust Danny's judgment?"

"Well enough," she said, "but your brother has a tendency to see the best in people whether it's there or not."

"Mama!" I groaned.

She exchanged a smile with Mabel's mother, and I realized she'd been playing me all along. Why was it I never caught on when people were funning me?

"I suppose, if the whole county has decided to take him in, I might as well go along with it," she said. "It's not as if he could get up to anything in broad daylight."

I threw my arms around her, then saw Danny and Mr. Cullowee looking over with amusement. Why could I never master an air of mystery when it was most useful?

When I got back, Glynis pushed off the truck and sauntered away with her yapping dog. I could pick up a thing or two from her about showing off one's backside to best advantage, I thought.

Mr. Cullowee opened his passenger door. "If you're ready."

I climbed up and slid across the sun-warmed seat to the middle, tugging my skirt down. Danny climbed in after me, and Mr. Cullowee walked around and sat behind the wheel.

"Which direction?" Mr. Cullowee asked.

"Right at the next corner, then right again," Danny said. "We'll head out the way you came in." I was glad Danny answered him, since I'd been struck mute.

As we got further from town, the distances between the houses began to increase, populated by fields of new corn and empty ones awaiting tobacco and cotton.

"So what brings you to Cooper County, Mr. Cullowee?" Danny asked.

"Research, Danny," Mr. Cullowee replied. "I've searched the country to find locations that would benefit most from this opportunity, and your fine community is right there at the top of the list." There was something grand about the way he spoke that filled the cab with a warm, golden magnificence.

Danny nodded. Sometimes he referred to asking questions as "collecting data." "And where do you come from originally?"

"All over," Mr. Cullowee said. "My father's a career army man. I've seen more of this grand country of ours than most long-distance haulers."

Danny leaned against the door, his knees accidentally pushing me closer to the Kudzu King. I could feel every quarter inch of closing distance. "So tell me about this kudzu," Danny said. "How much water does it actually need?"

Mr. Cullowee smiled. "As much as naturally falls from the sky."

"And if there's a drought?"

"Then that's how much it needs," Mr. Cullowee said. "Kudzu likes drought. Kudzu likes rain. It's the puppy dog of cash crops. It requires only the slightest encouragement to make itself at home."

Their conversation continued, interspersed with directions from Danny. I snuck a look at Mr. Cullowee's sculpted chin and nose and high cheekbones. When he parked in front of the Johnsons', I couldn't recall whether I'd taken a breath the entire trip from town.

The front yard sported a paltry crop of pea gravel, dotted with tufts of singed crabgrass. The occasion seemed to require some ceremony, so I led Mr. Cullowee and Danny up the crumpled cement path to the front door, lifted the brass knocker and let it fall.

The door jerked open to reveal Mr. Johnson in the dark hallway, with Mrs. Johnson behind him and the girls ranging up the stairs. Mrs. Johnson stepped around her husband to the door. "Welcome to our home. We're pleased to have you."

The Kudzu King took her hand in both of his. "Thank you for your hospitality, Mrs. Johnson," he said. "I'll try not to be a burden on your generosity."

"You couldn't possibly be a burden." She looked over her shoulder. "Girls? Come get Mr. Cullowee's things and carry them upstairs."

"Oh no," Mr. Cullowee said. "I wouldn't dream of letting these delicate flowers lift those heavy bags. I've got them."

"I'll give you a hand," Danny said.

"Me, too," I volunteered, before remembering that I was a delicate flower too.

Mr. Cullowee and Danny retrieved a leather valise and an army duffel from the truck. Mrs. Johnson held the door for them. "It's straight up the stairs, first room on the left."

Lynnette, Aggie, and Catherine pressed to the wall side of the staircase to let Danny and Mr. Cullowee by. "That's *your* room," I whispered to Lynnette. "Where will you sleep?"

"Sleeping porch," she said.

Danny came downstairs. "He's getting settled. He'll be down shortly."

"Did he need anything else?" Mrs. Johnson asked.

"I don't think so," Danny said. "It's real nice of you all to put him up."

Aggie looked up at Danny. "Hey, champ," he said, giving her a light punch in the arm. She cut her eyes at him and rubbed her arm, less like she was trying to rub away the hurt than like she wanted to rub in the memory of Danny's attention. He swung Catherine high over his head. "Hello, Miss Madame." When he put her down, she giggled and hid behind Lynnette's legs.

"And you, pal," he said to me. "I'd best be getting you home before Mama and Daddy think we're trying to slide out of our chores."

As we walked home down the middle of the road, Danny threw pinecones at trees, providing his own commentary. "Eighty-eight miles an hour. That Danny Watson has a fast ball that would peel the paint off your house. And it's strike one!" He picked up another pinecone. "He's shaking off the catcher's sign. There's the wind-up and…strike two!" He bent again. "Looks like it's going to be—no. He's shaking off the sign again and—"

"Danny?" I looked into the trees where strike three was headed.

He paused in mid-pitch. "Yeah?"

"What do you think of Mr. Cullowee?"

He lobbed the last pinecone in an underhand softball toss. It bounced off a dogwood. "He's all right. Bit of a smooth talker."

"No, I mean, do you think he's good-looking?"

"Not the kind of thing I notice," Danny said. "But I suppose a girl would think so."

"I think he looks like a movie star," I said. "Not just how handsome he is. It's like he's bigger than anybody I've ever seen."

"I doubt he's much more than six foot," Danny said.

"I don't mean his height," I told him. "It's something else, something in his character."

We walked without speaking for a while. Little dust ghosts spun at our heels after each step on the dirt road. From the fields on either side of us, the hum of cicadas rose like walls. Currie Creek kept us company to our left.

"You know he's too old for you, Matts," Danny said gently. "He's probably twice as old as you."

"I'm very mature for my age," I protested.

He cuffed the side of my head. "Not exactly."

When we got home, I asked Mama if I could spend that night with Lynnette, but she'd reached her daily limit on granting requests.

"I'm sure Mrs. Johnson has enough on her hands without taking on a foundling this evening."

"I'm not a foundling," I protested. "I'm practically a member of the family. I help out all the time."

"Oh, you mean like you help out around here? Voluntarily and without complaining?"

I could hardly say that I helped Mrs. Johnson more than my own mother. But Mama wasn't sick, like Mrs. Johnson. She was, if anything, so entirely competent that it was hard to find anything left to do.

"Besides," she said, "I've got a use for you right here."

"What?" I wasn't exactly sulking, but I wasn't exactly not.

"You're going to help me test gingersnap recipes. I can't have my own daughter going around in public saying store-bought cookies are an improvement over mine."

"Testing as in tasting, or testing as in having to cook?" The horrors of junior high school home economics were never far from my mind.

"Mattie," she sighed. "Someday you'll have your own children, and it might be good if you knew how to prepare something other than a jar of peanut butter with a spoon stuck in it."

"Peanut butter's nutritious," I countered. "Anyhow, Daddy eats it." It was true. Daddy often sat at the kitchen table after he'd finished work, watching Mama put the finishing touches on supper while he spooned peanut butter into his mouth. Mama never chided him for spoiling his appetite the way she did us. As far as I could tell, his appetite was unspoilable.

"It's not the balanced diet you'll have to prepare for your family someday. Think of it as a science experiment."

"Fine," I huffed.

The rest of the weekend passed with excruciating sluggishness, with the Kudzu King staying at my best friend's house and me forbidden to visit. I occupied myself by tending the kudzu with Joey, but honestly, it seemed to be growing just fine on its own.

On Monday, things sped up when the door to history class slammed open and a freshman girl stumbled into the room. She was the sort my mother called a pixie, with her bowl-cut red hair.

"Announcement!" she panted as if she'd been running down the hall with the Olympic torch. "Assembly. Seventh period. Gym. Required," she gasped. "Mr. James T. Cullowee will speak about the benefits of kudzu and the upcoming festival," she blurted out, stringing the words together in one breath.

The pixie darted to the next class, leaving the room buzzing like an overloaded party line. "Students," Mr. Kerr droned. "I'm sure this is all very interesting, but the Eighteenth Amendment awaits our attention." He returned to the board to write more factors leading to the amendment. We'd be tested on them whether we paid attention or not.

Mr. Kerr had made it to the Women's Christian Temperance Union. I knew from my reading that he had years to go before the Anti-Saloon League. I whispered to Lynnette, "Do you know what Mr. Cullowee is going to speak about?"

She gave a quick headshake. "I've hardly seen him since Saturday," she whispered. "Mama said he's been out talking to people."

"Like who?" I asked.

"Like Principal Lassiter," she said, "and the mayor."

After sixth period, students mobbed the halls, herded by teachers toward the gymnasium like cows in a chute. In the gym, the bleachers were full, chairs in rows on the basketball court held the principal and teachers, the volleyball net was rolled around its stanchions and stowed in a corner, and the climbing rope was tied up. The "Cooper County Consolidated High School" banner hung from the rafters, with the banner from the Kudzu King's truck hanging beneath. It was uncanny how perfectly they went together.

Usually in assemblies, the principal had to hush everyone as best he could and hand over the unstable quiet to the speaker like a poorly wrapped present. That day, as soon as we saw the Kudzu King alone on the stage, everyone stopped talking. He stood in front of a microphone, gazing out as if we were his loyal subjects. What was he waiting for? A late-arriving class? An introduction? The principal had already taken a seat in the front row, along with the secretary and cafeteria ladies. Even Mr.

Sykes, the custodian, sat there. I'd never seen Mr. Sykes sit down.

I'd thought we were unusually quiet before, but as we waited, a hum I hadn't noticed died out, leaving us completely still. Into that stillness, the Kudzu King spoke.

"Ladies and gentlemen, I bring you your future." His voice boomed through the speakers. No one breathed. "One small and powerful plant is going to rule the South in years to come, and you, my friends, will be its kings and queens."

The breath we'd all been holding flew out as a collective sigh.

"You, the future of the South, will lead this region to the greatness it deserves."

Here was this man, saying that we—pimple-faced, too pudgy or too tall, voices breaking or shrill—were the future.

"I've heard tell," his voice deepened, "that cotton is king. Well, my friends, the day of cotton is over. The day of kudzu has dawned. Anything cotton can do, kudzu can do better. It wears longer than cotton and weaves finer than the finest flax linen. Can you eat cotton? Can it cure a sick headache? Can you put it in your pipe and smoke it?" A laugh blurted out of some of the boys. "The King is dead," Mr. Cullowee said. "Long live the King!"

This was the future. And here was the man to lead us to it.

"This week we'll begin classes for any girl interested in entering the Kudzu Queen competition, culminating in the crowning of your very own queen on the fourteenth of June. Every young lady in this auditorium—" I liked how he called it an auditorium instead of the gym it was—"is invited to attend these classes Wednesday afternoons at 3:15, free of charge, with bus service to your homes afterward. I'll expect to see you Wednesday at the mayor's home, where he and his wife have generously offered to accommodate all who join us."

He paused and looked around. "Now, boys, don't you go feeling left out. You too will have the opportunity to engage in extracurricular higher education. Each and every Thursday afternoon, we'll meet at the farm of Mr. Leroy Johnson, where you'll learn the latest advances in kudzu farming. I hope to see as many of you as can be spared from chores for a few hours each week."

He stepped back. "I thank you for your time. And I thank your principal, Mr. Lassiter, for the opportunity to speak to you. I look forward to seeing you all this week."

We applauded as if to bring down the bleachers, clapping until our hands hurt. We were ready to dress in kudzu, eat it, and hand it out as Christmas presents. We only hoped there'd be enough to go around.

That night, over catfish—caught by Danny after church the day before, and battered and fried by me with Mama's help—Danny talked about the assembly. "You should have seen him, Daddy," he said. "The man's got a knack for getting people stirred up."

"I noticed that knack on Saturday, myself," Daddy said. "I can think of a few other men with that knack. As I remember, Mr. Huey Long down in Louisiana was quite adept at it."

Danny stared at the fish lying on his plate, took a deep breath and tried again. "Well, he says kudzu's going to be king of the South. He believes cotton's on its way out."

"What does it take to be a king?" Daddy mused. "Wisdom? Restraint?"

"Don't make fun, Will," Mama said.

I figured it was time for me to contribute to the conversation. "They're going to be giving Kudzu Queen lessons. On Wednesday afternoons."

"That's great!" Joey said. "Where do you sign up?"

"I don't think there's anything our Mattie has to learn about being a queen," Daddy said.

Mama refilled my glass with milk. "What will they be teaching?"

"Oh, I don't know." I shrugged. "How to talk with marbles in your mouth, how to walk with a book on your head—" When I saw the milk pitcher hovering over Joey's glass, I took advantage of her momentary distraction. "How to put on make-up."

"Well, you're welcome to go if you want to, Mattie," she said absently.

After supper, Joey shooed Mama out of the kitchen. "Why don't you take it easy, Mama? Me and Mattie will clean up."

"Oh?" She raised an eyebrow at the mess I'd made: a fallen cavalry of pots and pans, bowls dripping with egg-and-flour gore, sticky spoons, and encrusted forks.

"We're happy to do it," he said with wide-eyed sincerity.

"Mattie," she asked. "Are you in on this generous offer?"

"Sure," I said.

I waited until the kitchen door had swung shut. "If you're trying to raise her suspicions, you're doing an excellent job," I said.

"I'm working out a plan," Joey said.

"A plan for what?" I turned on the tap and poured a snowfall of Lux flakes into the sink. Bubbles piled into foam. "To help me become the Kudzu Queen of Cooper County?" I started scrubbing a bowl encrusted with eggy flour. Best to get the worst done first.

"That's not a bad idea, but this is bigger." He picked up a dishtowel. "You can be a spy."

"A spy?" I handed him the bowl and dumped the silver in the water.

"It's not about being the Kudzu Queen." He plucked silver out of the soapy water. "It's about finding out how we get rich off our kudzu. You can get information when you see him."

"You know who could help us a lot?" I asked.

Joey rolled his eyes. "No, we're not telling Lynnette."

"But we need her," I insisted. "And he's staying at her house, so she might hear things."

Joey dropped the glasses into the water, where they listed like sinking boats. He tipped one with his finger and it dropped to the bottom. "Mattie," he said, "could we not tell anybody for now? Not even her? I've never had one thing in my life that was just mine."

I started to tell him this wasn't his either, that it was both of ours. But then I thought about what it would be like to live in the shadow of Danny, and even, sometimes, me.

"All right," I said. "For now."

# 5

After school on Wednesday, I sat with Lynnette on our usual bench in front of the school while she waited for the bus. Despite the fact that her family was hosting the Kudzu King, her father hadn't even contemplated letting her go to Queen School to "prance around like you think you're somebody."

I scuffed the toe of my oxford in the dirt. "So what's happening at your house?"

Her face lit up. It wasn't every day she had good news. "Mr. Cullowee's planting the fallow field between the cornfield and the creek so the boys can learn to grow kudzu. He's going to pay us fifty dollars to let him use the land, plus the government money."

"Fallow" was in the eye of the beholder. My daddy would have said Mr. Johnson was too lazy to plant all the way to the creek. But this was Mr. Johnson's lucky year. He was going to have half the boys of Cooper Consolidated working as farmhands without paying a nickel, and make money off the kudzu besides.

When the bus arrived, I waved goodbye to Lynnette and walked the three blocks to the mayor's house. Seventeen girls had shown up, all juniors and seniors except for me. The town girls had gone home and spruced up in dresses a notch above school outfits, while the county girls looked wilted in the late April heat.

At precisely 3:15, Mrs. Sampson opened her front door. "Welcome, girls!" she trilled. She led us down a hall lined with wallpaper of huntsmen chasing foxes. I'd never been inside the mayor's house, or any house so fancy. We stopped in the doorway to the sitting room, with its flocked wallpaper and mahogany furniture, like the Pinesboro Historical Museum, where we took a field trip every year. I expected her to point out a gold rope and tell us to stay on our side of it. But she ushered us in with an expansive gesture. "Please sit anywhere you like."

The town girls followed Mabel like ducklings and sat on two green sofas on opposite sides of the room, separated by cream satin pillows that dotted the sofas like marshmallows. I perched on a chair upholstered in slippery yellow silk, gripping lion paw arms to stay in place.

The rest of the country girls trailed in afterward, and were left with straight-backed chairs, which seemed designed for the sole purpose of making you sit up properly, and stood among the luxurious furnishings like infantrymen among officers.

Mabel, sitting on my left, leaned over her lion's paw. "Do you think Mr. Cullowee will be here?" she whispered.

"I hope so," I whispered back. "He's the only one who knows how things are done."

Mrs. Sampson waddled to the front of the room where she stood before a life-sized gilt-framed portrait of herself holding a Siamese cat.

The actual Mrs. Sampson held something far more interesting than a bored cat: the Kudzu Queen tiara, resting on a white velvet cushion. "This, my dears," she said, "is the crown one of you girls will be lucky enough to wear." Up close, it looked even more striking than it had from a distance: a big emerald framed by rubies and sapphires, diminishing to a narrow circlet of gold. Could those be actual gems? I wished Lynnette were there so I could ask what she thought.

To the right of the portrait, a door opened, and the Kudzu King stepped out, wearing the blue suit he'd worn when he first arrived in Cooper County. "Mrs. Sampson." He bowed in her direction, causing her cheeks to flame. "Ladies." He made a second bow toward us.

A few girls giggled and gawked at him being right in the room with them, which I figured didn't bode well for their Kudzu Queen training. I bestowed on him my best closed-mouth smile. Mrs. Sampson balanced the cushion on a side table where the jewels glistened in the lamplight.

"Ladies." Mr. Cullowee clasped his hands behind his back. On his lapel, he wore a tiny sprig of kudzu as a boutonnière, like Fred Astaire. "In two months' time, one of you will be crowned Cooper County's first Kudzu Queen, and will carry that mantle of responsibility for an entire year, as you invite your community to reap the benefits of kudzu. The rest of you have a task almost as important. Through your natural beauty and gracious ways, and the lessons in decorum you'll receive in the coming weeks, you will become ambassadresses for the crop that will transform the South. I'm honored to meet you all, and I look forward to getting to know you in the coming weeks." He gestured toward the mayor's wife. "And now, I'll leave you in the capable hands of the lovely Mrs. Sampson."

My heart plummeted. What was the use of giving up every Wednesday afternoon, if James Cullowee—in my head I was already calling him James—planned to abandon us to the pudgy clutches of the mayor's wife? When he started toward the door, I tried to think of something to keep him there. "Mr. Cullowee?" I called out, raising my hand as an afterthought.

"Yes?" he turned around. "Miss Watson, isn't it?"

"You can call me Mattie," I said.

"Mathilda," Mrs. Sampson said sternly. I wasn't sure whether she was reprimanding me for being forward or saying that a gentleman should call a lady by her proper name.

"I just wanted to know, if a person can't come to these lessons because of other obligations, could that person still try out for the Kudzu Queen?" I wasn't sure what Lynnette's chances were, but I would have been a sorry best friend if I didn't ask.

"Absolutely," he said. "Any young lady between the ages of fifteen and twenty-two is eligible. These lessons are simply an opportunity for us—"

"—to teach you to be ladies of *quality*," Mrs. Sampson interjected.

"But can we tell other people what we—"

"Mathilda," Mrs. Sampson pronounced, "I'm sure Mr. Cullowee," she sent a simper in his direction, "has obligations beyond our own little gathering. We wouldn't want to keep him."

Yes, we would, I thought, but Mrs. Sampson tucked her arm through Mr. Cullowee's and walked him to the door, her tiny feet scurrying under her rotund body to keep up with his pace.

When she returned, she reverently lifted the crown. "Now, to give you a taste of what's in store for one of you lucky girls, you'll get to try on our tiara."

"Mabel?" Her voice was as syrupy as a fruit cocktail. "Would you be so kind as to assist me?" The year before, when Mabel came back from modeling in Raleigh, the mayor and his wife had held a tea for her, inviting the town council. I didn't begrudge Mabel the attention. There are some spotlights you'd just as soon not have shining on you.

Mabel smoothed her turquoise-and-cream striped taffeta skirt and stood up. She crossed the room with her Hudson-Belk walk to stand gracefully next to Mrs. Sampson. As far as I could see, Mabel didn't need queen lessons. But despite Mabel's edge, there wasn't a girl in that room—spindly, overly tall, broad in the backside or completely unblessed by any bosom whatsoever—who didn't clutch a small belief that she, somehow, might be chosen.

Beyond being pretty, I wasn't sure of the qualifications for Kudzu queenliness. In the Miss America pageant you had to demonstrate a talent, charm, and poise. I figured I could manage charm and poise for brief spurts, but I wasn't sure what to do about the talent. Most of us had a party piece for social occasions, though, from what Danny said, when you got older, there were fewer party pieces and more rounds of Spin the Bottle. A party piece was usually a song or a poem you could recite by heart. Mine was mimicking a mourning dove by blowing through my cupped hands. At dusk, I'd have ten-minute conversations with birds that didn't know I was an imposter. I doubted this was a talent that would impress the judges.

Mrs. Sampson reached up to place the crown gently atop Mabel's head. She brushed Mabel's hair back for better effect and stepped away so we could see Mabel in all her glory. The mayor's wife's eyes were shiny with tears. She didn't have children of her own. It was easy to see that Mabel was the daughter she'd always wanted. They stood before us, allowing us to drink in all that splendor. Then Mrs. Sampson took a mother-of-pearl hand mirror from a side table and held it up so Mabel could see her future. Mabel touched the crown with the tips of her fingers, the corners of her mouth rising slightly, before she smiled at the rest of us, as if to say, *Really, any of you could be queen.*

Seeing how natural it looked on her, I was surprised the other sixteen of us didn't just admit the futility of all this and get up to leave.

Wistfully, Mrs. Sampson lifted the tiara from Mabel's head. "Mabel, dear, I'm sure the other girls would like to see how they would look if they were crowned queen." She walked to the next girl, a tall stork of a town girl named Alice Tomlinson. Alice stood.

"Oh no, dear." With a duchess-like tilt of the head, Mrs. Sampson gestured her down. Alice sat with a thud on the overstuffed sofa. As if she were Cinderella's fairy godmother, Mrs. Sampson guided the crown toward Alice's head, stopping two inches short of her stick-straight brown hair. Alice sat up straighter, and tried to lift herself up by pressing her palms into the cushions, but the crown remained tantalizingly out of reach.

"Mabel?" Mrs. Sampson called. "Would you be so kind as to bring the mirror? I'm sure this young lady would like to see how pretty she looks."

Mabel followed Mrs. Sampson, holding the mirror so each girl could see her own hope or disappointment. But there was no gentle hair tucking for Alice or any of the girls who followed. With each of us, Mrs. Sampson repeated the procedure, careful not to let the tiara touch one stray hair on our unworthy heads.

Glynis Carpentier neither rose nor sagged. Instead, she slouched like a boy, stretching out her legs and crossing them at the ankles, and tipping her head back against the sofa so Mrs. Sampson had to lower the crown. Mrs. Sampson gave her a glare that would have made most girls cower, but Glynis stared back, leaving her legs sticking out so Mabel and the mayor's wife had to pick their way over them.

By the time Mrs. Sampson got to me, Mabel looked embarrassed at her complicity. I'm sure if you'd asked Mrs. Sampson what she thought of our chances, she'd have said in a sweet songbird trill, "I don't envy the judges their decision." But instead of trying too hard, or waiting in perfect humility, or giving up on the whole thing, I looked straight at myself in the mirror that wavered in Mabel's hand and judged the exact distance of the chasm I was going to leap to become Kudzu Queen of Cooper County. I liked Mabel, and I wished her all the best, but I had more experience than she did leaping across Currie Creek when it was swollen in spring, and I was determined that on the other side of this competition, I would be queen.

When we finished our first Kudzu Queen class, Carla Ann had the bus waiting in front of school, having dropped off the other kids and returned. Most of the town girls were picked up by mothers or boyfriends, or walked home. The bus deposited the other town girls at their houses and headed out into the county with the rest of us.

I asked Carla Ann to leave me at Lynnette's driveway. When I opened the kitchen door, she was putting a chicken into the oven to roast. "Mr. Cullowee's talking to *him*," Lynnette said, without looking up, "about what they'll do tomorrow for their first kudzu class with the boys." She closed the oven door as gently as if she'd just perched an angel food cake on the center rack. "Mama asked me to kill a chicken so we could have a special supper."

I was glad I'd missed that part. I didn't like chickens, but I didn't care to witness their executions. For all Lynnette's gentleness, she had no difficulty taking care of practical things. She'd have made sure that Catherine was napping and Aggie safely off by the creek before she did the job, and she'd have sharpened the axe so the chicken's end would be quick.

We sat on the kitchen steps snapping green beans while I told her about the tiara. In the distance, I could see Mr. Cullowee and

Mr. Johnson walking between spindly stalks of corn. In the field by the creek were freshly plowed tracks. Mr. Cullowee must have done it himself. Mr. Johnson had about as much precision with a plow as I did with a sewing machine. I wondered about the "no plowing needed" part of Mr. Cullowee's first speech, but figured since that field hadn't been touched in years, maybe it needed more attention than most.

"Do you think they were real gemstones?" Lynnette asked.

"Probably paste," I said. "He can't very well go around giving out emerald and ruby crowns in every county in the south."

We settled on semi-precious, and went on to discuss what I'd learned about how a lady behaves in polite company: appropriate skirt lengths for every occasion, proper posture while sitting and walking, and the correct way to drink tea—demonstrated by Mrs. Sampson using an invisible cup and saucer—with the pinky as far as possible from the other fingers, as if the rest of the hand suffered from a contagious disease.

Joey was waiting, eager for news, when I arrived home. I hated to disappoint him, particularly since he'd been unusually generous in offering to do all the work for both of us on Wednesdays—not only the kudzu-tending and his usual pig feeding, but also the chickens and milking, well beyond what he owed after daring me into Aunt Mary's house. At least my imitation of a pinky-extended, haughty-voiced Mrs. Sampson made him laugh.

That night at supper, Danny surprised me by asking Daddy, "Do you think you could spare me one afternoon a week? I'm considering doing that kudzu course with Mr. Cullowee."

Daddy took a sip of sweet tea. "I might be able to, if you think it's worthwhile."

"Could give me a leg up next fall," Danny said.

"Let me know if you learn anything useful," Daddy said.

"I could come, too," Joey said, his face stiff with the effort of trying to act casual.

"Sorry, pal," Danny told him. "It's just for the big boys." When he saw Joey's crestfallen look, he added, "But if I find out anything especially good, I'll let you know."

I wanted to watch the first kudzu cultivation class the next day, but I didn't want Danny to think I was spying. When Joey and I headed toward the woods, we waved at Daddy as he walked the rows of the cornfield alone, holding leaves up to the sunlight to look for spider mites. He looked cheerful enough, even without Danny. Daddy, Mama, and Danny were alike in that way, happy enough in solitude, and equally happy in company. Joey and I needed companionship, Joey with his school friends and me with Lynnette, and now for the first time in our lives, with each other. As far as the family was concerned, I was being unusually thoughtful, spending my afternoons with Joey in the woods. I was earning big sister points, which I hoped to cash in for something important, like permission to wear lipstick.

At the table that evening, Danny was full of "Jim this—" and "Jim that—" how Mr. Cullowee had shown them color photographs of kudzu in bloom, with its purple flowers and wide leaves, and had explained that you could plant kudzu between your corn rows to increase the nitrogen intake of the soil and improve your corn crop. Though kudzu didn't need any special tending, Danny continued, "Jim said you can water and weed it in the first few weeks, to improve its viability."

"Water and weed," Joey repeated, sneaking me a triumphant look.

"Was Mr. Cullowee there the whole time?" I asked.

"Sure," Danny said.

"You mean he didn't leave you with Mr. Johnson?"

"Why would he do that?" Danny said. "Johnson doesn't know anything about kudzu—or about farming at all, for that matter."

"About as much as Mrs. Sampson knows about being a beauty queen," I snapped. How was it that Danny got Mr. Cullowee while I had to settle for the mayor's wife?

"Manners, Mattie," Mama warned.

"How come you didn't tell Danny to mind his manners when he said that about Mr. Johnson?" I demanded.

Mama and Daddy traded a look. "You too, Danny," Mama said.

"Did he tell you anything else?" Joey asked. I kicked him under the table. It wouldn't do for either of us to look eager about kudzu. "I'm just curious," he amended.

"We're all curious," Mama said. "What else did you learn today, Danny?"

"Well, you can graze a cow for over two months on an acre of kudzu," he said, "though it's best used to supplement your regular feed, rather than replacing it." I wasn't planning to waste our kudzu on cows, particularly Sassafras. That was no way to get rich. He went on, "And you can grind the roots into meal for chickens," which seemed an even bigger waste to me.

"Sounds interesting," Daddy said. "I'll look forward to seeing how it does around here."

"We could plant some and see for ourselves," Danny said, sipping his tea, to show he didn't care one way or the other. "I mean, as an experiment."

"I've got this year's experiments pretty well planned out," Daddy told him, "but I'll keep it in mind for next season."

"You know I won't be here next season," Danny reminded him, as if Daddy ever needed to be reminded of anything.

"All the more reason for me to have a new project to occupy my mind in your absence," Daddy said, which was as close as he was likely to get to telling Danny he'd miss him.

Daddy had been to college himself, in Delaware, not to study modern scientific methods of farming, but to read Shakespeare and other famous literature. He could have been a professor, but when he married Mama, her daddy told them he'd give over his 320 acres of cotton, corn, tobacco, and tenant farms if they'd settle on it. You'd have thought in a place like Cooper County, Daddy would have been an outcast, coming to farming from books and being from up north besides. But he had a way about him that made men respect his opinion. He was a listener before he was a talker. When he opened his mouth to say something, other people shut theirs.

He'd approached farming the way he'd approached Shakespeare. He'd read the land, seen its beauty, then sat down and figured out what made it work. There was plenty of talk when word got out that Daddy and Mama were paying to send Danny to Ag School. A waste of good money, people said, and even more, of the boy's life. Danny was a natural farmer already, having inherited an eye for weather and perfect timing for planting and harvesting from Mama's daddy.

Everybody liked Danny—girls, boys, parents, farmers, teachers, preachers. Easygoing, smart, captain of the baseball team and handsome as a film star, with dark hair that always fell in his eyes, he had the sort of local fame that allowed a person to pass easily through the membrane between town and country.

There were plenty who felt they were in a position to give him counsel, not just farmers who lectured him on staying home to help his father, but also his friends—boys who told him schooling was a waste of time, and girls like Ann Marie Walker, Glynis Carpentier's best friend, looking up from under her lashes and, saying, "Aren't you going to be lonely?" when what she meant was, *Those girls up in Raleigh won't do for you what I will.*

That night, on my way to bed after brushing my teeth, I lingered outside Danny's bedroom. I watched him sit at the pine table he'd built in shop class, reading his course catalog by the light of his desk lamp. I wanted to tell him about the field Joey and I had planted. We were doing all right, but we'd do better if we let Danny in on it. I couldn't, though. If Danny took it over, Joey would get no credit at all. It would just be another thing Danny had done right.

"Come on in, Mattie," Danny said without looking up. "I know you're out there."

I padded in, silent in the thick wool socks I preferred to house slippers, and sat on the floor at his feet, drawing my knees up under my nightgown. Danny kept reading. The circle of lamplight spilled onto the floor, leaving shadows below his desk. When I was little, I was afraid of the shadows that lived in the undersides of furniture. I pulled my toes beneath my nightgown.

"If I take an extra course a semester," Danny said, "I could finish a semester early."

The idea of voluntarily taking more courses than required seemed to me a cruel kind of self-inflicted punishment, but I appreciated the simple math of it.

"It would save money on tuition and boarding," he added.

"How far away is Raleigh?" I asked, meaning, but not saying: *I don't want you to go.*

I'd sworn I'd never say that. My reasons for wishing he'd stay were selfish. Danny was the best listener I knew, even better than Mama or Daddy or Lynnette. If I wanted to talk about something, but didn't want it inscribed in the permanent record book in my mother's head, he was the one I could tell. When he went away in September, the house was going to feel empty.

"I might be able to come home weekends," he said, as if he knew what I wanted to say.

I leaned against his leg, content to sit while he studied his future. Danny thought like Daddy, looking at problems with interest rather than frustration, and trying to figure out equally interesting and useful solutions. Danny called it "thinking like the variable." If he and Daddy wanted to keep squirrels from clattering on the roof, they'd think: What's a squirrel afraid of, and how can we make sure he has to face it every time he climbs up there? In the end, they made a hawk weathervane, wings outstretched like it was about to dive for a kill. Danny painted that hawk so lifelike, you couldn't have told it from a real one.

In less than a month, every family within ten miles had hawk weathervanes. They weren't as good as Danny's, but nobody had a problem with squirrels on the roof after that.

A person like Danny needed to go to school. One idea could grow to a hundred in his mind. He needed to be where people talked about what was happening now, instead of telling him to do things the way they'd been done for generations. I didn't know if he'd come home a farmer, or even if he'd come home at all. But I knew if he didn't go, he'd wilt, wither, and die.

# 6

Mr. Cullowee likes my room," Lynnette declared after school on Friday, while we were waiting for Carla Ann to grind the school bus gears to announce her arrival. "He said he'd know a beautiful young lady slept there even if he'd never met me."

We were sitting on our bench, swinging our bare legs to get some sun. I'd read in a beauty magazine if you moved your legs you got a fuller exposure to the sun's rays.

"He always says good night to me before he goes up to bed," she added. "And sometimes I see him before he's fully dressed in the morning."

I wondered if Lynnette felt left out because she couldn't go to Queen School. It wasn't like her to brag. "What do you think he's doing in your room anyway, between the time you say good night and the morning when you see him half-naked?" I asked.

"He'd never sneak someone in there," Lynnette protested, tucking her legs under her mustard-colored dress. She sewed the prettiest clothes, though she tended to pick drab colors.

I tried on my shoes to see if my legs were dark enough to go to church without stockings. Not yet. I pulled my skirt higher to shock Lynnette, who secretly liked to be shocked.

She straightened my skirt, pretending it had accidentally gotten hiked up and she was putting it right before I embarrassed myself. "Besides who'd do it with him anyway? Glynis?"

"You're right. I can't think of any girl who'd do it," I said. Except maybe me, I thought, and I had only a technical idea of "it" as it pertained to people rather than farm animals.

I took off my shoes and examined my toenails. My mother wouldn't let me paint them. She said painted toenails looked cheap. "But he's got company in there just the same."

"But you said—"

"He's got the whole family," I told her. "Little Miss Thumb and her four sweet sisters."

"Mattie!" Lynnette glowered. "That's disgusting."

"Fine," I told her. "Don't believe me. Check the sheets when you go to wash them. See if they aren't a little stained in the middle." Since Lynnette didn't have brothers she could be shocked by things I took for granted.

"You're just jealous," Lynnette said.

"I'll tell you what," I said. "You have me over to your house tonight and we'll both see him in his undershirt tomorrow morning and I won't have anything to feel jealous about."

She kept her eyes down, pretending to sulk. "But we can't sleep in my bedroom."

"I'll stay with you on the sleeping porch," I said. "Maybe your mama will make kudzu flour pancakes for breakfast. With kudzu syrup."

"Disgusting!" she said, but she smiled at a little.

Mama was happy to let me stay over at Lynnette's that night. "It's been a few weeks, hasn't it? I'm sure you girls have some catching up to do."

"And can I miss town tomorrow too?" I asked.

I figured if I came early, and stayed late, there would be plenty of chances to catch sight of Mr. Cullowee, maybe even at supper, though I couldn't count on that. From what Lynnette had said, he spent a lot of time in meetings with the mayor and council members, which often extended through suppertime.

I arrived at Lynnette's house with Danny's old Boy Scout sleeping bag tied up with a shoelace, and the train case filled with essentials: nightgown, bathrobe, toothbrush, hairbrush, and clothes for the morning. We stowed my stuff on the sleeping porch, on the cot I'd come to think of as mine whenever Lynnette and I stayed out there. Some families had full-sized daybeds on their sleeping porches, but the Johnsons had rickety cots that creaked when you rolled over.

After I'd unrolled my sleeping bag, I curled up in the white wicker rocker, staring dreamily at the empty field out back. "Soon, that field will be full of beautiful green kudzu."

Sitting on the edge of her cot, Lynnette kept her feet flat on the floor, knees pressed together. Even with me she sometimes had a prim way about her, though it was usually worst when I first arrived, as if she had to start from scratch every time. She tended to relax late at night, when we lay on top of our sleeping bags in our nightgowns, giggling.

"Mr. Cullowee's promised ours'll be the first field planted," she told me.

"Uh-huh." The first official field, I thought.

The smell of pork chops and greens drifted out to the porch. The sunlight slipped down the side of the barn as we debated whether kudzu jelly or syrup would be tastier. After awhile, Mrs. Johnson called, "Lynnette? Aggie? Catherine? You girls come to supper."

Mr. Cullowee wasn't there, which made the pork chops drier and the greens more vinegary. But I got to drink Mrs. Johnson's tea, which was so sweet you didn't need dessert, though that never kept me from taking a helping of her lemon pie or pound cake. With this not being a company night and Mr. Johnson out drinking on the stoop, we made do with oatmeal cookies. Mrs. Johnson had a generous hand with the raisins.

When we had our cookies, I asked if we could be excused, something Lynnette would never do until the last person at the table finished the last bite. "I suppose so," her mother sighed.

"Come on," I told Lynnette, as we stuffed our cookies in our skirt pockets. "Let's go to your room."

"It's not my room now. It's Mr. Cullowee's."

I was going to have to be persuasive, but I was planning to be a lawyer, so it was good practice. "All right." I pulled her down beside me on the bottom step. Breaking my cookie in two, I handed her the bigger half. Lynnette loved sweet things even more than I did, which was saying something. "Do you have everything you need from your room?" I asked.

She shook her head. "Not everything."

"What're you missing?"

"Well, I could use my other two school dresses." She'd worn the same dress to school all week, but I wasn't low enough to mention that—if she hadn't said it first.

"Let's go get it, then." I stood, pulling her to her feet.

"Mama said not to go in there," she said. "A man needs his privacy."

"That's why we're going in while he's not here." I started up the steps, leaving her no choice but to follow. "We'll just grab your school dresses. We won't be a minute."

"All right, then." She stuffed the rest of the cookie in her mouth. "Just for a minute."

When we got to her bedroom, we both froze in the hall.

"You first." I pushed her toward the closed door.

Her feet skidded on the worn pine floor. "Not me."

"It's your room," I said.

"But it was your idea." She folded her arms across her chest, a sure sign she wouldn't do anything I asked no matter how reasonably I asked it.

"Fine." I was about to open the door when I wondered if he'd been there the whole time. "Mr. Cullowee?" I knocked. "Are you there? Lynnette needs to get in her room for a minute." No answer.

"Why'd you say it was me?" Lynnette whispered.

"That's why we're here, isn't it?" I said.

"Fine!" She swung the door open, marched in, grabbed the dresses from the dowel rod and a crumpled gray cardigan from a chair and marched out. "That girl," she said, "she leaves her things strewn everywhere." I scurried to catch up as she strode down the hall, making a detour to toss the sweater on Aggie's bed. "We're done."

"Lynnette," I protested. "We haven't even started. What did you see? The whole point of coming up here was to find out about Mr. Cullowee."

She handed me the dresses, which I took without thinking. "And here I thought the whole point was to keep me from wearing the same blessed dress five days in one week."

Mr. Cullowee didn't come home until after midnight. Though I heard his step on the stairs, I didn't wake Lynnette. I thought of him in Lynnette's room, surrounded by her faded wallpaper. I imagined the bed creaking as he climbed in, wearing the blue-and-white-striped pajamas Lynnette had described, his jaw shiny with golden stubble. I imagined his long fingers untying his pajama string and slipping under the cool cloth. I felt excited and sad at the same time, like a child who's old enough to know that her birthday bicycle means no new dress for Mama this year, but it's too late to give it back and say she didn't really want it.

The cicadas hummed, one long chorus of the same note. There were so many cicadas that hundreds could stop to draw breath while hundreds more filled in the gap, never leaving a lull.

Lynnette snuffled occasionally in sleep, an arm's reach away. I lay on my back, staring at the beadboard ceiling. It was, I knew, painted pale blue to keep the haints away.

"They won't cross water," my grandfather had told me when I was little. "And no more will they cross a porch ceiling painted blue like water, so they can't get into the house."

The ceiling looked silver-gray in the dark, but I liked the idea of lying underwater, languid as a mermaid, with no more responsibility for my actions.

I imagined the Kudzu King lying next to me on the narrow cot, balanced on his side, staring into my eyes like he was hypnotized. "May I touch your leg?" he would ask, and like a game of "Mother, May I?" where there's only one possible answer, I'd say, "Yes, you may."

"May I touch your thigh? Your hip? Your beautiful bosom?"

"Yes, you may."

What Lynnette felt for Bobby Mason was a crush, and crushes are made for confidences, but I was in love, a far lonelier thing. I looked at her skinny face in the moonlight. Poor child, I thought. I'm leaving you behind.

Through the open upstairs window, I heard Aggie calling out and thrashing in her sleep. Catherine, across the room from Aggie, tended to float all night like a log down a slow river.

I heard Mrs. Johnson tend to Aggie, heard her soft murmurs in the bedroom above, while in my mind the Kudzu King asked, "May I lift your nightgown?" and my bare arms and feet glowed atop white sheets. Sleep was something ordinary people did. Sleep, and touching the ground when you walked, and breathing regularly.

The room above quieted, and Lynnette rolled over, pressing her face into her pillow. We were the only ones awake, my imagined Kudzu King and I. I could tell him to stay or go, except the only thing I remembered how to say was, "Yes, you may." And then I remembered something else, about the real Kudzu King, James Cullowee. He was upstairs, a naked man under respectable pajamas. I wondered if he was lying in bed, thinking of me, thinking of asking, "May I touch your leg?"

# 7

Lynnette and I got up early and tended to the chickens before they began squawking. I wanted us to practice what I'd learned in Queen class before everyone was awake to see us.

It was easy enough to choose books for posture practice. There were only four in the Johnson home: the Bible, a tobacco pamphlet from the Department of Agriculture, Webster's Unabridged Dictionary, and a collection of children's stories from Mrs. Johnson's schoolteaching days. There used to be more, Lynnette told me, but Mr. Johnson had dumped the rest in the trash fire the last time they'd moved, saying he was tired of carting around useless junk. I tucked Webster under my arm while Lynnette carried *The Blue Fairy Book*, and we made our way through the dew-soaked weeds to her family's cornfield.

My head turned out to be a bit pointy, so I had to keep reaching up to steady the dictionary. Lynnette, on the other hand, had a perfectly flat head on top, which meant she could—and did—stride up and down the rows, faster and faster, until she was almost running.

"It's not a race," I complained as she sped by. "The object is to practice our queenly walk, not break the four-minute mile."

She slowed to my pace, lifting each foot deliberately and placing it flat on the ground. "Like this?"

I laughed and Webster went flying. "You look like a mule. Place one foot in front of the other, like you're walking on a porch rail, and your hips will follow naturally." I'd learned this from Mabel Moore, who'd learned it from her Hudson-Belk modeling. After Lynnette adjusted her walk, I had to admit she looked sexier, even if she didn't have much hip to work with.

"I think you should put your shoulders back to display your bosom a little more," she suggested, which was quite daring of

Lynnette. My bosom had come along since seventh grade. Lynnette's was more modest, but that suited her personality. It was thoughtful of her to suggest showcasing my bosom, having so little of her own to display.

"How much? I don't want to look cheap."

She paused to ponder, the book perfectly balanced on top of her head. "You should model yourself after Olivia de Havilland," she said.

"Maybe we could switch," I suggested, plucking *The Blue Fairy Book* from her head and handing her the dictionary. But *The Blue Fairy* was wobbly too.

"I think I'd be better off in your royal court." Lynnette tilted her head forward and the dictionary dropped neatly into her hand. "I'm not the queenly type."

"Come on," I said. "You'd be a wonderful Kudzu Queen." Which was true. What she lacked in womanly attributes, she made up for with a willowy elegance and pretty green eyes.

"It's going to be you," she said. "I can feel it in my bones."

"I can't even walk two steps with a book on my head," I objected.

"But you're beautiful." She said it as a statement of fact rather than an opinion. "Anyhow," she added, with that practical side I loved her for, "you won't have a book on your head in the pageant."

From the kitchen steps, her mother called us in to dress for breakfast. By the time we'd washed and dressed, everyone was seated at the table, including Mr. Cullowee. It felt strange to sit across from him after the things I'd imagined the night before. "Good morning, Miss Lynnette," he said. "And what a pleasure it is to see you, Miss Mathilda." I felt my cheeks go red, but hoped he might think I was sun-flushed.

For all Mr. Johnson's poor-mouthing, breakfast at the Johnsons tended to be substantial. Eggs, sausage, grits, biscuits and gravy, and—that morning—leftover peach pie. Mr. Johnson piled his plate high with eggs and sausage and ate steadily, head down, in his usual silence. The others generally followed suit, but that day Mrs. Johnson seemed inspired by Mr. Cullowee's presence. "Tell me about your people," she said, as she poured his coffee.

"My people?" He paused while lifting a forkful of eggs. "Well, we're pretty much mongrels all the way back, though you'd never know it to talk with my mother. She has a family tree tracing us to Charlemagne."

"She must be a sweet lady," Mrs. Johnson said, "to have raised such a good son."

"I'm her only child," he said, winking at Aggie, whose glance darted to the kitchen window, "so she thinks I hang the moon. Of course, she's a bit biased."

She patted his hand. "No mother's biased regarding her own children. And your father?"

"Career military. Salute when he enters the room," he raised his coffee cup, "and don't forget to say 'sir' at the end of every sentence."

Head bent over his sausage, Mr. Johnson nodded as if he approved.

Out in the driveway, gravel crunched under truck wheels. Aggie ran to the window. "Danny!" she called, and rushed to the screen door.

Sometimes Danny would swing by the Johnson house on his way to the river with a couple of fishing poles and ask if Aggie wanted to join him. He'd discovered in Aggie a quiet appreciation for nature that matched his own. Aggie could sit for hours in silence, taking in the river: the wavering reflections of trees, the conversations of birds, fish popping up with their mouths gaping for water bugs, the music of water over rocks. The two of them would come home with identical rolled-up jeans, matching sunburns, and a string of fish. Though Lynnette always sent her off wearing a hat, Aggie usually returned with it shoved in her back pocket, covered with dirt.

Danny's knock sounded just before Aggie opened the door. He smiled, his hand raised to knock again. "Agatha Johnson." He squatted to her level. "It's a pleasure to see your smiling face." Danny and Lynnette were the only people Aggie tolerated calling her Agatha. When she soberly climbed on his back, he carried her to the table and deposited her into her seat.

"You're just in time, Danny," Mrs. Johnson said. "Sit down and have some breakfast." She stood to get him a chair, but he'd already claimed half of mine.

"Don't mind if I do," Danny said. "It's my second one this morning, but since it's the most important meal of the day, two breakfasts are sure to be an improvement on one."

Mrs. Johnson brought him a plate, which he proceeded to fill in a haphazard pile, a breakfast sandwich with a biscuit at the bottom, peach pie on top, and everything else in the middle. "Morning, Mr. Johnson," he said. Mr. Johnson grunted without looking up.

Danny leaned across the table toward Mr. Cullowee, balancing a giant forkful of biscuit, sausage, eggs, grits, and pie. "Bunch of us are heading to the far end of the county, to the Lockabees'," he said. "Kurt Lockabee broke his leg last week and could use a hand getting his corn planted. Stopped by to see if you wanted to come along." He deposited his forkful in his mouth, chewed, and swallowed. "Be an opportunity for you to meet some folks, make a good impression. Lot of people wanting to hear more about this kudzu you're selling."

"I'm not selling it, Danny. I'm giving it away." Mr. Cullowee lifted his coffee cup in a toast. "I want to see Cooper County make a name for itself."

"I appreciate that," said Danny. "And I'm sure most people do. But with these fellows, you might want to tone it down. They're interested in practical information—what's the growing season, how do you tend it, where can you sell it, and what kind of profit can you turn?"

I was interested in practical information too. "Can I come?"

Danny sipped his coffee. "I thought you and Lynnette were spending the day together."

"We were. I mean, we are. But Lynnette wants to come too. Don't you, Lynnette?"

"I suppose so," she said. "But I have to watch Aggie and Catherine."

"You girls go, and take Aggie," said Mrs. Johnson. "I can survive a day without you." Aggie jumped up from the table and stood by Danny, ready to leave the instant he was.

"Can we help clean up?" Danny asked Mrs. Johnson.

"No, go on," she answered. "I'll get it done twice as fast with you all out of my kitchen."

"All right, then." Danny took a last bite and stood. The chair, deprived of his weight, tipped toward me, so I jumped up before it could fall over.

"Let's go," I told Lynnette.

Mr. Cullowee stood up, patted his mouth with a napkin, folded it, and placed it beside his empty plate. He laid his hand on Mrs. Johnson's shoulder like he was offering a benediction. "You make the best breakfast in the country, Mrs. Johnson," he said. "First, second, or third."

She smiled. "My pleasure."

"Anything we can get for you while we're out and about?" he asked.

"Not a thing," Mrs. Johnson said.

"You could get some rat poison on your way through town," Mr. Johnson said, still not looking up. "Those rats are getting into the chicken feed again." Mrs. Johnson gave her husband a quick glare, which he ignored, adding, "And you might as well get a sack of feed to replace what they ate."

"Glad to do it," said Mr. Cullowee. "Shall we?" He gestured us ahead.

"When should I expect you?" asked Lynnette's mother.

"Oh, surely by supper," Mr. Cullowee said. "If I could presume upon your hospitality?"

"Of course," Mrs. Johnson said. "You know you're always welcome."

Forgetting for the moment that Lynnette and I were delicate

flowers, I hoisted myself into Danny's truck bed and sat on a pile of feed sacks behind the cab, while Danny swung Aggie over the side. Lynnette, careful to avoid any revelation of her knees in mixed company, waited for him to lower the tailgate and help her in. We leaned back, tucking our legs under our skirts.

"Wouldn't you ladies like to sit up front?" Mr. Cullowee asked through the window.

"No, thank you." I wasn't sure I could manage that much proximity. Anyhow, riding in the back was more fun, especially when Danny drove fast and the wind whipped past like a highway hurricane.

Danny crunched out of the drive, aiming for the bumps in the road. With each bump, we flew up and landed squealing on the soft pile of sacks.

A trip to the east side of the county practically required a passport. We traveled from our dirt road to the country road to the county road to the state road that turned into Main Street as we passed through town, with a quick stop at the feed store. Then we did the whole procedure in reverse: state road, county road, country road, dirt road, Lockabee farm.

I didn't really know the Lockabees, though they attended our church and had a boy a year behind Lynnette and me in school, a redheaded scarecrow with feet as big as rowboats, who was so skinny I figured he'd break if he tried to carry a bucket of water.

We bounced into the yard and parked by the other trucks. Mr. Lockabee swung over on crutches to meet us. He had red hair like his boy, though his had a lot of gray in it, and wrinkles around his eyes from sun-squinting. "Danny, you're a good man." He leaned his right crutch against the truck to shake Danny's hand. "And who are these farmhands you've brought?"

I jumped down. "This is my sister, Mattie." Lynnette slid to the ground as Danny hoisted Aggie over the side. "And her friend Lynnette and Lynnette's sister, Aggie. And I expect you've heard of Mr. James T. Cullowee, the Kudzu King."

Mr. Lockabee pivoted on his good foot to shake Mr. Cullowee's hand. "Pleasure," he said. "I wasn't able to get into town last weekend, but I heard tell of you from my boy." He gathered up his right crutch and stuck it under his arm. "Come around to the kitchen. My wife's filling everybody up with coffee and biscuits before we head out to the field."

Aggie quietly gripped Danny's hand.

Ahead of us, I could hear Mr. Cullowee extolling the benefits of kudzu to Mr. Lockabee. "It's the ideal crop for a man in such a situation as yourself. You say you have a son?"

"Fourteen years old, and near as tall as me," Mr. Lockabee answered, swinging forward in long arcs.

"Couldn't be better!" The Kudzu King lengthened his stride to keep up. "A boy of ten could plant a field of kudzu. And with you to advise him? Why kudzu will see you through this rough patch, and by harvest time, you'll never want to plant anything else."

"I believe I'll take things one at a time," said Mr. Lockabee politely. "Right now my job is to get this corn in the ground."

"Absolutely," Mr. Cullowee said. "You just let me know where I can be the most help."

It took all day, gallons of sweet tea and sweat, and platters of pimento cheese sandwiches to get the Lockabees' field planted. Trucks pulled up well into the afternoon as neighbors arrived to pitch in. Lynnette, Aggie, and I helped wherever we could, making sandwiches and delivering glasses of tea. By quarter past four, the rows were cleanly planted, and the men were filthy dirty.

The men—eighteen or twenty of them—gathered by the pump, mopping sweat off their dirt-streaked necks with handkerchiefs, drinking beer out of bottles, and taking turns to splash cool water on their faces. The only one who looked fresh was the Kudzu King, who'd spent much of the afternoon chatting with Mrs. Lockabee while she made sandwiches and poured tea. He smiled and raised his bottle. "Gentlemen," he said, "and ladies—" nodding toward Mrs. Lockabee, Lynnette, Aggie, and me, "I'd like to propose a toast to our fine host and hostess—and young Kurt Lockabee, Junior. And to the spirit of neighborliness so evident in Cooper County."

A couple of the farmers halfheartedly lifted their bottles and drained them, ready to pack into their trucks and head home, where supper, baths, and wives awaited them. One by one, they deposited their empty bottles on the picnic table or beside the pump before they trudged to their trucks.

"Hey, Mike," Danny called after one of them, a young farmer who'd inherited twenty acres from his uncle, a few miles east of us. "How're your potatoes coming along? You got them in nice and early this year. When do you think you'll harvest?"

Mike paused and looked back to where Danny stood by the Kudzu King. "Another month or so, I'd say."

"You going to let that field lie fallow until next spring?" Danny asked.

Even from where I stood, I could see the gleam light up in the Kudzu King's eyes, but he had the sense to keep his mouth shut.

"Might as well."

"You could plant a cover," Danny said. "Feed the soil." Other men paused to listen. For all the ribbing they gave Danny over Ag School, they tended to pay attention to his suggestions. Some of his methods might come out of books, but he and Daddy were using them on our farm, and our crops were doing better than most.

"Suppose I could. What you think?"

"I'm thinking maybe kudzu," Danny said.

"Your daddy know you plan to plant that weed on his land? The way things've been lately, I'm not planting anything that don't bring in an income," another man said, taking a fresh beer from the tray Mrs. Lockabee was offering around. "No offense," he said to Mr. Cullowee.

"None taken," Mr. Cullowee replied.

"I see it as a cash crop," Danny answered. "Sure, it grows like a weed, but that just means it doesn't need a lot of care."

A few more men stopped on their way to their trucks.

"A cash crop," Danny leaned against the picnic table and

sipped his beer, "that can feed your livestock through the winter, doubling the return on each field, while it holds the topsoil in place and gives it the nitrogen it's hungry for."

The Kudzu King stood off to one side, a quiet smile on his face.

"You ever seen it grown?" Mike asked.

"Not yet," said Danny, "but I read up on it in one of my dad's USDA bulletins, and it's starting to sound like a no-risk gamble. What've you got to lose on a field you would've left fallow half the year anyway? Might as well pull its weight year round. Not to mention the fact that the government's offered to pay you to grow the stuff."

Mrs. Lockabee circulated, handing out more beer now that the men seemed to be staying. Lynnette and I slipped between the men, picking up empty bottles. Aggie stood at the edge of the crowd, transfixed by her hero at the center of all those grown men's attention.

"Anyone here try those kudzu cigarettes?" Danny asked.

A couple men tilted their heads, as if to say, *I might've done, but I'm not going to admit to it in public.*

"Well, I did," Danny told them. "I smoked one after supper yesterday evening. They weren't bad. I could get used to a smoke like that." He took a swig of beer. "Anybody try that kudzu jelly your wives brought home?"

A few more nodded. They'd admit to jelly. You could make jelly out of almost anything, but cigarettes in tobacco country? That was nothing to take lightly.

"I had some of that jelly for breakfast this morning," Danny said. "My first breakfast, that is, not my second—or the third I had here."

The men laughed again and tipped back their beers, relaxed now. Mr. Cullowee laughed along with the others, but in his face I thought I saw a little relief.

# 8

The next Wednesday afternoon, after I saw Lynnette off on the bus, I walked to the mayor's house, thinking how the Kudzu Queen class would be more fun if she could come. By the time I arrived, the comfortable chairs were full, so I sat on a hard wooden one in the back of the room.

"I have such a lovely surprise for you, girls!" Mrs. Sampson exclaimed. "Guess who's here to give you a lesson in 'The Grand Promenade'?"

If we'd been boys, or ourselves before starting Queen classes, we would have called out our best guesses, but Mrs. Sampson had drilled enough comportment into us that we knew when she said, "guess," she didn't mean guess.

"Mr. Cullowee and my handsome husband, the Honorable Mayor Sampson," she announced, as if Mr. Cullowee might be a treat, but the mayor was baked Alaska. I figured if things went according to form, we'd get to spend the afternoon watching Mr. Cullowee escort Mabel around the room.

Sure enough, Mrs. Sampson crooked her finger at Mabel. "Our Mabel will demonstrate 'Perambulation.'" When Mabel rose gracefully from her chair, Mrs. Sampson continued. "We've blocked off a portion of the street for you girls to practice. We'll go outside in a moment, but first I'd like to present 'The Gentlemen.'" She opened the door with a flourish and in walked the mayor, his tuxedo jacket stretching desperately over his belly. Mr. Cullowee waited in the doorway, much more elegant in a gray pinstriped suit.

We clapped politely as we'd been taught, fingertips to palm. When Mr. Cullowee's eyes lingered on me, my heart crashed against my ribs, trying to escape. I'm sure other girls in that room had feelings for the Kudzu King, but what I felt was so big I could barely contain it.

"Girls?" Mrs. Sampson called. Then, more sharply, "Girls!" I yanked my eyes away to see her scowling at me. "We'll go outside now. As I determine you've mastered 'Perambulation' and are ready to learn 'The Grand Promenade,' I'll send you in to practice with Mr. Mayor and Mr. Cullowee. While we perambulate, the gentlemen will enjoy a spot of tea."

She tinkled a brass bell and in walked Rose Moore, a girl about my age, in a black dress with a white collar. Rose and I had been friends when we were little. Even then she'd been distinctive, with dark brown skin, steady green eyes, and a quick mind. Rose was no relation to Mabel, though there were lots of Moores in the county, both colored and white.

Rose's daddy, Luther, was a tenant on one of the farms we'd inherited from Granddaddy, a couple miles from us. I used to go over to their house with Daddy whenever he needed to fix a pipe, or nail down a loose sheet of tin on the barn roof, or help out with the tobacco harvest. It took me years to catch on to the fact that most people with tenants didn't pitch in with planting or harvesting, but Daddy claimed he'd never felt quite right standing by when a man didn't have one grown child to his name and needed to get the tobacco in before the rain. While he and Luther worked, Rose and I could do anything we wanted as long as we stayed away from the juke joint and the river. We were fascinated by the juke joint, with walls that seemed to pulse to the music even in the middle of the day, and a bright red neon sign that alternated the words "COLD" and "BEER." But we obeyed, and spent most of our time creating amateur theatricals on Rose's front porch, forcing her cousin Evelyn to be our audience until our daddies finished and we could persuade them to watch our princess stories.

Some days, Rose's mother left her at our house on her way to work in town. We'd play tea party with acorn cups and gingko leaves, or climb trees and pretend to be pirates in the rigging. Rose was always head pirate, which meant she got to wear the eye patch. Until we were six, she was my best and only friend, but once we started different schools, we hardly saw each other.

Now, in her black uniform, she seemed to have invisible shutters in front of her eyes to keep whatever was inside her from being seen. I couldn't blame her. If I worked for Mrs. Sampson, I'd wear shutters too. Rose carried a heavy silver tray with two cups and saucers and a teapot decorated with fleeing shepherdesses pursued by grimly determined shepherds. She put the tray on a table and glanced up to give me a nod so small as to be invisible to anyone who wasn't looking for it.

"Young ladies?" Mrs. Sampson started for the front door. "If you'll follow me, we'll begin."

I took up the end of the line, behind Glynis Carpentier, who couldn't be bothered to look at me. Whenever I was near Glynis, I felt a strange hatred radiating from her. I had no idea what I'd done to make her hate me. I missed Lynnette. I gave a silent prayer that her father would stay in the fields until well past dark so she and her mother could have a few hours of peace.

At each end of the block stood two brass stanchions with gold ropes between them. "Line up, please," Mrs. Sampson said. "Three across, with your best posture."

We sorted ourselves out by our natures, with the brave and conceited in the first group and those who wanted to get it over with in the next. I found a place to be invisible: middle girl in the third row, next to Alice, and away from Glynis.

Women emerged from their houses to watch, wiping hands on aprons. Small girls and boys sat on the curb, elbows propped on knees.

"Chins up, girls," Mrs. Sampson called out. "Hands still, but not stiff."

Mabel glided ahead, each foot placed perfectly in front of the other, her hips gently swaying. Two of the three girls in the first row did their best to imitate her, clopping like draft horses, smiles rubber-cemented onto their faces. The third was Glynis.

Technically, her stride duplicated Mabel's, her hands so perfectly still they seemed to be encased in elbow-length white gloves. But her hips seemed to have more swing to them, and her bosom more thrust. She raised her chin a notch higher, and on her lips a small smile played, as if to say, *I've got something you want*, meaning one thing to us girls and quite another to the few boys and men who had trickled out to the sidewalk for the afternoon's unexpected entertainment.

Normally I walked pretty much like Daddy, to Mama's chagrin. But when my turn came, I recalled my practice with Lynnette and did my best to duplicate the length of Mabel's stride and the exact angles she made with her elbows and wrists. It came off stiffly at first, but by the time we'd reached the gold rope, I thought I looked elegant.

Once we'd all walked to the far end of the block and back, Mrs. Sampson called to Rose to bring out the music. Rose emerged from the house to the porch, struggling to carry a heavy black phonograph. She squatted to place the machine on a wicker table and started it going with something classical.

I tried to pretend I was strolling to the stage to accept an Academy Award, instead of walking up and down the street in front of the growing number of gawkers. The music helped. After we'd paraded for what felt like hours, Mrs. Sampson started to gesture to girls with a come-hither finger. She'd whisper something and they'd follow her up the steps to disappear inside. When she crooked the finger at me, I perambulated to the curb. "Mathilda," she said, "I believe you're ready to meet the gentlemen for your Grand Promenade."

Did that mean I'd be promenading with both of them? Or would I get to choose? To my surprise, I didn't know if I could stand the excitement of being escorted by Mr. Cullowee, whose merest glance could turn my knees to pepper jelly, all jiggly and spicy hot.

"Miss Watson?" Mrs. Sampson turned back to see me still on the curb. "The gentlemen await your presence." I scuttled behind her into the cool, dark house. As my eyes adjusted, I saw Mr. Cullowee at the end of the dim hall, lounging against the wall, his long fingers tracing the chair rail. Even in the shadows, his golden hair seemed to glow.

Mrs. Sampson paused, and I came to a quick halt to keep

from mowing her down. She looked around with evident dissatisfaction. "Is Mr. Mayor not available?" she asked. Did this mean she considered me second string, not worthy of learning proper promenade behavior with Mr. Cullowee, or did she offer her husband to only the best girls?

"He's gone out for a moment." Mr. Cullowee stepped away from the wall. "I'll be glad to work with Mathilda."

"Well," Mrs. Sampson considered, a bit flustered. "I suppose that would be all right." She drew me around in front of her. "Show Mr. Cullowee how you can walk, Mathilda."

I resisted mentioning the fact that I'd been walking since the age of two, and started down the hall at a perfect Mabel pace. "Very nice," Mrs. Sampson said, in a voice so full of pride you'd have thought she'd baked me from scratch.

As I drew closer to the dark end of the hall where Mr. Cullowee stood, I could make out his features. On the surface, he looked as approving as Mrs. Sampson, but underneath, I saw something familiar, but out of place. I was having a hard time deciphering it, my attention focused on creating a replica of Mabel's point, step, and glide. But halfway down the hall, I remembered where I'd seen that expression: on the face of Mr. Lindley, my ninth grade English teacher, when he gave us the same lecture on Shakespeare he'd given every year of his teaching career. I'd heard from Danny that when Mr. Lindley was young, he'd had dreams of being a famous poet. Boredom. That was what I saw.

So I threw a Glynis wriggle into my walk.

I was rewarded by Mr. Cullowee's raised eyebrow and Mrs. Sampson's sharp intake of breath. When her "Mathilda?" went up at the end, I lost my nerve and dropped into my plain old Mattie lope. Mr. Cullowee gave me a conspiratorial grin too small to reach the end of the hall, where I suspected Mrs. Sampson was reconsidering the wisdom of assigning me to him. If I had some Glynis in me waiting to wriggle out, who knew what corrupt, untoward behavior I might try?

But Mr. Cullowee knew how to placate her. "Mrs. Sampson, I believe young Mathilda is a fine example of your training. It will be my pleasure to add what little I can to the excellent work you've done."

"If you're sure?" she asked. "I can always get Mr. Sampson to—he shouldn't have stepped out when we're in the middle of—"

"That's quite all right." Mr. Cullowee strode past me to Mrs. Sampson and rested his hand sympathetically on her shoulder. Was it my imagination or did the thin layer of air between us tingle with electrical charge as he passed? "The mayor deserves a little breather. I'm sure he'll return shortly, in time to escort the next young lady."

"Well, if you think—" Mrs. Sampson began.

"I absolutely do," said Mr. Cullowee as he circled her around and out the door.

He turned to me and held out his arm. I started toward him with the Glynis hip-sway, then remembered I was supposed to be demure. When I reached him, he tucked my arm into his. I felt the fine cloth of his jacket, and under that, the way it slid over his soft white shirt, and under that, the hard strength of his upper arm. Touching him like that, I had a tough time catching my breath. My heart seemed to be clogging up my windpipe. Down below, a part of me that I generally ignored seemed lit up in neon. It was hard to believe it wasn't glowing straight through my skirt.

"Shall we walk, Mattie?" he asked quietly, his mouth close to my ear. I nodded. A person needed breath to talk, and I couldn't find any.

None of my walks seemed right for this situation—not Mabel's step-glide, or the hip sway Glynis employed or my own lope. I found myself trying to match his refined stride, until we were walking in time with each other.

"You move quite gracefully, Mattie," he said. I liked the way he called me Mattie in private and Mathilda in public. "Would you like to dance?"

I forced my heart out of my windpipe. "If you don't mind getting your feet trampled on."

"I'm willing to take the risk." He smiled.

"Then, yes, please."

He led me into the familiar sitting room, ringed with its gallery of chairs and sofas. Through the window, I saw the other girls making their dogged treks up the street in pursuit of Mabel's grace. Their steps dragged and their shoulders slumped in the heat.

But inside, we were cool and invisible. If Mrs. Sampson or any of the girls looked toward the windows, they would see only their reflections.

Mr. Cullowee held out his arms in invitation. I placed my right palm against his outstretched left. The warmth of his hand pressing into the small of my back spread until my entire body glowed. I looked up at his face, unable to believe the power of one hand placed in exactly the right spot, a spot I'd never thought about before, and one that could be touched in public without the slightest raising of eyebrows.

He smiled at me, as if he knew what I was feeling. "Ready?"

I nodded and he swept me into the dance, steering me with the confidence of my father's hand on the wheel. All I knew about dancing I'd learned from Daddy, in preparation for school dances and weddings. He'd taught me the box step in our sitting room, but that was nothing like this. Though the music from the front porch was all wrong for dancing, Mr. Cullowee made me feel as if it had been composed expressly for this purpose: for the two of us to dance in soaring circles around a sitting room full of empty chairs occupied by invisible Kudzu Queen judges, who radiated their benevolent approval, as his hand radiated heat throughout my body.

On the bus ride home from Queen School that day, I leaned my cheek against the dirty window, recalling my dance with Mr. Cullowee as if it were a movie I'd seen. The music from the porch mixed with Mrs. Sampson's calls of "Chins up!" and "Square your shoulders!" to the hapless girls outside, Mr. Cullowee's palm on my back, guiding me around the room, the way he'd held me a few beats past the end of the music, and his elegant bow at the end. Finally, he'd tucked my hand into his arm to escort me to the front porch. The outdoors seemed unbearably bright after the soft shadows of the sitting room.

After class, I'd heard girls complaining about having to dodge to keep the mayor from stepping on their feet while they promenaded. I'd waited for somebody to mention dancing with the Kudzu King, but Glynis said, "I'll have to soak my feet in Epsom salts for a week," and Mabel replied, "But he's such a sweet man." Was it possible no one else had danced with Mr. Cullowee?

"Watson! Mattie Watson," Carla Ann yelled, and I realized the bus had stopped in front of my house.

"Sorry," I said, and ran down the aisle.

Once I stepped off the bus, my feet slowed down. My senses seemed to be offering triple the information they usually sent to my brain. I had to move slowly to take it all in. The afternoon's brightness had traveled with me, infusing the white clapboard of our house with its own light. My mother's azaleas were enjoying their brief moment of pink glory before they subsided into wilted blossoms the color of old newspapers. Her red and yellow roses framed the banisters of our porch steps. I could smell the difference between the colors. I went around to the side of the house, where the brightness continued, bathing the pigsty, the chicken coop, and the hard-packed yard in a movie light so glamorous I had to cup my hand over my eyes to shade them.

The yard was empty except for Stevie rooting through the muck, while her piglets shoved under her, snuffling for milk. The smell of the pigsty, like the smell of the roses, was more powerful than usual, but not in a bad way. It smelled like pigs, the way the chicken coop smelled like chickens, as if smell were part of the definition of a thing. The chickens cooed, innocent-sounding for once.

I could have gone in to help Mama with supper, but I wasn't ready to face the everyday. I needed to confide in someone. Not Mama, who would tell me that it was sweet that I had a crush, but I should remember that the Kudzu King was a grown man, and I was a fifteen-year-old girl. Not Joey, who would pump me for kudzu facts I hadn't gotten, not Daddy or Danny, who would tease me for going all girly on them. I needed to talk to someone who understood longing.

I wandered into the woods. The path to Aunt Mary's was soft with yellow-green moss I hadn't noticed before, and nests of ferns cropping up under maples and pines. Birds called to each other as if they were playing Whispering Down the Lane.

When I emerged, the tangled mint in Aunt Mary's back garden seemed unexpectedly friendly, like a welcoming committee leaping in excitement at my arrival. Her windows shone sunflower gold in the late afternoon light. On her porch, new growth had appeared on the mums in her brass pots, forcing the dead sticks of last year's stems aside. I found the key where I'd left it. Without the swelling of humidity, the door opened easily.

Dust had gathered on the knickknacks again, but I went straight upstairs, ignoring the public rooms in favor of the private. Aunt Mary's bedroom had dried out, though there was a faint watermark on her bedspread from the rain. I took off my shoes and climbed onto her bed. I lay on my back in a wide X, legs and arms stretching toward the four corners, closing my eyes. If Aunt Mary had a ghost and that ghost was angry, now was the time to let me know, before I got too comfortable. I thought my heart could take it. I thought my heart could take anything—it was so loose and fluid from my dance with the Kudzu King. But her ghost was quiet, maybe listening. Maybe no one had ever confided in Aunt Mary while she was alive. When she was a girl, the other girls were probably afraid she'd take their heads off if they said anything to her. I slitted my eyes open, and looked at the picture of the young man in uniform. Maybe him, I thought. Maybe he'd told her his secrets, and she'd confided hers in him.

"I danced with the Kudzu King," I said out loud, experimentally. No white apparition. No eerie moans. She seemed to be waiting for me to go on. "I think he wanted to dance with me. I mean me, specifically."

Washed-out sunlight spread across the dusty pine floorboards.

"I don't know why me," I said, as if she'd asked. I was sensible enough to know that I wasn't as pretty as Mabel or a sexpot like Glynis. "He didn't stop when the song ended."

It felt as if parts of me were still glowing under my clothing, especially the parts covered by more than one layer. "Do you think Mrs. Sampson knows?"

Aunt Mary seemed to understand what I meant by that. I didn't get the feeling that she was asking, *Knows what?* Which was good, since I wouldn't have been sure how to answer.

"Me, neither," I said. "I don't think she suspects a thing."

I pressed my skirt down over my legs, thinking about how shocked Lynnette would have been at my position. Beneath my hands I felt the muscles of my thighs. The light on the floorboards had turned from honey to the warm yellow-brown of syrup.

"I have to go home now," I said. "Or Mama will start worrying."

I swung my legs over the edge of the bed, smoothing the bedspread where I'd lain, and stood on the edges of the darkening spill of sunlight. "I'll come back," I said. "If that's okay."

I waited, but I didn't hear any objections.

"You don't mind what we're doing, do you?" I asked. "I mean with the kudzu and all?" I looked around for a way she could give me a sign. "Maybe, if you're all right with it, you could do some sort of miracle or something, like make it so there aren't any weeds next time we come." I went on. It seemed only fair to give her an out. "And if it bothers you, you could singe the edges of the leaves and I'll know you don't want us using your field."

Technically, it wasn't her field any more, since she'd left it to Daddy, who would probably give it to Danny. But if I believed in an afterlife enough to confide in her about romance, it was only logical to assume she might still have opinions about the use of her property. Although maybe asking for those opinions hadn't been the wisest move. Joey would be livid if he knew I'd offered Aunt Mary the opportunity to put a curse on our kudzu. "Maybe just a few leaves," I amended.

The next afternoon, the school bus was full of boys heading to the Johnson farm. Town boys crowded in, though I couldn't imagine where they planned to grow kudzu. In their mothers' window boxes? Pick-up trucks trailed after us, carrying the entire baseball team.

"You all right having all those boys over at your house?" I asked Lynnette.

"It's nice," she said, staring at the back of Bobby Mason's head like she was memorizing his latest haircut for a quiz.

"How about your father?" I asked.

"What about him?" Talking with Lynnette about her father was tricky. Sometimes she'd be spitting mad about how he'd smacked her mama or barked at Catherine when she wanted more peas at supper. Other times she'd defend him, saying he was doing his best, and I had no cause to speak ill of him. Or even, on rare occasions, that her father was none of my business.

"I mean, is he—" Could I ask straight out if he was acting crazy mean or drinking in front of the boys, or being a normal person for once? I settled on, "How's he liking the extra help?"

"He doesn't mind."

"And what does he think about having his land planted in kudzu?" I continued, since my last question hadn't made her mad.

"Oh, he's real pleased. He thinks we'll do well this year."

Aggie got on the bus at the elementary school, last of all the kids, even the first graders. "What did you get on your spelling test today, missy?" Lynnette asked.

Aggie flashed her fingers ten times. "One hundred."

"Good going!" Lynnette crooked her arm around Aggie's neck and pulled her sister toward her, where Aggie remained until she drifted into Aggieland.

When we drew up at the Johnsons', boys spilled out into the cloud of dust raised by the bus. The rest emerged, slamming truck doors, to head up the driveway, talking over each other.

At the end of the drive stood Mr. Cullowee and Mr. Johnson.

If I'd had to pick one word to describe Mr. Johnson before that day, it would have been "looming." But beside the Kudzu King, he just looked scrawny and irritated.

We followed the boys, Lynnette idly swinging Aggie's hand in small arcs.

"How's it going, Lynnette?" Bobby Mason asked, which turned her pink and flustered. Her answer got stuck between her lungs and her tongue.

"Tell him you're fine," I whispered.

"I'm—" she started. "I'm—"

"She's fine," I told Bobby, "and she hopes you are too."

Bobby Mason's presence made it easier to convince Lynnette we should climb the live oak near the creek to spy on the boys. Lynnette put Catherine down to nap, and we climbed up to a high branch. Aggie sat on the skinny end, peering at a squirrel scolding us from the next tree.

The Kudzu King truck was parked at the edge of the field, full of mattocks, shovels, and crates. Mr. Cullowee pried open a crate from the top of the stack, and held up a small lumpy object for the boys to see.

Each boy chose a tool and headed to the field to dig holes along the plowed furrows. It looked like hot, hard work. Mr. Johnson sat on a rotten log at the edge of the field, chewing a grass stalk, and watching the boys work. Mr. Cullowee looked at him a few times, but when Mr. Johnson stayed put, Mr. Cullowee gave his attention to the boys, encouraging them.

They were just digging holes, so I leaned against the trunk to listen to Lynnette talk about Bobby Mason. I nodded in absent agreement as she went on about how good-looking and smart and nice he was, while I contemplated the differences between the way Mr. Cullowee was teaching the boys to plant kudzu and the way Joey and I had started ours.

"Of course you didn't embarrass yourself," I reassured Lynnette. "He likes you. The way you acted showed him you like him too. Boys aren't very intelligent creatures. You need to be a little obvious for them to get it."

The boys finally finished, though several looked done in long before their rows were dug. Mr. Cullowee examined their work, deepening a few holes made by younger and weaker boys. Then he walked to Mr. Johnson and asked him a question. Danny and the others watched. Mr. Johnson gave a one-shoulder shrug, as if to say, *So?*

Danny watched Mr. Johnson a moment longer, then gave a look of disgust and headed with Mr. Cullowee toward the Kudzu King truck. The rest of the boys followed.

I looked back at Mr. Johnson and saw him give Danny a look of pure evil. Lynnette's father was a man on whom your back shouldn't be turned.

Danny and Mr. Cullowee lifted crates from the truck, handing one to each boy. Whatever was in the crates, I suspected it might give the boys an unfair advantage over Joey and me.

"Can you tell what's in those crates?" I asked Lynnette, who had excellent eyesight.

"No idea," she said, grabbing Aggie's waistband without looking. "Uh-uh, Miss Agatha Johnson. You stay right here with me." She kept a firm grip on Aggie with her right hand, and looked again. "But it looks sort of dirty and gnarled up."

"What's your father doing?" The look he'd given Danny had made me uneasy.

"Sitting," she said. "No, he's getting up and walking to the house."

So he was, though not before he snagged three of the crates from the far end of the truck bed. Most of the boys were carrying their crates to the road, where the trucks and school bus waited to convey them home to chores, but a couple of them, including Bobby Mason, still hadn't received theirs. Mr. Johnson headed toward the house, crates stacked to his chin.

Bobby took a step as if to follow, then stopped. The other boy, a sophomore named Earl Ebhart, tugged on Mr. Cullowee's shirtsleeve. When he got his attention, he pointed at Mr. Johnson trudging toward the house with his stack of crates. Mr. Cullowee shook his head and pried open the last crate. He indicated that

Bobby and Earl should hold out their arms, and filled them with an armload of scraggly dirt. Mr. Johnson put down the crates long enough to swing open the screen door to the kitchen, then disappeared into the house with them.

Lynnette and Aggie watched their father quietly. "We've got to go," Lynnette said.

"Sure," I said. "I understand."

Whatever Mr. Johnson had done, it was another example of his not-rightness, and didn't bode well. When he felt the need to get his own back, it was usually Mrs. Johnson and the girls who suffered his rage at the injustice the world had dealt him.

"I'll see you on the bus tomorrow." Lynnette climbed out of the tree. Aggie slid down the trunk behind her.

I was about to climb down myself when Danny and Mr. Cullowee got into the Kudzu King truck and drove off, leaving the tools behind. I needed to help Joey with the field and chores, but he'd forgive my lateness if I came back with inside information. After ten minutes, they returned with more crates. They carried one to the head of each row. When the truck was empty, they started picking things from the crates and dropping one each hole, then tamping the holes shut. Around dusk, they finished the last row, shook hands, got in their trucks, and drove away. When the dust had settled behind them, I slid down the tree. I was tempted to dig up a hole to see what was inside, but someone might be watching. The last thing I wanted was to get caught out looking too interested in the propagation of kudzu.

Supper that night was pork roast, mashed potatoes, and pickled beets, my least favorite vegetable. Normally, I'd have turned up my nose, whereupon Mama would haul those starving children from China into the conversation. I'd tell her they were welcome to my beets and Daddy would ponder the mechanics of getting my beets to China while they were still edible. In the old days, when I was even more likely to speak before I thought, I'd have complained that they weren't edible in the first place and Mama and Daddy would have been forced to send me to my room without supper. I'd sit at the top of the stairs, listening to Daddy considering the fastest way to get beets to China, since most of the boats there were slow, and whether being pickled might give them extra time to make the journey, until Mama said, "That's enough, Will."

Later, Danny would sneak me a plate of leftovers. I'd know by the fact that the despised beets had been replaced with Mama's applesauce that the plate came from her. With regards to discipline, Mama was strict on principle, but soft on follow-through.

That night, however, I simply cut up my beets without comment and forked them into my mouth, relieved that I'd found our field free of weeds and our kudzu leaves unsinged, which I took as Aunt Mary's approval. I was trying to come up with a way to get Danny to tell about that day's kudzu cultivation, when Daddy solved my problem by asking, "So, what did you learn from Mr. Kudzu today, Dan?"

"Wait until you see it, Daddy." Danny shoveled potatoes into his mouth like his fork was a garden spade. "Turns out you don't plant kudzu with cuttings at all—" He shoved in another load.

Jocy and I exchanged a look of consternation. I looked away quickly when Mama glanced from me to him in puzzlement.

"Well, you can," Danny amended around the mashed potatoes.

"Chew, baby, chew," Mama said to him.

I could practically see the wad of potato lodged in Danny's throat. He swallowed with a gulp. "But if you're serious about it, you want to use crowns."

I suddenly had this image of the mayor digging a hole and his wife tearfully dropping in the Kudzu Queen tiara. Then I remembered the mess of tangled dirt Mr. Cullowee had piled into Bobby and Earl's hands.

Danny cut off a piece of meat. "But why—" I interjected, trying to catch him before his mouth was full.

The advantage to family is that you don't have to finish your sentences. Danny paused, a hunk of pork poised outside his mouth. "Why'd he bring a truckload of cuttings?"

Across the table, Joey slumped in his chair as if he'd just learned that he'd be required to attend school the entire summer. Seven days a week.

"To catch people's interest." He bit into the meat and chewed.

I wasn't giving up. "And?"

Danny swallowed. "You can grow kudzu from cuttings. But it roots quicker from crowns. Still, I've heard of people who planted those cuttings in their gardens, and they're doing fine."

I cut my eyes at Joey while Danny examined his plate to decide what to shovel in next. I glanced at Mama and Daddy, but they too were occupied, Daddy pouring gravy onto his mashed potatoes and Mama helping herself to beets. *See?* I mouthed to Joey.

"And where can you get these crowns?" Daddy asked. His potatoes were now in a one-to-one ratio with his gravy, so he was free to rejoin the conversation.

"Jim's giving us the first box for free," Danny said. "All the fellas in the class, and any farmer who wants one. He gets them from the Department of Agriculture. I can get him to give you a box if you want one, Daddy."

"That's all right," Daddy said. "If I decide to go into kudzu, I'm sure I can afford a few boxes of crowns to get started."

I wondered if Mr. Cullowee would give Joey and me a crate too. Then I decided no, we didn't need crowns, not with our field already brimming with kudzu. I imagined leading Mr. Cullowee there, blindfolded. I would stop to untie his blindfold, whereupon he would place his hand firmly in the small of my back and we would promenade into that glorious tangle of green.

# 9

That Saturday the air was hot and humid as bath water, finally warm enough for Lynnette and me to take our first swim of the year at the old quarry, our secret swimming hole. We generally went there Saturdays after chores, whenever Mrs. Johnson felt well enough to look after Aggie and Catherine.

We'd pull our blouses over our heads, unzipping skirts as we ran, and be stripped to our underwear by the time we jumped in the water. It was the only time I could get Lynnette to stop fussing about propriety, since nobody ever saw us. We'd swim and chat for a while, then climb onto a rock and lie there, silent as gutted fish, for the sun to broil us dry.

But halfway down the trail that day, we heard voices and laughter. A bunch of town girls, including Glynis and her sidekick, Ann Marie, lolled about in our swimming hole. Glynis's yapping little dog strained at his pink rhinestone leash, which was tied to a tree.

"Let's come another time," Lynnette suggested.

I toed off my shoes and yanked down my socks. "I'm not letting them chase me off."

Lynnette stood there, her fingers paused over her top blouse button.

I tugged down my skirt. "Do I have to do this by myself?"

"You're right." She undid the button. "It's our place."

We tucked our things behind a tree and slid into the water. When the town girls saw us, they giggled and splashed to show what fun they were having. After that, they paid us no attention, as if the line between town and country extended to the swimming hole. That was all right. I could ignore them as easily as they ignored us.

Which I managed quite well until a herd of boys came bellowing through the woods, tossing shirts aside and kicking shoes in high arcs over branches. They jumped into the water with wild yelps, emerging with their jeans plastered to them. Lynnette and I scrambled onto the shore and dashed to our clothes. The town girls did the same, cowering behind a stand of pines. When we were dressed to the top buttons of our blouses, I peered from behind the tree.

"What are they doing?" Lynnette whispered.

I couldn't believe it. "Taking off their jeans in the water and throwing them on the bank."

Lynnette shook her head. "Those boys don't have a lick of sense."

"Do you think they saw anything?" I asked.

"We moved pretty fast," she said.

"Let's just go home," I said. "The afternoon's ruined, anyway."

"All right." Lynnette smoothed down her skirt, then her hair. I bent to tie the laces of my oxfords, but when I stood up, she cried, "Wait!"

"What?" I whirled around, sure there was a bear behind me.

"Your brassiere," she pointed. "It's soaked straight through your shirt. Every blessed thing is showing."

"Damn," I said.

"How about mine?" she asked, turning in a circle.

"Right down to the hook in the back."

She sat down on the ground. "We're not going anywhere until we dry out."

In the muggy heat, our shirts would take a while to dry to decency. I'd just come to this conclusion when the rain started. Not a downpour, which might have concealed us, but a steady soak. Crops would be grateful for it, but we were not.

But if we were trapped, so were the boys. Their bravado in tossing their pants to shore was going to bite them in their soggy-boxer butts. Sooner or later one side would have to declare a no-look truce.

The rain fell in a lukewarm shower, pleasant enough once we stopped resisting it. We watched the boys dunk each other as rain bounced off the water. Eventually we gave up trying to keep clean, and lay on our stomachs, chins propped on our hands. "Which one do you think is the cutest?" Lynnette asked.

"Not a one of them," I told her.

"But if you had to pick?"

"They're all pretty immature," I said, "but if I had to pick—"

"BOO!"

We leapt up, crossing our arms over our chests. I was fully prepared to bless Joey out, because this was exactly the kind of no-brain thing he would do, when I realized it wasn't Joey at all, but Carl Davis, a senior boy who played outfield on Danny's team and went to my church.

"Carl Davis," I snapped. "What do you think you're doing, sneaking up on us like that? You could have scared us into a heart attack." Just because it was Carl instead of Joey, I didn't see any reason to waste a good mad. "Didn't your mother teach you any manners?"

Carl looked flabbergasted. Clearly this wasn't the reception he'd expected. Maybe other girls would have simpered and blushed, but I wasn't the simpering sort. "I— I just—"

"You just *what*?" I glared at him.

"My dad turned me loose." He dug a hole in the loam with the toe of his work boot. "Said I could go swimming once I finished working. I wasn't expecting to find you two here."

"Us two, a bunch of town girls, and a whole mess of boys," I said. "You knew precisely what you were doing, coming down to embarrass us with your *friends*." I spat out the last word.

"I didn't know anybody was down here until I got close enough to hear all the yelling," Carl insisted. "I always go swimming on hot days. That's my house, just up there."

"Mattie," Lynnette said quietly. "I think he means it."

"Then how come we've never seen you down here on a Saturday before?" I demanded.

He went all red and stammery, which raised my suspicions even more.

"You've been spying on us, haven't you?" I said. "Hiding behind trees to catch a peek?"

"No, I haven't." He got indignant. "I knew y'all were here. I could hear you talking and laughing. But I stayed away to give you privacy."

"So why didn't you stay away this time?" I demanded.

"Because I didn't know you were here," he said. "I thought it was just boys."

The heat left my face and my temper at the same time. Carl was clearly a better breed of boy than those whooping and hollering in the water, hoping to see us with our clothes plastered to our bodies and—I realized that Carl's gaze kept dropping to my chest.

"Carl," Lynnette said. "I think this would be a good time to let Mattie and me have some of that privacy you were talking about."

Carl blushed. "Sorry." He ducked his head and disappeared into the woods.

"What should we do?" I asked Lynnette.

"I think we should keep our arms crossed and run for home," she tried.

I sighed, considering the situation.

"I need to get back and help with supper," she said. "My mama—"

We heard a rustling, and Carl stepped into the clearing, his eyes fixed above our heads, holding out a couple of old flannel shirts. "Brought you something to cover up with," he said.

"Thanks," I said, as he handed me the blue one.

He gave Lynnette the red plaid. "That was real nice of you," she said.

He stood on the edge of the clearing, his eyes still averted in a gentlemanly fashion. "I can take you out the back way, through our property."

He led us up the hill toward a field. I heard girls laughing, and figured Glynis and Ann Marie were sitting on the bank, arms clasped around their legs, flirting.

Carl's shirts reached halfway down our thighs and flapped against our skirts in the light breeze. We trudged between rows of new tobacco. Though the rain had stopped, we couldn't help kicking up mud, which stuck to our legs like lumpy red-brown stockings.

"I could walk you home," Carl offered.

"That's all right." I patted his arm. "You'd only have to turn around and come back."

"We'll bring your shirts to school on Monday," Lynnette said, which meant she'd bring the one she was wearing washed, ironed, and wrapped in brown paper so as not to embarrass him.

"Come back whenever you want to," Carl said.

"Thanks," I said, and Lynnette echoed. We walked along the edge of the road. As our skirts dried in the bright after-rain sunlight, they hung stiffly. No matter how often we paused to brush off leaves and dirt, our clothes wouldn't be clean by the time we arrived home.

"That was nice of him," Lynnette said.

"Sure," I said, "after he scared the life out of us. I bet he was watching us before, those other times when we came down to swim."

Lynnette clutched Carl's shirt more tightly. "He swore he didn't."

"He's a boy," I said. "They can't help looking."

Cicadas droned in the grass alongside the heat-shimmered tarmac. We turned onto our road without speaking. When we got to Lynnette's house, she said goodbye at the driveway.

"Want me to come in?" I asked.

She shook her head. We both knew her father would yell at her for being late and filthy, and my being there would only make him yell louder and longer.

I watched until she opened the door, closing it gently behind her. I wasn't two steps down the road when I heard him. "Where the hell you been? What do you think you're doing, gadding about in front of the whole world like that, bringing shame on my house?"

As I kept walking, his voice was swallowed into the hum of the cicadas until I could imagine him a cicada, all skinny legs and hard shell, and with any luck—though it was ugly to think that way—gone by the end of summer. I imagined Lynnette's mother as a tiny dun pantry moth, fluttering around him ineffectually, forced to rest, all out of breath, between her flutters.

When my own house appeared around the curve, my heart got bigger in my chest. It looked so welcoming: porch swept, white wicker rocker shifting gently in the breeze, porch swing singing out a welcome as it creaked on its chains. Around the side of the house, the kitchen window glowed yellow. Mama had pulled the café curtains wide open, probably to watch the rain.

"Hey, Mama." I ran inside. "Sorry about—"

I stopped in mid-sentence. There at my mother's kitchen table sat the Kudzu King.

"Mattie," my mother said, turning from the stove. "You know Mr. Cullowee, don't you? Mrs. Johnson was feeling a little peaked, so I invited him to join us for supper this evening. Mr. Cullowee, my daughter, Mathilda, whom I believe may have gotten caught in the rain."

I stood there, spattered with mud from my birds' nest hair to my filthy white socks, wearing a size extra-large boy's flannel shirt over my wrinkled skirt, and wishing a trap door would open up and drop me straight into the core of the earth.

"Yes, ma'am," I muttered. "We've met."

Mr. Cullowee stuck out his hand. "Mathilda, it's a pleasure to see you again."

I glanced down, hoping to find a clean square inch of clothing on which to wipe the mud off my hand. My mother, taking pity, pulled the dishtowel from her shoulder. Gratefully, I wiped my hand and shook his. "Nice to see you again too," I mumbled.

He held my hand long enough for me to feel how warm it was, how nice it felt around mine—and how mortified I was that he was seeing me in this state.

"I think everything's in good shape around here, Mattie," my mother said. "Why don't you run upstairs and freshen up?"

With a quick nod I bolted upstairs, passing Joey in the hall.

"What happened to you? You look like you've been rolling in the pigsty."

I was moving too fast to do more than throw him a glare. In my room, I tore off my filthy clothes, scattering them across the floor. I gave Carl's shirt a kick that launched it into the air. It snagged on the window latch and hung like a flag proclaiming my humiliation. When I was down to the underpants and brassiere that had gotten me into this mess in the first place, I threw on my ratty pink robe and stalked to the bathroom, where I drew the hottest bath I could stand, climbing into the tub before it was a quarter full so I could start scrubbing the afternoon off of me.

I ran a steady stream of hot water, draining the tub when the water got clouded with dirt. By the time the water was clear, I had an idea. I would dress for dinner, as ladies did in the pictures. I whisked dry, bundled in my bathrobe and dashed to my bedroom. My Sunday dress—a pale blue that brought out my eyes—was definitely in order, along with my wedding-and-funeral heels and stockings. That would hit the right note.

I pulled on stockings and heels, yanked the dress over my head and zipped it up along my ribs. When I was ready, I hobbled—I didn't have much practice with heels—to assess myself in my mother's full-length mirror. My hair was still a disaster, hanging in damp drapes. I fluffed it with my fingers and decided to put on some of Mama's lipstick as a distraction. It occurred to me that I could use the lipstick to make up for what nature had failed to provide me in the way of a juicy, kissable top lip. Mama called me to supper as I was uncapping her lipstick.

"One minute." The Cupid's bow I made of my lips looked very tasty indeed. If you didn't know me, you'd never have known those weren't my natural lips. I gave my hair a final fluff, and teetered down to dinner.

When I arrived in the kitchen, I found it empty.

"We're in here," Mama called from the dining room, a room we used so rarely I forgot it was even in the house. I was pleased at this. The dining room suited my purposes quite well.

I tripped over the threshold, but righted myself, only to find my family gaping at me—except my mother, who was smiling. You'd think no one ever dressed for dinner in our house.

My father recovered first. "You look lovely, Mattie," he said.

"Indeed," the Kudzu King agreed. He stood as I approached the table.

"Beautiful." My mother beamed at me, managing to slip a glare at Joey in the middle to forestall any smart comment he might make.

Mr. Cullowee pulled out my chair. "Thank you." I smiled. He pushed me in like I was a feather pillow. If high heels got me this kind of treatment, I resolved to wear them more often.

In honor of our company, Mama had made chicken and gravy, which meant one less chicken to feed in the morning, and chicken pot pie tomorrow.

"What portion of this bird may I serve you, Mr. Cullowee?" Daddy asked, carving knife poised.

"I'm partial to thighs," the Kudzu King answered. "And please, call me Jim."

Daddy carved off a plump thigh and forked it onto Mr. Cullowee's plate. Mama added a helping of parsnips. She ladled gravy over the chicken and passed his plate, followed by a bowl of applesauce still radiating cinnamon steam.

Once Mr. Cullowee was served, the rest of us piled food on our plates, though with more grace than usual. Mama had put out Aunt Mary's ivory linen cloth and her mother's silver. The scent of lemon oil emanated from under the cloth.

"So, what sort of reception is kudzu getting around here?" Daddy asked, once everyone had gotten in the first few bites.

Joey and I snuck a glance at one another.

"It's a little slow," said Mr. Cullowee. "But once flyers for the festival are posted, interest will pick up." He smiled across the table. "My mother's been looking her whole life for the perfect applesauce. What would it take to persuade you to part with your recipe?"

Mama beamed. "It's hardly a recipe at all," she said. "Just apples, sugar, and cinnamon."

"Well, you must have the touch, then," he told her. "I've never tasted anything like it."

"The secret's in the apples. I'll be glad to send your mother a crate."

I had my eye on a second helping, but after weighing tonight's chicken and gravy against tomorrow's pot pie, I decided to abstain. Plus, I didn't want Mr. Cullowee to think I was a pig.

I felt a poke in the ribs. When I whipped around to glare at Joey, he pointed to his mouth. "What?"

He pointed again and I dabbed my face with my napkin, which came away Cranberry Red. I guessed I could add lipstick to high heels as another area in which I needed practice.

*Thanks*, I mouthed to him. Ever since we'd become kudzu partners, Joey had been surprising me with moments of genuine niceness.

"How does your success here compare with your experience elsewhere?" Danny asked.

"Things are going quite well here," said the Kudzu King. "I've had a lot of interest."

Daddy leaned back and rested his hands on his belly. "So how do you go about selling the stuff? I've yet to hear of a kudzu auction."

"I'm glad you asked, Mr. Watson," said the Kudzu King. "They're springing up all over. So far, we've had two auctions in Tennessee, one in Georgia, and a couple coming up in Virginia. I'm looking to see one in North Carolina in the coming year, but it takes a real community leader to make that happen." He stopped and patted his mouth with his napkin, leaving his sentence floating in the air.

Daddy ignored the bait, but I wasn't worried. Once he saw the success Joey and I made of kudzu at Aunt Mary's, I was sure he'd move into the modern world right along with us.

"How do you prepare it to sell?" Danny asked. "Does it need to be dried like tobacco?"

"You can dry it right alongside your tobacco. In the same shed to pick up the flavor."

"And are people bringing in a profit from it yet?" Daddy asked.

"Some." Mr. Cullowee tilted his head. "It takes a while for a new crop to catch on."

"And how about you, yourself?" Daddy continued. "Seems to me you're putting in an awful lot of work on something that hasn't shown any return."

Mr. Cullowee smiled. "Good work is its own reward."

Daddy quirked his mouth to one side, the way he did when he hadn't entirely bought a person's story. "But it doesn't put gas in your truck."

The smile on Mr. Cullowee's face held, but it seemed to be straining against gravity. "I have a little money set aside for the time being," he said. "The point is to benefit the people who need it most. It's been a rough few years for farmers, as I'm sure you know."

"This is all well and good, you gentlemen talking profits and such," Mama said, changing the subject. "But Mattie and I want to get to the important part. I hear you have some pictures of queens from other counties. I don't suppose you could be persuaded to show them over dessert."

Now Mr. Cullowee's natural grin flashed across his face. "Well, that all depends on the dessert you have hidden away, Mrs. Watson."

"I have a very persuasive cherry pie," Mama told him. "With homemade vanilla ice cream for the a la mode."

"I believe that would do the trick," he said.

When I stood up to clear the table, Mama said, "Mattie, honey, why don't you sit here with your father and Mr. Cullowee while I get dessert? You look too pretty to clear the dishes."

Joey snorted, but began stacking plates, mashing the leftover food between them, while Danny collected glasses by sticking a finger in each one until he had them gathered like petals.

"I'll only be a minute," said Mr. Cullowee. "The book's in the truck."

After he stepped out, Daddy asked, "So, Mattie, are you going to be the Queen of Cooper County?"

"I'd like to be," I told him, "but I don't know what my chances are."

"You clean up pretty well." He rubbed his thumb over his bottom lip, considering. "I'd say your chances are excellent."

"Which would be helpful if you were a judge," I told him, "but I suspect you won't be."

Mama cleared the last few dishes and retrieved her pie. Danny followed with the frosty cylinder from the ice cream freezer, as the Kudzu King arrived with his picture album.

"Perhaps Mr. Cullowee would do the honors," said Mama, handing him the scoop.

"I'd be delighted," he told her. "Reminds me of my sophomore year of high school, working the soda fountain."

Mama sliced the pie into Danny-sized wedges and passed each plate to Mr. Cullowee. When each of us had been pied and ice-creamed, she beckoned with a finger. "Hand it over," she ordered Mr. Cullowee. "Come here, Mattie. You know you want to see this."

I scooted my chair around the table. Mama brushed her fingers over the leather, tracing the gold letters, "Kudzu Queens of the South." Mr. Cullowee glanced at Daddy and Danny, who'd started talking baseball, then tipped back his chair, smiling.

Mama turned to the first page, where an 8 x 10 glossy was held neatly by four ornate black metal corners. "Macon, Georgia. September 16, 1939. Miss Nora Cunningham." The picture looked like a wedding photo: a pensive girl framed by a tall window, long blond hair flowing over her bare shoulders. Her white satin dress was fitted at the bodice and pooled at her feet. On the next page, Miss Cunningham stood in sash and tiara, surrounded by her smiling retinue.

More pictures of queens and their courts, marked by location, date, and name. The pages went through November, skipped Christmas and leapt to April 1940 in Lafayette, Louisiana. The last was from Williamson County, Tennessee, a tiny redhead with springy curls and an expression that said she could stir up more trouble than Joey. Clearly Kudzu Queens weren't a type, which was a relief, but after paging through the book, I was discouraged about my chances.

"Quite a bevy, wouldn't you say?" Mr. Cullowee said.

"Oh my, yes," said my mother. I nodded. My shoes had begun to pinch my baby toes.

"You know, Mathilda's been doing quite well in the classes we're holding for young ladies," he told Mama.

"I'm glad to hear it," Mama said.

I dragged my attention from my aching toes. I wondered if he was thinking of our dance together, and hoped he wouldn't mention it to my mother.

He shifted his gaze to me. "Mrs. Sampson speaks quite highly of you. 'That winsome girl,' she calls you."

I almost blurted, "You must be joking," but chose the more ladylike, "You mean Mabel."

He shook his head. "I know she's fond of Mabel, but it was you she was describing."

"What subjects are you offering in these classes?" Mama asked. "We can hardly get a word out of Mattie." She meant she could hardly get me to say a word that wasn't a complaint about Mrs. Sampson. I was going to have to think twice about all the mean things I said behind Mrs. Sampson's back, if she was saying nice things behind mine.

"Poise, stage presence, elocution," Mr. Cullowee said. "Mrs. Sampson's doing a fine job. Next week she'll be holding a ladies' tea." He smiled. "No gentlemen invited."

"What's Mattie good at?" Joey asked.

Please don't say dancing.

"She's a charming conversationalist," Mr. Cullowee said. He turned to Mama. "Thank you, Mrs. Watson, for a superb meal. Your cherry pie was the best I've ever tasted."

He shook Daddy's hand. "It's been a pleasure discussing kudzu with you, sir. I'm sure a man with your depth of knowledge will know how best to adapt this fine crop to your native soil."

Daddy smiled, his lip quirking to the side. He didn't mention that he'd left his native soil in Delaware.

# 10

The following Wednesday I emerged from the cafeteria line with my Salisbury steak to see Danny waving me to the window side.

I carried my tray to the baseball team table and sat between him and Carl Davis. On game days, the team ate with the sophomores and wore ties and white shirts with dark trousers, except Carl, who wore his army-green Junior ROTC uniform.

His flannel shirt still hung on my window latch where I'd kicked it.

Danny gestured across me. "You know Carl, don't you, Matts?"

"Good to see you again, Mattie," Carl said, going red under his uniform collar.

I stared at my Salisbury steak, while all the boys except Carl talked about the upcoming game. I hunched my shoulders and pushed soggy carrots across my plate.

Danny patted my shoulder. "Tell Mama I may be late for supper. I'm heading over to East Cooper with Jim Cullowee after the game. He wants to talk with some fellas about intercropping kudzu."

"Uh-huh," I said, scratching a tic-tac-toe in my mashed potatoes with my fork. The boys picked up their trays. "See you later, Mattie," they called.

"Mattie?" I slid my eyes to the right. Army green pants.

"Um, Mattie?" Carl repeated. "Danny told me you liked the movies. I was wondering if you might want to go to the picture show sometime?" I snuck a glance at him. His face was as red as mine felt. I hoped nobody was watching. "I mean with me," he added.

"I don't know," I mumbled. "Maybe."

He seemed to take that as encouragement. He spoke quickly,

staring over my head, as if the words were written there. "They say that *Lady Eve* picture with Henry Fonda and Barbara Stanwyck is pretty good. This is the last weekend, so maybe you'd want to go Friday night?" He went on without pausing for a response. "You haven't seen it yet, have you? I haven't either."

It was just as well he kept barreling onward. My brain had stalled. On the one hand, this was the first time I'd been asked out by a boy. Would Mama let me go or say I wasn't old enough? Was I supposed to accept or keep him dangling? On the other hand, I'd recently skipped boys entirely and graduated to men. I wasn't sure, even if Mama did grant her approval, whether I wanted to waste my time. But maybe I should do it anyway, to get some practice. Mr. Cullowee, being grown, was surely used to girls with more experience.

Finally Carl looked directly at me. "I know girls have rules about asking, and I should have asked you on Monday, but I wasn't sure you'd want to talk to me after last weekend."

Last weekend wasn't a subject I wanted to discuss. "What time?" I asked.

"Um, 6:15?" He seemed startled, as if he'd expected a tougher negotiation, which made me wonder if I should have played hard to get. But the longer he stood there, the more likely we were to attract the attention of Glynis and Ann Marie and Mabel, who occupied the prime table in the middle of the cafeteria, in a direct line of sight from where Carl loomed over me.

"6:15. Yes, fine," I said, and fought the urge to snap out a military, "Dis-missed."

"I'll pick you up at your house," he said.

"Right." Glynis glanced over. My skin itched. Would he ever leave? "See you later."

Someone slid into the seat beside me. I looked down. Mustard yellow cotton dress, hand tugging hem over pale freckled knees. Lynnette, who'd never have sat with all those boys. She must have eaten across the cafeteria at our usual table.

"What was that all about?" she asked.

"Carl," I mumbled. "Danny told me to come over."

"Does Danny know?" she asked. "About Saturday?"

"I don't think so."

"That speaks well for him. Carl, I mean."

"I guess." I wiped my mouth. "But it was still embarrassing."

"Well, it would be, wouldn't it?" she said matter of factly. "I mean he could practically see straight through your shirt."

I groaned. "Don't remind me." I gripped my tray, glancing down to reassure myself that today's shirt was sufficiently opaque. "Anyhow, he could see straight through your shirt too."

She dabbed her mouth with her napkin. "Oh, I don't think there was anything under my shirt that he was particularly interested in looking at."

I stood to carry my tray to the dish line. "He asked me on a date."

"What?" Lynnette ran after me. "Are you going? Does Danny know? Will your mother let you go? Do you like him?"

Scrape plate, stack plate. Slide silverware into tepid gray dishwater. Stack tray. "Yes. No. I don't know. And I have absolutely no idea."

The afternoon had heated up considerably, as if a day had been dug out of August and transplanted to early May, which made the walk from school to Queen class feel like swimming through sludge.

Rose let me in to the mayor's cool hallway. From the sitting room I could hear Mrs. Sampson's voice rising and falling. "Don't worry, they've only just started," Rose whispered.

I stood outside the parlor door until I heard polite gloved applause. Gloves. Mrs. Sampson had told us the week before that "as young ladies of quality," we were supposed to start wearing gloves to Queen School. Late and barehanded, two strikes.

I slipped into the room only to discover that, like some horrible game of musical chairs, there was not an empty seat to be had. The wooden chairs were gone. Glynis and Ann Marie had spread their skirts to claim a sofa that should have seated three. There were fewer chairs because there were fewer girls. I found myself in enemy territory, surrounded by town girls, with Mabel representing Switzerland.

"Come sit by me, Mattie." Mabel scooted over on the opposite sofa to make room between her and Alice. I was impressed with Alice's staying power. If I'd looked like her, I'd have given up after the first week. Not to speak ill, but her junior yearbook picture had looked more like an Audubon painting than a Kudzu Queen. Still, I was grateful to her and Mabel for making room.

"A lady is always prompt, Mathilda," Mrs. Sampson chided. "Never early and never late." She lifted the brass bell. "Rose?"

Rose wheeled in a two-shelved cart crowned by the shepherds chasing shepherdesses teapot, a creamer and sugar bowl, and a three-tiered stand held together by a fluted gold rod.

Plump chocolate-covered strawberries were arrayed on the top plate. On the middle plate sat assorted confections: almond cookies, shortbread, and little iced cakes decorated with pink roses and green leaves. Tiny cucumber sandwiches fanned in a circle around the bottom plate. On the cart's lower shelf were gold-rimmed cups and saucers, small plates, white linen napkins, and silver.

I predicted all sorts of calamities: blouses ruined by spilled tea, a riot of pink and green icing staining the cream-colored sofa pillows, teacups chipped, saucers shattered, girls cast out into the street, forever banned from the dream of becoming the Kudzu Queen of Cooper County.

"Ladies," Mrs. Sampson said. "Today we'll be drinking a special Oolong tea imported directly from China. Mabel, dear, would you do the honors?"

Rose wheeled the cart to Mabel. "Milk and sugar, Mrs. Sampson?" Mabel asked.

"The hostess is always the last to be served, dear," Mrs. Sampson corrected.

Mabel's cheeks pinked. I didn't like to see her embarrassed, but it was reassuring to discover that even Mabel could occasionally put a foot wrong. She turned to me, "Mattie?"

I'd been drinking tea my whole life, but I'd never tried it hot with milk in it. Why ruin perfectly good tea? "Just sugar, thank you, Mabel," I said.

"One lump or two?" Mabel asked, holding a pair of tongs over the sugar bowl, which was full of little cubes. I thought about asking for three, but Rose, who knew my sweet tooth from way back, gave me the slightest headshake.

Mabel poured tea for the rest of the girls. Mostly they asked for one lump or two and milk, so they wouldn't offend Mrs. Sampson, but Glynis had to be different. "I'll take mine black," she said, which seemed a perfect fit for her low-cut magenta blouse and short black taffeta skirt. It was just as well that Glynis hadn't wanted any sugar. There wasn't enough sugar in the world to sweeten her disposition. Ann Marie made a face, but took hers black too.

Rose moved the dessert plates and napkins to the top shelf. Then she rolled the cart in front of me. Mrs. Sampson gave a significant glance at the plates, from which I figured I was meant to take one and fill it from the three-tiered stand. I could have used more thorough instructions.

"Mathilda," Mrs. Sampson said with an unexpected gentleness. Maybe she, too, had once been faced with learning to be ladylike without any aptitude for it, though I doubted it. "Just choose an item or two that appeals to you."

I looked at her gratefully and spread a napkin on my lap with one hand, then picked a plate from the pile and balanced it on my knees. After I had the plate settled, I reached out, stopping before I touched a chocolate-covered strawberry to check whether I could use my bare hand.

"Go ahead," Mrs. Sampson said. I put the strawberry on my plate and added a small cake.

"Thank you," I said to Rose, hoping she'd take the cart away before greed got the better of me. She handed me a fork and rolled the cart to Mabel.

"I see you like the petits fours." Mrs. Sampson smiled. "They're my favorite too." I wasn't much fond of pettiness in anything, but maybe she meant the cakes, since the strawberries were obviously strawberries dipped in chocolate and probably didn't have a fancy name.

"Yes, ma'am," I said. "They look delicious."

Ann Marie, in an unexpected fit of rebellion, took two of the little cakes even after Glynis clearly established by example that they would be dining on cucumber sandwiches that afternoon. Mabel left the last cake for Mrs. Sampson, since she'd established a clear preference for them, and chose an almond cookie and a small wedge of shortbread.

After that, it was simply a matter of leaving the dessert plate balanced on my knees, holding my saucer in my left hand so I could eat and drink with my right, and sending up a prayer that I wouldn't have an attack of the clumsies. Around me, polite conversation came and went in the choppy waves you might expect from girls who hadn't been raised on it. Whenever the talk veered into gossip, Mrs. Sampson steered it to the weather.

The parlor door opened and the mayor peeked in. "Just wanted to see how you're doing."

"No gentlemen allowed, Mr. Mayor!" Mrs. Sampson scolded. "This is a ladies' tea."

He didn't seem perturbed. "You're saving me one of those chocolate strawberries, aren't you, Beulie?" he asked.

She glanced at her plate, where an extra strawberry sat off to the side, and back to him with a look of such sweetness that I thought better of them both. They'd been young once and had fallen in love, before they became dumpy and pompous.

When Rose brought the cart around to collect the dishes, I surrendered my teacup, saucer, plate, and silver and sank into the cushions. Tragedy averted.

Mrs. Sampson stood. "What a delightful afternoon this has been. I'm pleased with the progress you've all made." We followed her to the front door, where she clasped the hands of each girl and thanked her for attending. "Mabel, you're a credit," she said. "Alice, you're coming along nicely. Your mother will be proud."

I was two girls behind Glynis, who stood with her hip cocked and arms crossed, so Mrs. Sampson couldn't take her hands without prying them free. "Glynis," she said, and again, simply, "Glynis." Even through the back of her head, I could see Glynis's eyes rolling.

Ann Marie didn't have the nerve for hip cocking or eye rolling. "Thank you, Mrs. S."

When it was my turn, Mrs. Sampson made a sandwich of our hands. "Mathilda," she said. I suspected I was in for a repeat of the disapproval she'd shown Glynis. "I look forward to your interview question. I suspect you're a young lady with a great deal to say."

I wasn't sure whether that was an insult or a compliment, but she seemed to mean it kindly. She pressed my hands together one last time and released them. "You're a lovely girl," she said. "Now run catch the bus. I'm sure your mother has plenty of chores waiting."

A more immediate chore awaited me between the mayor's house and the bus.

Glynis.

I didn't know whether she'd uncrossed her arms or uncocked her hip since she and Mrs. Sampson had bidden their not-so-fond adieus, but she was standing in that exact position two blocks from the mayor's house.

"You need to cut it out." The side of her mouth lifted in something that was not a smile.

"Cut what out?" I was prepared to do whatever was needed to get safely on the bus. Glynis had a reputation for using her fingernails in a fight.

"You know."

I looked around, hoping I'd be struck by the ability to read minds or that someone would walk by and rescue me.

"If I knew, I'd quit it," I said. I meant it. If Glynis escalated from scratching to biting, I could catch rabies. I'd heard about those shots in the stomach.

She thrust back her shoulders. "When I want something, I get it." Her sharp bosom jutted above her crossed arms.

"Like what?" I asked.

"You will never get to be queen," she sneered. "And he will never go for a child like you."

"Mr. Cullowee?" I asked, too astonished to consider the fact that she seemed to think I stood a chance against Mabel to be queen. "What makes you think—?"

Then I realized. In Cooper County, everyone knew who had dinner where, not to mention whose brother was hanging out with whom and who was staying in whose best friend's house.

Of course, I dreamed of being the recipient of Mr. Cullowee's affections, but I also had more sensible moments when I knew that no amount of my mother's lipstick would make me a grown woman. But instead of appeasing her, I felt unwisely required to point out facts. "You're not even a year older than me, anyway," I said.

"And a lifetime more mature," she told me.

Whoever decided that men were the ones in charge of throwing down gauntlets didn't know girls. And if Glynis thought I'd be afraid to pick hers up, she didn't know me.

"Oddly enough, 'mature' and 'slutty' are not synonyms," I said. "And I have a bus to catch." As I strode past, I glanced over my shoulder. "And by the way, if you keep sticking out your hip like that," I borrowed a line from my mother, "it's going to get stuck that way."

I walked in the door to find the telephone ringing on the hall table. When Mama didn't answer it, I ran to get it before it inched its way off the edge. "Hello? Hello?"

"Miss Eleanora Dunne," the operator said—and my heart froze up, "calling for Mrs. Lydia Watson." Was she calling to retroactively retract the B- I'd finally earned in Junior High Home Ec? "One minute," I said gruffly, hoping I sounded like Daddy.

I rested the receiver on the table and ran out back to find Mama in her garden.

"Telephone," I blurted. "Miss Dunne. For you."

"Oh. I've been expecting to hear from her." I followed her

back inside and stood next to her, waiting for elucidation, but all she said was, "Hello…Yes, of course…I'd be delighted."

"Mama!" I followed her into the kitchen.

"Yes?" She picked up a bowl of green beans from the counter and sat at the kitchen table.

"What?" I stood beside her, impatient. Her attention was on snapping the beans with as little waste as possible. Mama could get more eating out of a green bean than anyone I knew.

She dropped a stem into a bowl and looked up. "What what, Mattie?"

"What was all that about?"

"Oh," she said. "Eleanora's putting together a sewing committee for the mothers of the girls in the competition. She asked if I'd like to join."

"But you don't even know her."

"Mattie, Eleanora and I have been friends since the third grade," she said.

"But you never speak together for more than a minute. You never have her over for coffee or anything," I protested. "You don't do any of the things friends do together."

"That you know of," Mama said, returning her attention to the green beans.

This was a disturbing thought to ponder, that my mother had a secret life I knew nothing about. Maybe everyone had secret lives other people knew nothing about. Maybe our lives were the stems and leaves and flowers of things, and there were whole underground root systems that people kept secret from one another.

The beans flew from her hands, trimmed beans in one bowl, trimmings in another. "Are you going to do it?" I asked.

"I don't see why not," she said. "It would be nice to spend more time with old friends."

I straddled a chair, resting my chin on the back. "Is Mabel's mother going to be on it?"

"Mattie, could you for once sit like a young lady?" she asked. "Aren't you learning anything from Mrs. Sampson?"

"Is she an old friend? Mrs. Sampson, I mean? How about Alice's mother? And Ann Marie's and Glynis's?" It would be too much if Mama was friends with Mrs. Carpentier and couldn't get Glynis to be nice to me. "Will they be on the committee too?"

"Yes on Mabel and Alice's, and Ann Marie's, though she's younger than we are. I knew her older sister, who married and moved to Iowa. Mrs. Sampson has more than enough to do, trying to make ladies out of the lot of you. Anyway, she's from Charleston."

"What about Mrs. Carpentier?"

"Eleanora will invite her, of course, though I doubt she'll join us," Mama said. "I don't think she particularly wants to hear from me." She dropped the last bean into the bowl.

"Why doesn't she want to hear from you?"

"Ancient history, Mattie," she said, carrying the bowl to the stove.

"What kind of ancient history?" I persisted.

Mama dumped the beans into a pot of water. "Let's just say that apples and trees rarely find themselves far from one another," she said, proving yet again that she knew more than I gave her credit for.

There were twelve years between Danny and the Kudzu King, but you wouldn't have known it the next day at the Johnsons' as they leaned over the hood of Mr. Cullowee's truck, looking at a pamphlet, Danny's dark head beside Mr. Cullowee's golden curls. If anyone had asked me, I'd have told them that Danny and Mr. Cullowee were the very definition of "forward-thinking," a picture of what the South would be when every farmer grazed his cattle in lush fields of kudzu. The years they could see into the future made the years between them a finger snap.

From our perch in the tree, Lynnette and I watched them walk the field, each with his hands linked behind his back, examining the kudzu. The boys trailed after them like rambunctious ducklings. Their kudzu was coming up pretty well, though nowhere near as far along as Joey's and mine.

Weeding and watering seemed to be the day's tasks. The Johnsons' pump was by the house, so the boys refilled their buckets from the creek. Danny and Mr. Cullowee worked with the boys, encouraging the younger ones, who had to lean backward to lug their buckets. I felt sorry for them. The day was hot enough to boil the water they were carrying. Mr. Johnson was nowhere to be seen.

Aggie sat among the roots at the foot of the tree, tracing her fingers over the bark as if it were a Braille map to Aggieland, while Catherine napped up at the house. Catherine was the sleepingest child I'd ever known, which was nice since it freed Lynnette up to spend more afternoons with me as long as we took Aggie with us. Today, we were also accompanied by Lynnette's book bag, hanging from the broken stub of a branch.

"You planning on doing homework up here?"

"Maybe a little," she said.

For the rest of the afternoon, she fiddled in her notebook, occasionally looking down to see what Bobby Mason was doing. At one point she leaned against the trunk, and propped her notebook against her raised knees, while I swung my legs to stir up a breeze. When she'd finished, she tore the page from her notebook and handed me an excellent drawing of Mr. Cullowee. "You can have it, if you want. I'm practicing my portraits."

"Really?" It looked just like him, in pencil over the faint blue lines of the paper. "When'd you get so good at this?"

She shrugged, then slid down the tree to check on her mother, who'd been feeling poorly. I had nothing to learn from watching the boys weed and water, so I left too.

When I got home, the house was empty: Mama in her garden, Daddy in the field, Joey tending our kudzu, and Danny still with Mr. Cullowee. I unrolled Lynnette's picture, which I'd rolled up for safekeeping, and Scotch-taped it to my bureau mirror. It really was an amazing likeness. She'd gotten Mr. Cullowee's elegant cheekbones exactly right.

The chickens were unusually subdued, drugged by the late afternoon heat, and Stevie lay on her side in the remains of a puddle, her piglets sleepily suckling. I fed them for Joey, and put straw in the pen. Even Sassafras was less unruly, telegraphing her kicks so I could catch the bucket before it tipped. I let her out of the barn and she meandered into the pasture, nibbling as she went. If that were a kudzu field, I thought, she'd hardly even have to lower her head to graze.

By the time Mama returned to the house with a basket of greens and strawberries, I had the milk strained and skimmed and the table set.

"I seem to have misplaced my daughter." She dropped her basket on the counter. "But I'm pleased to meet you, Miss.... What did you say your name was?"

"Mama," I groaned.

"Miss Mama?" She scooped strawberries into the colander by the sink. "I thought I was the mama around here. That's excellent. If you're the mama, I can go to the picture show."

"It's not as if I never do anything around here."

"You do seem to be maturing nicely these days." She handed me the colander. "As long as you're here, why don't you wash these? If you'll help out, we can make strawberry shortcake and whipped cream for dessert."

I ran cool water over the berries, letting it waterfall over my palms. "Mama," I stared into the colander, "do you think I might be mature enough to go on a date?"

I felt her look up sharply, though I didn't have the nerve to glance over. "I'd say that would depend on the boy you think you'd like to date."

I dug my hands in under the berries. "Well, I'm not sure I'd use the word 'like,' but Carl Davis from Danny's team asked me to go to the pictures. Tomorrow."

She gave a deep sigh, though it was hard to tell whether it was a sigh of relief or annoyance. "Well, it's pretty short notice to be asking permission," she said, "but there's probably enough maturity between the two of you to merit my approval. What's showing?"

"*The Lady Eve*," I told her. "With Henry Fonda."

"Hmm," she said. "Not exactly to my taste. But I don't expect you'll be paying too much attention to the picture anyway."

Lately Joey and I had been skidding into our seats for supper, our faces and hands still wet from a quick scrub after chores and kudzu labors, so it wasn't until that night, when Danny wasn't at the table when we sat down, that I realized he'd been late every night that week.

There's probably a rule that says parents have to love their children equally. If you have three children, each gets precisely one-third of their parents' affection. Our parents were nothing if not fair. But Danny had been Daddy's right-hand man for as long as I could remember. I knew Daddy didn't hold any great expectations of Joey or me filling Danny's shoes when Danny left for Raleigh, but I hoped once he saw what we'd accomplished, he'd see us differently.

"Why don't you bring Mr. Cullowee to supper with you next Thursday?" Mama asked when Danny slid into his seat just as she set the strawberry shortcake on the table. "Maybe the two of you could manage to get here on time."

"He's got to make the rounds. Everyone wants to have him to supper," Danny said, stuffing his mouth full of shortcake. Half a strawberry toppled from his fork. "He wants every family in the county to feel right about coming to him for advice."

"Well, your family would like to have you for supper occasionally too," Daddy said with a snap in his voice. We all looked up from our shortcake in surprise. Daddy never snapped.

I studied Daddy after everyone else resumed eating. He was staring through the kitchen door at something I couldn't see. His face was drawn, as if he hadn't slept well lately.

He's lonely, I thought, which was a revelation. I hadn't thought parents could feel abandoned. Everybody liked Daddy, but he didn't seem to need other people much. Maybe his standards were high, or maybe coming from Delaware had made him an outsider. But he really only had two friends—Mama and Danny—to talk with about things that interested him, instead of repeating the same tired conversations about whether it was hot enough. Two friends, and now one of them appeared to be disappearing months earlier than planned.

Lynnette would have known what to do. She could always perk up her mother after a hard day or tease Aggie out of a sulk. She could even sometimes calm her father out of his dark rages with a hand on his arm or a question about the Crimson Tide's chances in an upcoming game. I didn't think my father would know what to do if I put my hand on his arm and he wasn't fond of football. Anyhow, he wasn't in a rage, just sad. I looked at Mama, but she was talking with Joey about a report on the Lost Colony and didn't notice anything wrong at our end of the table.

"Daddy?" I offered him the shortcake plate. "Would you like some more? There's one last serving left. I think you should have it."

He broke his stare, and looked for a long moment at me. Then he gave a smile that stopped just short of his eyes. "Thank you, Mattie," he said. "I believe I will."

# 11

The next day, Lynnette passed me notes in every class. *Are you ready for your first date? Are you nervous? What are you going to wear?* Each one got me more wound up. By seventh period, Carl might as well have been Cary Grant. I tried on eight outfits in my head before I settled on my blue plaid skirt and cream-colored sweater.

At precisely 6:15 p.m., there was a knock at the door. I ran to open it, but skidded to a stop when I saw my mother's act-like-a-lady look. I snuck a look around the corner. In the doorway stood Carl in his Junior ROTC uniform. A uniform to go to the movies? I wasn't sure whether to be flattered or embarrassed.

"Who are you and what do you want?" Joey demanded.

If I'd thought Carl awkward before, he surprised me now. "Carl Davis, Cadet First Lieutenant." He snapped Joey a salute. "Here to escort Miss Mathilda Watson to the picture show."

With that, he won Joey over completely, so instead of taking advantage of Carl's use of my full name to bawl out, "Ma-TILL-da," he said, "Wait here. I'll see if she's ready."

I'd thought this was going to be nothing much. Not a real first date, just practice. But I was having trouble swallowing the cotton ball stuck in my throat.

"Mattie." Mama nudged me toward the door. "Your young man is waiting."

"Could you tell him I'm not here?" I asked.

"Invite him in, honey," she said. "He's a boy, not a fire-breathing dragon. We'll sit him down and have a glass of lemonade before the two of you head off to town."

This sounded all right. The movie wasn't until 7:15. Maybe we didn't even have to go to the movies. I could have my first date right there in the comfort of my own home.

"And I know your father wants to speak to him," Mama added.

"Daddy?" I croaked. "Wants to speak to him?"

"To make sure he passes muster," she said.

"Passes muster?" I gurgled.

"You used to be such an intelligent child." She shook her head sadly and propelled me toward the door, where Joey stood gawking at Carl, waiting for him to do something military. "Good evening, Carl." Mama held out her hand for him to shake. "It's a pleasure to see you. You've got a few minutes to sit down, I hope?"

"Yes, ma'am, Mrs. Watson," Carl said. "You look real nice, Mattie. Like a movie star."

I did look nice. At least I'd done my best to look nice, with my hair curled and the pale peach lipstick Mama had bought me after my escapade with hers. She'd suggested I wear Mary Janes rather than heels because "it would be such a tragic end to your first date if you were rushed to the hospital with a broken ankle." She'd also loaned me her gold bracelet. Now she touched me on the shoulder, like a doll that needed winding up to walk and talk.

"Um, thank you," I said.

Joey trailed after us into the sitting room. "I'll fetch Daddy," he said, "and Danny."

"You don't need to—" I called after him, but he was already out of earshot. Great. I was sure Carl had been looking forward to being grilled by my entire family.

"Have a seat on the sofa, while I get us some lemonade," Mama told him. "Mattie, you can sit down too. On the sofa," she added, in case I got any bright ideas about sitting safely in the armchair opposite.

"Why don't I help with the lemonade, Mama?" I asked, hoping for a last-minute reprieve.

"Oh, that's all right," she said over her shoulder. "I think I can manage."

I kept a good eighteen inches of sofa between Carl and me. I knew my mother. She'd take her time pouring out lemonade, slicing the lemons into perfect wheels and cutting a radius in each one, so it would balance neatly on the rim of the glass. Then she'd have to arrange the gingersnaps we'd baked, the ones I'd finally agreed were an improvement over store-bought, and she'd finally admitted were a sign I might not remain a hopeless cook for the rest of my life.

"I like your hair like that," Carl said. "All curly."

"Thank you," I said automatically. "I like yours too." What a stupid thing to say. His hair looked the same as always: short, brown, and side-parted. "I mean, your uniform looks nice."

Mama finally appeared with a tray of lemonade, Daddy carrying the cookies behind her, followed by Danny and Joey: the Watson family parade.

Daddy and Mama did their best to put Carl at ease. "I heard you made a nice play on that fly ball last week," Daddy said.

"Carl, you have to taste Mattie's gingersnaps." Mama handed him a glass of lemonade, the lemon wheel balanced on a sugared rim, and held out the cookies. "They're her personal recipe."

"Not really," I corrected. "I just changed a couple of ingredients."

"It's nice of you to take Mattie out," Danny said. Great. Now I was a charity case. If he went on to mention to Carl that I'd never been on a date before, I'd have to kill him.

Joey, still awestruck by Carl's uniform, said nothing, for which I was grateful. Even the new-and-improved version of Joey was no guarantee he wouldn't say something mortifying.

Daddy looked at his watch. "I guess you two need to get going, don't you?"

"And you'll have her back by ten?" Mama asked, with some starch ironed into her voice.

"Yes, sir," Carl answered. "Yes, ma'am."

Carl helped me into the passenger seat of his truck. My family watched from the doorway as if seeing me off on the *Queen Mary*.

"I don't know a lot about this picture, do you?" he asked as he eased onto the road.

Not only had Mama decided the film didn't meet her standards, but I'd also overheard every detail about it the day before from Ann Marie Walker, who'd sat behind Lynnette and me in the school cafeteria. However, it didn't seem polite to say so. "Not really," I said.

Carl tried again. "I hardly ever go to the movies. But you like them, don't you?"

"Uh-huh." I went whenever I could wheedle Mama into taking me, at least once a month. If this was all the conversational ability I could muster, the drive would last for weeks. I did, however, have one subject that might interest him. "What do you think about kudzu?" I asked.

He rested his hands on the steering wheel. "I doubt it'll amount to much."

"But think of all the things it can do," I protested. "Feed the soil, fix erosion. We can eat it about six different ways and so can cows. Weren't you listening at the assembly at school?"

"Uh-huh," he said.

"Well, if you went to the kudzu lessons you'd know," I told him. "Danny's going, and he's crazy about kudzu now." I didn't mention that I'd also attended the kudzu-growing classes, from a balcony seat. I also didn't mention Mr. Cullowee's name. I didn't want to sully it by saying it out loud on my first date with someone else.

"Danny's pretty smart," he agreed, watching the road. I appreciated the fact that he was a responsible driver, but I wished he'd show more enthusiasm for the conversation.

"So don't you think if Danny believes in kudzu, there's bound to be something to it?"

"My dad can't spare me to study something that's probably just a fad," he said.

"A fad?" I sputtered. "People already have kudzu auctions in other states. We have to catch up and move ahead, put North Carolina on the kudzu map."

"I expect they can do that catching up without my help," he said.

I looked at him, all crisp and unruffled in his JROTC uniform. "Well, you and your daddy are going to discover how wrong you are."

We made the rest of the drive to town in silence. How could I spend the entire evening with a boy who had so little sense? As agitated as I felt, Carl seemed entirely calm, driving with his eyes on the road.

He found a parallel parking space on Main Street, a block from the theater. Despite my annoyance with his opinion of kudzu, I was impressed by the deft way he slid into the space.

The sidewalks were crowded with people heading for the movie theater or barbecue and hush puppies at Ginger's BBQ. We walked side by side, though whenever a crowd came our way, Carl ushered me in front of him. Everybody else must have had the same idea about the movie, because the line stretched for half the block. "Do you think we'll get in?" I asked.

"Sure. It's a big place, isn't it?"

The crowd was mostly families, I was relieved to see, not anyone who might give me grief, like Glynis. The line inched forward until we were in front. "Two tickets, please," Carl said to Miss Edna Winnicutt in her glass ticket booth. I knew Miss Edna from Lynnette's church. She taught the Tinies, and had such patience with all those little children crawling in different directions, that if Baptists had saints, I'd nominate her.

"That you, Mattie?" she peered over her pince-nez. "Where's your mama?"

"She's giving this one a pass, Miss Edna," I told her. "She says she doesn't like to see Henry Fonda being played for a fool."

"I see," she said, looking at Carl. "And who's your boyfriend? He's awful good-looking."

"He's not my boyfriend," I said, but it was no good. This was how rumors got started, and Miss Edna, for all her talent in keeping toddlers in check, hadn't mastered the same talent with regard to her own tongue. "His name's Carl Davis," I said. "He's on the baseball team with Danny. Carl, this is Miss Edna Winnicutt. She goes to Lynnette's church."

Carl reached through the small arch-shaped cutout in the glass and shook Miss Edna's hand. "Pleased to meet you, Miss Winnicutt."

"Would you hurry it up?" said the man behind us. "We don't want to miss the newsreel."

"Sorry," Carl said. He retrieved his hand and pulled two quarters from his pocket.

As we walked away from the ticket booth, Carl said, "I thought you hadn't seen it."

"I haven't," I said, "but my mama hears about every film that comes through."

The line inched toward the door, where the usher stood in his red uniform.

"Mathilda Watson?" I heard a familiar voice behind me. Mrs. Sampson. "What on earth are you doing here on a Friday night?"

I would have thought it was self-evident. Maybe she assumed that once she sent me home each Wednesday I disappeared until she conjured me up the next week. I was about to tell her I was going to the picture when I realized she was attended not only by her husband, who was chatting with his constituents, but also by Mr. Cullowee, who gave me a thin smile. "Movies," I stammered.

"And who is your handsome beau?" Mrs. Sampson smiled beneficently.

"Carl," I mumbled. My introduction wasn't up to Mrs. Sampson's standards, but it was the best I could do when I desperately wanted to wind this particular movie back to where I'd said I'd go to the movies with Carl and tell him, "Not if you were the last boy on Earth."

"Carl," Mrs. Sampson crooned as she took his hand. "I'm delighted to meet you. We do love our Mathilda. She's such a charming girl." She looked around. "Mr. Mayor, come over and meet Mathilda's darling young man."

"Pleased to meet you, Mrs. Sampson." She might not have known who Carl was, but everyone knew the mayor and his wife.

"An honor to meet you, son," Mr. Sampson said. "Good to see a young man willing to step up and represent his country."

"Thank you, sir," Carl said.

"Will you be joining the army, then?" the mayor asked.

"Yes, sir." Carl hadn't told me that. It would have been decidedly more helpful for me if he'd joined up a week earlier, before he saw Lynnette and me at the swimming hole.

Mrs. Sampson pulled Carl to Mr. Cullowee. "Carl, this is Mr. Cullowee, who's teaching all of Cooper County about the benefits of kudzu. Mr. Cullowee, Carl is Mathilda's sweetheart."

"Not my sweetheart," I muttered.

"Carl." Mr. Cullowee nodded coolly, but didn't shake Carl's hand. "Haven't seen you at our kudzu cultivation class. You from around here?"

Go ahead, I thought, tell him you think kudzu's a fad. Ruin my life.

"Yes, sir," he said. "My dad keeps me pretty busy on the farm."

"Well, stop by if you can find the time. We're always glad to have another young farmer join us," Mr. Cullowee said, though without his usual warmth. It almost seemed as if he were saying the opposite. He looked past Carl. "Mathilda."

"I've got our tickets, Beulah." Mr. Sampson waved three tickets in the air.

"Well," Mrs. Sampson said, "can't miss the shorts! A pleasure to meet you, Carl. And, Mathilda, you're looking particularly lovely this evening." Mr. Cullowee did not look back.

"Do you want popcorn and a Coca-Cola?" Carl asked.

"The movie's about to start," I said. Another usher stood by the door, waiting to close it.

"It's not a movie without popcorn," Carl said. "Come on. There's hardly a line at the concession stand at all. Large popcorn and two Cokes, please," he said to the concessionaire. "Coke all right for you?" he asked me belatedly.

"Fine. Can you get her to hurry?"

"She's a talker, isn't she?" Carl asked as we surveyed the remaining seats. I didn't think Carl was the necking type, but I was happy to see the back rows filled. "The mayor's wife."

"Not really." I felt the need to defend her. "She's a very nice person. She's doing the Kudzu Queen classes for any girl who wants it, purely out of the goodness of her heart." I didn't actually know her reasons for teaching the Kudzu Queen classes. But at that point I was willing to ascribe the purest motives to anyone Carl criticized.

Carl, being a boy, plowed on ahead. "And that Mr. Cullowee. He seemed all right in the assembly, but up close, he's kind of cold, don't you think?"

"Carl Davis, are you a complete idiot, or just trying to get on my bad side?" I snapped.

Carl stopped looking around and gazed at me, startled. "Did I say something wrong?"

"Forget it," I said. "We've got to find seats."

We had to squeeze past a dozen people's knees, holding our popcorn and Cokes over our heads, to make our way to two seats in the center, three rows in front of Mr. Cullowee and the Sampsons. To make my humiliation complete, the lights dimmed before we sat down, and people had to peer around us to see the short. Daffy Duck. Perfect.

During the newsreel I covered my eyes, though what I saw between my fingers made me glad we weren't in the war overseas: squadrons of airplanes dropping bombs, and people running on the ground through the smoke, holding their hands over their heads.

Once the picture started, though, I became Barbara Stanwyck—sticking my foot in the aisle to trip Henry Fonda into falling for me, wearing racy outfits that showed off my midriff. Henry Fonda reminded me not of Carl, whom I managed to forget for the first half of the movie, but of Lynnette, as he tugged Jean Harrington's skirt more demurely to her knees while she tried to seduce him. Then, just as the Lady Eve confessed to Charles Pike's father that she found his son handsome, something heavy settled across my back. Carl's arm. Startled out of my trance, I jerked forward. "What do you think you're doing?"

Carl snatched his hand away. "Just stretching." I turned around to see who'd noticed, but everyone was caught up in the film. Everyone except Mr. Cullowee, who watched us with the closed-mouth smile he'd had outside the theater. I considered crawling under my seat until the ushers swept up the spilled popcorn. Instead, I squeezed as far as I could from Carl and spent the rest of the movie making sure no part of my body touched any part of his.

We left the cinema and walked to Carl's truck in silence. I'd gone on this date hoping to gain some experience, so I'd know how to be sophisticated when the time came, but now it seemed certain that time would never come.

It wasn't Carl's fault. If I'd gone out with him for better reasons, I would have been happy people thought we were a couple and ecstatic when he put his arm around me. He'd done everything possible to ensure I had a good time, and I'd done everything I could to punish him for it. He opened the door for me.

"Carl," I said. "I'm sorry I snapped at you."

To his credit, he didn't ask, "Which time?" Instead he said, "You had every reason to."

"No, I didn't. You were thoughtful, and I was horrible."

He didn't answer. We drove down Main Street, away from the streetlights. Soon, they'd be festooned with kudzu, but I didn't want to think about that. My eyes adjusted as the brightness of town faded behind us. I stared out the window as the stars began cropping up in the dark sky.

"Did you like the picture?" I asked, in an attempt at a peace offering.

His right hand shifted around the steering wheel from 2:00 to 5:00. "You have a thing for him, don't you?"

I jerked upright. "For who?"

He gripped the wheel and wiggled it from side to side, but there was enough play in it that the truck didn't waver. "The Kudzu King."

"No," I protested. "I definitely do not."

"It's okay." He turned onto the county road. "All the girls do." He veered around a possum staring from the center line. "I just thought you had more sense."

I felt my face go hot and red, and was glad it was dark inside the cab. I wanted Carl to believe he'd been right, that I did have sense, even though the thought of Mr. Cullowee generally dissolved me from the inside out, even though I'd imagined him sliding his hand from my ankle up my thigh, even though— "I do like him," I said, "but I like you too." As I said it, I realized I wasn't being nice to make up for being awful. It was true. What was more—and this was a strange thought—I found myself thinking that Aunt Mary would have liked him, and—an even stranger thought—that whether she would have liked him mattered a great deal to me.

# 12

The next morning, I woke up early and couldn't go back to sleep. The humidity lay on me like an extra blanket. I kicked my bedclothes to the foot of the bed, braced my heel against the rucked-up quilt, and thought about the end of the evening.

At the front door, Carl had touched my hand. "I had a nice time, Mattie."

"Seriously?" I'd asked.

"Seriously," he'd answered.

He hadn't tried to kiss me, even on the cheek. He'd walked to his truck and driven away.

My mother had stood at the top of the stairs, with messy hair and a face soft from sleep, her nightgown glowing in the moonlight. "Did you have a good evening?" she asked.

I knew better than to tell her that it had been interesting, which would only have brought her fully awake, wanting to know details. "Yes, Mama, thank you. Go back to bed."

Now I lay in bed and pulled my nightgown to my thighs, hoping for a breeze to cool my sweaty skin. If I got up now, I'd have to face Mama on my way to chores. I'd have to tell about my date over and over: to Mama, to Danny, to Lynnette. I wanted to get it clear in my head first.

I thought about how lightly Carl had touched my hand. What would that same touch feel like on my leg now, if he were sitting on the edge of my bed, drawing his fingertips up my calf?

Carl would never do that. Carl was the sort of boy who'd have to go steady for a year before he'd touch my leg. And I didn't want him to. I didn't like him like that.

I'd tell everyone the truth: Carl had behaved like a gentleman. He'd bought me popcorn and a Coke. I'd seen Miss Edna and Mrs. Sampson and the mayor. The movie theater had been crowded. The film had been entertaining and Henry Fonda hadn't seemed at all like a simpleton by the end of it.

Rehearsing my story made it unnecessary, at least with Mama, who was making coffee, and just wanted to hear that I'd enjoyed myself. At breakfast, Danny stuffed fried eggs into his mouth. "How'd you like Carl, Matts?" he asked between bites. "Good guy, isn't he?"

"He's nice." I waited for him to demand more details, but he just gulped down his coffee and wiped his mouth with his sleeve.

"Got to get going," he said. "Jim and I have to drop off some kudzu crowns in East Cooper. We've finally got fellas at least willing to try it for the government subsidy."

"You've got tobacco and corn requiring your attention here, Daniel," Daddy said.

The use of his full name should have warned Danny, but he stood up. "We'll back by three. That'll give me a couple hours before supper."

"Is Jim Cullowee planning to send you to college?" Daddy asked slowly, tipping onto the rear legs of his chair.

"No." Danny paused at the door.

"Because the man who's paying for your education could use some help around here," Daddy said, landing his chair square on the floor. "And your mother could use you in town this morning, to carry groceries. I expect Jim Cullowee can make do without you today."

When we got home from shopping, Joey and I went to our field. Mama was so used to seeing us go off together that she didn't even comment on it. As we headed into the woods, we saw Danny and Daddy lugging flats of seedlings from the seedbed to the freshly plowed tobacco field. Danny's back was hunched in a way that made him look sulky. It occurred to me that Daddy had done all the plowing himself this year while Danny was off with Mr. Cullowee.

It had been days since I'd seen our field, what with queen

lessons and spying and getting ready for my date. The kudzu looked lush and happy, leafy stems curled around each other. The individual cuttings we'd planted had grown into a mass as high as my knees. I had to look hard to see any cowpeas, but was reassured when I found them hidden among the kudzu.

"You're doing a good job," I told Joey.

"Haven't done much," he said. "It's pretty much growing by itself."

We filled our buckets at the pump. "You think it needs thinning?" Joey asked.

It was an excellent question and one for which my spying had provided no answers. The boys and Mr. Cullowee were weeks away from this kind of growth.

I propped my bucket on my hip and studied the field. "Where would we start?"

Joey rested his bucket on the toes of his boots. He lifted his toes and dropped them, sloshing the water. "You still want to do this?"

Startled, I looked at him, but he was staring at the surface of the water, where the waves hit the edge of the bucket and bounced back. "Why wouldn't I?"

"I don't know," he said. "You seem awful busy."

"But we agreed," I reminded him. "I'd do the queen lessons, since I was the only one who could, and the spying, because of Lynnette being my friend. I thought you wanted me to."

"I did." He lifted his toes and the bucket almost tipped over. "But now you've got a boyfriend and all. You probably don't want to mess with any stupid kudzu."

"He's not my boyfriend. He's just Carl." I put my own bucket down. "And since when is kudzu stupid? What happened to being the richest man in the county?"

"Come on, Mattie." He pulled his feet out from under the bucket and slipped his hands into his pockets. "Who's going to buy kudzu from a ten-year-old kid?"

I put an arm around him. "Anybody who sees it. It's glorious. And it's mostly you who's done it."

He looked at me slyly. "So does that mean I should get a bigger cut?"

I slapped his back so hard he stumbled into his bucket. "Learning to be girly is twice as hard as weeding and watering. Now come on, this kudzu's not smart enough to water itself."

I'd learned a new word in biology class that week: homeostasis. It meant that things tended to want to stay the way they were. In the middle of all the changes in my life, I needed some homeostasis, so I asked Mama if I could spend the night with Lynnette.

I needed to tell Lynnette about my date with Carl and seeing Mr. Cullowee, so she could help me make sense of it all. The thought occurred that I might well see him again at Lynnette's. I wasn't sure whether to hope for that or dread it.

Mama must have needed some homeostasis herself, because she just said, "Supper here or there?" I didn't want Mrs. Johnson to think I believed they were too poor for guests, so I told Mama I'd eat at the Johnsons. The smell of collards on the stove had nothing to do with it.

When I got to the Johnsons', Mr. Cullowee's truck was gone, and I discovered I was more relieved than disappointed. I found Lynnette and the girls on the sleeping porch. Lynnette was teaching Aggie to play Concentration on the rickety card table while Mrs. Johnson finished making supper. Since it was a Saturday night with no men, she wasn't making a full-out meal, just ham biscuits and tomato soup from a tin.

Catherine was occupied with an old naked Shirley Temple doll of Lynnette's, quietly singing a made-up song composed equally of words and babble. Shirley's hair had warped to one side, showing her horrible doll roots. Catherine was walking the doll across the porch, trying to get her to take the width of each chipped gray floorboard at a single stride. Shirley, neglected since Lynnette had outgrown her and never of interest to Aggie, was doing her best to oblige.

Meanwhile, Aggie displayed an astonishing talent for

Concentration. Lynnette turned over a card: the jack of hearts. "Where's another jack, Aggie?"

Aggie pointed to a card on the second row, two in from the right edge, then another card in the middle of the fifth row. Lynnette turned over both cards. The jacks of diamonds and clubs.

"Where's the last one, Aggs?" Lynnette asked.

Aggie stuck her finger in her mouth and lightly bit it, something she did when she was thinking. But before she could answer, we heard a crash from the kitchen.

Catherine looked up from Shirley Temple in mid-stride. "Mama!"

Lynnette grabbed her and ran to the kitchen, with Aggie and me right behind. In the middle of the floor lay Mrs. Johnson, eyes fluttering, with a soup pot clattering to a stop beside her and tomato soup splattered across the linoleum.

Lynnette crouched down, setting Catherine on the floor. "Mama, are you all right?"

Mrs. Johnson lifted her hand weakly, as if trying to quiet us, but she didn't say a word.

"I think we should call an ambulance," I told Lynnette, "or at least find your father."

Mrs. Johnson's mouth made the word "no," but only the "oh" came out, in a soft breath.

Lynnette held her mother's hand. "Mama, can you say anything? What happened?"

Aggie crept closer to Lynnette.

"She's cold," Lynnette said. "Can you get a blanket?"

I ran to the girls' room and snatched up Aggie's orange and brown afghan and Catherine's baby quilt with a rabbit embroidered on it. I laid them carefully over Mrs. Johnson. The baby quilt barely stretched from her shoulders to her thighs.

"I really think we should call the ambulance," I said again.

Mrs. Johnson made that "oh," sound again, barely a breath of it.

"I'm going to drive her to the hospital," Lynnette said. "Can you stay with the girls?"

This was not the time to remind Lynnette that she'd never driven anything but a tractor before, and that she was two months shy of her sixteenth birthday.

"All right," I said.

She reached for the hook where her father kept the car keys. This was probably also not the time to ask if she knew where her father was. Sometimes he wandered into the woods with a bottle. Other times, he walked down the road until he met someone driving in the direction of the juke joint down by the tenant farms.

She glanced at her mother, who was lying with her eyes closed, the rabbit blanket rising and falling with her harsh breathing. Lynnette picked Catherine up from the floor and lowered her into her high chair. Catherine opened her mouth to wail, but Lynnette popped a biscuit into it.

"Keep feeding her. She'll hush." She detached Aggie from her leg and bent down. "Now, Miss Agatha, you be good for Mattie." She turned to me. "I'll pull the car around."

I sat cross-legged beside Mrs. Johnson. "You're going to be all right." Through the screen, I saw Lynnette drive up to the kitchen door, jump out, and open the back door of the car.

"Do you think she's broken anything?" she asked, as the screen slapped shut behind her.

"She's not bleeding," I said. "And no bones seem to be sticking out of her."

She bent down and draped her mother's left arm over her shoulder, lifting her up to sitting. "You get her other side." I ducked under Mrs. Johnson's right arm and we stood up, bringing her with us. Aggie and Catherine watched, quiet and wild-eyed. When we got halfway up, she moaned and twisted, almost falling, but I tightened my grip around her waist, feeling Lynnette do the same. Mrs. Johnson was a slight woman, but at that moment she was pure deadweight.

She was taller than either of us, so we had to stand as straight as we could and drag her feet. When her right house slipper fell off, Aggie ran up and grabbed it. We managed to get Mrs.

Johnson partway onto the back seat. I held her steady while Lynnette ran to the other side, crawled over and pulled her in.

"I'm afraid she'll fall," Lynnette said. "Can you get some—"

I ran inside and grabbed every pillow I could find. When I got back, Aggie was trying to put the slipper onto her mama's stocking foot, but her foot was hanging out the door, and the slipper kept falling to the ground.

"Here, Aggie." I handed her the pillows and eased Mrs. Johnson's foot into the car. Then I stuffed the pillows between Mrs. Johnson and the front seat, while Aggie slid the slipper onto her mother's foot. At least she'd be warm. And if she fell, she'd have a soft landing.

I eased the car door shut as Lynnette started the engine and ground it into gear.

"Call when you get there," I said.

Aggie and I stood in the doorway while Lynnette wove down the drive into the dusk. She finally remembered to turn on the headlights when she got to the road.

Inside the kitchen, Catherine wailed. I ran in to find the biscuit fallen to the floor, crumbs soaking up spilled soup, and Catherine pounding the tray of her high chair with flat palms.

"She doesn't like her chair." Aggie's quiet voice slid beneath Catherine's screams. "She's scared."

Which meant Aggie was scared, too, as was I. I was almost as scared about Lynnette driving to the hospital as I was for their mother. I grabbed Catherine under the arms.

"You have to unlatch her tray first," Aggie said, lifting the tray off and putting it on the table. I reached for Catherine again, but I should have braced myself. A solid, thrashing little girl was more difficult to handle than a solid, placid one. Her hand flung out and popped me a good one on the cheekbone. I staggered back, but hung on tightly, setting her down on the floor, where she sat screaming amidst the milky tomato mess of soup and soaked biscuit parts.

"What now?" I asked.

"She'll stop if she has her passy," Aggie told me.

I couldn't believe anything would make her stop. When Lynnette watched over the girls, Catherine always seemed so quiet and content. "Do you know where it is?"

Aggie skirted the mess and plucked the pacifier from the dish drainer. I'd seen Lynnette pop it into her own mouth before putting it in Catherine's, so I did the same. Her mouth closed automatically around it and, like a miracle, the wails subsided to sniffles. I looked at Aggie, amazed. "You're a smart girl."

Mucus ran down Catherine's face and clogged her nose. I grabbed a napkin from the table and loosely pinched it over Catherine's tiny nose, the way my mother had done when I was little. "Blow," I said, and she did. I mopped up the snot that had run past her mouth and onto her chin, then found a clean spot on the napkin and blotted her damp eyes. "There you go. All better." She glared at me, unconvinced. But at least the house was quieter and she wasn't suffocating on her own snot. Tomato soup stiffened a clump of her fine blond hair against her cheek. I wet a dishcloth and cleaned the soup out of her hair, leaving it damp against her cheek, but I wasn't sure what to do about the rest of her.

"Should I put her to bed?" I asked Aggie.

She looked out the window. "It's not dark, and we haven't had supper."

"How do you feel about cornflakes?"

"All right," she said.

Aggie must be terrified, I thought, though she wouldn't show it. I knelt and put my hands on her shoulders. "Your mama's going to be fine."

I poured giant bowls of cornflakes and goat milk for the girls. Holding Catherine on my lap, I tried to feed her, but she kept sagging forward. Aggie stirred her cereal until it became a soggy mess. "I'm not hungry," she said.

"Are you sleepy?" I asked.

"Not really."

"Help me get Catherine to bed, and you can sit up with me until Lynnette calls." I hoisted Catherine onto my hip, trying to ignore the way her diaper squished against my hipbone. When Lynnette did it, she made it look effortless, but I found myself trembling as I climbed the stairs, Catherine's head lolling on my shoulder.

In the girls' room, Aggie extracted a diaper from the second drawer in the tall bureau. She felt around on top until she found the talcum bottle.

"Can I change her on your bed?" I asked Aggie.

"Mama does," she said. "Lynnie changes her standing up."

This seemed an impractical approach for a beginner.

"Wait," Aggie said. She grabbed a towel and spread it on the bed. "Lay her on this."

Between us, we were able to get Catherine cleaned up, powdered and changed. It was probably a more efficient process when Lynnette did it, but I was proud. And exhausted. Catherine fell asleep somewhere in the middle.

"Now her nightie." Aggie handed me a wash-thinned one of bleached cotton.

"Can't she sleep in her clothes for tonight?" Extracting an unconscious Catherine from her blue gingham dress and putting her in a nightgown seemed a lot of unnecessary trouble, even though the dress was stained with porch dirt and tomato soup.

"She won't sleep right." Aggie held out the nightie until I took it.

I lay the sleeping Catherine on the bed and peeled off her dress, then pulled the nightgown over her head and wriggled it down.

My mother had a lot more experience with small children than I did. If I called her she'd be right over, full of concern. I ignored the desire and hoisted Catherine over my shoulder. "Crib?"

"On her back," Aggie instructed.

I hoisted Catherine over the crib rails and laid her down. Since her blanket was still on the kitchen floor, sopping up soup, I covered her with my cardigan. Thumb in her mouth, she flung her other arm over her face. I reached for the pull string to turn out the light. "We done?"

"You have to tell a story," Aggie said.

"But she's already asleep."

"You have to tell a story," she repeated.

"I don't know any stories," I told her.

"Make one up, or she'll have nightmares."

I sat down heavily on Aggie's bed. "I'm not good at making things up." She didn't answer, but stood at the foot of Catherine's crib, holding the bars. Somebody needed a story, but I wasn't sure it was Catherine. "Once upon a time..." I sighed, unable to think of anything else.

"There was a princess," supplied Aggie, more experienced than I was.

"Right. There was a princess named Aggie."

"Named Catherine," Aggie corrected. "Princesses aren't named Aggie."

"Catherine." I wondered what title Aggie had in Aggieland.

"And a handsome prince, Prince James." I would brook no argument on this one. "Princess Catherine lived in a castle."

"A shack," Aggie corrected, with ruthless honesty. She let go of Catherine's crib, and sat on the floor, leaning against the bed.

"Maybe you should tell the story, since you know it so well."

"It isn't made up yet," she pointed out. Catherine kicked off my cardigan, her foot getting tangled in the sleeve. I freed her foot and sat back on the bed.

"She's having bad dreams," Aggie said. "This is how it starts. You better get on with the story, before they turn to nightmares."

I found myself envying Lynnette her natural storytelling ability, and the Bible stories and fairy tales cataloged in her head. "So this Princess Catherine lived in a shack, but a nice shack, with her two sisters and her mother and her father."

"She didn't have a father, just her mother and her sisters," Aggie corrected.

"Anyway, Princess Catherine was very beautiful, the way all princesses are, with long blond hair and eyes as blue as the summer sky."

I paused for any objections, but Aggie seemed satisfied. There was something magical about how she was talking to me. "There was only one problem in Princess Catherine's life." I stopped, not sure what the problem should be. It didn't seem to be lack of a father or living in a shack. "The problem was," I was struck by sudden inspiration, "that when this princess was born, she was so beautiful that a witch who came to her christening got jealous. This witch had warts all over her nose and gnarled-up hands and pointy feet—"

"And hair like dry hay," Aggie added, "and squinty black eyes and—"

In the kitchen, the phone rang.

Aggie and I leapt up and rushed down the stairs.

"Hello?" I grabbed the receiver. "Hello? Lynnette?"

Aggie pressed close, as if she could get to Lynnette through me.

"Hello?" said a strange woman. "To whom am I speaking?"

"This is Mattie. Mattie Lee Watson."

"Miss Watson," the voice said. "This is Miss Garner, from the hospital. I'm calling on behalf of Lynnette Johnson."

"Yes?" When Aggie heard Lynnette's name, rather than her voice, she jerked away from the phone.

"She wanted me to let you know that her mother's condition is stable, but guarded."

"What's wrong with her? Is she all right?"

"We'll know more tomorrow," she said. "Miss Johnson will be staying at her mother's bedside tonight. She's asked if you can remain at home with her sisters until she calls in the morning, around eight. Can she count on you to do that?"

"Yes, ma'am," I said. "She can."

"Thank you," Miss Garner said crisply. "I'll let her know. Good-bye."

I held on to the phone after she disconnected. This would be the time to call my mother, to tell her what had happened and enlist her assistance. The phone was in my hand.

But I found myself looking for a new homeostasis, where I acted like a grown-up. As far as Mama knew, Lynnette and I were having our usual Saturday night sleepover. There was nothing she could do for Lynnette or her mother by being there. For once I felt as if I might do some good for Aggie and Catherine. This recent invitation into Aggieland felt fragile, like something written on old parchment in disappearing ink. I didn't want it to fade away in the light of my mother's efficiency. I dropped the telephone receiver in its cradle and squatted, eye-level with Aggie. "Your mama's doing fine, but she needs to rest," I said. "We'll talk to Lynnette in the morning. It's you and me and Catherine tonight, Aggs. That all right by you?"

Aggie looked at the top corner of the screen door. I followed her gaze but all I could see was a place where the paint had peeled away. "I guess," she said.

Around midnight, Aggie fell asleep on the sitting room sofa. We'd sat there for hours, not talking, just listening to the creaking house and Catherine's sleeping murmurs. Occasionally the murmurs turned to whimpers, and I'd tiptoe up to stroke Catherine's hair until she stilled. I'd never noticed how soft her hair was, like corn silk. Then I'd walk downstairs and curl up in the armchair. Sometimes headlights filled the window, making us squint. Then we'd get used to the darkness again. By the time Aggie fell asleep, I hadn't seen a car in over an hour.

Danny would have been able to carry Aggie upstairs, but I couldn't, so I straightened her out on the sofa and sat beside her. At first she curled up like a roly-poly, but after awhile she stretched out again, her feet resting on my lap. The house settled into itself. Several times I heard a train whistle, once alternating with an owl, as if they were calling back and forth.

My own eyes started to droop. I kept snapping them wide again. If Lynnette was staying up by her mama's bedside, I should too. Plus, one of the girls might wake in a state.

I didn't realize I'd fallen asleep until I heard a new creak. My eyes opened and I saw Mr. Cullowee in the armchair, looking at me. You know how sometimes when you wake from a sound sleep, you say whatever comes into your head? "How long have you been watching me?" I asked.

"About ten minutes," he said.

"You're out late." If I'd been more awake, I'd never have spoken so boldly.

"I was at a meeting in town, with the pageant committee."

"Mrs. Johnson's in the hospital," I told him. "With Lynnette."

"I heard," he said, "in town." I couldn't see his expression. "And Mr. Johnson?"

"Out," I said simply. He'd been there long enough to know Mr. Johnson's habits.

He stood and peered down at Aggie. "Shouldn't she be in bed?"

"Probably," I said, "but she's too heavy."

He picked her up, one arm behind her back and the other under her knees. I followed them upstairs and stood in the doorway as he lowered her to the bed. She didn't wake. It made me think of times I'd cried myself to sleep, so worn out by a storm of misery that I couldn't move. I'd never seen Aggie even glaze over with tears. But she seemed as weighted as if she'd been crying for hours, as if she'd sunk to the bottom of a pond of grief.

"What about her nightclothes?" he asked.

"She can stay dressed this once," I said. It felt wrong to undress her in front of him. I slid the sheet out from under her and pulled it to her chin. Then I stood beside him, watching her as if we were a strange little family: the handsome father, the mother only a few years older than the daughter, and the toddler in her crib. A wet breeze blew through the open window, bringing a promise of rain. Aggie curled up, drawing the sheet around herself. "Would you mind," I asked, "seeing if there are any extra covers somewhere? I'm afraid she'll catch a chill."

I watched Aggie sleep while he was out. Her hand lay on the pillow near her cheek. Mr. Cullowee returned with a quilt. I wrapped it around her and watched her limbs unfurl. "Thanks." I left the girls' room and closed the door, heading down to catnap on the sofa. I didn't want to be on the sleeping porch and not hear the phone.

I expected Mr. Cullowee to go into Lynnette's bedroom, but

instead he followed me downstairs. He returned to the armchair and stretched out his legs. His cuffs fell perfectly, the creases as crisp as they must have been that morning. I couldn't very well lie down in front of him, so I found my shoes under the sofa. I slid my feet into them and pulled up my socks, then sat primly with my knees together, my mind scurrying for something neutral to say.

I'd considered and rejected the weather, the movie we'd both seen and how his day had gone, when he spoke. "Your name came up in discussion, Mattie. At the meeting this evening."

That was the last thing I'd expected him to say. "Why—?" I began. "Who—?"

Instead of answering, he stood up and crossed to me. "You're a lovely girl, Mathilda."

How long had I rehearsed for this moment? Now I wasn't sure I wanted to see what the next would hold. "Mrs. Johnson—do you think—will she…?"

He held my chin and tilted my head back until I looked up at him. "You shouldn't waste yourself on immature boys." When he dropped his hand, my jaw dropped with it. He turned and climbed the stairs.

I lay awake on the sofa the rest of the night, still in my shoes, afraid to undress even slightly. The storm hit around three a.m. I thought of our kudzu, hardy enough to withstand the pounding of the rain, and the newly planted field behind the Johnsons' house, which might get washed out. The rain gradually ended as sunlight seeped into the room, lighting up the faded upholstery. I listened for noises, but heard nothing. In the side yard I gathered eggs, accepting the hen's pecks as if they were penance for some sin I might have committed.

The goats were pure comfort. I rested my forehead against their rough fur as I milked them, drifting into dreams of dark-suited men in hospital rooms. I was carrying the steaming pail of milk across the muddy yard when I heard Mr. Cullowee's truck ease down the drive.

By the time the girls came down at seven, I had the kitchen

cleaned and breakfast on the table—eggs fried too hard and greasy and warm goat's milk with a little coffee in Aggie's and mine to cover the smell. I lifted Catherine into her high chair and slid in the tray as if I'd been practicing for years.

At eight-thirty, Lynnette called. I stretched the phone cord into the hallway so Aggie and Catherine wouldn't see my face if something bad had happened. But Lynnette said the doctor thought her mother might be able to go home by evening. They didn't know exactly what had happened to her, but it was all part of her condition, which was still a mystery to me. I didn't ask. Even though Lynnette was my best friend, it felt like prying.

"Could you look after the girls?" she asked. "Until we get back?"

At some point their father would stagger into the house and stumble upstairs, but nobody considered him responsible enough to care for his own children. "Sure," I said.

Around four, Lynnette arrived home with her mother. An orderly from the hospital drove Mr. Johnson's car and a nurse followed in a brand new Pontiac. The orderly helped Mrs. Johnson up to bed, then waved as he climbed into the Pontiac.

"Is she all right?" I asked.

"They said she could come home," Lynnette said, which wasn't an answer. She trudged upstairs. I figured the best way I could help was to keep Aggie occupied, so I went back to the checkers game we'd kept up throughout the afternoon while Catherine slept.

I heard Lynnette call softly. "Mattie?" I stood at the foot of the steps and looked up. She was backlit by the bathroom window at the end of the hall. Her hair looked frazzled and her shoulders slumped. "You probably need to go home, don't you?"

"Either that or call," I said. "Chores." I suddenly felt as if I'd lost something, like I was back to plain old slapdash Mattie that no one counted on for anything. "I could stay."

"No, I've got it," she said. "There's not much you can do."

I felt a tiny flare of irritation. I'd done plenty when she'd needed it. But Lynnette hadn't meant to be mean. She just hadn't seen me rise to the occasion. "Will I see you tomorrow?"

"Maybe. I don't know for sure. I'll send you a note with Aggie if not."

I stopped by the kitchen. Aggie had abandoned the checkers game, leaving the kitchen door open on her way outside. She'd been one move away from winning, so I jumped her red over my black and closed the screen door. In the distance, I saw Mr. Johnson trudging through his kudzu field toward the house, the breeze lifting his hair from his hatless head and dropping it again. He didn't seem to notice.

# 13

Lynnette was out of school all the next week. Each morning, she sent a note by way of Aggie. *Maybe tomorrow.* All week, the bus was steamy from 90-degree weather and ongoing rain, but Aggie showed up wearing the same heavy wool cardigan buttoned up to her neck. I wondered if she was practicing some kind of Aggieland magic to help her mother get better. After handing me Lynnette's notes, she stared out the bus window, swinging her leg, which would sometimes touch mine and stay there.

In Queen School that week, I sat as far from Glynis as I could. I still wasn't sure why she hated me so much, since if by any chance Mabel wasn't selected to be the Kudzu Queen, Glynis would get it on looks alone.

Mrs. Sampson cleared her throat delicately. "Ladies?" The usual before-class whispering subsided. "You're coming along nicely in the etiquette and poise departments. However, to rise like cream to the top of our society, a young lady must have something that makes her distinctive. She must have a talent."

I was doubtful enough about my ability to master etiquette and poise. I didn't think dove calls would meet Mrs. Sampson's standards for a talent. What was I doing there, anyway? I wasn't any closer to becoming the Kudzu Queen, it had been two weeks since my dance with Mr. Cullowee, and I certainly wasn't picking up any tips on growing kudzu.

To be honest, Joey and I didn't need any kudzu advice. If I had a talent, it seemed to be the one I shared with Joey for growing the lushest, greenest crop of anything I'd ever seen. Joey now spent all his free time taking care of our kudzu, though "taking care" meant "admiring," since our kudzu was entirely self-sufficient. He'd stand on the edge of the field, daydreaming about his plan to reveal our brilliance to the world, then move on to how we'd harvest, cure, and market the kudzu. And, saving the best for last, what he planned to do with his millions.

"You'll work in small groups," Mrs. Sampson interrupted my thoughts, "to help determine which talents you should cultivate." I looked from Mabel to Alice, on each side of me.

"I thought it would be enlightening for you to chat with partners you might not ordinarily choose," Mrs. Sampson went on. "So I've divided you accordingly, to liven things up a bit. Mathilda? You'll work with Ann Marie and—" Please no, I thought. "Glynis." She swiveled a stern stare between us. "A lady is cordial in any company," she said to both of us.

It seemed to me that a lady should be able to choose her own company, but it wasn't up to me. I sat next to Ann Marie. She wasn't nice, but she didn't have enough brains to reach the level of mean Glynis achieved just by waking up in the morning.

"So, girls." Mrs. Sampson waved her hands like she was stirring us around. "Discuss."

Ann Marie scooted to face Glynis. Her tight olive-green sweater stretched over her brassiere, outlining the hardware on the straps, not to mention her spine. The sight of her back told me nothing about my talents or hers, but it did demonstrate that along with a lack of brains, she also had miserable manners. Still, it was nice to know she had a spine.

"So," I addressed the air between us, "what do you think you're talented at?"

"Squashing little bugs that think they're something." Glynis had mastered the art of speaking just loudly enough to be heard by her victim without attracting the attention of adults. Meanwhile, Mrs. Sampson beamed at Mabel, who was earnestly eliciting a list of talents from Alice. How had Alice gotten Mabel, while I had to partner with Fire and Brimstone?

"That's not bad," I said, "but you might want to try something with more crowd appeal."

I saw Rose passing the doorway and sent her a desperate look. If anyone could help me figure out my talents, it would be Rose, though I didn't think that was the sort of pairing Mrs. Sampson had in mind.

"Mrs. Sampson?" Rose called softly. "Um, there's a message for Mattie Lee."

"For Mathilda?" Mrs. Sampson asked. "What sort of message?"

Glynis and Ann Marie mockingly mouthed, *What sort of message?*

"From her mother." Rose had never been as good a liar as I was, though once she picked up steam, she was able to lie more smoothly. My early years of teaching Rose to keep her lies simple had paid off. Nothing messed up a good lie like unnecessary embellishments.

I followed Rose down the hall to the kitchen, where she lifted a couple of sugar cookies from a cooling rack. "May we?" she asked the Sampson's cook, a tall woman named Raquel.

"Sure," Raquel answered. "There's plenty."

The kitchen door was ajar, letting out some of the oven heat. Rose opened the door and I followed her to the stoop, where we sat down. She handed me a hot cookie.

"That girl is a piece of work," she said.

I juggled the cookie from hand to hand to cool it down. "She hates me."

"That she does," Rose agreed. "What're you going to do about it?"

"I don't know."

"Well, you better do something," Rose told me. "She's not a good enemy."

I took a bite of the cookie. Sweet, with pink sugar crystals on top. "Do you think I have any talents, Rose?" I asked.

She bit into her cookie. "Haven't seen all that much of you lately."

"Well, did I then?" I asked. "When we used to play together?"

She thought for a moment. "You were pretty good at telling people what to do."

Coming from her, that didn't seem like an insult, just a statement.

"I don't want to go back in there," I told her.

"Don't, then," she said.

"But Mrs. Sampson will have a fit."

"Maybe, maybe not. She's smarter than you think." She shoved her cookie in her mouth, stood, and reached down with both hands. "Come on. Time for you to get out of here."

After a brief stint of sunshine on Wednesday afternoon, the rains resumed in Biblical fashion. The Thursday afternoon kudzu cultivation class was canceled due to downpour.

"Cullowee not up to farming in the rain?" Daddy asked at supper.

"Our kudzu's doing pretty well on its own," Danny said, a defensive edge to his voice. "And Jim has some meetings, about the festival."

"Meetings," Daddy mused. Mama gave him a look over the squash casserole.

The rain hadn't kept Joey and me from our kudzu, which lifted its leaves to the sky like a field of hungry baby birds. By now it was as tall as my thighs. I wouldn't say I gloated over the boys missing their kudzu class, but I wasn't unhappy to see them fall behind.

"Kudzu doesn't need to be coddled," Danny said, jabbing irritably at his Brunswick stew.

"Mrs. Johnson seems to be doing a bit better," Mama said mildly. "I took some soup by this afternoon."

"Did you see Lynnette?" I asked. "Does she want me to—?"

Mama laid her hand over mine. "I think you'd best give them a few days before you stop over, Mattie. Lynnette's got a lot on her hands, with her mother and the girls, and—" She gave Daddy another look, one I couldn't read.

"And what?" I asked.

"And just that. I know you'd like to help, but Lynnette needs to take care of things on her own right now."

Now, of course, I was dying to know what "and" meant. Maybe I couldn't go over, but the telephone still worked. Or at least it did until my mother, the mind reader, added, "And don't call her, either. I'm sure by Saturday you can visit."

"Could I—"

"I'd rather you not stay the night," she answered before I'd finished asking, "until Mrs. Johnson is on her feet again. You can stay for an hour or so. I don't want you to tire her out."

That night the rain pounded on the roof like it was trying to force its way into the house. My dreams were full of animals, two by two.

Friday morning Joey and I picked our way around puddles to get to the bus. Through the rain I saw Danny and Daddy in the cornfield.

On the bus Aggie handed me Lynnette's note, *Monday, for sure*, then watched the rain sheet down the windows as her fingers gripped the top button of her cardigan.

In history, we were ensconced in Prohibition. I wished Lynnette were there so I could pass her a note about how Mr. Kerr's lecture on the Eighteenth Amendment made me want to take up drink in the worst way.

At the end of the day, everyone spilled into the downpour, holding book bags and umbrellas over our heads, but the rain got us by slanting sideways. After almost five days of it, I worried that my skin might mildew. I gazed out the bus window, hypnotized by drops snaking down the glass. When we pulled up at the stoplight at Main and Third, I looked at the truck beside us. Through the rain, Mr. Cullowee's profile wavered. I watched him until my stare drew his gaze to the window. When he saw me, his mouth sidled upward into a slow smile. He winked. I jerked my head away, and the light changed to green.

Lynnette wasn't in town on Saturday morning, but I had business to keep me occupied while Mama shopped. I was beginning to think I might need some remedial work in manners, if I were to have even a hope of beating Mabel to the Kudzu Queen crown.

Between Aronson's and the library, the wind blew my umbrella inside out. I hauled open the heavy library door and dripped in the foyer. My intention was to skip the tedious card catalog and go straight to Miss Perkins, the librarian, for advice.

But Miss Perkins wasn't at the checkout desk. Neither was she polishing windows or dusting the tops of books, which she did regularly even though Nettie, the janitress, was in charge of such things. Nothing Nettie did met Miss Perkins's standards. I never saw two women bicker so over a little dust. She wasn't perched on a low stool, legs tucked under her skirt, putting away biographies on the bottom shelf or alphabetizing books people had misshelved. I even checked the ladies' room, looking for her silk-stockinged calves under the stall doors.

Finally, from behind the closed door of the meeting room, I heard men's voices, with Miss Perkins asking questions. I heard "revenue" several times, and "kudzu." Someone said, "…could be a problem" and Mr. Cullowee soothed, "…not a thing… worry…" Miss Perkins asked, "Have you considered…" The mayor replied, "That's an excellent…" I edged closer.

Miss Perkins must have had a sixth sense about people in her library, because she swung the door wide open. I jumped, trying to look as if I were up to anything but what I'd been doing: snooping. My mother would have been appalled to find me listening at keyholes.

"May I help—" Miss Perkins began, then saw that it was me. "Oh, hello, Mattie. What can I do for you?" She closed the door and leaned against it, in a smart forest-green suit and pearls.

"I was just…I kind of need—I can use the card catalog."

"That's all right," she said. "I can take a moment."

"It's just, well, I was wondering if you had any books about manners?"

She went directly to a shelf by the window. I had no doubt that, if pressed, she could recite every title in the library in order by shelf. "This is the classic," she said, selecting a book with a blue cloth cover and *Etiquette* at the top in fancy gold letters. "I think you'll find it enlightening—and perhaps entertaining." She carried it to her desk, wrote my name on the card and stamped the date due slip, then handed me the book. "Good luck in the contest," she said with a wink, and disappeared into the meeting room.

I sat at a table and read while the rain poured outside. I hadn't expected a book on etiquette to be a page-turner, but when I finally looked up, it was going on 11:30. Mama would have finished shopping, and everyone would be gathered at the car. I stuffed the book in my book bag. The door to the meeting room was still closed.

That afternoon, I wore Danny's old slicker so I could tent it around the platter of roast chicken Mama had made for the Johnsons. She'd covered the chicken with a bowl to keep it as dry as possible when I cut through the cornfields. It felt warm against my chest.

"One hour," she'd warned, "or I'm sending Joey to fetch you."

"One hour," I agreed, though I could stretch it another fifteen minutes before she made good on her threat. When I arrived, the kitchen door was shut. I knocked with my elbow.

Lynnette eased the door open. "Come in, but be quiet. I've just got her to sleep."

I opened the slicker and gave her the chicken. "Mama sent this over. Another chicken down. Two, actually. One for you and one for us."

"Thanks," she whispered. "She shouldn't have, but I'm grateful. The girls were hungry."

"What do you mean?" I asked, forgetting to keep my voice down.

"Shh," she reminded me. She tilted her head toward the stairs, listening for a sound that might indicate her mother had wakened. When nothing came, she carried the chicken to the cutting board. "There hasn't been much around but biscuits and fatback."

"But you've got chickens," I protested.

"We're saving them," she said, "and selling all our eggs now," she went on before I could bring those up too. With a sharp knife, she began slicing the chicken and chopping up the slices.

"But you need to eat something," I argued. "Where's Mr. Cullowee?" Surely she wasn't serving fatback and biscuits to a guest.

"Moved to the mayor's house. He didn't want to be a burden while Mama was mending."

"What about your father?" A dangerous line of inquiry, but I couldn't help it.

She filled a pot with water, put it on the stove, and began dropping in the chicken.

"What are you doing?" I asked. "That chicken's cooked."

"It'll go further as soup, and Mama needs to get her strength back." She chopped a couple of sprouting onions, and some old potatoes. All that went into the pot.

"You haven't seen him, have you?"

"Not since I brought Mama home," she said, her shoulders hunched.

I put my arm around her, but her shoulders rose more sharply. "Is there anything—"

"No," she said, still facing the stove. "Thanks. I'll see you Monday."

Of the hour my mother had given me, I'd used eleven minutes.

# 14

After a week of rain, I considered scouting around the barn for spare lumber, in case we had to build an ark. Most people think all a farmer has to worry about are bugs and droughts and freezes, but too much water and crops can drown, especially early in the season when they're not deeply rooted. Danny was spending more time at home, working with Daddy every morning and afternoon in the downpour to trench the fields and direct water away from the plants. Cotton was a fickle crop, and the corn and tobacco leaves were going yellow, even with their efforts.

Despite Lynnette's promise, she wasn't in school on Monday. I worried about her. How could she pass sophomore year if she kept missing school?

On Wednesday I left school as quickly as I could, before the bell had finished ringing, and arrived at the Sampson house at 3:00, well ahead of the other girls. When Rose answered the doorbell, I whispered, "She mad?"

"Don't know," Rose said quietly, "but she doesn't usually keep a grudge this long."

From the sitting room, I heard Mrs. Sampson call, "Rose? Who is it at the door?"

I tugged down my skirt, and smoothed my hair. "Do I look all right?"

"Good enough." She opened the door wide. "Go on in and get it over with."

Given my slight inclination toward willfulness, I'd had some experience apologizing. It worked best if you looked sorry, so I stood in the doorway with my head bowed, as if the weight of my transgression were too much to bear.

Mrs. Sampson sat in an armchair, reading a pamphlet. She looked up.

"I'm sorry to interrupt, but I wanted to say, before the other girls got here, how much I regret my behavior last week. I shouldn't have left in the middle of class."

She placed the pamphlet on the table beside her. "Come here, Mathilda."

When I stepped into the room, she tilted her head toward the rug in front of her. Was this what "being called on the carpet" meant? I shuffled closer. "I'm really sorry."

She took my chin in her hand, angling it toward the lamp. "Good bone structure," she murmured. She dropped her hand. "I understand why you left, Mathilda. I'm sorry. I'd hoped—"

In four weeks of Kudzu Queen classes, I'd never once heard her apologize. I waited for what she'd hoped, but she just said, "The other girls will arrive any minute now, won't they?"

"Yes, ma'am," I said.

She gestured me into the chair opposite hers. "How much do you want this?"

"How much do I want what?" I was having trouble understanding this conversation.

"Learning to become a lady. Winning the Kudzu Queen competition."

"Honestly?"

"Yes," she said.

"Not much."

"The etiquette lessons?" she asked. "Or becoming Kudzu Queen?"

I leaned back in the brocade chair. "I'm not sure how I feel right now. At least about all the manners stuff, and how to walk and talk and drink tea. I liked the little cakes and things, though." I hesitated, then added, "When Mr. Cullowee first came to town, the only thing I wanted was to be the Kudzu Queen of Cooper County."

"You could be, you know," she said.

I snorted before I caught myself. "I don't think so, ma'am. We all know it'll be Mabel."

"Mabel's a sweet girl," she said, "quite lovely."

If there were two words that fit Mabel, they were "sweet" and "lovely."

"Which is why they're going to pick her as queen," I said.

Mrs. Sampson continued, "But she doesn't have your..." she looked toward the ornate molding in a corner of the ceiling, as if the rest of her sentence might be engraved there, "intelligence."

Right, I thought. I'd been told I was stubborn, bossy, and impulsive, but I'd never heard anyone call me intelligent. I didn't think that was a quality likely to impress the judges.

"I'm not pretty," I said flatly, "and, as I figured out last week, I don't have any talents."

"That was my mistake. I'd hoped—" And she stopped again.

I got up the nerve to ask, "Hoped what?"

"That you might be a good influence on Glynis," she said.

"Me? Influence her? That's like asking a rabbit to influence a rattlesnake."

"A good lead horse and a mule might be the example I'd choose," she went on. "I'd hoped you might at least sway Ann Marie from Glynis's influence. She's not a bright girl, Ann Marie, but I don't think she's bad at heart. She's a follower."

"I'm not exactly a leader," I confessed.

"Really?" she asked. "Maybe you should spend some time observing yourself."

She stood. "And now we really do have to prepare for the others." I glanced at the pamphlet on the table. It was not, as I'd thought, a treatise on proper behavior for young ladies. Instead, it was a booklet from the U. S. Department of Agriculture, *Kudzu: A Forage Crop for the Southeast.* Mrs. Sampson unexpectedly gave me a co-conspirator's smile. "A little light reading. We have to keep up with the men, don't we?"

I followed as she walked to the doorway to greet the other girls. "Mrs. Sampson," I asked. "Could a person really become queen, if she hasn't come to any classes?"

Her smile lingered, as if she'd forgotten and left it there. "Mattie, I'd say a person can be anything she chooses to be."

When the others arrived, Mrs. Sampson handed us notepads and pencils, and explained our task: an essay on why we hoped to become Kudzu Queen. "It's wise to be prepared, should the judges inquire." I wasn't thrilled about having to write an essay, but I kept that to myself. My talk with Mrs. Sampson had been so unexpectedly pleasant that I didn't want to upset her. I'd thought I was coming over to eat crow, and instead she'd fed me caviar.

She asked each of us to find a private place, "to commune with your own thoughts, girls."

The kitchen wasn't private, but it offered privacy from Glynis, and kept me from having to look at Mabel, embarrassed that Mrs. Sampson didn't think she was as smart as I was.

"This all right?" I asked, as I set my notepad at the kitchen table opposite Rose, who was rubbing a pile of teaspoons with murky gray polish.

"Help yourself," Rose said.

"You want anything?" Raquel lifted her soapy hands from the dishwater. She was washing pans in the porcelain sink. The kitchen smelled of roast lamb and peas.

"No, thank you." I propped my elbows on the table. "Why do I want to be the Kudzu Queen?" I asked Rose.

Rose smeared more polish on the spoons. "Because you like power."

"What?" I sat up and crossed my arms. "I absolutely do not."

"You absolutely do too."

Behind her, Raquel nodded, which struck me as unfair. She hardly knew me. But it was hard to argue with two people who'd made up their minds. Maybe they saw something I didn't.

"What's wrong with liking power?" I asked.

Raquel reached for a dishtowel. When her hands were dry, she started sprinkling flour on the counter. "Not a thing. Depends how you use it."

"Anyhow, there's no power in being the Kudzu Queen," I told them.

"That's what you think," Rose said. "Why do you think Glynis wants it?"

Maybe it would be better to enter the subject from a different angle. "Okay, why do I deserve to be the Kudzu Queen? Not that I'm going to get it, of course."

"Nobody *deserves* to be Kudzu Queen," Raquel said. She lifted a damp cloth off a bowl and pulled out a ball of dough. Dusting flour on top, she proceeded to flatten it into a circle.

"Well," Rose said. "You're pretty fair. You wouldn't be mean to anybody."

"Not if they didn't deserve it."

"No." Rose gathered the silver in an old towel and carried it to the sink Raquel had vacated. She laid it all in the sink and pulled the towel out from beneath. The spoons tinkled like wind chimes. "Besides," she added, "you're smarter than Mabel Moore."

"You're the second person who's said that today," I told her. "Anyhow, it's not about smart. It's about pretty. And I'm not that, I mean not compared to Mabel."

"Smart's part of pretty," Rose said.

"Well, what about Glynis? She's smart *and* pretty," I protested. Rose didn't even bother answering that one. She just raised her eyes to the ceiling. "Anyhow, I'm only fifteen. Nobody's going to pick a sophomore to be Kudzu Queen."

"Maybe not," Rose said. "But they would if they had sense." She ran cold water over a spoon, and held it up to inspect it. She shook her head and rubbed at a dark spot of tarnish in the bowl of the spoon. "So why are you here, if you don't think it makes a difference?"

I couldn't exactly tell her the whole truth, so I said, "Because there's stuff I don't know. And I want to find out about it."

"See?" Rose said, raising the shiny spoon for emphasis. "That's why."

"That's why what?" I asked.

"That's why you should be queen. If you don't know something, you want to learn about it. That's who should be queen." She dried the spoon and laid it on the drain board, then lowered her hands over the remaining spoons in the sink, like she was preparing to heal them.

Raquel ran her floured hands over a rolling pin to coat it lightly and began to roll out the dough. "Tell her," she said.

Rose rinsed another spoon, dried it, and placed it by the first. "No, I don't think so."

"Tell me what?" I demanded.

Rose shook her head. "It's private."

"Oh," I said. There was a difference between Rose's private and Lynnette's. It wasn't just that I saw Lynnette all the time, while I'd only recently rediscovered Rose. Behind Rose was a whole world of private. It wasn't my place to invade it.

"You stop that." Raquel pointed her rolling pin at Rose. "You know that's not the truth."

"It is," Rose insisted. "Anyhow, it's not going to help her to know. She's trying to write why she wants to be queen. We should let her get on with it."

"How can a thing be private when more than a hundred people know about it?"

Over a hundred people knew about something and I didn't?

"Fine," Rose snapped. She dried her hands on the dishtowel, and turned around to lean against the sink, crossing her arms. "We've got our own contest."

"What do you mean?" I asked.

Enunciating each word, she repeated. "We've. Got. Our. Own. Contest."

It took me a minute to grasp what she was saying. "You mean you've got a whole other Kudzu Queen contest? For colored girls?"

"And I'm in it," she said defiantly, as if I might object.

"She's going to win it too," said Raquel, proudly.

"When is it?" My brain whirled at the thought of another competition, parallel to the one I knew about.

"Night before yours."

"Does Mrs. Sampson know about it?"

Rose shrugged. "I don't always know what she knows about."

"And do you have Queen classes?" I asked. "Like we do?"

She looked around the kitchen, piled with silver to be polished, dishes to be washed, greens to be cleaned and sorted. "Do I look like I have that kind of time?"

"Does Mr. Cullowee know?" I asked. It seemed a big thing to keep from the person in charge of kudzu for the whole county.

"Of course," Rose said.

Raquel, satisfied, returned to her piecrust, lifting the dough circle onto a pan and pressing it in place. With a fork, she pierced tiny holes in the bottom and crimped the edges. She poured dry beans in the center and slid it into the oven. "So what're you going to say on your paper?"

I looked at my blank pad. In fifteen minutes, everyone but me had accomplished something: Raquel had a piecrust baking, Rose had polished the spoons, and I hadn't written a word.

"You're going to win your contest, aren't you?" I said.

Rose rinsed the rest of the spoons and gathered them in a clean towel like a bouquet, plucking out dried spoons one by one. "More than likely."

"And not just because you're pretty," I added.

"Though she is that," Raquel called as she opened the oven door to check on her piecrust.

"You're smart too," I told Rose. She nodded. No false modestly for Rose. "But you're my age."

"Three months older," she reminded me.

"Three months?" I scoffed. "That's nothing."

"Three months more mature," she corrected. I started to object, but she was probably right.

"Maybe you need to ask yourself what you want," Rose said, "and why you want it."

When I returned to the parlor, Mabel sat on a sofa, her notepad covered with neat Palmer loops, but Ann Marie's paper was scribbled over as if she'd had trouble too. I held my pad by my side, the empty page pressed against my thigh.

Just as I was trying to manufacture an excuse for not having completed my assignment, Glynis and Alice stumbled into the parlor, laughing. Ann Marie's brows pressed together.

"Miss Carpentier and Miss Tomlinson, is there an occasion for humor the rest of us have missed?" Mrs. Sampson asked. As far as I could tell, the occasion was that they'd gotten into the mayor's liquor cabinet. It had to be Glynis, inciting Alice, but where had Ann Marie been?

Alice covered her mouth with her fingers, but the giggles escaped. "No, ma'am," she said earnestly.

"Nope," Glynis smirked. "Nothing," snicker, "funny," snicker, "at all."

"Alice," Mrs. Sampson said. "Come to me." Alice staggered to stand in front of Mrs. Sampson. "Please recite the alphabet."

Alice's eyes widened. "Sure. I mean, yes, ma'am." She thrust back her shoulders, which made her teeter. "A, B, C, D, E, um, E, um F." On F, she breathed out with a huff and Mrs. Sampson took a step backward. Even from six feet away, I could smell the gin.

"That will be enough," Mrs. Sampson said. "I'm calling your mother to take you home." She glanced over at Glynis, who was fascinated by her own fingernails. "And yours, too, Glynis. We'll discuss the consequences of your actions when you're more... yourselves."

Glynis looked up from her nails. Her head jerked back as she adjusted to focus on Mrs. Sampson. "You can't call my mother," she said airily. "She's off—" She waved her hand as if the conclusion to her sentence were self-evident.

"Then Rose will walk you home," Mrs. Sampson said. She rang her little bell, but Rose was already standing in the doorway with an umbrella. "Please walk Miss Carpentier home," she said. "And make sure she's inside the door before you return."

"Yes, ma'am." Rose took Glynis by the arm, as if Glynis were an old lady requiring assistance. Glynis carried herself with a stiff upright posture as she high-stepped out the door with Rose. By the time Alice's mother arrived, Alice had progressed from giggling to crying. She was likely to be whupped into next week when she got home. Her parents were complete teetotalers.

After Alice left, Mrs. Sampson spoke into the silence. "I feel as if, perhaps…" she said with a quaver. Her voice turned brusque. "I feel sure that the remainder of you will redouble your efforts. We have much to accomplish. You, my girls, are a long way from silk purses."

Glynis's absence made the parlor feel smaller. Mrs. Sampson seemed smaller, too, as if she'd inflated herself to combat Glynis, but now shrank in her absence. I think she missed Alice, too, the girl who would never be queen, but had tried to learn everything she was taught. The rest of us thanked Mrs. Sampson quietly, and let ourselves out the front door.

Carla Ann had stopped making an extra bus run, so Mama waited in her car outside the mayor's house. It was comforting to see her white-gloved hands resting on the steering wheel. When she opened the door, I slid in.

"How was your day, Mattie?" Mama asked.

"It was all right," I said.

Thursday morning started with what seemed like two good things. The rain finally let up. And when the bus stopped at the Johnson house, Lynnette got on with Aggie.

For the first ten minutes, Lynnette said nothing. She just watched out the window over Aggie's head. I was afraid to break the silence. Finally, as the river came into view, sluggish and brown alongside waterlogged tobacco fields, she spoke, quietly. "He's gone."

"What do you mean?" I asked.

She glanced at Aggie, who was safely in Aggieland: pressed to the window, watching rows of wilted tobacco whirring past. "Mama hasn't heard anything from or about him in days."

I gripped her hand, but it lay limp in mine, like a caught fish that's realized it's not going to find its way back to the water.

She shrugged. "He's got his money from Mr. Cullowee."

On top of the fifty dollars Mr. Cullowee was paying the Johnsons for the privilege of using their land, he'd also distributed the government money the day before. He'd driven around the county, bringing cash to everyone to save them the trouble of going to the bank to deposit a check. Five dollars an acre for every farmer in Cooper County who'd been willing to take a flyer on kudzu with a spare bit of land. Except Joey and me, of course.

"Mama begged him to put it in the bank." Lynnette studied her palms.

I should have let the subject drop, but I couldn't resist picking at the scab. "Do you think he'll come back?"

Lynnette looked again at Aggie, whose hands were splayed against the window like starfish. "How would I know?" she snapped.

"Do you want him to?"

Her shoulders gave a quick spasm.

"I'm really sorry," I told her.

She bit her bottom lip, and I realized that kudzu lessons would surely resume, since the rain had stopped. "What will you do when the boys and Mr. Cullowee come today?"

"Lie," Lynnette said.

That afternoon, half a dozen boys spilled off the bus with Lynnette, Aggie, and me. Along with Danny and his truck-riding buddies, they all trooped past the house to the Johnsons' fields. Their kudzu was nowhere near as far along as Joey's and mine, but it was the greenest crop I'd seen there in three years, particularly compared to the soggy corn alongside it.

Lynnette and I walked silently to the house, while Aggie paused to peer at the edge of the driveway where gravel met crabgrass. She was looking, I supposed, for anything small, interesting, and alive that might emerge after all that rain. I followed Lynnette through the screen door into the kitchen, closing it gently so it didn't slam and break off any of the frayed pieces where the screen was black and rotting. We left Aggie squatting over a fresh anthill.

Mrs. Johnson stood at the stove, stirring something in a big pot with a wooden spoon, over a low flame. The kitchen had an odd smell to it.

"Good to see you up and about, Mrs. Johnson," I said.

"They're here, Mama," Lynnette said to her mother's back.

Mrs. Johnson nodded slowly. She rested the spoon in the pot. When she turned, her face was as still as the spoon. "Keep an eye on this," she said. "Don't let it burn." Then she extracted Catherine from the high chair and settled her on her hip, sagging from the effort. She stepped out of the kitchen, pushing the screen door open with a flat palm against the peeling wood.

Lynnette went to the stove. "Mattie," she said.

I looked over. Except for the spoon, the pot was empty.

Lynnette turned off the flame and we followed Mrs. Johnson out the door, sidestepping Aggie, who was drawing wide circles around the anthill with a stick. Any other ten-year-old would have been stirring up that anthill to send the ants scurrying into a tizzy. But these ants seemed to be going about their business as Aggie went about hers: embellishing their architecture with a series of gentle moats.

Mr. Cullowee crouched in the Johnsons' field, tipping a kudzu leaf to show the boys, who squatted around him. The closer Mrs. Johnson got, the more upright she stood and the less tightly she clutched Catherine. By the time she reached the field, her stride was long and loose-limbed. "Mr. Cullowee?" she called. Even from the doorway I could hear the smile in her voice. "I'm sorry to tell you Mr. Johnson won't be joining you today. He has business to attend to."

Mr. Cullowee stood and tipped his straw hat.

Mrs. Johnson let Catherine slide to the ground, took her hand, and walked back to the house at Catherine's pace. It was the longest walk I'd ever seen anyone ask of Catherine, practically a hundred miles in Catherine steps.

The boys hunkered down to examine their kudzu, looking to see the effects of the rain, I supposed. Their kudzu, like ours, had thrived in the deluge. Mr. Cullowee gazed past the boys, beyond Mrs. Johnson. It was too far away to be sure, but I knew. He was looking at me.

With her father gone and her mother stirring empty pots, there was no question of Lynnette going to school. Unless she stayed home to tend the paltry corn, they wouldn't earn enough to buy groceries, no matter how many eggs she coaxed from their chickens.

I knew Daddy would tell the Johnsons not to worry about the rent until things improved. I heard him talking with Mama late Friday evening. I wanted to ask if I could give Lynnette the good news, but the quiet way they spoke made me think they'd probably talk with Mrs. Johnson themselves. I only hoped she'd bring her right mind to the conversation.

Saturday afternoon, Mama sent me to the Johnsons with a meatloaf, along with some applesauce and a chocolate sheet cake. "You can have supper over there," she told me, "but it would be best if you didn't stay long afterward. Give them some time."

Lynnette met me at the door. She put the meatloaf in the oven to keep warm.

"Tell your mama thanks," she said.

I left the applesauce and cake on the counter, and followed Lynnette to the sitting room. Mrs. Johnson sat tucked into the armchair, eyes closed, the orange and brown afghan wrapped around her despite the lingering heat from the day. Her eyelids were pale as onionskin. Aggie played jacks on the floor at her feet. *The Blue Fairy Book* lay splayed facedown on the sofa by Catherine. Lynnette sat beside her and picked up the book.

"'No evil ever befell them;'" Lynnette read, "'if they tarried late in the wood and night overtook them, they lay down together on the moss and slept till morning.'" She looked over as if she'd just remembered I was there. "Sit down," she said. "We're resting."

Her eyes still closed, Mrs. Johnson said, "Don't you want to stay to supper, Mattie?"

I looked at the four of them, like creatures washed up on the riverbank after a storm, and thought of the food I'd brought over. Enough to last a couple of meals if I didn't eat any.

"Mama asked me to get back to help her," I lied, "but thank you anyway."

After church, Sunday stretched ahead, full of nothing. Mama immersed herself in baking a pineapple upside-down cake. Danny was upstairs, looking at his course catalog for the millionth time, though he'd decided on his courses weeks ago. Daddy lay on the sitting room sofa with the newspaper opened over his face. "That way I can read a whole page at a time," he'd said, before he started snoring. I changed out of church clothes and found Joey in the pigpen, making an obstacle course for the piglets with sticks. Mostly they ran straight through his obstacles. Stevie lay on her side in the mud, profoundly uninterested in the goings-on of her offspring.

"Let's go see our kudzu," I told Joey.

From Daddy's study, I borrowed the Kodak camera he used to take pictures of his experimental cotton. When he retired, he'd told us, he was going to make a living on the lecture circuit, giving slide presentations and letting other men do the farming. I could drop the film at the drugstore on Monday before school and replace it before he even noticed.

Since the rain, the path was likely to be full of snakes sunning themselves, so we went the long way. On the tarmac, crystals sparkled in the sun. I heard the peepers, their calls rising and falling in waves, and felt the sun making freckles on my nose. The air smelled green. An engine shifted into a lower gear.

"What's he doing here?" Joey asked.

Before I could look back, Mr. Cullowee pulled up beside us, slowing to match our walking pace. "Afternoon," he said. "Need a ride?"

I remembered how I'd imagined leading Mr. Cullowee blindfolded to our kudzu field to reveal its glory. But not yet.

"No, thank you," I said, "but thanks for offering."

"You sure? How far do you have to go?"

"Not far," I said.

"She needs the exercise," Joey told him.

I glared at him, then smiled sweetly at Mr. Cullowee. "Thank you anyway, but it's such a lovely day. We're enjoying our walk."

"Nice weather for it," Mr. Cullowee said. "I'm sure I'll see you soon." He tipped his hat and drove off.

*I'm sure I'll see you soon.* I could have pondered that in bed for a whole week before falling asleep, but it popped out of my brain when I whirled on Joey. "She needs the exercise?"

He shrugged. "He was going to follow us all the way to the field."

You can't fault a ten-year-old for saying the first dumb thing that jumps into his head, even if it makes you look bad. "You don't think he suspects, do you?"

"He stopped because you're a girl," Joey said.

"He was being nice," I corrected, though I wasn't sure why I felt the need to clarify.

Our kudzu field had doubled. The eruption of green leaves and vines after the rain had eradicated any sense of order. I took picture after picture, trying to capture its vastness.

We would have needed a scythe to get through it, so we walked around, stepping over tendrils that snaked along the ground toward the woods. When we reached the front porch, I saw that the kudzu had reached it, too, creeping up columns like a cat burglar about to make a second story break-in. "Think we should pull it down?" I asked Joey.

"Are you kidding? That's pure profit right there."

I felt funny, like I was leaving Aunt Mary's house defenseless against an invasion. I picked at a vine, pulling it away from the column.

"Mattie?" he raised an eyebrow. "Don't be stupid."

When I let the vine go, it snapped back, as snug as if I'd never tugged on it. "Well, what should we do, then?" I asked him. A breeze blew through the field, rippling it in waves.

For once Joey was stumped. The rain had taken care of watering. Weed it? No weed could hold its own against that kudzu. Even the cowpeas had been swept away in the tide. "I guess there's nothing we *can* do," he said.

We sat on the top porch step, looking out over a green kudzu sea. "Think we'll see it grow if we sit here long enough?" Joey asked.

The leaves tilted their faces toward the sun, drinking in the light. "When should we tell Mama and Daddy?" I asked.

He stretched out his legs to the step below, and I noticed that he'd grown too. His feet rested a full step lower than they had a month and a half before. "When we tell everybody else. The day after your Kudzu Queen thing."

"Shouldn't we give them some warning? In case Daddy's mad?"

"He won't be mad," Joey assured me. I wasn't convinced. But even though we were splitting the field, it really was Joey's kudzu.

"So is this all we do for the next three weeks? Watch it grow?"

"It's like watching money grow, Matts," he said. "The easy way."

Another breeze rolled through the kudzu.

Joey stood up and brushed off the seat of his pants. "I never saw a crop like this in my whole life."

"Mr. Cullowee was right," I agreed. "It's the best crop I ever heard of."

"This is the future of North Carolina we're looking at," Joey said, surveying his territory. He reached down to give me a hand up, another thing he'd grown into.

I handed him the camera. "Put this away before Daddy notices. I'm going to stay a little longer."

"Suit yourself," he said.

I thought about Danny leaving as Joey wandered down the road. Maybe having just Joey at home next year wouldn't be as bad as I'd thought.

I retrieved the key from under the brass pot. It seemed to stick in the lock, probably from the rain, but I wondered if Aunt Mary was telling me not to get too complacent about my welcome. Inside, everything was covered with a fine yellow-green dust of pollen. No matter how tightly you close the windows, come spring, pollen will sneak indoors.

It seemed unfair that Aunt Mary's house should be neglected

when the kudzu was doing so well. At home, it would have taken an Act of Congress to get me to clean without being asked. I couldn't understand why anyone felt required to clean a house when it would only get dirty again. But the idea of dust collecting on Aunt Mary's pretty things made me sad.

Under her kitchen sink, two rows of bottles stood next to a stack of rags. I found the lemon oil, dampened a pink flannel with it, and began dusting my way from the front door to the picture windows, knickknack by knickknack: silver tray, horse and rider, sun and moon clock. I poured Pine-Sol and water in a pail, and lugged the bucket out to attack the floors with a mop.

Once finished, I looked around the room. "And she saw that it was good," I said out loud, hoping the Lord wouldn't strike me down. But it was good, and I knew the reward I wanted. "Aunt Mary?" I called. "I'm just going to go upstairs, if you don't mind."

The house groaned and settled, the way Daddy did when Mama rubbed his shoulders in the evening. I thought maybe Aunt Mary's ghost had forgiven me for letting kudzu creep up her porch pillars "When we harvest," I promised, "we'll start from the house."

I opened the door across from her bedroom. The ghostly apparitions were as I'd left them. The furs smelled dry, like a book that hadn't been read in a long time.

I started with the mink stole. The claws scratched my bare arms, but I could tolerate some discomfort. On the back of the door, I found a tall oval mirror, its edges darkened with age. The stole made me look like a little girl playing dress-up, so I put it back.

My next option was the rabbit fur jacket. But the pale gray-brown made my freckles stand out in a most unsophisticated manner. I tried the red fox jacket, which was too tight in the shoulders. The silver fox cape started shedding like it was molting season.

Finally, I reached what my mother would have called the *piece d'*, the ankle-length mink coat. I slid my arms into the silk-lined sleeves and lifted it onto my shoulders. It hit the tops of my brown oxfords, covering my white ankle socks. In the mirror, I looked elegant, the way I'd felt that evening at supper when Mr. Cullowee pushed in my chair like I was a feather pillow.

I yanked the sheet off the second rack, setting the hats to trembling, like they were all hoping to be chosen. But I knew the one I needed: the exotic peacock feather cloche, with its sultry whisper of *woman of mystery.*

In the mirror, the cloche grazing my right eyebrow, my hair brushing my mink-clad shoulders, I looked like Marlene Dietrich. I only needed the right lipstick and shoes, and I knew where to find those: in my own bedroom. I hung the coat and hat together to await my return.

As I crouched by the door to slide the key under the pot, I heard the porch swing creak in the breeze. Next time, I'd oil the chain and wipe the wood with polish so it didn't dry out.

"Nice crop."

I froze.

His legs, lean and elegant in gray pinstriped trousers, were crossed at the ankle. Red socks today. He wore a matching jacket and a straw hat tipped down, shadowing his eyes.

"How—?" I stood up so fast the blood rushed to my head. "What are you doing here?" Where was his truck? Why hadn't I heard him drive up?

"Visiting." Mr. Cullowee idly bent his knees and straightened them. The swing eased back and forth in a controlled glide. "Thought I'd see what you and young Joseph were up to."

He patted the seat beside him. "Come sit, Mattie. Let's have ourselves a visit."

"How long have you known?" I asked, not moving.

"Oh, only a day or so. You're better at keeping secrets than I would have anticipated."

I felt tendrils tightening around my gut. This was far from the revelation I'd dreamed of. "We were just having fun." I forced myself to look casual. "Kid stuff."

He shook his head. "Oh, I don't think so, Mattie. This is quite an accomplishment. You seem to have inherited your father's gifts for propagation, as well as your mother's looks." He stilled the swing, bracing his feet on the porch floor. "Come sit," he said again.

Why wasn't I floating toward him, arms outstretched like wings? "No, thank you."

He clasped his hands behind his head, beneath his hat brim. "So what does your father think of all this? He must be proud of the two of you."

I gave a quick little headshake.

"He doesn't know, does he?" The Kudzu King's voice was like honey pouring from the jar, sweet and slow. "So you get your ability to keep secrets from your mother? Must be hard for her to keep this from your father. They strike me as being uncommonly close."

"She doesn't know either," I mumbled.

"No?" he asked. "What about your friend, Lynnette?"

"I haven't told her. We're waiting for the festival. We were going to surprise everyone."

He tipped up his hat brim with one finger, and his eyes widened. "Oh, my. That's a big secret for a little boy and a beautiful young lady to keep to themselves. The finest kudzu crop in Cooper County and the three of us are the only ones who know about it."

These were the words I'd dreamed of hearing from Mr. James T. Cullowee—beautiful, young lady, finest kudzu crop in Cooper County—and all I could think was, "the three of us?" It was supposed to be the two of us, Joey and me, until we were ready.

"How'd you find this place?" I asked. He might be the Kudzu King, but that didn't mean he was entitled to come on our property without permission.

"You're not subtle, Mattie," he said. "Did you think I wouldn't notice somebody growing such a healthy crop of kudzu in one of my counties?"

His counties?

"I'm concerned." He frowned. "Has the lure of kudzu led

you to deceive your parents? Perhaps I've inadvertently led you astray." He let the swing glide back. "I feel responsible. I think I should do the right thing and tell your parents that you and young Joey are illegally farming someone's land." He glanced at the brass pot. "Not to mention breaking and entering."

"It's ours," I blurted. "It belongs to my aunt Mary."

He sat up abruptly and looked around. "Your aunt Mary?"

"She's dead." I slid down the door and sat on the porch, pulling my skirt over my knees. I suddenly felt alone, as if by saying out loud that Aunt Mary was dead, I might have banished her presence. Maybe she hadn't realized she'd died.

"Ah." He resumed his former position. "You'd rather, I imagine, that I keep your little secret, wouldn't you?"

I pulled my calves tightly toward my chest.

"Then you should come sit by me, so we can discuss the matter." This time it was an order, not a request. "You can explain to me why my silence is in everyone's best interest." That lazy tone eased into his voice again, and snaked around my belly like a python. "You can persuade me." His voice hardened. "Now."

I started to scramble up, but, thinking of Mrs. Sampson, I tried to stand gracefully. When I reached the porch swing, I waited for Mr. Cullowee to slide over, but he didn't. So I squeezed against the armrest to preserve the few inches between us. In a gesture that would have comforted Lynnette, I placed my ankles side by side. I couldn't quite rest my feet flat, so I pressed my toes to the floorboards and stared at my shoes.

Mr. Cullowee eased his arm over the swing, brushing my shoulders. I could feel the wiry golden hair on his arms. The hairs on the back of my neck rose to meet his warm skin. Then his hand clenched the back of my head. He kissed me hard, crushing my lips against my teeth. He moved away slightly, breathing hard. "How persuasive can you be, Mattie?"

I'd once seen a newsreel of lava roiling in a volcano, steaming and thickly molten. Part of me wanted to run away, while another part wanted to roil. He pushed his mouth against mine again, while his free hand grasped my breast like a vise. This was no game of "Mother, May I?" He wasn't going to ask if he could touch parts of me. He was going to do what he wanted.

I pulled away as far as I could with his hand gripping my head.

"Mattie," he said hoarsely. "Let's go inside."

"No." I summoned my mother's firmest voice, trying to summon her backbone with it.

"I saw you coming out the door," he insisted, "hiding the key."

"I'm not going in that house with you," I said. I thought of all the things I'd heard a girl could say in a situation like this: "I'm not that kind of a girl." "It wouldn't be right." "How dare you?" But they all sounded silly, not like anything I'd normally say. Plus, in my dreams, I was that kind of girl. I stood up, and crossed my arms over my chest.

"I'm just not," I said. There she was, the stubborn Mattie my family knew and loved, even when I made them crazy. I looked down. His hat had tumbled to the porch floor.

"You need to go," I said, stern as Moses. "Now."

"And if I tell your parents about this field?"

"You won't." Whether I believed it or was bluffing, I wasn't sure, but I suddenly, fiercely, felt I had to keep the secret for Joey. "Or I'll tell them about you attacking me."

"I attacked you?" His laugh came out a touch brittle, but he was regaining his composure. "Who do you think they'll believe, the man who's come to raise this entire region out of poverty, or their deceitful daughter who's been doing all this—" He waved his hand to encompass the scope of evidence: the undulating field of kudzu, Aunt Mary's house, my rumpled blouse—"behind their backs?"

"Me," I said flatly. "They'll believe me."

He gathered his hat from the floor, lightly dropped it on his head, and tipped it at me. "I look forward to our next encounter, Miss Watson." He smiled. "It would be foolish of me," he made the same gesture he'd made before—field, house, me—"to walk away from all this."

I watched him stroll to the road where his truck waited,

bending once to lift a kudzu vine to his face and inhale, as if he were breathing in the perfume of an elegant woman. He climbed into the truck and gave me a jaunty wave.

I waited until the truck was out of sight. Then I grabbed the key, jammed it into the lock, and dashed upstairs to launch myself onto Aunt Mary's white counterpane, convulsing with sobs. I didn't know why I was crying—for finally getting what I wanted or not wanting what I'd gotten—but I couldn't stop for the longest time.

Before I left, I strung the key to Aunt Mary's house around my neck, on the chain with my grandfather's watch.

# 15

When I was little, Taylor Wagner told me you could kill ants by focusing sunlight on them through a magnifying glass. He'd later gotten the tar whupped out of him by his daddy, his mama crying and trying to pull Mr. Wagner off him the whole time, for starting a fire that almost burned down their barn.

In school on Monday morning, I felt a burning between my shoulder blades, as if Glynis Carpentier had narrowed her glare through a magnifying glass. She started before first bell and caught me again in the hall between history and English. In gym, she shot her burning stare at various parts of my body—forehead, chest, legs—as I ran sprints in my baggy uniform. Why was she mad at me? I hadn't poured liquor down her throat. Did she think I'd tattled?

Surely she didn't know what had happened on Aunt Mary's porch. I hadn't told a soul, and I couldn't see Mr. Cullowee stopping Glynis on the street to say, "Oh, by the way, you know that girl Mattie Watson? The one you hate? Well, I thought I'd let you know that I kissed her."

I waited for her to pin me against a locker and give me what for, but either she was too mad to speak or she thought I knew what her glares meant. Still, I should have been prepared when she dug her fingers into my arm outside the mayor's house on Wednesday afternoon.

"Act like we're still friends," she said in a hard whisper, her mouth by my ear. *Still?* I thought. "I'm going into Queen class with you."

"Sure." I'd seen enough movies to know that when the bad guy has his weapon on you, you do what he says until you can escape.

"Don't turn around." She maneuvered me up the steps. "Act normal." Right. Like Glynis and I normally walked around together with her crushing my arm into jelly.

When I lifted my hand to ring the bell, she swatted it down. "Wait!" she said. "We're best friends." She spoke reasonably, as if she were reminding me of facts instead of inventing a highly improbable fiction. "And you can't possibly go to Kudzu Queen class without me."

I almost laughed, except my arm hurt so much I was afraid I might burst out crying instead. "What? Nobody's going to believe that."

"Mrs. Sampson is," Glynis said flatly, "because you're going to make her believe it."

"What about Ann Marie?" I asked. "Why not get her to convince Mrs. Sampson?"

"Mrs. Sampson doesn't give one tiny rat's turd about Ann Marie," Glynis said. "But she thinks you walk on water."

"Glynis!" I wasn't a Bible-toting zealot, but there were certain things you didn't say.

She jabbed the doorbell. "Best friends," she hissed.

Rose opened the door. She kept her face in a flat mask of politeness, but I knew her well enough. When she let us in, she murmured, "Not what I'd have recommended."

She preceded us to the parlor and announced our arrival. I was surprised to see Alice doing her best to look invisible. I guessed Mrs. Sampson considered her behavior a first offense.

"Mrs. Sampson," I squeaked. "Don't you look lovely today?" Behind me, I felt Rose shake her head. "Um, look who I ran into outside." Glynis had let go, but I could feel the hot skin of her upper arm burning mine. "My best friend, Glynis." I said a silent prayer to the Lord for forgiveness and to please tell Lynnette I'd only lied to save my own skin.

I couldn't tell if Mrs. Sampson was angry or disappointed. Mostly, she looked curious.

"Um..." No way to get around it but to get it over with. "And I don't think I can keep coming to class unless Glynis comes back, because she's my inspiration." Was I spreading it too thick? "And she's really sorry and…" The skin on Glynis's arm went up another ten degrees. If I got one more thing wrong, I could forget about Kudzu Queen class. I'd be spending the rest of the week in the hospital. "Anyhow, if you'd let her back in, I'd really appreciate it."

Mrs. Sampson let the silence gather. The other girls were frozen in whatever gesture they'd been making when we came in, lifting teacups or reaching for a cookie from the cart.

"Glynis is your best friend," Mrs. Sampson repeated.

I nodded. It wasn't a lie if you didn't say it out loud.

"And you can't continue with this class unless she is allowed to return."

I nodded again, eagerly. This could all work out. Mrs. Sampson would let Glynis back in class again, my arm would heal, and we'd all live happily ever after.

"No," Mrs. Sampson said.

Glynis shoved me hard, elbowed Rose out of the way, and ran out the front door, leaving it wide open. She was gone so quickly I had to touch my arm to believe she'd been there at all.

"Mathilda," Mrs. Sampson said, "perhaps you could sit down so we can begin?"

I scuttled to the sofa beside Mabel, staying well away from Ann Marie. I wasn't sure how she'd react to my calling Glynis my best friend, even if I'd done it under dire threat.

"Mrs. Sampson?" Mabel tentatively raised her hand. "Does that mean Glynis won't be able to enter the Queen competition?" It was just like Mabel to look out for somebody else, even Glynis Carpentier, instead of thinking, as I had, how this might improve her chances of winning.

Mrs. Sampson's lips narrowed to thin lines. "Completion of the Kudzu Queen course is not a prerequisite for entering the competition." She continued, "Your task today is to learn how to behave toward your elders and betters." If she managed to instill that in me, Mama would be purely delighted.

Behaving toward our elders meant a lot of ma'am-ing and

sir-ing, which wasn't news. More surprising were Mrs. Sampson's directions to pause after someone spoke. "Savor each word you hear as if it were a bonbon," she instructed.

Of course this came naturally to Mabel. She pretty much had a college degree in behaving well toward her elders. But for once, Mrs. Sampson didn't use Mabel as a shining example. Instead, she aimed her attention at Ann Marie, as if afraid of losing her too.

After class, I waited close to the mayor's house for Mama, keeping an eye out for Glynis.

My heart pounded when I heard a truck pull up, but it was just Carl, his arm resting on the window frame. "Can I you drive you home?"

"My mama's coming," I said. "She'll worry."

He held the door. "I called and told her I'd fetch you after practice."

I wondered when he and my mother had become such good pals, but I kind of liked the idea of a boy driving me home.

Just before we got to the Johnsons' driveway, I asked, "Can you drop me here instead?" "Sure." Carl turned in past the mailbox, and cut the ignition.

Aggie squatted under the pecan tree, digging a tiny hole with a piece of nutshell.

"Hey, Aggie," I said, "where's Lynnette?"

Without looking up, Aggie tilted her head to the cornfield. She hadn't gotten much from her father, but she'd certainly inherited his tendency not to waste words. Still, after the night Lynnette had taken their mother to the hospital, I'd have expected her to spare a word or two.

Carl walked with me around the house. The screen had peeled away from the kitchen door in the top right hand corner. Normally Lynnette would have taken care of it.

Out in the field Lynnette crouched like Aggie, but when we got closer, I saw she wasn't digging holes, but picking beetles off corn stalks and dropping them in a water bucket to drown.

"There are pesticides that'll take care of those," Carl said. "They're a lot less work."

"Mmm," Lynnette answered without looking up.

I squatted beside her and started picking beetles off an adjoining plant, and dropping them in the bucket. Pesticides cost money. Picking beetles was free.

"You'll never get them all," Carl said, still standing beside us.

"You can talk," I said, "or you can help."

He crouched beside me, pulling off beetles and reaching past me to drop them in the water. The beetles climbed on top of each other, scrabbling against the sides of the bucket until they stilled and floated. I could have felt sorry for them, but I didn't.

We picked beetles until it was time for me to go home for chores. Then I patted Lynnette on the back. Her dress was so thin I could feel the individual threads in the cloth. "I'll come by before school tomorrow," I said, standing up. My knees felt creaky from squatting for so long.

"Want me to take you the rest of the way home?" Carl asked.

"I'll be all right," I said.

I left them crouched in the field, picking off beetles in the late afternoon light.

The next morning I milked Sassafras early. In the henhouse, I tried Lynnette's soothing nonsense, "cooey-cooey-cooey," and not one of the hens pecked me. By 5:15, as the house began to stir, I was running across the cornfields to Lynnette's, cramming a biscuit from yesterday's breakfast into my mouth, the butter clammy and thick in the morning cool. I wanted to help her finish picking beetles and tell her what had happened at Aunt Mary's, if I could do it without revealing our kudzu field. I needed her advice.

But when I emerged from the Johnsons' sickly cornstalks to see Mr. Cullowee walking out their kitchen door in khakis and a blue shirt, I almost spit out my biscuit.

I ducked back and crouched between the corn rows until he'd made his way to the far side of the field, down by the educational kudzu. Then I made a dash for the door and slipped inside.

Lynnette was stirring oatmeal on the stove, while Aggie did an old dot-to-dot on the kitchen table. The lines on the puzzle had been erased and still showed through faintly, but Aggie persevered as if figuring it out for the first time.

"What's he doing here?" I blurted.

Lynnette lugged the pot to the table and took a plate and bowls from the cupboard, while Aggie drew her lines so deeply I wondered if she'd leave grooves in the table. "Boarding."

"But he's living in town now," I said, as if she needed reminding.

She placed the plate at the head of the table, with a linen napkin and silver fork, the only silver I'd ever seen in the Johnson house. "He came by yesterday evening and asked if Mama could use a renter for a while, to tide her over." She shook out the napkin and refolded it. "Told her kudzu was well on its way in the county, so he had some time on his hands and wouldn't mind helping out around the place."

"Did he say anything about your father?" I asked.

"No, just that he hated to be idle and was missing the country air."

"What about the mayor and Mrs. Sampson?" I picked up a bowl and ladled some oatmeal into it. "Should I do one for Mr. Cullowee?" I asked.

She shook her head. "We've got extra eggs." They hadn't had extra anything since Mr. Johnson had left. "Said they'd been real generous, but it was time to pay his own way. He offered Mama seven dollars a week for room and board."

"Seven dollars?" I asked. "And helping out too? What did she say?"

"She said yes, of course." Lynnette poured goat milk into a pitcher. "When a miracle happens, only a crazy person would argue with it." She went quiet. I wondered if she was remembering what I was: Mrs. Johnson stirring an empty pot over a gas flame. "She isn't crazy."

"No one said she was." I finished filling the bowls and laid them out. "How's she doing?"

"She's doing," Lynnette said. "Mostly resting."

I sat at the table while Lynnette fetched Catherine. Aggie had almost completed the picture: a rabbit with one ear at attention and the other folded down. Though it was obvious what the result would be, she connected each dot as if nothing would be revealed until the last line. With her left hand, she ate her oatmeal. Lynnette and Catherine trudged downstairs, Catherine planting both bare feet on each step before attempting the next.

"Can you put her in her chair?" Lynnette transferred Catherine's hand to mine. "While I take this up?" She scraped brown sugar out of an almost-empty Ball jar into a bowl of oatmeal and poured goat milk on top. "If I'm not down in a minute, go ahead and give her the cereal."

By the time Lynnette came down I'd washed the dishes, leaving her bowl and the empty plate at the head of the table. She spooned her oatmeal back into the pot. "Not a good morning."

I waited, afraid to set her off by asking questions.

"She's fretful," Lynnette said finally. "And hot." She carried her bowl and spoon to the sink and began to rinse them. "I think she's got another fever."

"Does she need to go back to the hospital?" I asked.

"I put a cool compress on her forehead." She dried the bowl with a dishtowel. "It'll break after a while."

With that settled—though a fever a few weeks after leaving the hospital didn't seem promising—I recalled my purpose. "I came to help you pick beetles," I announced. "Maybe Aggie could help too." Aggie was carefully erasing the lines of the rabbit, dot-from-dot, in the same order she'd drawn them. Silently, I mouthed to Lynnette, *If she doesn't see us kill them.*

Lynnette shook her head. "No need. Mr. Cullowee and the boys will spray them this afternoon. He's driving into town after breakfast to pick up the spray and some groceries."

I ran my finger along the table edge. "Then you don't need me."

"No, we're fine. But I appreciate your help."

With that as my consolation prize, I left without telling her about Aunt Mary's. In the past, no matter how romantic a light I cast, she wouldn't have looked kindly on Mr. Cullowee's behavior. But this was a more practical Lynnette. I wasn't sure whose side she'd be on. For that matter, I wasn't sure what side I was on.

# 16

All around town, flyers had begun to appear in shop windows, proclaiming in circus-style letters that the parade would begin promptly at three p.m. on Saturday, June 14th, followed by the First Annual Cooper County Kudzu Queen Pageant at the high school at six that evening. On Sunday, all the churches in the county would hold covered dish dinners after services, and tours would be held at the Model Kudzu Field that afternoon from two to five p.m.

The seniors were fixed on the future, with the school year fading like a dusty road in their rearview mirrors. A few, like Danny, were going to college, though mostly junior college. Some were heading up north to look for work in factories. But for most of the country boys, the coming of summer would mean what summers always meant, working on their daddies' farms from dawn to evening, though this particular summer would go on for the rest of their lives. The town boys would follow their fathers, too, only instead of farming, they'd fix cars or work at the hardware store.

For girls, summer meant a rash of weddings, as those who'd bet their junior and senior years on going steady cashed in and became wives. The rest would find jobs as secretaries or clerks, teachers or librarians, and hope to avoid becoming old maids.

After school on Thursday, Mabel sat with me on the school steps while I waited for the bus. Without Lynnette, our private bench felt like purgatory. "Aren't you excited?" Mabel asked.

"About what?" I liked Mabel, but I found myself hoping Carla Ann would show up soon.

"Everything!" She gazed around in wonder, as if her particular "everything" might be gathered in a circle around us. "The Kudzu Queen pageant, the summer, the rest of our lives."

My best friend is hardly speaking to me, her mother is sick and may well be sick crazy, the man I thought I loved scares the snot out of me, and the rest of my life won't start for two more years, I thought. But it seemed wrong to smear her happiness, so I asked. "What are you doing after graduation?"

"Well," she propped her heels on the step below, "Hudson-Belk invited me up to Raleigh to try out for more modeling work." I pictured a portly man named Hudson Belk, in a pin-striped suit with an old-fashioned watch chain, studying Mabel as she perambulated up and down a runway in a variety of outfits—ladies' business suits, party frocks, ball gowns, bathing suits. "There may be a full-time model position opening up," she said, excitement sparking her eyes, "but I'd be happy to work as a clerk." It was just like Mabel to assume they'd invite her to Raleigh to audition as a model and then stick her behind a counter to sell ties.

"You know Danny's going to be in Raleigh this fall," I said. I didn't know why I reminded her. Every senior girl in school knew Danny was going to Raleigh.

She sighed. "Yes, I know." For a moment I imagined what life would be like if Danny married Mabel. She wouldn't be a bad sister-in-law, though I thought Danny should concentrate on college until he got through it. I didn't want him distracted by girls, not even Mabel.

I flinched at the sound of a nearby engine. Maybe Glynis had gotten hold of a car and was going to drive up the steps and run us over. I could see Mabel and me dashing around like cartoon characters while Glynis, gripping the wheel of a massive Chevy, chased us down. But it was only Carl, that reliable boy, trusted by parents and big brothers alike. I supposed he and my mother had been plotting out my life behind my back again, but I was relieved to see him.

A warm smile lit Mabel's face. "It's Carl." I wondered if Carl rated even higher in her estimation than Danny. "He's here to drive you home," she announced.

I was surprised to find I liked having Mabel's approval. I

wondered if she'd approve as much of the type of attention Mr. Cullowee had recently been paying me.

"He's the sweetest boy in the world," Mabel sighed. Since she believed that every girl was the nicest and every boy the sweetest, I didn't put much stock in it.

Carl helped me into the truck. But instead of starting the engine, he reached across me toward the glove box. "I've got something for you. Hold out your hands and close your eyes."

I stuck my hands out, squinting between my lashes.

He paused, mid-reach. "I mean it, Mattie. Close your eyes."

When I squeezed them shut, he placed something smooth and heavy in my hands, weighted on one end.

I opened my eyes: a gavel, just like the ones I'd seen in the movies.

"Where did you—?"

"Made it in my dad's woodshop," he said. "Danny told me you want to be a lawyer." He closed my right hand around the carved grip and pointed at the glove box. "Here, try it out."

Though I tapped gently, the gavel gave a satisfyingly thunk.

"Thank you," I said. "That's the best present I've ever gotten."

Friday night, after I'd gone to bed, I woke to a clicking sound. I crept to my window and looked down to see Lynnette pitching gravel at my window, with Catherine swaddled in a blanket in her arms. Beside her stood Aggie, dressed in footie pajamas.

I ran downstairs and opened the kitchen door. "What's going on?"

"Can you look after them?" Lynnette said. "She needs to go to the hospital again."

"Sure," I said.

"I can only leave her a minute. It's bad."

I reached for Catherine, who was struggling to disentangle herself from the blanket. Aggie was sleepy enough to take my free hand. "Call when you know something," I said.

Lynnette was already running toward the cornfield. She nodded without looking back.

"All right, young ladies," I said brightly. "Let's get you into bed." Catherine leaned against my shoulder, drifting to sleep. Aggie trailed half a step behind me. When we got upstairs, I considered waking Mama and Daddy, but they'd find out in the morning.

Aggie climbed into my bed and turned to the wall. I laid Catherine beside her and squeezed onto the outer edge, resting my arm across them. I woke once to find Aggie thrashing and kicking, mumbling like she was in a nightmare, but I ran my hand down her arm and she settled. When she woke, she'd wriggle away, but in the meantime, I was keeping them safe.

The next morning, I opened my eyes before Aggie or Catherine to see Mama by my bed. "Children are popping up like mushrooms around here," she said. "Is their mother all right?"

By some miracle, both girls were still tucked under my arm. I gave a miniscule shake of my head. If they woke up, I didn't want them to be more scared than they had to be.

"I know these are serious circumstances, but I've never seen a sweeter picture. I just had a moment," she said, smoothing the hair from my forehead, "imagining you with your own little girls."

Aggie blinked, forcing herself out of sleep, and sat up, pushing my arm away. At the movement, Catherine burrowed deeply into my side, like she was trying to squeeze in between my ribs to hibernate. "Looks like you can handle things up here," Mama said. "I'll go down and put together breakfast for everyone."

Aggie rubbed the heels of her hands against her eyes. "Can you pour a big glass of milk for Aggie?" I asked Mama. "She hates goat's milk, so real milk would be a treat for her."

"Chocolate?" Aggie asked, peeking one eye from behind her hand.

"Absolutely," Mama said. "I think we can find some Bosco for such a good girl."

In the hall, I heard Danny's rumbling voice, "Is that Miss Agatha Johnson I hear? Could it be true, right here in my very own home?"

Dropping her hands, Aggie jumped down and ran to Danny,

who hoisted her over his head. I always forgot how strong he was. He plopped her on the ground, squatting to face her. "This must be a miracle," he told her. "I was just thinking, today is a perfect day for fishing. I wish I had someone to fish with. And lo and behold, you appear before my very eyes."

I knew for a fact that it was actually a perfect day for weeding cotton, which was what Daddy and Danny had been planning to do. They'd been talking the night before about how they'd have to take care of it before the weeds settled down to raise families. But the one thing guaranteed to distract Aggie from fretting about her mother was fishing with Danny.

"How many fish are we going to catch, Aggs?" Danny asked.

"A million?" she ventured.

"At least," he told her. "I was thinking more like two million."

She laughed, a sound I heard so rarely that I almost didn't recognize it.

"How many can you eat?" he asked.

"Six," she announced.

"Excellent. That means six for you and one million, nine hundred ninety-nine thousand, nine hundred and ninety-four for me." Danny tugged her sleeve. "This your fishing outfit?" She looked down at her orange footie pajamas and shook her head. "Let's see if we can find you something to wear that won't scare the fish," he said. "Then we'll fill up with breakfast so we won't have to eat worms to stave off starvation. I could eat a hundred and fifty pancakes. How about you?"

"A hundred and sixty," she claimed. "With chocolate milk."

"Naturally," he agreed. "Your chariot awaits, mademoiselle." He crouched down and she climbed solemnly on his back.

I lugged the sleepy Catherine downstairs. As Danny and Aggie veered off for the kitchen, where they'd be more trouble than help to Mama, I heard a knock at the front door.

I opened the door to find Mr. Cullowee standing there.

"Ah, so they're under your care," he said, "the young ladies."

I shifted Catherine on my hip, though I wasn't sure whether I was trying to protect her or use her as a shield.

He went on, all charm and smiles, as if nothing had happened at Aunt Mary's house. "With Mrs. Johnson in the hospital, I was concerned that no one was caring for the little girls. I'll be happy to take them home." He reached out to Catherine, who clenched her legs around my waist, blinking at Mr. Cullowee like a baby owl.

"I think she's fine here," I said.

"As a guest of the Johnsons," he began, "it's the least—"

"She's good here," I said. "Thanks anyway."

"Well, what about young Agatha?" She would have hated that, being called Agatha by anyone but Lynnette and Danny. "Surely I can ease your family's burden by taking one of them off your hands?" He looked beyond me into the hallway. "Aggie?" he called.

I gripped Catherine more tightly. "She's fine, too."

Danny came lumbering down the hall with a heavy clomp, pretending to be an elephant, Aggie on his back. "What have we here?" he pretend-growled. "Could it be Mr. Jim Cullowee?" Aggie buried her face in Danny's neck.

"Thought I'd see if I could cadge a bite of breakfast from the world-famous cook who runs this household," Mr. Cullowee said.

"Come on in," Danny said. "Aggs and I will be sharing three hundred and ten pancakes between us. We'll see if there are any left over."

Danny and I carried our parcels into the kitchen. Mama had placed a pillow on a chair, so Catherine looked like a baby princess on a throne, her legs sticking out in front of her.

"We brought you a surprise," Danny said. "Look what Mattie found on the doorstep."

Mama looked up from her batter and smiled. "I hope you'll stay for breakfast, Mr. Cullowee. I'm making enough pancakes to feed the county."

"Or at least two hungry fishermen," Danny said, winking at Aggie.

"Nothing I'd like better," Mr. Cullowee said.

"Mattie," she said, "why don't you go see what the chickens have graced us with this morning?"

I raced through the henhouse, displacing chickens and gathering eggs in record time. Who knew what Mr. Cullowee might choose to discuss while I was gone?

I met Daddy in the hallway, wiping his just-washed face. He slung the towel over my shoulder. "Best wash up, sport, so you don't face a lecture." When I got to the kitchen everyone was crowded around the table, with one empty chair squeezed in for me.

"I heard something about a fishing expedition," Mr. Cullowee said, after the flurry of buttering and syruping had subsided. "I could use a little fishing myself." He cut a bite from his pancake stack and observed it at the end of his fork. "Now that we're at a lull in the kudzu cycle."

"A lull?" Daddy asked.

"Yup," Mr. Cullowee said. "The kudzu's doing well on its own, doesn't need tending at the moment. There's not much on me right now." He ate his bite of pancake.

"So kudzu doesn't need any tending right now?" Joey asked, all big-eyed innocence. If he could have stuck his thumbs in his front pockets and whistled at the table, he would've.

"Not a bit, Joseph," Mr. Cullowee proclaimed. "As I've been saying, kudzu's the most cooperative crop in the world. Once it gets going, you don't have to hover over it. Now's the time to get that fishing in. You should come along."

I had to tell Joey. Not what had happened on Aunt Mary's porch, but that the Kudzu King knew about our crop. I'd wanted to tell him all week, but didn't know how. The longer he didn't know, the worse I felt.

"That's interesting about kudzu," Daddy said. "Cotton, on the other hand, does need to be tended. I've lost my farmhand today, Mr. Cullowee. Perhaps you might care to join me in the field. I could use a man with your agricultural knowledge."

"I'll help you, Daddy," I said. The two of them together in the field all day? Not a good idea.

"That's a nice deal," Daddy said. "Lose one farmhand, gain two. Mr. Cullowee?"

"Who needs more pancakes?" Mama held out the plate. "I heard a certain little girl wanted a hundred and sixty." Aggie had met her match in a stack of four, while Catherine had distributed pancake mush to the outer regions of her plate. "Anyone? They're going cheap."

"I'd be happy to offer whatever assistance you need, Mr. Watson," Mr. Cullowee said. "Danny, maybe I could take a rain check."

"Sure," Danny said. "Any time." Aggie seemed relieved to have Danny to herself. She leaned against him, cutting suspicious glances at Mr. Cullowee.

Then I remembered we were supposed to be going to town. "Mama?" I asked.

She answered before I had to say any more. "I think we'll stay close to home today. Pinesboro can make it through one Saturday without us. How about if I keep Catherine with me? You can help mind her, Joey."

Joey gave a *why me?* look.

"You'll come get me, Mama?" I asked. "If you hear anything—?" I glanced at Aggie and Catherine, so I wouldn't have to finish my sentence in front of them.

"Of course," she said.

Danny and Aggie went to the garden to unearth worms. Aggie couldn't bear to deter an animal from its appointed rounds, much less kill one, but when Danny crooked his finger, she was willing to run hooks through as many as necessary.

Mama fed a few forkfuls of pancakes into Catherine, then wiped her down and lifted her onto the floor.

Daddy pushed back his chair. "You ready, Mattie? Mr. Cullowee?"

"Jim," Mr. Cullowee reminded Daddy.

"Mr. Cullowee," Daddy went on, "those are some smart trousers you've got on, and a mighty nice shirt. I'm sure Mattie could dig out some more practical clothes from her brother's bureau, if you'd like. Maybe some clodhoppers so you can keep your good shoes clean?" Daddy rarely used country words like "mighty" and "clodhoppers." I wondered what he was up to.

"That's quite all right," said Mr. Cullowee. "These are my work clothes."

"Well, that's fine, then," Daddy said. "If you're ready?" We followed him to the shed, where he handed each of us a hoe. Mr. Cullowee looked startled, as if he hadn't been prepared for farming tools. Daddy had two cotton fields, the experimental one across the road, close enough so he could keep an eye on it, and the traditional one over by the tenant farms. Today we were heading to the traditional field to employ some traditional elbow grease.

Daddy led us through acres of corn. I looked back a few times to see Mr. Cullowee leaning on his hoe. Daddy and I kept up the same pace, so Mr. Cullowee fell progressively farther behind until we stopped at the border between corn and cotton to wait. When he caught up, he was breathing hard. His white wingtips were crusted with red mud, with more mud splattered on his wilting khakis. "A bit warm," he panted.

"About average," Daddy drawled. "You need a minute, Mr. Cullowee?"

"Nope," Mr. Cullowee said, still winded. "I'm fine." He rested his hoe on the ground. He seemed to be summoning his will to keep from leaning on it. "So what are we planting today?"

"We're weeding." Daddy pointed toward the field in front of us. "Cotton."

"Of course," Mr. Cullowee said. "I meant weeding."

"Maybe you don't know too much about cotton, being a one-crop man and all."

"Oh no," said Mr. Cullowee. "I know it well. Done a lot of reading on it."

"Reading," Daddy considered. Of course, Daddy himself was not only college-educated, but known for reading Department of Agriculture pamphlets as soon as they left the presses, not to mention anything he could find about cotton propagation in other countries. "So you know all about pigweed."

Mr. Cullowee agreed enthusiastically.

"And common cocklebur," Daddy went on.

"Of course."

"And Gossypium hirsutum," Daddy added.

"Absolutely," Mr. Cullowee said. "A blight."

"Then I'd say you're ready." Daddy gestured to the field with an *after you* sweep of his free hand. "Have at it. We'll follow your lead."

Mr. Cullowee gave a tight smile, then slung his hoe over his shoulder and headed into the field. Daddy and I watched as he proceeded to hack at the first cotton plant he came across, neglecting the thriving cocklebur beside it. Cocklebur loves rain, so during the downpour it had established itself quite nicely. But after a rain is the best time to haul it out, when the ground's still muddy and loose. That's when you can catch the root on the blade of your hoe and pull the whole thing up. It's the only way to get rid of it for good, and even that's no guarantee.

Daddy nudged me. "You want to tell him, or should I?"

"I'll do it," I said. "Um, Mr. Cullowee? You might want to move to your left. That's cotton you're digging up."

Mr. Cullowee used his shirtsleeve to wipe sweat from his forehead, hoe still in his hand. "Natural mistake," he said. "I'm used to a different strain of cotton."

"It's a slow grower at first, cotton is," Daddy said. "Easy to miss it among the weeds."

Mr. Cullowee nudged his hoe over to a cocklebur beside the cotton he'd recently decimated. He sized it up with a gentle tap, then swung the hoe like a golf club, whacking it cleanly at the base with a single swipe, and taking down the rest of that poor cotton plant.

Daddy nudged me again.

"You are going to get the root, aren't you?" I asked.

"Of course," Mr. Cullowee said. "Just clearing room so I can get at it." It was going to take him weeks to weed that row, at great cost to the surrounding cotton. "But don't let me have all the fun."

I took the row beside him and started digging out cocklebur and pigweed, avoiding the fragile cotton plants. Dig, pry, pull. Dig, pry, pull. Mr. Cullowee leaned on his hoe, watching.

"You do have quite a technique, Mattie," he said drily.

Daddy took the row on the other side of Mr. Cullowee. "She's got the touch," he agreed. "I'll be counting on her next year, when her brother's gone." This was news to me.

"You must have had a lot of practice farming in the past few months or so," Mr. Cullowee said, with a close-mouthed smile.

I bit my lip. "Your row looks tougher than mine," I said, hacking at the weeds beside him. "Let me help." Stab, pry, yank. I aimed my hoe close enough to his muddy shoes that he took a step back.

"Hey there," a voice called from the far side of the field. "Will Watson." I held my hand over my eyes and squinted to see Rose's daddy standing on the boundary where our crops gave way to the tenants' farms, and cotton gave way to tobacco.

"Luther Moore," my father called. "How's it going?" He laid his hoe on the ground and headed down the row.

"Who's your father's talking to?" Mr. Cullowee asked.

"Rose—who works for Mrs. Sampson—that's her father."

"Introduce me," he ordered.

I considered telling him to introduce himself, but I wasn't sure what he'd do. So I trudged to the tobacco field where Daddy and Mr. Moore stood talking. Mr. Cullowee followed with a jaunty step. His exhaustion had evaporated, leaving in its place the resurrected Kudzu King.

"Good morning!" He reached past me with his right hand. "I'm James T. Cullowee. I expect you've heard of me." He smiled with self-deprecation. "They call me the Kudzu King."

Mr. Moore shook his hand, though his face went blank. "Luther Moore," he said. "They call me Luther."

Daddy looked slowly back and forth between them.

"That's a fine crop of tobacco you've got growing there, Luther," Mr. Cullowee said, his voice bright and confident. "Have you considered planting kudzu between your tobacco rows to improve your nitrogen content? I'm here to tell you that the U. S. Government will pay you five dollars an acre, just to plant the stuff. It's never too late to plant kudzu. Ask anyone. I'll be happy to provide you with everything you need to get started."

"Uh-huh," said Mr. Moore.

The Kudzu King waited, but Mr. Moore said nothing else.

"Luther." Daddy nodded.

"William." Mr. Moore nodded back.

"Say hey to Rose for me," I called to Mr. Moore.

"Will do," he said.

We worked the whole morning, pulling pigweed and cocklebur. Mr. Cullowee managed one row for every three of mine, and five of Daddy's. By midday, we had enough weeds to start a bonfire, and Mr. Cullowee's clothes needed wringing. We sat in the shade by the creek, eating ham sandwiches Mama had packed, and scooping up cool water to wash them down.

After we finished, Mr. Cullowee stood and brushed his trousers. "I'd best get back to the Johnsons' farm. With Mrs. Johnson in the hospital, and Mr. Johnson gone—" He let the sentence hang, but the implication was that the entire farm would go to seed if he didn't attend to it.

"You know how to find your way?" Daddy asked.

"Of course," Mr. Cullowee said.

I was beginning to think his "of course" meant exactly the opposite. We watched him cross the cornfield, getting smaller and smaller in the distance.

"That man doesn't have a jot of stamina," Daddy said.

"He was trying," I answered, not sure why I felt the urge to defend him.

"That he was, Mattie." Daddy smiled. "That he was."

We worked together to the sound of crows overhead and the soft jabs of our hoes in the ground, faster without Mr. Cullowee's lagging. It was mid-afternoon when Mama's voice floated across the field. "Matt-ee? Matt-eee?" I put down my hoe and headed to meet her.

I found her running toward me, her skirt gathered up in one

hand. When she got to me, she pressed her hand tightly over her mouth.

"What?" I said. "What?"

She dropped her hand. "You need to come now."

Mama drove into town at about a hundred miles an hour. I sat in the front passenger seat, watching the fields whiz by, pressing my feet to the floorboards as if I could keep everything in place that way. "Is she still alive?"

"Just, when I left to fetch you," she said. "They called from the hospital."

"Catherine?"

"With Joey."

"Shouldn't we get her and Aggie?"

Mama shook her head. "It's going to be hard enough on those girls. It's better if they don't see this part."

"Did Lynnette ask for me?"

"No, but she needs you."

At the hospital, we threaded through white halls, following a nurse in a starched white dress, white stockings, and low-heeled white shoes. She stopped outside a door and turned the knob without entering. "Miss Johnson," she called softly through the crack. "You have visitors."

She opened the door a little wider and we stepped into the dim room. Lynnette sat on a chair by the bed, bent over her mother, her face pressed into the place where their hands met. Her mother lay flat and still, eyes closed, as small as I'd ever seen her.

"Lynnie?" I said, tentatively. She didn't move.

I walked around the bed and laid my hand on her shoulder.

"She's done," Lynnette said.

"Honey." Mama stood in the doorway. "Why don't you let us bring you home? Mattie's daddy and I will help you take care of things."

Lynnette shook her head without lifting it. "We're done."

My mother went to Lynnette's other side and crouched,

draping her arm around Lynnette's shoulders. "I know how hard this is for you. You and the girls will come stay with us."

"I have to take care of her." When Lynnette raised her head, her face was as bleak as drought. I don't think she saw either of us.

"That's our job now, honey." Mama helped her to her feet. As she stood, Lynnette stretched so her fingertips continued to touch the back of her mother's hand.

I wrapped my arm around her waist. "It's going to be okay, Lynnie," I said. I'd heard the sorts of lies people make after something terrible happens, but I'd never known how easily they slid out. "I mean, I know it's not, but we'll help you."

Lynnette's fingers slipped off her mother's hand, and she drew in a sharp breath, as if she'd dropped something fragile off a high place and was waiting for it to hit the ground.

"Breathe deep, baby," Mama said. "We've got you now."

While Mama made arrangements, I stood with my arms around Lynnette, inside the glass doors to the emergency department. Stretchers, wheelchairs, urgent conversations, flowers, visitors, nurses, doctors—everything flowed around us as if we were a rock in a stream.

Finally my mother finished. "She's in good hands, Lynnette. We can go now." With Mama holding Lynnette's shoulders and me clasping her waist, we guided her to the car. I eased her into the front seat and got in after her. The whole drive home she stared out the windshield, not at the scenery, but through it, as if a vast hole had opened up beyond the fields and trees and river.

When Mama turned off the ignition, Lynnette finally spoke again. "The farm?"

"Is taken care of," Mama said firmly.

"Aggie and Catherine?"

"Right here. You'll see them in just a minute."

We walked her through the door. When Aggie saw Lynnette shake her head, she tore loose from Danny and ran to Lynnette, wrapping her arms around her waist. Lynnette held one hand around Aggie and cupped the other against the back of her head. She touched her lips to the place where she parted Aggie's hair every morning. "Shh, shhh," she said. Aggie, who hadn't made a sound, erupted in convulsive silent sobs. "It's all right," Lynnette told her. So easy to lie.

Mama took Catherine from Joey, who was straining under her weight. "Here's the baby."

Without looking up, Lynnette reached out, gathering Catherine in her free arm. "You're okay now," she said into Aggie's hair. "We're all right."

Mama sent Daddy and Joey over to the Johnsons' house to tell Mr. Cullowee. "Ask him to keep an eye on the place," she said. When they got home, Daddy told her they hadn't been able to find him, but they'd put the goats in the barn and fed the chickens and pigs.

At supper, we crowded into the kitchen for comfort, with Catherine on Lynnette's lap. Mama served only soft foods—mashed potatoes, applesauce and brisket with gravy, with vanilla pudding for dessert—the kind of food you could swallow without chewing.

It didn't seem possible that there could be a world without Mrs. Johnson in it. I thought of her trudging up the stairs, shoulder blades showing through her thin nightdress, and Lynnette propping her up. I thought about how two trees can grow together and even if the weaker one falls, the stronger still leans in the same direction.

Lynnette slept with me, and we made nests of quilts on my bedroom floor for Aggie and Catherine, so Lynnette could hang her arm over the edge of the bed and touch them. For once, we went to bed well before dark. Everyone was so tired.

Late that night I woke to warm drops on my arm and heard Lynnette sniffling. I wrapped my arm around her and pulled her close. "Do you want to talk?" I asked.

She shook her head and buried her face in the mattress.

Mama went to the Johnsons' house early the next morning to feed the animals and pack clothes for the girls. We squished into the car to go to their church, where the congregation crowded around them—big-bosomed women enfolding Lynnette in warmth and skinny men nodding at Aggie and patting Catherine awkwardly on the head—and the preacher spoke of the loss of their dear sister, Virginia Johnson, and how the good Lord had gathered her into his arms. From there, we went to the late service at First Baptist. It must have been different for the Johnson girls: the stained glass and organ music soaring above, compared with the crowded clapboard building and enthusiastic choir they knew.

That evening, we ate in the dining room. The kitchen felt too close. Lynnette spent most of the meal with her fork suspended in mid-air, full of food, but lost on the way to her mouth.

After the rice pudding, I volunteered to do the animals at the Johnsons'.

"I should…" Lynnette trailed off, staring at the hole that apparently existed in our dining room wall over Danny's shoulder.

When I cut through the cornfield, the sky was still light, a color between robin's egg and cornflower. It always seemed like winter was dark forever until late spring, when suddenly daylight went until bedtime.

By the time I arrived, the sky had made its way to violet. The Kudzu King truck sat parked in the yard, its engine ticking as it cooled. I might have been able to stable the goats and feed the chickens and pigs without being seen, but I found I didn't want to. The light over the kitchen doorway was on, but the house was dark. By pressing my palms gently against the rotting screen and peering between them I could make out a figure sitting at the head of the table. "Mr. Cullowee?"

"I think we know one another well enough for you to use my first name, Mattie," he said.

I tried to shape the word with my mouth—starting with Jim and then James—but it wouldn't come out. Instead, I said, "You know Mrs. Johnson died yesterday, don't you?"

"Yes. I'm aware of that."

"About the time you left." It sounded like an accusation. Mr. Kerr had said over and over in history class that correlation didn't imply causation. Mr. Cullowee's abdication from the cotton field hadn't killed Mrs. Johnson, but somehow they seemed connected.

"You can come inside," he said. "I won't bite." I wasn't convinced of that. But I hated being afraid. I stepped inside, closing the door gently behind me. That screen was getting worse every day. Once rot starts, it's got nothing to do but spread.

He had a plate of ham and beans in front of him. "Did you cook that?" I asked. I didn't like the thought of him making himself at home in Mrs. Johnson's kitchen when she hadn't even made it to the grave.

"These are leftovers. I'm not much of a cook." Somehow that seemed worse, him living off what the Johnsons had left, when they had so little to leave.

"You weren't here," I accused, "when my father came to tell you about Mrs. Johnson."

"Meeting."

Because he hadn't responded to the blame in my voice, I upped the ante. "I thought you were coming back here to take care of things for the Johnsons."

"The kudzu was in good shape, as I told you before. There wasn't much to do and I had business to attend to." This seemed the worst sort of betrayal. Mr. Johnson had abandoned his family to a farm that couldn't support them. Mrs. Johnson had gotten sicker by the day until she'd died. Lynnette had given up school to make sure her sisters didn't starve. And this man's only concern was that "the kudzu was in good shape." He believed "there wasn't much to do."

I didn't bother asking if he'd fed the chickens or pigs or brought in the goats or why, if he knew Mrs. Johnson had died, he hadn't come by our house to pay his respects to her daughters.

When I'd spent that night on Lynnette's porch, all those weeks ago, and dreamed of him touching me in some magical game of "Mother, May I?" I'd imagined his golden curls would glow in the dark, his alabaster skin would gleam from inside, the touch of his fingers would leave luminescent trails. Now, in the shadows, his cheekbones looked sharp, his shoulders slumped. He wasn't as handsome as he'd once been.

They held the funeral for Mrs. Johnson at Mount Sinai on Tuesday afternoon, with the viewing beforehand. Mama made over one of her black dresses for Lynnette to wear. That and the bleak expression engraved on Lynnette's face made her look like a grown woman.

Some people say that children shouldn't see their parents dead, but there was never any question as to whether Aggie or Catherine would be at the viewing. Lynnette held their hands as they walked at the head of the line. When they came abreast of the casket, Lynnette lifted Catherine to see. Aggie stood on tiptoes, bracing her fingertips on the edge. She stared in at her mother for a long time, then sank back to her heels and leaned against Lynnette.

On the way to church, I'd offered to walk with Lynnette, but she'd said, "People will remember. How you act at the funeral is the kind of thing people talk about for years."

If so, they'd have nothing but good things to say about Lynnette and her sisters. She put Catherine down and held her mother's hand, leaning over their joined hands for a moment, as she had in the hospital. Then she gathered her sisters and moved on, allowing the line to proceed behind her. The church was hot and still, as quiet as I'd ever known it to be.

When I reached the casket, I wanted to give Mrs. Johnson a quick sidelong glance, to keep from having nightmares. But this was my best friend's mother, so I made myself look. Her hair was neatly parted and carefully brushed, lying on the white satin pillow. She wore her navy blue church dress, its cream buttons carefully aligned from neck to hem, and her good navy heels. But her face seemed strange: perfectly calm, with the lines between her eyebrows smoothed away as if someone had taken wet hands to dried clay and rubbed out all the cracks. Lynnette looked decades older than her young, dead mother.

Late the night before, I'd heard my parents' quiet voices drifting upstairs. "Do you think he'll be there?" Mama asked.

"I don't know," Daddy answered. "Nobody's seen him. I don't know if he knows."

Being the mourners, Lynnette and her sisters sat in the front pew, bookended by my parents. I sat next to Daddy, with Danny beside me. As people finished their viewing, they came by to offer respects and handclasps to Lynnette and kiss Catherine on the head. Everyone at church knew better than to touch Aggie unnecessarily, but they murmured, "Sorry for your loss," while she sat with her shoulders hunched, unblinking eyes fixed on the casket.

When Miss Edna stopped by the pew, she handed Lynnette a white satin-covered box. "We took up a collection," she said.

Mechanically, Lynnette lifted the lid. Inside sat a white leatherette Bible, with "Holy Bible, King James Version" inscribed in gold on the cover.

Lynnette dragged her eyes upward. "Thank you."

"Open it up," Miss Edna ordered.

Lynnette's hand looked small and pale, even against the shiny white cover of the Bible. On the inside page, someone had carefully written:

Virginia Lacey Johnson

Born September 12, 1904

Died May 31, 1941

A small pile of money was stacked below, neatly fanned out to show fives and tens and a couple of twenties.

"That's your money, now," Miss Edna said. "You don't let anybody else get a hold of it, not your father, not anybody. That's for you and those girls."

The preacher ascended to the pulpit and everyone found seats. I caught a movement from the corner of my eye as Mr. Cullowee slid into the pew behind Lynnette and Aggie. He placed a hand on each of their shoulders. Aggie ducked away from his grasp. “I’m terribly sorry,” he said. Lynnette didn’t even look back.

The preacher spoke of what a good woman Mrs. Johnson had been. No one could argue with that. While he didn’t give a litany of what she’d had to put up with—a mean-as-a-snake husband who’d deserted her, raising three girls on nothing, an illness that sucked the life out of her—people knew. “Our sister Virginia is sitting at the right hand of Jesus this very moment. He is thanking her for her good works on Earth, and telling her that her troubles are over.”

While Lynnette’s troubles, I thought, are a whole lot worse.

As the choir sang, “What a Friend We Have in Jesus,” I held my face in my hands and cried for Mrs. Johnson, tears leaking between my fingers.

Daddy laid his warm palm on my back. “You’re a good friend to that girl,” he said quietly. “She’s going to need you.”

# 17

Lynnette curled up on our sitting room sofa throughout the rest of the afternoon and into the evening, staring without seeing. Mama, Daddy, and I went in and out, bringing her sweet tea and pecan pie, gingersnaps and lemonade, sitting beside her, asking if she wanted to talk. Comforting words flowed over her, but didn't sink in. Full glasses and plates of untouched food crowded the side table. Even Mama couldn't persuade her to come into supper.

But when Aggie silently strayed from Danny's side to Lynnette, or Catherine staggered over, holding out her arms to be lifted up, Lynnette would slide her hand down Aggie's thick brown hair, or Catherine's blond curls. That night she read to them from my old *Peter Rabbit* stories. Her mother's *Blue Fairy Book* still sat in the Johnson parlor, but no one felt much like fairy stories any more.

Finally she came upstairs, where she cried herself to sleep in the cot Mama had set up beside my bed. I stared at the ceiling, feeling helpless. Sometimes you need to be alone, but there's no alone to be had, so the people around you have to pretend they're not there.

It didn't seem right that an ordinary Wednesday should arrive the next morning. Or that the kudzu parade and queen competition were only ten days away. Mama let Lynnette sleep in the next morning, but drove us to school at noon.

"I know how hard it must be," she told Lynnette as she handed her a paper sack of sandwiches and sweets, "but the everyday is the only tonic for grief." When she told us she'd pick us up from the mayor's house, I reminded Mama that Lynnette wasn't in the class. "She is now," she said.

As we walked to the Sampsons', Lynnette finally spoke for the first time since the funeral. "It's not too late to catch the bus. I should just go to your house."

She said "your house" and not "home," as if it could never be home to her. In truth, nobody knew what would happen, whether the Johnson girls would stay with us forever, or something else I didn't want to imagine—foster care or a home for abandoned children or going to live with distant relatives they hardly knew. For all Mr. Cullowee's fine talk, he hadn't stopped by our house once to ask after the Johnsons. There was talk about seeing if Mr. Johnson could be found, but nobody looked very hard.

I didn't particularly want to go to Queen class either. But Mama had decreed that we attend.

Lynnette stopped at the bottom of the steps. "It doesn't make sense. I'm not going to be queen of anything."

"You don't know that," I said.

I looked for Glynis before I lifted the brass knocker, hoping she was off with some boy, doing things she wouldn't tell her mother. Or maybe she'd found a new best friend, and was now complaining bitterly about Mrs. Sampson and calling me a teacher's pet. The only person I saw scurrying down the street was Alice, anxious to remain in good standing with Mrs. Sampson.

Rose answered the door. "Here comes the queen," she smiled. But when she saw Lynnette behind me, she shuttered her expression. It hadn't occurred to me that they might not know each other. It was as if I'd kept them in different pockets, both close to me, but separate from one another. As a newly minted young lady, it was my obligation to introduce them. "Miss Rose Moore, may I present Miss Lynnette Johnson. Miss Johnson, Miss Moore."

Lynnette held out her hand: politeness overcoming grief.

After a moment, Rose took it. "Good to meet you," she muttered.

"You, too," said Lynnette.

Rose paused, her other hand resting on the doorknob, as if she hadn't decided whether to let us in. "Is your daddy Mr. Leonard Johnson?"

Behind me, I felt Lynnette stiffen. "Yes, he is. Why?

Rose shrugged. "Just wondering. Sorry about your mama." In Cooper County, you didn't have to know a person to know their tragedies. She let go of the knob. "Go on into the parlor. She's in the library. She'll be with you in a minute."

"Why was she asking about him?" Lynnette whispered as she followed me down the hall.

"No idea." I led her past the closed library door to the parlor, where Mabel sat with Ann Marie.

"Oh, Lynnette, you poor thing!" Mabel cried, leaping up to take Lynnette's hands. Alice scooted into the parlor with an *I've been here this whole time* look.

A shrill voice erupted from the library. "I will not tolerate it." Mrs. Sampson's voice, already on the high side, had climbed up the register. "I absolutely will not permit it."

A soothing male voice answered her. The man spoke so quietly that only snippets of what he said found their way to the parlor. "…Don't you… deserves a…. grateful if…"

"I see no reason why I should be required—" Mrs. Sampson sputtered, mad as a wet cat.

"…not quite… reconsider…" the man interrupted gently. "… best for the community…"

"Fine," Mrs. Sampson fumed. Decisive steps strode down the hallway, accompanied by the sound of another person skittering to keep up. I yanked Lynnette onto the sofa just as Mrs. Sampson steered Glynis into the parlor by the arm. Glynis had the oddest expression on her face, a cross between a grimace and a gloat.

"Ladies," Mrs. Sampson announced, having regained control of her voice. "Miss Carpentier will be rejoining us for the duration of our lessons." She propelled Glynis toward the sofa where Lynnette and I sat, and backed her against it until her knees buckled and she had to sit between us. Then she crossed her arms over her bosom and glared. "If you even think—"

"Now, Mrs. Sampson." Mr. Cullowee had eased into the room while we were engrossed in the drama. He leaned against the flocked wallpaper, ankles crossed neatly. Today he wore pale blue socks, and the wingtips he'd had on in the cotton field. His shoes had been restored to pristine whiteness. "It's so late in the preparations to lose one of our contestants, isn't it?"

Mrs. Sampson, in an uncharacteristic fit of rudeness, didn't answer. Instead her lips thinned to slivers. Meanwhile, Glynis gave Mr. Cullowee a sideways glance and settled more comfortably into the sofa, forcing me to scoot further away to avoid touching her. Her gloat gained ascendance over the grimace.

Mr. Cullowee continued. "I'm sure Glynis has learned her lesson, haven't you, Glynis?"

Glynis looked down demurely, the perfect parody of a good girl. "Yes, I have, Mr. Cullowee," she simpered. "I'm so grateful to be allowed to rejoin my friends." What friends? The only one she'd had to start with had been Ann Marie, two if you counted Mabel, since Mabel was friends with everyone.

Mr. Cullowee seemed to notice Lynnette and me uncomfortably flanking Glynis, and gave me a smile that made me uneasy.

The mayor stepped into the room and said something quietly in Mr. Cullowee's ear. The two of them spoke briefly, then Mr. Cullowee said, "Ladies? Mrs. Sampson? I regret that I have to leave your charming company, but the work of the festival calls."

As soon as he left, Mrs. Sampson snapped at Glynis, "Miss Carpentier? Posture."

Reflexively, Glynis started to sit up straight, but it must have occurred to her that with Mr. Cullowee on her side, there was no need to mind Mrs. Sampson. So she stretched out her legs and admired her spectator pumps. Mrs. Sampson shook her head and looked away. One could only imagine what Glynis had said, or more likely done, to make Mr. Cullowee champion her, but she was now, like some evil fairy tale princess, under his protection.

Mrs. Sampson saw Lynnette for the first time and her face softened. "Lynnette Johnson," she said. "I'm so terribly sorry about your mother."

Lynnette sagged. I understood. Sometimes you can take anything but kindness.

Mrs. Sampson brushed a wisp of hair from Lynnette's

forehead. "How wonderful that you've come to join us." She studied Lynnette for another moment.

Then she turned abruptly to the rest of us. "Well, we're off to a late start, so we need to begin work promptly. We have only a week and a half before the pageant. I want every one of you," her gaze swept the room, stumbling only slightly at Glynis, "to do me proud."

Mrs. Sampson proceeded to hand us each a piece of paper with what must have been twenty questions on it. "I have here a list of questions that may be asked in the interview portion of the pageant. Each young lady will be asked only one question, but you must be prepared to answer any of them or, indeed, one you've never seen, as new questions may be added at the discretion of the master of ceremonies."

It didn't make much sense to have to figure out twenty answers when we'd only get one question, which might not even be on the list. I was about to point out that this seemed like a big waste of time, when Alice, eager to grovel her way back into Mrs. Sampson's good graces, raised her hand and saved me from embarrassing myself. "Mrs. Sampson, ma'am," she asked, "should we memorize our answers?"

"Excellent question, Alice," Mrs. Sampson replied. "It would be best if you commit to heart the spirit, but not necessarily the substance of your answers. You should respond as if hearing your question for the first time, but your answers should be gracious and considered, which means some advance preparation is in order."

She paired us up, and sent Lynnette and me to the kitchen to practice, for which I was grateful.

"I think I should leave," Lynnette whispered as we walked down the hall. "I'm not going to do this."

"Why not?" I whispered back.

"It's about looks. I don't have them, and you know it."

"That's not true," I insisted. "You have classic bone structure and beautiful eyes."

"Mattie." Her eyes dropped to the floor. "I just can't."

"Please," I said. "Just come in with me. You don't have to do anything." She followed me into the kitchen, where Rose stood ironing table linens and Raquel sliced tomatoes.

"Sit over there," Raquel said. She pointed to the far side of the kitchen table, near the open window. "It's cooler. I've got a pork roast in the oven." Once she mentioned it, I could smell the pork, heavy over the smell of starch. Raquel didn't bother asking, just pulled a couple lemon cookies from the jar and put them on a plate between us. "What does she want you to do this time?" she asked.

"Pretend interviews," I explained.

"Aren't you a little old for pretend?" Raquel asked.

I took a bite of the cookie, tart and sweet. "Not according to Mrs. Sampson."

"Have you told her?" Rose asked, as if Lynnette weren't in the room.

"Not mine to tell," I said.

Raquel, fed up already, put down her tomato knife. "We got a contest too," she said, "and Miss Rose here is going to win it." Would Rose's people have a parade? I wondered. I couldn't imagine that they'd be part of the town parade, but it seemed to me that Rose deserved her own float. Lynnette betrayed no surprise about a second Kudzu Queen competition that white people weren't talking about.

"It's not much of a contest," Lynnette said, "if you already know who's going to win."

I could see Rose starting to get her back up. As far as I knew they'd just met, but it seemed as if she already had some quarrel going with Lynnette that she wasn't talking about. "Just because you expect a thing," Rose said, "doesn't mean you don't deserve it. And sometimes it doesn't mean you do. Depends on the situation, doesn't it?"

I didn't want my oldest friend and my closest friend to dislike each other. "Will you have to do what we're doing?" I asked, to change the subject. "If you're going to be interviewed, you can practice with us."

"I won't be practicing," Lynnette said stiffly. "I'm not competing."

"I've got work," Rose said. She lifted the napkin she'd ironed and folded it in precise, angry creases.

"Let's go ahead and try a few of these, Rose," I said, "just in case. Humor me." I broke off a piece of cookie and pointed at Rose with it. "What adjective would other people say most accurately describes your personality?"

"Irritating," Raquel muttered.

"I heard that," Rose snapped.

"What about, 'doesn't take guff from anybody'?" Lynnette asked quietly.

Rose ran her iron over a fresh napkin, erasing the wrinkles. "That'll do," she said.

Relieved, I popped the bite of cookie in my mouth.

"If you could have one wish, what one thing would you ask for? And you can't ask for more wishes."

Lynnette's face froze. Of all the stupid questions.

Rose didn't turn her head, but I saw her glance at Lynnette out of the corner of her eye. "Shoes that don't give me blisters," Rose declared, "and I'll ask for as many wishes as I want to, Mattie Lee Watson."

Lynnette gave a hiccup-y laugh. I could have hugged Rose for it. "Fine," I said. "Be that way."

And it was then that I saw it, what made Rose queen material: her unique combination of confidence and awareness of other people. She never let herself be diminished: not as a Negro girl, not as the daughter of a tenant farmer, not as a servant.

That glance at Lynnette seemed to flip a switch inside her. "Your father—" Rose said into the silence.

Lynnette stared at her. "You've seen him?"

Rose nodded.

I was caught by surprise, unsure if it was the best or worst time for this to come up. "When?"

"While back. He came by our neighbor's house, looking for whiskey."

Lynnette looked both scared and curious. "We haven't seen him, didn't know if he was alive or dead."

"Alive or dead, you're better off without him," Rose said. "He's got the evil that won't wash out, no matter how many times the preacher dips him in the river."

Even with her troubles, Lynnette couldn't help smiling at this.

"Next question's yours, baby girl," Rose told Lynnette. I could have hugged her again for changing the subject.

"But I'm not—"

"Give her a good one, now," Raquel said. "Something she has to think about."

I ran my finger down the list, trying to choose a question that would make her think hard but not about hard things.

"What sets you apart from other people?" I asked.

Lynnette sat so long, tracing circles around the cookie plate, I almost forgot what I'd asked.

"Knowing things other people don't know," she said. "And wishing I didn't."

Mr. Cullowee showed up at our house with Danny just before suppertime that evening. The two of them stood at the kitchen door, covered with a layer of sawdust glued to them with sweat. My mother's reflexive, "Surely you'll stay for supper?" was met with Danny's, "Too much to do. We'll grab a sandwich or something."

"Daniel?" Mama said, the end of his name rising dangerously. She wasn't pleased when her children missed meals without notice.

"You've no idea how much work that place needs," Danny said.

"What place?" Mama asked.

He gave her a *where have you been?* look. "The Johnson farm. We have to fix it up if Jim's going to stay there with the girls."

"If Jim is going to do *what*?" Mama came down hard on the last word.

"Stay at the Johnson house. And look after the girls," Danny repeated as if explaining to a slow learner, not the best approach to take with Mama.

"It's the least I can do." Mr. Cullowee had been content to let Danny speak for him, but now he seemed to feel the need to pipe up. "After all Mr. and Mrs. Johnson did for me."

"And plant more kudzu. Anybody can tell Johnson's corn won't make it," Danny added, "but you can plant kudzu any time. And there's the subsidy. If we plant the place in kudzu, that'll go a long way toward supporting Aggie and Lynnette and Catherine."

The whole time Danny had been going on, Mama's jaw had been winding tighter than a watch spring. It was an indication of how fired up he was that he hadn't noticed. He wasn't used to upsetting our parents, so he didn't look for the signs the way Joey and I did.

"Don't worry," Mr. Cullowee chimed in. "I plan to pick up the rent where Mr. Johnson left off. In fact I'd like to go ahead and pay you any back rent the Johnsons owed, so you and Mr. Watson won't be out anything."

"No," Mama said.

"Beg your pardon?" Mr. Cullowee asked.

Mama forced the words between clenched teeth. "You are not taking my children."

"Mama," Danny protested. "He's not talking about taking Mattie or Joey. Or me."

"He already has you, Daniel," she said quietly. "He will not have my girls."

"You can't be serious," Danny said. "You're going to keep them here? Raise Aggie and Catherine?"

"Yes," she said. "We are."

"Does Daddy know about this?" he asked incredulously. Mr. Cullowee was shifting from one foot to the other, clearly uncomfortable with the direction this conversation was taking.

"Yes," she said. "He does. It was his idea."

"Where are you going to put them? They can't keep sleeping in Mattie's room. They have their own rooms over there. They have their own *house*."

"That house, and the land with it, belong to your father and myself," Mama said. "And we will decide how to dispose of it."

"I thought you liked Jim," Danny pleaded, as if the man weren't right beside him.

"I did," Mama said.

Danny didn't notice the past tense. "Well, it's a good thing he's offered to do, out of the kindness of his heart."

"That remains to be seen," she answered. "If you'd like to discuss the matter, I'd be happy to do so, among family. After Mr. Cullowee leaves."

"Where do you want him to go?" Danny asked, somewhat petulantly. "Since you've barred him from the Johnsons?"

"That will do for the present," Mama said. "It's time for you to wash up, Daniel." Without turning her head, she spoke to me. "As for you, Mattie, I'd like you to stop gaping and take care of your chores before the cornbread burns." She looked past Danny to the doorway. "Mr. Cullowee," she nodded, as neat a dismissal as I'd ever seen.

"Mrs. Watson," he said, and left.

From the yard outside the chicken house I could hear the truck for a long way, until the engine sound got swallowed up by the swell of cicadas.

Thursday afternoon, after the last day of school ended, the boys' kudzu class took place as usual at the Johnsons' farm. I didn't especially want to go watch them, but someone needed to know what Mr. Cullowee and Danny were up to. I left Lynnette in the kitchen, baking chocolate chip cookies with Mama and Catherine, while Aggie wandered our yard, claiming her new Aggieland. At first, Mama had carried Catherine on her hip from morning to night. But after a while, she started putting her down, and Catherine's thumb would emerge from her mouth to grip the folds of Mama's skirt as she toddled along beside her. Aggie seemed less skittish around Mama than she was with most people.

I cut through the woods so Danny and Mr. Cullowee wouldn't catch sight of me. But when I peered out, their field was empty. Lots of kudzu, a few spray canisters scattered around, no boys.

The cornfield was empty too. Mr. Johnson's puny corn stalks had been tilled under. I guessed they were getting ready to plant kudzu crowns.

Past the fields, the Johnsons' house swarmed with boys: on the roof replacing shingles, on ladders with paintbrushes, and on the sleeping porch swinging hammers. It looked like the baseball team was there, though I didn't see Carl, which was fine. I didn't like the idea of him helping Mr. Cullowee, not that I thought he would.

Danny stood by Mr. Cullowee in the yard, both of them giving directions. First the fields and now the house, I thought. A prize-winning field of kudzu to show off to farmers, boys to preach the kudzu gospel across the county, and the house, already transformed to a shiny white from the foundation to the second story windows.

Sometimes a rain will start so quietly that after a while you realize it's been raining for some time and you hadn't even noticed. By the time I grasped the fact that I was crying, I'd progressed to wet hiccups. I sat on the ground and pulled my knees up to my chest. Why hadn't anyone done this for the Johnsons when Mrs. Johnson was alive? I felt so sad for her, this lady who'd never had one thing go right in her life from the day she'd married. I cried for my friend who'd tried to keep her family safe. And even for Mr. Johnson, who must always have felt like the world was piling rocks on top of him to hold him down. I felt homesick for the days before all this had happened, when we took sleepovers for granted, when Lynnette was as grateful as I was that we were friends and neither of us felt any reason to keep secrets from one another.

I cried into the knees of my jeans, soaking the denim with tears and snot so it stuck to my legs. I didn't just want Mrs. Johnson back. I wanted Mr. Johnson, too, and I wanted Joey to be the annoying brat he'd always been and Danny to be my big brother who could do no wrong and I even wanted Aunt Mary to be the same hateful witch I'd known. I wanted there to be no such thing as kudzu or queens or festivals. I wanted the movie to reel backward from the day Mr. Cullowee first drove his shiny green truck into town.

That night at supper, I waited for Danny to bring up the changes at the Johnson house. Surely such a transformation was worth mentioning, but he said nothing. Like so many secrets these days, it wasn't mine to tell. Even my own secrets weren't ones I could share. I found myself quieter than usual. Secrets were expanding to fill all available space.

Friday evening, the seniors marched into the gym to "Pomp and Circumstance," so solemn in black robes and mortarboards you'd never have known they'd been cutting up all week. Being a Watson, Danny brought up the end of the line. The bleachers were filled with families, and "Kudzu! The Crop of the Future!" hung over the "Cooper County Consolidated High School" banner above the stage.

When the seniors reached their front row seats, Principal Lassiter led the Pledge of Allegiance. This was followed by a speech from Mr. Kerr, the history teacher, about how the senior class was about to join the ranks of history and should act accordingly.

A state judge from Morganton named Mr. Sam Ervin told funny stories. I knew judges started out as lawyers, so I listened closely for anything that would help me. Now that I had my own gavel, I was starting to consider becoming a judge some day.

Entertain your audience, I learned, and slip in serious things at the end, while they're laughing. He got the whole gym guffawing at a story about a mule that went to college but, being a mule, refused to learn a thing. "I hope I've learned a thing or two in my life," he said when he finished, "and maybe I can pass a little something on to you. The world is in flux these days, and I'd say it's our duty as American citizens to seek out wrongdoing and make it right.'"

Through it all, Mr. Cullowee sat on the stage, with a smile I'd come to hate, acting as if he'd somehow made all this happen.

As the seniors crossed the stage to receive their diplomas, I couldn't help but think about the war in Europe. If President

Roosevelt decided America should join, every boy called to the stage might be called up to war and sent overseas. Every boy. Including Danny.

# 18

People always say, "It woke me up in the middle of the night," as if anything momentous has to occur at the stroke of twelve. But when the roaring sound barreled through my bedroom window, it was 3:47 in the morning. I knew because I jumped up, dodging Lynnette's cot and the girls wrapped in blankets on the floor, and grabbed the alarm clock.

Once I was awake I barely heard it. But in my dreams, it was monstrous.

I ran into my parents' bedroom and shook them, shouting, "Get up! Something's happening at the Johnsons' farm!"

Daddy burrowed deeper into his pillow, but Mama jolted upright. "What's wrong?" Beyond the cornfields, a bright orange hole glowed.

By the time we got there—Daddy in overalls he'd pulled on top of his pajamas, Mama and the Johnson girls and me in our long white nightgowns, and Joey in a T-shirt and pajama bottoms, all of us in unlaced boots—the fire in the Johnsons' kudzu field was blazing with wicked glee. We weren't the only ones who'd rushed over. Luther Moore and other farmers from down the road were already there, forming a bucket brigade to bring water from the creek.

"Keep the children away," Daddy shouted. Mama kept Aggie and Catherine close and Lynnette hovered alongside. I grabbed an abandoned bucket and ran to the creek. The fire was gobbling dried grasses and sending runners toward the house.

"Danny!" Mama suddenly wailed. I realized he hadn't come with us. I hadn't heard him come home the night before, which meant he was asleep in one of the beds at the Johnsons'. And so was the Kudzu King. I dropped the bucket by the creek and dashed after Mama as she raced to the house, Catherine in her arms, Aggie and Lynnette behind her. She pounded on the door, yelling, "Danny! Daniel!" The fire behind us grew more confident, eating up weeds and volunteer saplings. "Daniel!" Mama screamed.

The door opened and there stood Danny, his hair sticking up and a slow-witted look on his face. "Mama?" he asked. "What are you doing here?"

Behind him, the Kudzu King looked much the same, with a day's growth of beard and a misbuttoned shirt.

"Fire!" Mama pointed at the hungry tongues of flame licking at the peeling paint of the woodshed. "Get out of the house right now!"

Aggie darted from behind Mama's legs and pulled at Danny's hand, while Lynnette, beside me, stared as the fire cracked open the woodshed like a nutshell and dug into the sweet meat of split logs inside. Catherine wailed like a coyote.

Mr. Cullowee dashed back into the hall.

"Where's he going?" Mama stroked Catherine's hair to calm her.

"Papers," Mr. Cullowee called, running upstairs.

"There's no time for papers," Mama yelled. "Get out here now! Those men need help!"

But he was down in a few seconds, a crate of neat file folders in his arms. He and Danny ran out of the house, and veered in opposite directions: Danny toward the fire, grabbing a bucket from the yard and filling it with quick spurts of the pump, Mr. Cullowee away from the fire with his precious box of papers. The chickens ran around in a frenzy. The two goats in the barn cried like babies for their mothers. Danny fought the fire while Lynnette opened the henhouse door and Aggie shooed the chickens out, waving her hands and yelling. They fled in an explosion of feathers, maybe never to return, but at least not trapped inside and burned to ashes. Mama and I ran for the goats and grabbed their collars. Mama, still holding Catherine, led them across the road where the fire would have nothing to eat. "Get a rope," she called, and I found one looped over the fence. She threaded it through the collars of both goats and tied them to a tree. "Remember they're here. We'll move them if we have to." She kicked at the hog pen until the fence came down and the hogs squealed off into the woods.

Meanwhile the men were putting out the fire in one part of the field only to have it erupt in another. Mr. Cullowee joined Danny at the pump, and took the bucket from him as soon as he could fill it, running for the woodshed. Lynnette and Aggie gathered more buckets from around the yard. "You fill," Lynnette told Aggie, who took Danny's place at the pump, freeing him to attack the fire directly with Lynnette and me. We waited for Aggie and Mama, who'd joined her, to pump the water as quickly as they could.

"Forget the shed!" Danny shouted. "It's gone. Keep the fire away from the house!"

But there was no keeping the fire away from the treat it had been saving for dessert. It licked up the new paint and dug into the old boards beneath it, climbing walls and racing through doors, eating window frames raw, hungry for everything it could reach.

The house became a flare that brought people from miles away. The bucket brigade lengthened as more neighbors joined, and divided, as if by mitosis, into several lines: creek to house, creek to woods, creek to field of formerly thriving kudzu. The pump was abandoned—too close to the house, too slow, too dangerous. We stopped the fire before it could move beyond the Johnson farm, but not before it ate their house alive, leaving only charred bones.

Lynnette cried throughout, a steady stream of tears running down her soot-covered face while she passed buckets, while she stomped hungry little flames, while she held the little girls way too tightly. She never stopped to wipe them away. I don't think she even noticed.

Dawn had come and passed—chickens unfed, cows unmilked, pigs unslopped, mules and horses and goats not let out to graze—by the time the fire was well and truly gone and all the burns had been tended to. Nobody had been badly hurt, thank goodness, and no one, thank the Lord, had died. Just one hard luck farm.

Neighbors trudged to their welcoming homes, and we to ours, the Johnson girls clutched in our midst, just before midday. There was no Saturday shopping trip to town. For most of the people who'd helped at the fire, there was no Saturday. Those who couldn't sleep through it sleepwalked through it.

Danny stayed with Mr. Cullowee, to tend whatever was left to tend on the farm that wasn't a farm anymore, by the house that had stopped being a house after it had ceased to be a home.

Mama made a big pan of scrambled eggs and another of bacon, poured milk for everyone, including Daddy, and sat at the table with her head in her hands. We ate in silence, without Mama ever raising her head. Then Daddy carried the little girls upstairs, one in each arm, Catherine asleep with her head on his shoulder, Aggie's wild-eyed gaze darting everywhere. Lynnette trailed after them, leaking tears, as she had throughout breakfast, reaching up every few steps to smooth Aggie's hair. Joey and I went out to do our morning chores without being asked. I touched Mama's curved back on the way out and kissed the top of her head. Her tangled hair smelled like smoke.

The chickens were mildly stirred, clucking quietly, as if in sympathy for their sisters on the next farm. I found the Johnson rooster, a red banty with half of his comb torn off in a long-ago fight, scratching around the yard in search of scraps. I gathered him up in the canvas from the woodpile and held him at arm's length so he wouldn't peck. Having no better place to put him, I dropped him in the empty stall between Sassafras and the Johnsons' goats, and left him there until we could figure out what to do with him.

When I came out, Joey was staring into the pigpen, where Stevie wallowed. Her piglets shoved against each other to get at her teats.

"Our kudzu's all right, isn't it?" he asked.

"I'm sure it's fine," I told him. "Aunt Mary's is nowhere near the Johnsons'."

"But what if...? I mean, could it have...?" He kept starting sentences, like he was turning over a dying car battery.

"You stay," I told him. "I'll check and come right back."

Hiking up my nightgown, I ran down the path. There it was, Aunt Mary's house, perfectly whole and oddly inviting. Relieved, I walked more slowly around to the front to see the kudzu shining green in the sun, as if to say, *You were worried about me? Really? I can take care of myself.*

Then I heard a creak.

There sat Mr. Cullowee on the porch swing, his arms across the back as before, except this time, a bucket sat at his feet, spilling over with lengths of kudzu. Our kudzu. Joey's and mine. Neat knife-cuts marked where it had been severed from the porch pillars.

Somehow—maybe at Aunt Mary's pump—he'd gotten cleaned up and had found one of his tailored suits that had escaped burning. Maybe he kept a valise of them in his truck.

"What are you doing here?" I asked. "Shouldn't you be taking care of things at the Johnsons'?"

"Nothing there to take care of anymore," he said mildly. He straightened his legs, pausing the swing. "I don't suppose you had anything to do with that fire?"

"Me?" I sputtered. "Why would I burn my best friend's house to the ground?"

He crossed one leg over the other, resting his left ankle on his right knee. Plain black socks today. I guessed he didn't carry spare fancy socks in that valise I'd imagined. "Maybe you thought you could burn my field and leave your friend's house alone."

I was tired and sad and that was just plain stupid. "Why would I want to burn your field?" I snapped. "And it's not your field, anyway. It's Mr. Johnson's. Actually—"

"Yes, I know," he said wearily. "It belongs to your parents. As does this property. As do most of the properties in this part of the county."

"It's not like I'm bragging. It's just a fact." I sat on the top step, leaning against the pillar. "So you think somebody set that fire?"

"I do. Nice get-up, by the way."

I looked down at my soot-stained nightgown and muddy boots with no socks. "Nothing you didn't see last night. You and half the county."

"You know, for a girl your age, you're rather—how shall I say it? High-spirited."

"So I've been told. What are you doing with our kudzu?"

"Pruning. Even kudzu needs to be kept in check from time to time." He examined the bucket brimming with our kudzu. "And borrowing."

"You're planning to return it?"

"With interest. That's why I'm here." He put both feet on the ground and leaned forward. "You have things I need. I have things you need. I'm prepared to make a deal."

I crossed my arms over my chest. "What do you think I need?"

"Let's talk about what I need first. I need kudzu."

"But it's not your kudzu," I said. "You didn't grow it. Joey and I did."

"So you did," he agreed. "And a fine crop it is. Which is precisely what has led me to this proposition. Will you hear me out, Mattie?"

I gave a grudging nod and brushed dried mud off my boots.

"I need kudzu," he went on, "a big thriving field of it, to persuade the holdouts in this county—your father, among them, and his tenants—that kudzu is the crop of the future." He began pacing the porch. "Model kudzu field propagated by bright young farmers tragically burns to ashes. But look! A thriving field of kudzu springs from those ashes—well, it doesn't actually spring from the ashes, we'd have to work on the wording. Anyhow, this thriving field? Why it was grown by mere children. And if children can grow kudzu, with only their bare hands and innocent labor, think of how much more you, farmers with battalions of tractors, can do."

Calling us "mere children" seemed insulting, but I kept my mouth shut.

He went on. "In secret, to surprise their parents with their ingenuity and diligence—that ought to get you off the hook with your father—" Since that had been our plan anyway, I couldn't object. "These two babes in the wood—that may be too much," he interjected, "planted an entire field of kudzu by—" He stopped pacing to consider. "How *did* you plant it, anyway? This field is much further along than the one at the Johnsons'."

I couldn't keep up with the way he leapt back and forth, one minute declaiming for an invisible audience, then interrupting himself to ask how it sounded.

"Um, the day you first came to town? Remember?"

"Of course," he said.

"All that kudzu you brought in your truck? The cuttings?"

He nodded, impatiently.

"We planted them."

He pointed to the field in disbelief. "All that came from two cuttings?"

I shook my head. "Joey collected the ones people didn't take home."

"You planted them," he said reverently. "Not crowns, cuttings. And they grew."

"Well, we watered them," I admitted. "I know you're not supposed to, but we didn't think it would hurt."

He swept that aside with a flick of his hand. "Doesn't matter. Water or no water. Wait! How did you carry the water?"

"In buckets," I said.

"Perfect!" He resumed his pacing. "Bucketful by bucketful, these little children, their backs bent by their labor— Do you think that's too much? I don't want to give people the impression that you have to work too hard for kudzu. And it would have grown either way."

"But not so well," I insisted.

"Maybe not," he agreed, not at all disturbed by my injection of truth into his declamations. "How many cuttings?"

I wondered if it would bother him to hear how many of his cuttings had been discarded. "About a hundred."

"Hmm." He didn't seem perturbed at all. "And none of them died?"

"Maybe one or two, but the others grew over them pretty fast."

"Right. Fertilizer?"

I shook my head.

"Insecticide?"

"We didn't see any bugs." I remembered what Lynnette had said. "You sprayed the Johnson kudzu, didn't you?"

"Just a precaution. There were beetles in their corn. Didn't want them to make the jump to kudzu."

"Do beetles eat kudzu?" I asked, professionally curious.

"I haven't seen it happen, but you never know."

"Anyhow," I said, "you knew that stuff was flammable, didn't you? They had a whole shed of it go up at the feed store downtown last year. Maybe it was you who started the fire."

He stopped mid-pace. "Really? Pesticides? How flammable?"

"That shed was gone before the fire truck got there, and the station's only a block away."

"Interesting." It was as if he'd opened a filing cabinet in his head, pulled out a file and stored the information to examine later.

"You said you had 'things,' you wanted from me, but so far you've only told me about one thing, and that belongs—"

"Yes, I know," he sighed. "It belongs to you and your brother, and, if we're being precise, to your parents and Danny as well. And your dead aunt Mary."

My eyes darted toward her door, hoping she hadn't heard him. "This *is* her house."

"Things," he repeated. "Some of which are better reserved for later in the discussion, when we discuss what you need from me, as it may happen that our needs coincide." I started to ask what he meant, but he held up his hand. "We need to form an alliance."

I waited to hear, pulling my knees closer to my chest and yanking down the hem of my nightgown to the tops of my boots. The white muslin was stretched so tightly I could see my skin through tiny windows in the fabric.

He sat on the wicker settee and began to trace the weave with a finger. "You have influence over your parents—"

"Please," I scoffed.

"More than you know," he said. "You can help persuade them."

"Of what?"

"That it's in Danny's best interests to delay college for a year and work for me."

"No, it's not!" I leapt up. "He's going to college. And you can't do anything to stop him!"

He stopped me with a word. "Why?"

I thought of a million answers, but couldn't find one that was convincing enough. So I said the one thing I could, though I knew it wasn't true. "You can't take him away from us."

"I've no intention of doing that," he protested.

"You already have," I said quietly.

The breeze stirred the bright leaves at the tops of the trees all around the kudzu field, and swung the empty porch swing on its chains. Joey must be worried, I thought. I'd told him I'd be back soon. Lynnette and the girls might be awake by now, sad and scared. And Mama, was she still sitting at the table?

"Are you through with the things you want from me?" I said. "Because I'm not going to help you steal Danny."

He ignored the second part and answered the first. "Not yet, but it might help you to know what's in it for you." He tipped his head at the empty seat on the settee beside him. "Sit?"

"Uh-uh." I needed a clear head.

He nodded as if I'd given the answer he'd expected. Finally, he said, "I'll make you the Kudzu Queen."

"That's ridiculous," I told him. "You're not one of the judges. You can't do that."

He gave me a look that spoke as clearly as if he'd said it out loud: *You are such a child.*

"Oh." A quick lesson in how the world worked. "And anyway," I added, determined to reclaim my pride. "I've been told I might win on my own."

"You might," he said. "But do you want to take that chance, or do you want to win?"

"It's not winning if you tell the judges who to choose," I argued. "It's not even a contest."

"Let me rephrase that. Do you want to be the Kudzu Queen?"

I did. Not enough to pray for it, because it was wrong to ask the Lord for something to benefit myself, and not enough to betray Danny, but I still wanted it with a fierce, uneven hope.

I thought he'd say more about my being the Kudzu Queen. Wasn't the devil supposed to tempt you with fancy words? But he moved to the next subject.

"Of course, I'll make sure your parents see that your appropriation of their property—"

I interrupted. "My family's property, so it's Joey's and mine too."

"Point taken. I'll make sure they see your unsanctioned use of your family's property in the best possible light." He continued as if explaining to them. "'I asked Mattie and Joey to do this for the benefit of Cooper County. I requested they keep it a secret so we could astound the county when they revealed it. I served in an advisory capacity to help them grow this fine crop.'"

"Technically—" I spluttered.

"Technically," he corrected, before I could finish my sentence, "I did. Didn't you and your brother use the kudzu I provided? And didn't you care for it more or less in the ways I recommended? It would be helpful if you'd say that whenever anyone asked."

Helpful to whom? I wondered.

"There is one other thing. But I need you to sit beside me, Mattie." He patted the spot next to him. "Please?" His face was drawn, skin taut over his cheekbones, blue eyes deepened by the porch shadows, golden hair darkened to bronze.

A Greek god shouldn't have to say please, I thought.

As if marionette strings were tied to my shoulders, I walked unsteadily to the settee and took the place beside him.

He brushed back my hair. His hand was soft, not a calloused farmer's hand like Carl's. "You're such a pretty girl," he said softly.

This was what I wanted, I thought. This. I am being made love to.

He leaned over and kissed me so gently that if I hadn't seen his face coming toward mine, I might not have known he'd been there. He pulled away and watched me, but I was too busy paying attention to my insides to speak. How was it possible that a kiss could cause ripples in my stomach, like the creek spilling over rocks in dappled sunlight? I closed my eyes and felt another kiss, like the first, as if instead of the nucleus of the cells of our lips touching, it was only the electrons, glancing off each other. He lifted my hair off the back of my neck, so I could feel a soft breeze.

My feet hovered a couple inches off the ground. His breath smelled like peppermint. I smelled smoke from the fire, too, but whether it came from him or me, or both of us, I couldn't tell. He kissed my neck below my ear. I held still as a deer, while he navigated kisses toward my throat. If I moved, if I said or did anything or shifted my weight, he might stop.

His hand slid to my shoulder. Not forward, toward the dangerous regions where he'd gone before. Instead, he slipped his hand down my back, flattening his palm to hold my shoulder blade, which felt as if it might start growing tiny pinfeathers under his touch.

"Mattie," he breathed into my neck, "let's go inside."

I stood like a sleepwalker and pulled the key from around my neck. He stood behind me, his hand resting lightly on my back. I tried three times to slide the key into the lock, but kept dropping it. Finally he took it from me and opened the door. It creaked like a horror movie.

Just humidity swelling the wood, I reassured myself.

His hand slid to the base of my spine, guiding me over the threshold.

I took a step, a little higher than necessary. My ability to gauge dimensions had vanished.

"Upstairs?" he asked.

I looked past him to the stairway, which led to Aunt Mary's private rooms: her bedroom, which I wouldn't dare enter with him, the room where she kept her finery, her washroom. Down here: public, safe. A door upstairs rattled in its frame as if in agreement. *Not. Up. Here.*

I was used to doors doing as they wanted in this house, but he jumped. "Is someone here?"

"Just the wind," I said, relieved to have gotten my voice back. "It does that."

He peered into the sitting room, assessed the furniture. "Come sit on the sofa."

I almost giggled. The sofa looked made for courting, not modern courting, but a hundred years ago when a boy and girl would have sat primly side by side, sipping tea.

He led me by the hand and sat down. But instead of sitting me beside him, he pulled me sideways onto his lap. He lifted my hair off my neck again and nuzzled me there, which tickled. I couldn't help giggling, though I felt myself blushing.

He drew away and looked at me. "You've never been with a man, have you, Mattie?"

I wasn't sure what "been with" meant. Was it what the boys called third base, where a girl let a boy touch her down there? Or was it a homerun?

"Mattie?"

I blinked. I hadn't answered him, had I? "No, sir."

"Mattie," he laughed. "I don't think you need to call me 'sir.'"

He returned to my neck. Meanwhile, under my right hip, things seemed to be shifting, jutting into me. He gripped my shoulder. "I wish this could be perfect for you," he said hoarsely. "A nice dinner, flowers. You should be treated like a princess." His other hand pushed my sooty nightgown up my leg and pressed my bare right thigh onto the hardening underneath me. "You understand, don't you? I would if I could."

"I understand," I said. Upstairs, the door rattled like it was trying to break free. His left hand moved from my shoulder to my breast. He gripped it like it was a stuck faucet knob he was trying to turn. Where had the sweet kisses gone? Could I ask him to be softer?

It's okay, I thought. In the olden days girls were married by twelve or thirteen. You were probably an old maid if you made it to fifteen and nobody'd betrothed you. There were even girls nowadays who got married at my age. There was a girl I'd gone to junior high with who'd—

The door upstairs broke loose and slammed. Twice. I leapt up. "I've got to go," I stammered. "My mama…Joey…"

"Mattie?" he reached for me, but I stepped away. "Come back."

"I thought boys were the ones who couldn't control their urges," I said. "Not grown men. Carl's never even touched me."

"Carl?" he scoffed. "He wouldn't know what to do with you." His voice shifted to pleading. "Come on, Mattie. You know you want this. This is for both of us."

But it wasn't. Like the rest of his deal, there was deceit under it. I wanted kisses, not this. I pushed him up and out the door, and shoved his bucket at him. "Take your stinking kudzu!" I said. "Take it and get off my family's property. And don't come back."

His chiseled face looked hard now, like the rest of him, except his hands, which were too soft for any man I could ever respect. "If you say anything to anyone, you'll be sorry."

"And if I don't?" I taunted, sassy Mattie back in full force now. "Will you make me the Kudzu Queen?"

"I will make you *nothing*." He slammed the bucket onto the porch so hard it cracked a floorboard. Lengths of kudzu vines spilled everywhere. He was off the porch in three strides and heading out to the road where his truck waited.

"You stay away from our kudzu!" I yelled at the dust behind his truck. "And you stay away from Danny!"

# 19

At church on Sunday, I prayed for saints and sinners. I prayed for Mrs. Johnson to be happy in heaven, and for Mr. Cullowee to stay well away from me. If his soul could be improved, I left that in the hands of the Lord. If you leave a sweet peach out long enough, it starts to turn. My love for Mr. James T. Cullowee had reached the stage of powdery mold.

At breakfast Daddy had offered to take Lynnette and her sisters to their church, but Lynnette surprised me by saying they'd rather go to ours.

"Are you sure?" I asked before we got in the car. "He'll take you to Mount Sinai. It's no trouble. They don't care where we go, as long as we get in some church time."

"No," she said quietly. "We're done with Mount Sinai." She slid next to Joey and pulled Catherine onto her lap. Aggie sat beside her and I squished in, pulling the door shut.

When we got to church, Danny stood by our pew, talking with Carl. Mr. Cullowee wasn't there, for which I was grateful. Danny wore black pants about an inch short, probably Carl's.

"Morning, Mrs. Watson," Carl said. "Mr. Watson."

"I see you've found our son," Mama said.

"Yes, ma'am," said Carl. "He was safe with me."

"Good to know," Daddy said.

Around one o'clock that morning, I woke because I thought I heard something. I listened, but heard only Lynnette's snuffling snores, the girls' breathing, and the katydids in the trees. It didn't feel like the night of the fire, but it still felt urgent, as if someone kept calling my name. I pulled a pair of overalls over my nightgown and went down to the kitchen. Through the screen door, I saw a shape on the stoop, so I pressed my nose to the mesh.

Danny. The door creaked when I opened it, but he didn't look up as I sat beside him. In the coop, the chickens muttered. Off in the woods, an owl called. A piglet squealed as Stevie rolled too close. From the barn, Sass's bell tinkled. She wasn't awake, just shifting from side to side as she slept. All around me, things seemed to be making little adjustments to settle.

"What if I put off school for a year?" Danny asked.

It sounded like one of those rhetorical questions I'd learned about in English class, the kind you're not expected to answer. The old Mattie would have been all over him with, "I can't believe you'd do something so stupid!" But a lot had changed in the past few months. People appearing, disappearing, changing, dying.

"This thing's too big for one person." Danny leaned back, hands braced behind him, and looked at the sky. The moon was full of cool light. "Jim says there's a lot to be made in kudzu, that it's about to break loose as an agricultural industry."

There were rhetorical statements too. I kept quiet.

"If I worked with him for a year, I'd be able to bring more to my studies."

"Or you might not to go to college at all," I blurted.

"Maybe I don't need college," he said. "If I go, and then start promoting kudzu after I graduate, it might be too late to be part of what's happening now."

I thought about Mrs. Sampson, and her way of keeping a conversation going with questions. "Are there other people like him, going around to get people to plant kudzu?"

"A few." He reached into his back pocket and pulled out a newspaper article, the edges soft where it had been folded. I unfolded it. *The Atlanta Constitution.*

"'The Miracle Vine,'" I read, "by Channing Cope." I read down to where Mr. Cope had written about how kudzu was the new king of the south.

I handed him his article. "I thought Mr. Cullowee made that up."

"It doesn't matter whether he made it up," Danny said. "It matters that people know it."

"Is he going to pay you?" I stretched out my legs, and adjusted my nightgown where it had gotten bunched up in my overalls.

"We're going to be partners."

I decided to practice my new question-asking approach, instead of offering my doubts as to whether Mr. Cullowee would make a good partner. "What does that mean, exactly?"

"We're still figuring that out. He says he needs someone like me, someone farmers trust."

Because they don't trust Mr. Cullowee, I thought. "What about outside Cooper County? Will farmers who don't know you trust you?"

Like Daddy, Danny had always struck an easy balance between modesty and honesty, at least when we used to talk more, before Mr. Cullowee got between us. Now it felt like he had that balance back. "Maybe not as easily, but I think so."

"Where would you live?"

"Like he does, renting rooms in counties we go to help."

It didn't seem the right time to point out that the last room Mr. Cullowee had rented had been burnt to cinders. "What will you get if you do it?"

He stretched out his legs beside mine. As far as I could tell, he'd never changed into his pajamas. His work boots made my bare feet look small.

"Experience," he said. "The chance to be in at the start of something big, to help people. Kudzu's going to make a difference, Mattie. I can tell."

"And what will you lose?" I looked over at him. The side of his face closest to me was in shadow, while moonlight outlined his eye socket and nose and mouth. I could see how girls could fall in love with him.

"Daddy's good opinion, and maybe Mama's."

"That's a lot to lose," I said.

"But probably only for a while," he mused. "They don't like him. I don't know why. But once they see what we can accomplish—"

I didn't know why they didn't like him either, though I sensed they had different reasons from each other, which were different from mine, at least the parts of me that didn't like him, which were also different from the parts of me that were still strangely in love with him and wished he would ask me to run off with him instead of Danny, though for different reasons.

"Can you keep a secret?" I asked.

"Sure," he said.

I stood, pulling Danny to his feet. "Come on." I grabbed my boots from the stoop, and shoved them on my bare feet. "I want to show you something."

"Where are we going?" he asked. "Is this the fort you and Joey are building?"

"You'll see," I told him.

In the dark, the path seemed like a tunnel, with patches of ground lit by moonlight. I went ahead, holding branches so they wouldn't snap in his face. Animals skittered in the undergrowth, maybe some species I'd never heard of, which only came out after midnight—small mammals with huge eyes that paused in their scrabbling for food to gape at these monsters stomping through their world, then darted off. Finally the woods opened up to Aunt Mary's back garden.

"You're braver than I thought," Danny said. "I'd never have believed you'd come here on your own. I'm not sure I'd have done it."

I looked up. "That's not it," I said, "the house, I mean." I didn't want Danny to know I'd been in Aunt Mary's house. That was between her and me. I took a deep breath of cool night air, so moist it felt like I was drinking it. As we came around to the front, the tangled sea of kudzu appeared. I stepped aside so Danny could see.

"Oh," he breathed. "It's beautiful."

I crossed my arms, pleased and a touch smug.

"Who did this?" Danny asked.

"Joey and me," I told him.

"But who showed you how?" he asked. "Has Jim been helping you in his free time?

My smugness deflated with a pop. "No," I snapped. "We did this on our own."

"But how did you know what to do?" So much for impressing Danny.

"We grew up in the same family you did," I said haughtily. "We listen to Daddy talking about his crops. We see Mama gardening. We're not stupid."

"I never said you were, Matts." He was too awestruck to be ruffled. "But this—"

"This is what Joey and I've been doing while you all thought we were playing." There was still some huffiness in my voice, but I was calming down. When faced with the impossible, Danny was pretty good at figuring out how it might be fathomable. He walked into the field.

"Careful," I called out. "The vines like to trip you up."

He stepped over a thick kudzu vine, and lifted another. Smaller branches brimming with leaves trailed over his arm, cascading to the ground. "This is something else. I still can't believe you did this—" He corrected himself before I could snap again. "Not you and Joey, Matts. Anybody. I've never seen anything like this."

It wasn't just the moonlight or coming onto something unexpected well past midnight. There was nothing like our kudzu in Cooper County. Maybe there was nothing like it anywhere.

"You see?" he said. "This is why I have to do it."

I'm not sure what I'd expected, but I hadn't thought Danny would take our kudzu as evidence that his future lay with Mr. Cullowee.

He waded through as if walking into the river, up to his knees in kudzu. Lifting another vine, he breathed in, as Mr. Cullowee had done. "This is good, Mattie. This is really good."

Seeing him in that moonlit green, I thought about how I'd be losing him, one way or the other, by the end of the summer. He'd come home to visit, and maybe settle down in Cooper County, take over the farm from Daddy or buy his own, but he wouldn't be the Danny I'd always understood. He'd have experiences I wasn't privy to, that would change him in ways I couldn't anticipate. He'd be a grown-up, and someday, not long after that, so would I.

"Can I tell Jim about it?" he asked.

It used to be, when Danny learned something, the person he wanted to talk it over with was Daddy. I sat, and pulled some trailing vines over my lap like a blanket. "He already knows."

Danny looked up from the kudzu. "You told him?"

"Not on purpose."

"Then how'd he find out?"

"Followed me here," I said.

His look was sharp, but he didn't ask any more. "How about Mama and Daddy?"

"Not yet. We're sort of doing it as a surprise for them."

"It's just you and Joey? You did this? And you've kept it a secret since—since when?"

"Since the first day the Kudzu King came here, when he brought all those cuttings."

He looked around the overflowing field. "That paper sack of Joey's? In the car?"

I nodded.

"Fertilizer?" he asked.

I shook my head.

He laughed and made a deep sweeping bow, almost toppling into the mass of vegetation. "I bow to you, Mathilda Lee Watson. You are indeed the Queen of Kudzu."

When he stood up, he said, "Maybe you should be the one to give up school and travel around with Jim. You seem to have the golden touch."

The complications of that made my head ache. "It's been Joey mostly. You know how you said I'm braver than you thought? Well, Joey's smarter than I thought. This was his idea."

"He's ten, Matts. He couldn't have done all this without you." He began to wade toward me. "What are you going to do with it all?"

"Sell it at one of those markets Mr. Cullowee was talking about."

"You can call him Jim, you know, Matts. He doesn't mind."

"I know," I said, "but it feels funny. Danny?"

He looked over, and the kudzu vines appeared to be holding him upright.

"He wants to use this field, to show everybody," I said.

"Makes sense," he said. "Since the fire."

"I don't want him to."

"Why not?" Danny resumed his heavy-legged trek through the kudzu.

"It's not his field." I didn't tell him any more.

He shook my hand. "I'll keep your secret, Mattie. It's yours to tell, yours and Joey's, whenever you want."

"I'll keep yours too," I told him. "It's yours to decide, though I know what I wish."

He held down his hand to pull me up. "What do you wish?"

"I know it can't happen, but I wish you could stay here."

"Yeah," he said, "me, too."

Our walk back was slow and silent. When the path was wide enough, we walked side by side. When it narrowed, Danny stepped ahead, pulling branches out of my way. The moon had lowered so I barely saw it behind the trees, though I felt comforted when it flashed between branches. I was collecting all the homeostasis I could find.

Danny held aside the last wisteria vines to let me step into the yard. I blinked at the sudden brightness. After my eyes adjusted, I saw the yard wasn't empty. Two people stood by the chicken coop: Lynnette and Rose. I had one of those moments when you can't connect the jigsaw puzzle pieces in your brain to make the picture on the box lid. I could see Lynnette waking to find me gone, maybe coming out to look for me. But what was Rose doing there at all, much less now, much less with Lynnette? Rose put her hand on Lynnette's arm.

Danny almost ran into me, and both girls looked up. They didn't seem startled, more like they'd been away and were coming back. "Lynnette?" I called. "Rose? What are you doing?"

"Talking," Rose said. Lynnette didn't answer. Her face was splotchy and wet, and she was choking out jagged sobs.

"Is she all right?" I asked Rose.

"She will be," Rose said.

"What did you say to her?" I accused. Danny rested his hands on my shoulders, but I didn't know whether he was trying to comfort me or keep me from getting riled up. I wasn't about to let anybody hurt Lynnette, especially now.

"It's for her to tell," Rose said. "If she wants to."

Secrets were whirling around me like planets. I wanted to come back down to Earth.

"Tell me." I could feel my eyes narrowing. No "please," no gentle cajoling. I needed to know. Danny's hands tightened on my shoulders. "Tell me now."

When Lynnette wiped her nose on her nightgown sleeve, Rose pulled a hankie from her sleeve and handed it to her. It was then that I saw Rose was still dressed for work, as if she'd never gone to bed. "Thank you," Lynnette said. "I'll wash it, and get it back to you."

Rose, never one to make false objections to be polite, said, "That's fine. When you can," though I doubted she had an extra hankie to tide her over.

Lynnette looked up at me across Rose's shoulder. "He did it. All of it."

"Who?" I asked. "What?" There were so many possibilities floating around that I couldn't figure out which "he" she meant, and what "it" she was talking about.

"Mr. Johnson," Rose said. I guessed once part of the secret was out, Rose no longer felt compelled to keep the rest of it, though the "it" still remained a mystery.

As if she hadn't spoken, Lynnette went on. "He did it, and he's dead. Drowned. In the river." She gave hiccup-y laugh. "Dead drunk."

I moved toward her, ducking out of Danny's grasp, but was stopped by Rose's downward gesture with her left hand. It said without speaking, *Give her room.*

The thought that someone else would tell me how to treat my best friend made me burn. But I still felt the imprint of Danny's hands on my shoulder, reminding me that I'd had a lifetime of acting precipitously, which hadn't always had the best results. I stopped by Stevie's pen.

"They found him," Lynnette said, gesturing at Rose with her head. "Her father and some of the others. He'd been staying down there, at the tenant farms, drinking and being a menace."

I'd never heard her speak that way, but it was such an accurate description that I wondered if she'd always seen him that clearly and for reasons of her own not said it out loud.

"What did he do?" I asked, keeping still as I'd have done for Aggie, afraid to spook her.

Rose slid her arm around Lynnette's waist, and Lynnette looked at me, wet snail tracks of tears ugly and shiny in the moonlight. She hiccupped another humorless laugh.

"He was bragging on it. Bragging about how he burned it all down. Burned his own place down. Meant to just do the kudzu, but he wasn't bothered by the way things turned out."

Her face hardened. The grief had burned out of her, leaving stony rage.

"He's dead?" She'd said it, but it was taking a while to sink into my brain. When he'd disappeared, I'd assumed he'd simply left Mrs. Johnson and the girls to fend for themselves.

"Yup," Lynnette drawled, a frighteningly cynical version of herself. "Guess there'll be another funeral, though I don't know who's going to pay for it—or who'll bother to show up."

"Don't worry," Danny said. "We'll take care of the expenses, our family will."

"And people will go, for you and the girls, and for your mother," I told her.

"What makes you think I will?" Lynnette spat. "Or my sisters?"

This shocked me. You were supposed to go to a person's funeral, even if you hated them.

"You don't have to, if you don't want to," Danny soothed. He put his arm around her shoulder. I noticed Rose didn't make the "stay there" signal to him. Lynnette melted into him, pressing her head against his chest, her back shaking with small earthquakes.

Rose slipped her arm from Lynnette's waist, and walked to where I stood by the pigpen.

"It's because of you that I'm here," Rose said as we watched Lynnette sob into Danny's chest. He circled his arms around her and let her cry, stroking her hair.

"Me?" I couldn't see what I had to do with it.

"I didn't know that girl," Rose said. "It's a bridge you built, Mattie, between her and me. That's what you do." It was the gentlest I'd ever heard Rose's voice, as if she thought I could use some comfort too.

"You mean that?" I glanced over at her.

"I don't say anything I don't mean, Mathilda."

Lynnette's sobs were diminishing, smoothing into long deep breaths.

"Did you see him?" I asked Rose, my voice low.

I felt her nod beside me. "It was awful, all bloated and white," she said, in the same low voice. "I'll have nightmares. You don't want to see a thing like that if you can help it."

I shook my head, though I'd have nightmares myself. "What was he like when he was down there, before..." I wasn't sure when "before" started. Before he burned his family's house? Before he washed onto the riverbank? "...before all that?"

"Mean and wheedling. Always trying to get my cousin Evelyn to go off with him."

Somehow that made it even worse, that while his wife was dying and his daughter was doing all she could to hold their family together, he was off sniffing after other women.

"What'd she say to him?"

"She couldn't stand the sight of him. But she couldn't tell him that. Not to his face. You know."

I did. No colored girl with an ounce of sense would tell a white man she didn't want to have anything to do with him. Especially not one as vicious and unpredictable as Mr. Johnson.

"She was polite enough," Rose went on. "But she started dressing ugly."

"Did it help?" I asked.

"Not much," she said.

# 20

On Monday, after Daddy and Danny finished off their fried eggs and headed to the cornfield, Mama announced that she couldn't go another week without groceries. "Girls, you want to go?"

Aggie and Catherine looked to Lynnette, who said, "I think we'll stay here, if you don't mind, Mrs. Watson. We need . . ." she trailed off. She'd been pale and muted all morning. When we'd gone to bed, neither of us had spoken of what we'd learned.

"You're absolutely right," Mama said briskly. "You just relax. We'll go." She glanced at the dirty kitchen table, the greasy pans in the sink. "Joey, you're on kitchen duty."

Before he could protest, she added, "Your sister and I need some time."

She turned to Lynnette. "You can practice for the competition while we're gone."

"Mrs. Watson?" Lynnette began, "I don't think I—"

Apparently, Mama no longer required people to finish their sentences. "Oh, you're going to be in that competition, Lynnette Johnson, if I have to dress you myself. You already know how to walk and talk, which is mostly what Mattie's been learning to do these past seven weeks, so I see no reason you can't be there on Saturday night."

I wasn't sure this bossiness on Mama's part was an improvement. She strode through the kitchen door to the car.

I shrugged at Lynnette. "Force of nature. Wish me luck."

"Luck." She gave a small smile and I saw my old friend under all that grief.

I pressed my lips together as Mama started the car. This was the first time I'd been alone with her in weeks, and all my secrets were bickering in my head like little kids in the back seat. I wasn't used to keeping secrets from my mother, not big ones anyway, except the kudzu field, which was starting to seem insignificant.

"So, Mattie, are you ready for the competition?" Mama looked at me sideways across the front seat.

"I guess." I opened my lips just enough to let the answer emerge. Maybe I could make it to town with my secrets intact.

"Any of the girls giving you any trouble?"

"Well, Glynis…" I wasn't sure how to summarize the trouble Glynis had been giving me.

"Hmm." She nodded.

I was curious enough to forget about secrets for the moment. "Hmm what?"

"Is she acting jealous?" Mama asked. "Like you're the cause of whatever misery she might suffer, and the object of whatever misery she'd like to inflict?"

I rolled my eyes. "She's got no need to be jealous. Everyone knows she's the second-prettiest after Mabel."

"Not true," Mama said, "and definitely not everyone. Besides, I suspect it's about a lot more than pretty."

"Like what?" I asked.

A half-mile down the road, she finally spoke. "Cora Carpentier went looking for a second husband after her first ran off. She thought she might like mine."

"Daddy?" I turned my whole body to face her. "Did he ever—"

"No." She shook her head. "He felt sorry for her. We both did. Nothing worse than pity in a situation like that. She never forgave me for it, though it's not as if we'd had much of a friendship in the first place."

In the silence, my mind kept veering to Glynis. And her mother. And my father.

"Tell me about Carl," Mama said. Did she have a whole list of interview questions she'd been waiting to ask once we were alone? Was Carl a safe topic, or were there secrets I should lock away before opening my mouth?

"He's nice," I said.

"Mm-hmm," she answered, in the way that meant: *go on.*

"He opens doors for me," I told her. Even though he hadn't opened one in a while, it wouldn't hurt for her to know his manners didn't evaporate out of her sight. "We haven't done anything."

"That's good," she said, which made the part I wasn't telling her, about what I had done with the Kudzu King—or what he had done to me, particularly to my breast, on Aunt Mary's porch and in her parlor, about my even being on Aunt Mary's porch and in her parlor and about the whole kudzu field in front of that porch and parlor—loom uncomfortably over my shoulder.

"He's a nice boy," I repeated lamely. "I wouldn't—" I said, though my stomach winced at how close I'd come to doing exactly that. I watched the road, feeling her speculative gaze.

Daddy had once told me how Catholics had to sit every Sunday in a dark closet next to a priest and confess every bad thing they'd done or thought. I didn't need a priest. I had my mother. I had to tell her some secret or they would all come spilling out. "Mama," I blurted, still staring at the road. "I found out something, about Lynnette's father, and the fire."

"I know," she said quietly. "I know, sweetheart."

"He's dead." My words spilled out over each other. "And he's the one that burned their house. He didn't mean to, but he was happy about it. But now he's dead and—"

"I know." She rested her hand on my thigh.

"Rose was here last night. I meant she came over to tell Lynnette. Late, after midnight—"

"Really?" she asked, as if it were interesting but not particularly extraordinary that Rose should be visiting our house after all these years, late at night. I realized she'd saved me from explaining that I'd been outside with Danny, and where we'd been. "That was good of her."

"How did you know?" I asked. "About Lynnette's father?"

"Rose's daddy," she said. "He came by the house and told your father and me, after you went to bed. And apparently"—she added drily— "before you got up again."

"Lynnette doesn't want to go to the funeral," I said.

"There's not going to be a funeral."

I jerked my head to look at her. Her mouth was set like concrete. "But everybody has a funeral when they die," I protested.

"Not him. Not after what he did to his wife and children every day of their lives," she said in a hard, flat voice. "There'll be an interment. The girls won't be expected to go."

"But shouldn't he—?" I couldn't help pursuing it. There were rules about dying, even if you were mean. Terrible things might happen if people started breaking those rules.

Her voice rose over the engine. "Mattie, that man never set foot in a church his whole life. Do you think the church would have him?"

I thought about Mrs. Johnson driving us to Sunday morning services, humming "What a Friend We Have in Jesus," while Mr. Johnson was off getting drunk. I thought about the congregation, all those big-bosomed women squishing Lynnette against them in perfumy hugs.

"I'd bar the doors," she said, her cheeks flushed, "before I'd allow that man's body to be carried into church to be prayed over."

I so rarely saw Mama angry that I didn't know what to do. We drove in silence.

When the state road became Main Street, she spoke again. "Mattie, whatever happens Saturday night, I'm proud of you."

"But I haven't done anything."

"You've changed," she said. "You've always been different from me, but now you're different from the way you were." A smile crept into her voice. "I don't know what's caused it—the classes with Mrs. Sampson, or maybe even Carl—but you've grown up."

I carried the shopping basket so Mama could add to it more efficiently. You wouldn't have thought three girls would eat that much, but apparently we needed six times our usual amount of groceries. Mama liked her house well-stocked. Even in the years when there hadn't been much money, she'd always made sure we had plenty in the pantry.

After we finished at Aronson's and filled the car trunk with paper sacks, we went to the hardware store to pick up some bits and pieces for Daddy and Danny. They'd been talking at breakfast about a contraption to make weeding easier on the back. Mama knew Daddy well enough that he had only to say, "Steel, about yea long, and so wide. Serrated if you can find it." It had been nice to hear Daddy and Danny inventing together again at breakfast, though it seemed unfair for Danny to lead Daddy along when he might be going off with Mr. Cullowee.

I'd been so distracted by my mother's pride that it took two trips to the car to realize that Main Street was done up like Christmas, only instead of tinsel and lights, green bunting was draped across shop awnings and huge green bows hung on every lamppost. In the drugstore parking lot, a wooden viewing stand had appeared. Two months ago, Mr. Cullowee had painted this picture, and now here it was, right in downtown Pinesboro.

As Mama closed the trunk, I saw men carrying lumber past the library, which reminded me I'd left the manners book in my purse. "Mama?" I asked. "Can I meet you in a minute? I have to do something."

She brushed off her gloves, and picked up her handbag from the roof of the car where she'd left it. "Dress shop. I'll see you in ten minutes."

The library was cool and thick with quiet after the warm bustle of the street. I found Miss Perkins sitting on a wooden stepstool in the Fiction H-N section, engrossed in a book. As usual, she wore a smart suit straight out of *Vogue* magazine, this one the color of ripe blueberries. I stood politely between the shelves, not wanting to interrupt. After turning the page, she looked up. "Mathilda." She stuck her finger in the book. "How nice to see you. What can I do for you?"

"I wanted to thank you for your help with the manners book." I took it out of my purse. "It was funnier than I thought it would be."

"I'm glad you came by." She pulled a slip of paper from the pocket of her suit, substituting it for her finger. "It occurred to me that I have something you'll like."

She led me to the periodicals section and pulled out an *Atlanta Constitution* hanging from a bamboo spindle. When she opened it to the society news section, I saw a picture of girls in white ball gowns gathered around a girl in a tiara with a dark green sash over her gown. "Miss Kudzu of Atlanta," the headline read, "Miss Irene Dunhill, daughter of Mr. and Mrs. George Dunhill, Atlanta's Queen of Kudzu."

"You could take her." Miss Perkins smiled, sounding surprisingly like one of my brothers.

At the bottom of two columns praising Miss Dunhill's many virtues, from her "raven tresses" to her "dulcet singing voice," was a line: "See page 4 for related story."

There I saw a column by Mr. Channing Cope, about the wonders of kudzu. I skimmed down the page. Nothing I hadn't heard from Mr. Cullowee or figured out with Joey or seen in Danny's clipping, until I came to the sentence, "Farmers: The United States Federal Government will pay you eight dollars for every acre you plant with kudzu."

"Is this right?" I asked. Miss Perkins followed my finger, which I saw had dirt under the nail. Mama and Mrs. Sampson would have despaired of me. "Eight dollars an acre?"

"I believe so," she said. "Let me check." It was a known fact that nothing entered the library—book, magazine, newspaper or advertising flyer—without Miss Perkins reading it first. She went to the newspaper shelf and pulled out the third from the top. She opened it and ran a finger down the page as if it were written in the Braille alphabet, which of course she'd be fluent in. "Mm-hmm," she murmured. "Yes, I thought so. One more, for corroboration." She replaced that newspaper and extracted a third from the stack beside it. "Yes." She slid it back into place. "Eight dollars per acre."

"But Mr. Cullowee's been telling everyone that it's five dollars," I said. I supposed she couldn't be expected to know that, since he'd been telling farmers, not people from town. But I was oddly disappointed to discover that she didn't know everything.

"Then Mr. Cullowee is—" She paused, tapping her manicured finger against her lip, without marring her perfect lipstick with the smallest smudge of newspaper ink "—mistaken."

I wondered if "mistaken" was the best word. Mama and Daddy always let us off the hook if we made an honest mistake, as long as we made an honest apology. It seemed likely that Mr. Cullowee's misinterpretation of the government's bounty was neither honest nor a mistake.

In the quiet, I heard the clock above the circulation desk click over to the next hour. Of Mama's ten minutes, I'd been gone fifteen. "Thanks, Miss Perkins," I said. "You've been very helpful."

"Good luck, Mattie." She gave me a smile that could have meant anything from *You're not a bad girl for all your flightiness* to *I know you'll do something useful with the information I've given you.* I suspected it meant all of the above.

When the bell over the dress shop door announced my arrival, Mama and Miss DeWitt, the owner, looked up from a glass counter covered by an ominous pile of white lace. I advanced slowly, prepared to agree to anything that would keep me from being trapped in a dressing room with a stack of brassieres.

But before I reached the counter, Mama gathered up a selection and said, "We'll take these, Noreen." Miss DeWitt nodded approvingly, as if Mama had shown impeccable taste in making those particular choices. I guessed the way to keep people coming back for more clothes was to give them the impression that their taste was exquisite.

Miss Dewitt wrapped Mama's purchases in white tissue paper and slipped them into a white bag with a gold cord handle, inscribed in gold script with *DeWitt's Elegant Ladieswear.* She handed Mama the bag, and gave her change in coins rather than dollars. Clearly, elegance didn't come cheaply. Then she reached behind the counter, and handed more bags to Mama.

"What'd you get?" I sidled beside Mama to sneak a look, but

she held the loaded bags well away from me. They spread out like a fan in her grip.

"I'm starving. Let's have a ladies' luncheon at the drugstore, shall we?" she asked instead of answering. As far as I was concerned, food rated higher than undergarments, so I followed her.

The whir of the milkshake machine greeted us as we entered the drugstore. "I'll be right there," I told Mama. It wasn't exactly a lie, since I hadn't actually said I was going to the restroom, though I'd implied it. Instead I went to the counter where I'd left the camera film two weeks earlier. I thanked the clerk and stuck the little box of slides in my purse.

In the soda fountain section, I was surprised to find Mama in a booth. The few times we'd eaten at the drugstore, we'd sat at the counter, which had stools you could spin around until you got queasy and your milkshake threatened to come up. Maybe she thought I'd outgrown such childish things with my newfound maturity.

Maybe I should.

"Mama?" I slid into the seat opposite her. "What would you do if you believed a person was lying to a bunch of people and you were maybe the only one who knew about it?"

She pondered as the waitress handed us menus. "Two coffees, two ice waters," she told the girl. Coffee, I thought. She really did think I'd grown up. "What shade of lie?" she asked.

I used to think everyone did this, but in elementary school I learned that, unlike our family, most people only believed in white lies and real lies. I looked around the drugstore until I caught sight of a businessman in a blue suit with a dark gray tie. "About like that." I tilted my head to indicate the man. "Like his tie." It was a sign of how much I'd learned from Mrs. Sampson that I didn't point, as I'd have done a couple months before.

"Pretty bad, then," she said. "Any extenuating circumstances?"

"Not that I know of. Maybe the opposite. Is there such a thing as un-extenuating circumstances?"

The waitress unloaded two glasses of water onto our table,

followed by coffees, sugar and cream. "You ready to order?" she asked, canting her hip in a decidedly Glynis-type fashion. I recognized her, a county girl who'd graduated a few years ago. Not particularly smart or pretty or nice, though she probably had qualities that weren't visible to strangers.

"We'll need to look at the menus," Mama said, in a voice that wasn't exactly chastening, but seemed to say: *you might want to pay closer attention, young lady*. Mama looked pointedly at my elbows resting on the coffee-stained menu. I snatched them away. "If you could give us a minute or two," she told the girl.

I picked up my menu to study it. Hamburgers, grilled cheese, fried egg sandwiches. French fries. If I could have eaten french fries at every meal, I would have.

"Is this something you want to talk with me about?" she asked.

"I don't know if I can," I told her. I might be lying to my mother about any number of things at the moment, lies of both commission and omission, but at least I could be honest about the fact that there were things I wasn't telling her. "It's pretty complicated."

The girl returned, plucked her order book from her apron pocket and slouched into her hip-leaning pose again, slightly more sullen than she'd been on her last visit. "I'll have the sliced peach and cottage cheese salad," my mother told her, without glancing at the menu.

French fries and hamburger, french fries and grilled cheese, french fries and—

"Me, too." At a stern glance from Mama, I corrected myself. "I mean I'll have the same, please. Thank you." The girl scribbled something indecipherable on her notepad, her handwriting as bad as her posture. When she'd left, my mother resumed our conversation. "Is anyone in any danger?" she asked. "From these lies?"

"Physical danger, no," I said. "Financial danger, maybe. But not much, at least not yet."

She leaned across the table. I didn't point out that her elbows were now firmly planted on her paper placemat. "Are you in any danger, Mathilda Lee?"

When she called me Mathilda Lee, I definitely couldn't lie to her. But I hadn't figured out enough to know how to phrase the whole truth. "Um, no, not really," I stalled. "I mean, nothing I'd call actual danger." She didn't look convinced. "Nothing I can't handle."

"You'd tell me?" she asked.

"I would, I mean I will—when I can," I stammered. "Soon. I think I can handle it."

The waitress returned with our platters and stood impatiently until we leaned back to allow her to slide them onto our placemats. "Anything else?" she asked, bored.

"No, thank you," Mama said. "That will be all for now." She scrutinized me over our plates: scoops of cottage cheese resting on lettuce leaves, upside-down canned peach halves sitting at a rakish angle to the cottage cheese. Curds. I'd ordered curds. She seemed to see something that satisfied her. She raised her spoon, and sliced it into her peach. I did the same.

In the middle of chores on Tuesday morning, I pulled Joey behind the chicken coop. "There's something I've got to tell you—about our field." I grabbed his arm before he lit off down the path. "Don't worry. Nothing's happened to it, but a couple of people know about it now—one on purpose and one by accident."

He scowled. "Who?"

"The Kudzu King," I said, "and Danny."

"Which one was the accident?"

I stared at the dusty ground, remembering the porch swing, the sofa. "The Kudzu King,"

"You told Danny?" he accused.

"I had to," I said. "I was trying to convince him not to do something. Anyhow, he's not our problem. He knows it's our field and he thinks it's great. I told him it was all your idea."

"Well, how can the Kudzu King be a problem?" he asked.

"It's kudzu. He's the king of it." That was one of the things I'd grown to like about Joey. Logic trumped disappointment.

But he didn't know everything. "He wants to use it. Our field, us starting it, everything. He wants to say it's all him and use our field to show off to everyone, since the Johnsons' one is gone. He even cut some of our kudzu off the porch."

"I thought it was you who did that." He scuffed the dirt with the toe of his sneaker. "What'd you tell him?"

"Not a chance."

"It's our field." He stared toward Aunt Mary's, as if he could see it through the woods. "It's ours."

I leaned against the henhouse, kicking it absently with my heel. Inside, the chickens cackled their complaints. "What if we show it off instead?"

"How?"

"I'm going to be onstage Saturday night," I reminded him. "In front of the entire county."

The smile slowly rose up his face. "That you are, Mattie."

When my eyes opened at 4:45 the next morning, I eased out of bed, my bare feet flat on the floor so I wouldn't wake Lynnette or the girls, dressed and tiptoed into Joey's room. My hand went over his mouth before I shook him awake. His eyes were wild, but he didn't speak. "Shh," I whispered. "Come on."

Glazed with sleep, he followed me downstairs, with a detour to Daddy's study so I could pick up a few things before we headed to the woods. As we stepped around Aunt Mary's house, our field emerged in the soft early light. I pulled him to the porch steps. "Sit with me a minute."

We sat on the top step, arms around our knees. Light seemed to rise from the kudzu, brightening the gray leaves to green. Behind us, the house breathed easily, as if Aunt Mary approved of what we'd done. Joey, caught up in his kudzu, didn't notice. "That's ours," I said.

"And everybody will see it," he said. "We're going to be famous, Matts."

"Here." I handed him a list I'd made, along with the wide-nib pen and ink I'd borrowed from Daddy's desk drawer.

"You want us to bring the kitchen table?" he asked.

"Well, you can take the silverware out of the drawer first," I said.

That afternoon we were to have our final Kudzu Queen class, Mrs. Sampson's last chance to transform us into well-behaved young ladies. At breakfast, Lynnette asked if Rose would be at the Sampson's.

"Probably."

Aggie carefully separated her eggs from her grits.

"How are you getting there?" Lynnette asked.

"Danny," I told her. "He and Joey are picking up some fertilizer at the feed store. Why?"

"Just curious," Lynnette said. "I'll come with you, if you don't mind." Aggie froze for a moment.

"I think that's an excellent idea," Mama said, ladling grits onto Lynnette's plate.

Aggie began eating again. In the past few days, I'd noticed Aggie listening more than she used to, as if she might be considering leaving Aggieland and applying for citizenship in the world with the rest of us.

Lynnette and I walked briskly from the feed store so we wouldn't be late, passing gardens of peonies and lilies, gardenias and hydrangeas, with lawns that ranged from perfect swaths of velvety green to clover patches erupting in dandelions. I heard a lazy click of heels behind us on the sidewalk: Glynis, in no apparent hurry to arrive on time.

Rose waited on the porch, the door shut behind her. She slipped me two molasses cookies wrapped in waxed paper and whispered, "These're from Raquel. No kitchen time for you today. Stick them in your purse." No kitchen time? Not even a minute? Lynnette looked even more disappointed than I felt, her shoulders collapsing as if she'd been deflated.

Rose rested her hand on Lynnette's shoulder. "It's a good thing," she said.

When Lynnette and I opened the door to the Sampson parlor, we discovered an entire trousseau of white dresses in chiffon, satin, and organza, laid out over every sofa and chair. Behind them stood a flock of beaming women: my mama and the other mothers—though not Mrs. Carpentier—plus Mrs. Sampson, Miss Eleanora Dunne, and Miss Edna from Lynnette's church. Each dress was gathered at the waist with a green sash the color of spring leaves. White satin pumps peeked out from under the dresses, identical except for size.

"It's fitting day!" Mrs. Sampson called gleefully. "Come in, girls, and see the magic these ladies have wrought for you!" Mama stood behind a sofa, where a dress in my exact size lay spread across the cushions. She sent me a Katherine Hepburn wink.

Lynnette pushed me forward. "Go in," she whispered. "Your dress is waiting."

But then I saw Mama give a small nod at the dress next to mine.

There was no way on earth Mama could have made that dress in the week and a half since Lynnette's mother had died. She had to have begun it weeks before. In that moment, I was grateful beyond all measure to be her daughter.

"So's yours," I said, reaching behind to take Lynnette's hand. "Come on."

Mama drove us home, with Lynnette and me sharing the front seat so our dresses could have the back seat to themselves. As we passed through town, I saw that Joey had modified the Kudzu Festival flyers according to my instructions, with Danny's help. *Location to be Announced* now appeared over the words "Cooper County Model Kudzu Field."

As soon as we arrived, the beaming mother vanished and the bossy one reappeared. She ordered us to take sponge baths and proceeded to spend the rest of the afternoon making adjustments.

It was a repetitive process: stand still to avoid being stuck, wait while she examined her alterations, at the crook of her finger remove dress and stand in our undies while she stitched or ripped a seam. Repeat, repeat, repeat. Even Lynnette's infinite patience frayed a little. I caught her sighing and shifting from foot to foot before we were released to set the table.

Joey was assigned chickens and milking on top of his usual pig chores, so Lynnette and I wouldn't get dirty. The girls got off easy, playing with spools in the corner. Aggie patiently constructed towering edifices, which Catherine gleefully swept into chaos.

After supper, Mama gave us a forty-minute reprieve with the admonition that we were to wipe our faces and under our arms with damp cloths and dry off. "I've put enough sweat into these dresses already. You girls are not going to perspire all over my hard-fought chiffon."

We flopped down, Lynnette on her cot and me on my bed, flat on our faces. "She's tough, your mama," Lynnette said.

"Now you know," I told her.

"But it was nice of her," she said wistfully. "Do you think my mama—?"

"She would've helped if she could," I said. "She would have wanted to make that whole dress for you."

"She would have, wouldn't she?" Lynnette said.

On that, we drifted off into pin-prodded dreams until we woke to Mama yelling from the foot of the stairs, "Girls! Get cleaned up and get down here. We have work to do."

Joey wisely vanished—Mama was never at her most cheerful with a needle in hand. She finally released us so Lynnette could read to her sisters. "Get out of my way." Mama brandished a threaded needle at us. "You are not to even dream of seeing these until Saturday, when I expect these beauties"— implying, I assumed, the dresses, not us—"to be ready for the cover of *Vogue*."

There was no kudzu cultivation class that Thursday, since there was no kudzu to cultivate, but I couldn't stay away. Once you start a habit, it's hard to get rid of it. Of Lynnette's house, only the chimney remained, awkwardly aiming for the sky. Everything else was mostly ash and charred lumber. I saw the Kudzu King truck parked behind what had been the sleeping porch, but no Kudzu King. I didn't see any reason to go looking for him.

After breakfast on Friday morning, Mama disappeared, assigning clean-up to Lynnette and me. As we were drying and putting away the last dishes, she called from upstairs, "Lynnette? Mattie? Aggie and Catherine? My room. Three minutes."

It wasn't until I closed the cupboard door that I realized there was no Catherine in her usual corner, playing with kitchen implements Mama had left with her, and no Aggie observing small creatures on the stoop. "Where are they?" I asked as Lynnette as we climbed the stairs.

"Playing house," she said. "With Joey."

We got to the upstairs landing in time to hear Catherine order, "Sleep, baby," as she and Aggie emerged from Joey's room, looking satisfied. Joey lay on his bed, afghan tucked to his chin, thumb in his mouth. Talk about your never-ceasing wonders.

In my parents' room, my mother stood with an array of familiar white and gold bags spread across her bed. "Aggie, you first," she said. "Close your eyes and open your hands."

Aggie, who'd never gone willingly to anyone besides Lynnette or Danny, went straight to my mother, eyes shut, palms spread. Mama drew Aggie's hands together to make a flat surface on which she placed a magnifying glass banded by black metal. "Open your eyes."

Aggie gripped the ridged handle and held the glass between her face and the bedspread. Over her shoulder I could see the ridges of the white chenille grown larger, like a field of cotton. Her face rose to meet my mother's and she smiled. Mama smiled back.

"And," Mama said, "one more thing." She reached into one of the Dewitt's bags, and pulled out something the bright green of new kudzu leaves. When she shook it out, I saw that it was a dress, smocked on the bodice, with a pleated skirt. Aggie never wore dresses if she could help it. But she laid the magnifying glass on the bed and took the dress by the shoulders. She held it at arm's length, turning it to examine it, and looked again at my mother.

"Thank you," she said.

"You're welcome," Mama said, rewarding Aggie's manners with her own, as she'd always done with me. Next, she took a large bag from the bed, held it behind her back and crouched down. "Now, Catherine, it's your turn. Which hand is your present in?"

Catherine studied my mother with the deep thought required by such a question. I wasn't sure she'd ever been given a present in her life, apart from used toys and clothes from the church donations bin. When she pointed to the left, Mama held out the bag to Catherine, saying, "What a smart little girl you are!"

Catherine looked to Lynnette, as if asking for permission.

"Go on," Lynnette said.

Catherine reached for the bag, which was as big as she was—and clutched it, unopened. "Thank you," she said, unprompted.

Mama laughed. "Don't you want to open it and see what's inside, sweetie?"

Catherine peered at my mother, as if that were a possibility she hadn't considered. Carefully setting the bag on the floor, she pulled it open. She extracted several pieces of white tissue, then a large doll with blond ringlets and a rosebud mouth, dressed in a frilly white frock.

When Catherine's eyes slid up, Mama said, "What are you going to name your baby?"

Catherine clutched everything tightly to her chest—doll, bag and tissue paper—and surveyed us slowly. "Lynnie."

From another bag, Mama pulled a smaller green dress, identical to Aggie's, and handed it over Catherine's head to Lynnette. "So there can be two pretty little girls in the family." Catherine, absorbed in laying her doll down to make its eyes close and standing it up so they'd pop open, didn't even notice.

"And now," Mama went on, "for my big girls." I wondered how Lynnette felt, hearing that. Had her mother ever said, "my girls"? Mrs. Johnson had kept such a tentative hold on everything, from her children to her own life, that the possessive pronoun might have felt presumptuous to her.

From inside a large DeWitt's bag, Mama pulled two smaller ones and handed them to Lynnette and me. "Now that you're young ladies," she said. I dreaded looking into my bag. I knew Mama was trying to be nice, but I'd seen what was on that counter. Underwear.

Lynnette drew something long and white from her bag. "Oh," she said. "Silk."

I looked in my bag, and yes, I had silk, too. A long slip trimmed in soft lace, with matching brassiere and panties, a far cry from the cotton Carters I'd worn my whole life. I drew the cool silk of the slip over my hand. Lynnette pressed hers to her flushed face.

"Keep looking," Mama said. "There's more."

Under loosely crumpled white tissue paper, we each found a blue leather box with a gold clasp.

"Open them," Mama said. She wore the expression I'd seen on Joey's face on Christmas morning. Watching us open her presents was like unwrapping one of her own.

I pressed the tiny gold button and the clasp popped open. When I lifted the lid, I saw a string of pearls nestled onto navy velvet.

"You, too, Lynnette," Mama urged, and Lynnette slowly opened her box.

"They're real," Mama said. "Here, let me help you." She unsnapped the two navy velvet ribbons that kept my pearls in place. "Lift your hair, Mattie." When I did, she clasped the pearls behind my neck and turned me to face her. "Beautiful," she breathed, then did the same for Lynnette.

Nobody had a mother like this.

# 21

Mama insisted everyone go to bed early that night. "And don't stay up all hours talking," she warned Lynnette and me. "If you don't get your beauty sleep, I won't be held accountable for the results. There's only so much cosmetics can do."

All through the house, lights were out at 6:15, hours before the sun thought about setting.

I meant to sleep. Really I did. But it was the night of Rose's Kudzu Queen competition. I lay still, waiting for everyone to fall asleep so I could go see, just for a little while.

The girls drifted off quickly, swaddled in their quilts. Catherine had her arm wrapped around her new doll, and Aggie lay with her head buried under her pillow. Lynnette pulled her cot close to my bed and leaned over. "Mattie, does Aggie seem different to you?" she whispered.

I thought back over the past few days. "Well, she's talking some. Not whole conversations, but when someone says something, she might answer."

She lay back and looked at the ceiling. "Your mama's good for her, but I think she misses ours. She's taken to disappearing a lot lately."

"Lynnette," I said. "Aggie's been disappearing her whole life."

I waited for her to say something else, but after a while her breathing deepened. I was just sticking my foot out of the covers when I heard Mama and Daddy talking down the hall.

"...told me that ... so I'm concerned about...," Mama said.

"Do you think we should...?" Daddy answered.

I jerked my foot back. Their conversation went on so long I started to worry about missing Rose's competition entirely. I couldn't catch the meaning of a single sentence, though my neck ached from straining to listen. I wondered if they were talking about me.

Finally, they stopped. When the whole house was heavy with sleep, I pulled on my brown dress and school shoes, invisible and practical, and slipped downstairs and out the kitchen door. I hoped I'd be there to see Rose get her tiara. Surely there was a tiara for her competition too.

It took fifteen minutes to get to the far side of Daddy's traditional cotton field, even running all out. At the edge of Mr. Moore's field, I paused, breathing in the sweet smell of tobacco while I wiped sweat off my face with the back of my hand. Under the gibbous moon, I couldn't see a sprig of kudzu in Mr. Moore's field, though a few of the neighboring fields had paltry patches of it planted amidst the corn and tobacco. His crops, like Daddy's, grew better than anyone's, so if he'd planted kudzu, he'd have had plenty of it by now. Beyond the neighbors' fields sat the juke joint, now quiet and dark. Even the flashing neon "COLD BEER" sign had been turned off.

Across the dirt road, the AME Zion Church stood shining by the river. The far side of the church was the darkest, so I snuck around and crouched under a thick azalea, a little ways from the side door. I could just see through a window, cracked open for the breeze: pews packed with families in Sunday clothes, mothers swatting fussy children. Over a hundred people sat inside that church and as far as I could see, not a one of them was white. The front doors stood wide open, but I wasn't going in.

On the chancel, a plump lady braced her hands on the pulpit, the sleeves of her purple chiffon dress riding up her wrists. "And I can tell you for a fact," she said, catching her breath as if she'd already spent a good bit of it talking, "that my Betty here is just smart as a whip. Smart and good, pure in word and deed—and isn't she the most prettiest girl you've even seen?"

I couldn't tell much about the purity of the girl standing beside her, but she was certainly well blessed with bosom, particularly for a girl that short. She fidgeted from one foot to the other, picking at her long lilac dress like she was trying to pry out a cocklebur, and staring over the audience as if she desperately hoped she'd get called up to heaven right then and there.

Five girls sat behind the pulpit, wearing dresses that ranged from peacock blue to cranberry to lemon chiffon. One of the two empty chairs beside them was surely for poor Betty, but where was Rose? I peered over the windowsill, but instead of Rose, I caught sight of Mr. James T. Cullowee sitting on the far side of the chancel, looking thoughtful and interested. Startled, I ducked below the window ledge. I'd known he knew about Rose's pageant, but it had never occurred to me he'd be part of it.

The side door opened and a yellow rectangle of light flooded out. "That child hasn't got the brains of a ground squirrel. I don't care what her mama says." I couldn't see who was behind the door, but the voice was creaky and sharp, an old lady's voice. "So do you want me to tell the truth or do you want me to make you look good?"

"The truth, Grandma. You know that." Rose. My heart settled.

"And that Clarissa Tilley?" her grandmother went on. "She'd drop her drawers at a wink from a blind man."

I tried not to laugh, but a small snort escaped.

"Who's there?" Rose stepped out in a gleaming ivory dress, her hair pinned up in a sleek roll, and her face pinned back in a severe scowl. She squinted into the darkness.

I crouched silently, afraid if Rose saw me she'd either tell me to go home or make me come inside. She waited another moment before going back to her conversation. "Grandma, you can't talk about people like that."

"Fine," her grandma replied. "I'll keep my opinions to myself. But you know Evelyn's the only other girl up there that counts besides you."

Evelyn, that was Rose's cousin, the one Mr. Johnson had tried to go after. I remembered her from when Rose and I made her watch our front porch theatricals, but hadn't recognized her, all grown up in her frothy yellow gown.

"Lord, it's almost as hot out here as it is in there," Rose's grandma said. "You might as well go on and bring me back in. They'll be calling us up there any minute now."

The door closed quietly and the rectangle of light disappeared. From inside came the sound of polite applause and a rich voice that had to be the minister. "Thank you, Mrs. Spivey, for that inspiring speech on behalf of your daughter." Though the window, I saw Betty's mother give a satisfied nod and march to her pew, while Betty slunk to the empty seat beside Evelyn.

"Once again," the minister continued, "I'd like to thank the Women's Missionary Society for using their considerable persuasive powers to convince Mr. Johnny Wainwright to close his juke joint on a Friday evening, thus ensuring you would all join us on the right side of the road."

The ladies in the front pew sat upright and stern, despite an "Amen!" from the back row, probably from a grateful wife whose husband wouldn't be spending the evening drinking.

"And now," the minister said, "we'll hear from Mrs. Ida Moore, grandmother to our final young lady, Miss Rose Moore."

Rose slowly guided her grandmother—who barely came to her shoulder—up to the pulpit and stood beside her, fingertips lightly touching the side seams of her skirt. Mrs. Moore stood on tiptoe to peer at the congregation, lips pursed, until she had everyone's attention.

"You've been here a long time this evening, so I'll be brief," she said to the crowd. "You probably expected Rose's mama or daddy to speak for her, but as most of you know, my son's not partial to all this kudzu mess. He tells me you're all going to be left wondering why you fell for such a foolish scheme." She looked over at Mr. Cullowee. "No offense meant, of course."

He smiled and tipped an imaginary hat to her.

"So Luther has asked me to speak for Rose," she went on, "since I know her as well as anybody, and better than most." She nodded to Rose's parents, who sat in the fourth pew.

"My granddaughter—" Her voice scraped like a tin spoon in a cast iron skillet, as if she'd been caught unaware by strong feelings. "My granddaughter," she said again, "is the only girl up here with a lick of sense. Except maybe her cousin Evelyn, if she'd just learn to speak up for herself."

Evelyn bit her bottom lip, as if she hoped that wouldn't count against her.

Rose's grandmother stared up at Rose for a long moment, as if taking her measure. "I don't have to tell you she's beautiful." It was true. The other girls were pretty enough, but Rose was in a different category. "And I won't, because it'll only sound vain, considering the stock she comes from." People laughed, but I was starting to see where Rose got her backbone.

"I have to say, though, it took her some time to grow into her looks. When she was little, she was skinny as a stick and twice as sharp. Not a favorite with the boys, though they all wanted her on their team when they were picking for relay races, with those long legs. There was this one boy—I won't go naming names, because I hope he's learned his lesson by now, but he took to mocking my Rose. Following her home from school most every day, yelling in front of everybody how she was black as a crow and skinny as a snake. But Rose, she didn't tell on him to the teacher. She didn't go crying to her mama or daddy. She just turned around one day after she got sick of listening and packed him a wallop. Broke his nose and blacked his eyes. She had herself quite a temper back then, though she's more or less gotten a handle on it by now."

I wondered if Rose regretted telling her grandma to be honest.

"Back then, it was all she could do to defend herself. But ever since, I've seen her look after others that same way, time and time again. Usually with those brains she's got, but if necessary—" Mrs. Moore grabbed Rose's hand and pulled her close. "This girl you see in front of you, she's got character, and you don't see that every day or in every generation. Good looks come and go. It's character that counts every time." She squeezed Rose's hand. "Every time."

Rose gazed at her grandmother, her face soft in a way I'd never seen. When she bent down to give her a kiss on the cheek, her grandmother pulled a handkerchief from her sleeve and dabbed at Rose's eyes. "Don't you get all weepy on me now." She pushed the hankie into Rose's hand. "You take this and put it to good use."

They leaned close together as Rose walked her grandmother down to her parents' pew, kissing the top of her head before she turned around to go sit with the other girls.

"Thank you, Mrs. Moore," the minister said. "We conclude with a few words from our esteemed judge, Mr. James T. Cullowee, and the crowning of the Riverside Kudzu Queen."

Mr. Cullowee shook the minister's hand and took his place at the pulpit.

"Well, this has been a very enlightening evening. You've set me a hard task, choosing just one queen from such glorious examples of young womanhood. Seven beautiful girls, spoken of so eloquently by their friends and family. But after careful consideration, it's clear to me that the young lady most qualified to be the first Kudzu Queen of the Riverside community is—"

The other girls gripped hands, but Rose held her grandmother's gaze.

"Miss Rose Moore." Mr. Cullowee placed the crown, a plain gold circle, on Rose's head.

"Mr. Moore," he continued, "I hope you're very proud of your daughter. Like you, she is a leader in her community, and I feel sure she will take her responsibilities as seriously as you yourself do." I snuck a look to see what Mr. Moore thought of all this, but his face was blank as polished granite.

I hoped Mr. Cullowee had chosen her because she deserved it, and not to win over her father. Rose was the one who'd carried bitter news to Lynnette and seen her through it, who'd held up a hard clear mirror for me to see myself, who'd rescued me from Glynis, and once, rescued Glynis from herself. Of all the people I knew, Rose was the only one who never tried to make the truth easier, but stood by you until you were able to take it in.

When the Kudzu King bowed and held out his arm to Rose, I was flooded by memories from the day I'd learned to promenade: my hand resting on Mr. Cullowee's arm, his palm warming the small of my back, whirling around the room with him while approving, invisible judges looked on. I wanted to be happy for Rose, but at that precise moment, even after everything that had happened, I wished I were the one arm in arm with the Kudzu King.

I watched them walk together to a barn with its front doors flung wide open, where I heard a band tuning up. The congregation became a party, shedding suit jackets and rolling up sleeves. Everyone seemed happy, even the girls who hadn't won. The band slid seamlessly into a crooning jazz tune. Mr. Cullowee made a frame of his arms, Rose stepped inside, and they began to dance.

# 22

Even potential Kudzu Queens have chores. If I'd expected Sassafras to have mercy on me, I'd expected wrong. She seemed almost gleeful when she kicked over her bucket halfway through the morning milking. The Johnsons' goats, on the other hand, were sweetly soothing. I leaned my face against the older one's haunch as I milked, and felt her rough coat, stiffened by dirt, against my cheek. By the time I left the barn with my bucket, Lynnette had the chickens fed, watered, and relieved of their eggs. That meant baths, first Lynnette and then me.

That morning I lingered, scrubbing parts I usually skimmed over: the spaces between toes and fingers, behind my knees. I lay in the water, listening to bubbles pop as they expired. These are my breasts, I thought, watching them float in the diminishing bubbles. They filled my hands, which they hadn't only a few months earlier. These are what the Kudzu King wanted. At a sound in the hall, I jerked upright, eyeing the door to make sure I'd remembered to lock it.

I climbed out of the bath, leaving my thoughts to drain out with the bath water.

Mama had laid out my new silk underthings beside a clean towel. The underpants felt cool skimming up my legs. The soft lace of the brassiere outlined the top of my bosom.

I wiped steam from the mirror. I didn't look like a woman, but I didn't look like a girl either. My skin between brassiere and panties was paler than my arms or face. Beneath the lacy waistband, my pelvic bones rose. The brassiere made my bosom look like something I was meant to have, not something I'd grown by accident.

Pulling on my bathrobe, I ran to my room. My dress lay on the bed, the skirt spread out as if I'd flopped down mid-twirl, even the pearls laid out in a curve at the throat. Mama stood at the head of the bed. "Not bad," she smiled, "for a ten-thumb seamstress."

I flung my arms around her. "Can I put it on now?"

"Not until just before the parade." We admired her handiwork until she snapped out of her reverie. "Now get into something clean and tidy while I put this in its bag. I have to find Aggie. It may take some wrestling to get her into her dress."

Just before breakfast, Aggie reappeared, thrown over Danny's shoulder like a sack of potatoes. She was smudged with black dust that looked suspiciously like charcoal, which got me wondering if she'd gone to her old house. Danny looked grim, but I would have felt the same way if I'd had to dig her out of whatever she'd gotten herself into. Struggling against Danny, she twisted out of his arms to the ground. He bent down, held her by the shoulders and looked at her, but she wouldn't meet his eyes. His face softened, then hardened again before he stalked out of the house without a word, slamming the kitchen door behind him. It occurred to me that I'd never seen him mad at Aggie before.

"Daniel?" Mama called. I heard his truck start, and Joey ran after him. Mama shook her head and turned to Aggie. "Bath," Mama told her. "Then breakfast."

After Aggie's bath, Lynnette dressed the girls in their new green dresses and sat down to pick at her scrambled eggs. "You finish those," Mama said. "Beauty pageants are grueling work." Lynnette ate dutifully, though she slipped her biscuit onto Aggie's plate, where it remained throughout the breakfast Aggie didn't touch.

Once the kitchen was tidied, Mama stood the girls before her and pushed Aggie's hair out of her eyes. "I believe you both pass muster. Mattie and Lynnette? It's time. Fetch your things." When we returned with the white and gold dress bags Miss DeWitt had donated for each contestant, Mama unzipped them. "Oh my," she sighed, pleased all over again at what she'd wrought. She smoothed the dresses, re-zipped the bags and shook them out for good measure.

She packed us in the car, Lynnette and me in front, the little girls in back, with my train case—which contained everything Mama had determined we'd need, from cosmetics to neatly rolled slips and bathrobes—at their feet and our dresses laid across their laps. "Can you be still the whole way?" she asked Aggie and Catherine. "I don't want those dresses getting wrinkled."

Mama drove as if the car were an extension of her body. The speedometer hovered at precisely twenty-five miles per hour. Her right leg fell and rose under her linen skirt in perfect and opposite reaction to the rise and fall of the road.

At the edge of town, Mama skirted the empty parade vehicles lined up behind the town limit sign. First was Miss DeWitt's white convertible Buick, gleaming in the sunlight with the top down. Even the red leather upholstery shone. As grand marshal, the mayor would lead off the parade in it, with Mrs. Sampson by his side. I imagined Rose being asked to polish the car that morning instead of the silver, but of course she'd probably been lying in bed, basking in the memory of her triumph the night before. Next, Danny would drive the Kudzu King truck, with Mr. Cullowee waving from atop a bed of kudzu. After that would march the Consolidated High School Band, with Bobby Mason on the snare drum. The *piece d'* would be us in our pure white dresses, on a float draped in green and white satin and covered in kudzu, followed by the town council and other vehicles important enough to be included.

The baseball team had volunteered to direct traffic, since downtown Main Street was closed for the parade. On the corner of Washington and Main, Carl stood in his JROTC uniform. He gestured to Mama to wind down her window. "Head down to the school lot. They'll let you in." He leaned into the window. "You look beautiful, Mattie. You're going to win for sure."

It's probably not a good idea to roll your eyes at a boy who could be your boyfriend, but I couldn't help it. Fortunately, he didn't see. "You look pretty too, Lynnette. Those your sisters?"

"Thanks." Lynnette blushed. "Aggie and Catherine, say hello to Carl," she said. Aggie gazed, unblinking, over Carl's shoulders. Catherine waved her pudgy fingers.

As we turned off Main Street, I saw green streamers woven around every porch railing and garlanding every streetlight. The viewing stand was jammed with spectators who'd arrived early to stake their claims. I could hardly see the curb for all the kids perched on it or the sidewalk for their parents. Carl caught me looking back and waved.

Mama eased into the parking lot behind the school. She handed me the train case, draped the dress bags carefully over our outstretched arms and led us around to the front, where we threaded our way through people who'd claimed front-row seats on the school steps.

Over the entrance hung three banners: Mr. Cullowee's "Kudzu! The Crop of the Future!" at the top, a "First Annual Cooper County Kudzu Queen Pageant" in the middle, and the Cooper County Consolidated High School banner at the bottom.

After weeks of Queen classes, I was about to get my face smoothed and improved, to wear a dress I couldn't have imagined owning six months ago, to walk as I'd learned to walk and talk as I'd learned to talk and to hope that out of six girls that evening, I'd be chosen the most beautiful and graceful and talented.

And at the same time, I hoped I wouldn't. It seemed foolish to think that any amount of lipstick and chiffon could make me beautiful or that I'd become graceful after a couple months of tea drinking and perambulating. And my feelings about the Kudzu King were so complicated that I didn't know what to do with them. What if I won? How would I know if I deserved it or if—despite everything I'd said—he thought we'd made a deal and rigged the contest?

I nudged Lynnette with my shoulder as we walked up the steps. "I think you should win."

Her close-mouthed laugh came out as a snort. "Not likely. It's going to be you."

I shook my head.

"You've got as much a chance as anybody," she said, "and more than some."

But first I had to spend the day standing and smiling and

waving in the hot sun, hoping Glynis didn't take a sudden notion to shove me off the float.

Downstairs, I discovered that an almost infinite amount of chaos could be created in a high school locker room by a few girls and their mothers, sisters, and brothers. Dress bags hung everywhere. Pancake make-up, lipstick tubes, mascara, and powder compacts lined the edges of sinks below smeared mirrors. Girls sat half-dressed on stools from the chemistry lab. Ann Marie's little brothers darted between us, and Alice's sister wailed in a bassinet beside a shower stall. Shouts and slamming toilet stall doors, courtesy of Ann Marie's brothers, echoed off the pale green tiled walls. In the center of this bedlam, Mrs. Carpentier perched on the stool her daughter should have occupied. In her fuchsia suit, she hunched over a yawning black patent leather purse, directing her sharp nose and sharper green eyes toward the contents as if she might have a tiny vial of patience lurking in there. Mama planted my train case on a sink and hung our dresses.

"Girls? Girls!" Mrs. Sampson's head appeared in the doorway, followed by the rest of her in a reassuringly calm blue dress. "Whatever you're doing, stop!" The silence was interrupted only by Alice's sister's mournful wail. Five girls and four mothers looked up. Mrs. Carpentier remained intent on exploring her handbag. "Ladies," Mrs. Sampson said. "I'll need to borrow your daughters to rehearse the order of this evening's pageant. Girls, please follow me."

Mabel raised her hand as if she were in school, which in fact she was. "Mrs. Sampson?"

In the doorway, Mrs. Sampson turned back. "Yes?"

"I don't think Glynis has arrived yet," Mabel said, with apology in her voice, as if she felt guilty about bringing Glynis's tardiness to Mrs. Sampson's attention.

Mrs. Carpentier looked up. "She's coming," she drawled. Having found a slightly bent cigarette in her purse, she lit it, took a long drag, and exhaled smoke in the direction of Alice's sister's bassinet. "She had to—" Apparently her waving hand, trailing smoke, was all that was necessary to explain whatever Glynis had to do.

Mrs. Sampson blinked. I could practically see her push down her anger. "Girls? If you'll come with me? Ladies, I'll return your daughters shortly."

We followed Mrs. Sampson up the locker room steps, with Alice and me at the end of the line. "Where do you think she is?" Alice asked, scurrying to keep up. Even with her giraffe legs, she struggled to match Mrs. Sampson's forced march. "Do you think she'll be here in time?"

I shrugged. "Don't know and don't care."

"But I thought she was your best friend," Alice insisted.

"I thought she was yours," I said, not very kindly. But at least my retort halted that line of conversation, and allowed me to continue the daydream I was beginning to entertain: the sash being lowered over my body, the tiara gently placed on my head.

The stage had stayed up since last week's graduation, though the scuffs of Sunday shoes had been waxed from the wooden floors. The podium now stood at a jaunty angle on the far side. A platform covered the back of the stage, with room for all of us to stand. A pleated white satin skirt hung from the platform, green ribbon sewn across it as if a continuous vine spread from one side to the other. A longer satin skirt hung from the stage itself, also garlanded in green.

Below the stage, in front, three seats were set apart with gold rope.

Mrs. Sampson led us by two rows of chairs between the locker room stairs and the stage. "You girls will wait here with your mothers to be called between events." She pointed to a table, on which sat a box with *Alfred Williams & Co., Raleigh, North Carolina* printed in ornamental script across the lid. "These are our programs for this evening. I'll have one for each of you," she said. "We'll leave your talent accoutrements here, so you can pick them up as you go onstage."

"Mrs. Sampson?" I raised my hand. "My brothers are bringing my things onto the stage. Is that all right?"

She looked over her glasses at me. "Are they responsible?"

"Yes, ma'am," I said.

"And will they be dressed properly?"

"They wouldn't dare not be," I told her, adding a belated, "ma'am."

"This isn't anything I should know about in advance, is it, Mathilda?" she asked.

"No, ma'am. You can trust me. This is my best talent."

We followed Mrs. Sampson up the steps to the stage. She arrayed us across the platform and told us to remember our places. Next she had us cross to the center of the stage, lifting the heels of our school shoes to mimic our pageant pumps, and stand behind the microphone as if being interviewed by an invisible master of ceremonies. No matter how nervous we felt, she reminded us, "A lady always displays a calm demeanor."

After our pretend interviews, Mrs. Sampson led us down to the locker room, but halted at the door. "If I let you in now, your mothers will get their hands on you and we won't finish. A pageant mother is a dangerous creature." She held up three fingers. "You'll have only three minutes to change into your gowns while the band plays one number."

We'd returned to the stage, to practice perambulating in our imaginary gowns, when Glynis strolled into the gym, wearing sleek black trousers, a lime-green blouse unbuttoned to her brassiere, black pumps, and lipstick the color of deoxygenated blood. Just inside the double doors, she struck a classic Glynis pose: hip cocked, head tilted, hands thrust in her pockets.

"Nice of you to join us, Miss Carpentier," Mrs. Sampson said. "Your mother is waiting downstairs." Mabel and I looked at one another. Wasn't Mrs. Sampson going to tell Glynis the order of events? Glynis gave a careless shrug and disappeared downstairs.

When we returned to the locker room, Mrs. Sampson abandoned us to our mothers, murmuring that she had things to attend to. I envied her easy escape.

Mama immediately ordered us to strip down to our underwear and put on our new silk slips and our bathrobes. Then she planted Lynnette on a stool. "Sit. I want to do this properly."

Mrs. Carpentier wet a washrag and handed it to Glynis. "Off. Every last speck. We're starting fresh." Glynis rolled her eyes before applying the wet cloth to her face. Ann Marie's little brothers had collapsed in a heap in a corner, and Alice's sister had finally worn herself out and gone to sleep, a stream of snot trailing from her nose to her mouth. Aggie and Catherine sat perched on the raised edge of a shower stall, watching.

Mama held Lynnette's chin in her hand and used it as a pivot to tilt her face until it caught the light to her liking. She dotted Lynnette's face with foundation and spread it in wide arcs with her thumbs. "How is it," Mama asked, "that you have absolutely no pores?" By this time she was brushing lip liner across Lynnette's mouth, with her thumb on Lynnette's chin to steady it, so she probably wasn't expecting an answer.

In the past, I'd certainly have said that Lynnette was pretty, but if pressed, I'd have had to explain that she had sort of a plain face. But under Mama's hands, Lynnette's face came alive. Her washy freckles disappeared beneath the smooth foundation. Her pale lashes, made visible by mascara, were ridiculously long, in dark contrast to her bottle-green eyes. I'd heard of actresses like that. On the street you'd never know them, but once the makeup artists started with brushes and tubes, their natural beauty emerged, as if it had been waiting for the right moment to come out of hiding. Myrna Loy, I'd heard, was like that. Lynnette saw me looking and smiled wanly. "How bad do I look?"

I let my breath out. I hadn't realized I'd been holding it. "You're beautiful."

"I do good work, don't I?" Mama said. "But I had good materials to start with." She spun Lynnette to the mirror. I'd expected her to be astonished, but she merely nodded.

"Good." Mama shoved Lynnette gently off the stool. "All right, Miss Mathilda."

Alice's mother was applying lipstick so close to the color of Alice's lips I wondered why she bothered. She'd drawn her daughter's hair into a tight bun that stretched the skin on her forehead and temples. Mabel did her own make-up while her mother offered approving murmurs. Mrs. Carpentier seemed to have forgotten the cigarette hanging from her mouth as she fiercely dabbed concealer on Glynis's neck. "I told you to be more careful," she said through clenched lips.

Mama smoothed foundation over my face and down my neck. Her hands felt cool and gentle, reminding me of times I'd had a fever, when she'd rest her hands on my hot face, leaving islands of comfort everywhere.

"Look up." She drew a line under my lower lashes while I surveyed the ceiling tiles. "Now close your eyes softly. Don't clench them." She brushed shadow over my eyelids. The eyeliner tickled as she drew it around my eyes. Finally she swept mascara over my lashes, combing out stray blobs with a tiny brush too small even for Catherine's new baby doll.

Lynnette sat beside Aggie on the edge of the shower stall and placed Catherine in her lap. "Front row seats," she said. Aggie pressed her face to Lynnette's shoulder as if the room were too bright for her eyes. Catherine patted Lynnette's rouged cheek. "Pretty," she said.

Glynis sneered over her mother's shoulder with a look that said emphatically, *I'm not here. I'm in a much better place with people far more entertaining than you.*

"Make a fish face," Mama said. I sucked in my cheeks and she touched the part that remained. "These are your apples, where the blusher goes."

Alice's mother stepped back to evaluate her handiwork and gave a brusque nod of approval. Alice looked exactly the way she always did. Mabel completed an improved version of her usual make-up, while Ann Marie's mother fluttered around her like an agitated bird, darting in to dab something on her daughter's face, which she immediately wiped off with a cotton ball. I wondered if Ann Marie's face would be finished before she had to dress, or if she'd end up looking like a bad paint-by-numbers kit.

Mama did my lips in layers, starting with a lip liner just outside my natural lips. She followed with my new red lipstick, and completed her masterpiece by painting Vaseline on my lips and eyebrows, switching brushes between the two. Then she covered everything with powder to set it. "Voilà!" she announced, spinning me to face the mirror.

Even in the warped streaky mirror I looked different: older, sophisticated, as if I knew things that up to this point I'd been pretty much guessing about. "Come here a minute, Lynnie," I said. With the two of us next to each other, you could tell the same hand had decorated us both, but Mama had used her brushes and powders and creams to emphasize what made us each ourselves. She'd heightened Lynnette's green eyes, while she'd featured my mouth, which looked as lush as if it had been made for the movies.

Mama stood behind us and wrapped her arms around our shoulders. "My two beauties," she said. "The judges are going to have to declare a tie."

At a knock, everyone froze and looked at each other, a hodgepodge of slips and robes, and faces in various stages of transformation. Then the door opened and Mrs. Sampson squeezed through. "Only me," she reassured. "One hour. Does anyone need anything?"

"Bobby pins, please!" called Ann Marie's mother.

"Have you got any smokes on you?" Mrs. Carpentier drawled.

Alice's mother, preoccupied with pulling Alice's hair back more tightly, said nothing.

"I think we're all right," Mama said.

Mrs. Sampson gave a grateful smile to Mama. "Bobby pins, coming up," she said before closing the door. I wondered if she missed the Queen classes, when all she'd had to manage was a bunch of unruly girls.

The next half hour passed in a blur of hairstyling. Pin curls were unpinned, brushed out and re-pinned into upsweeps and pompadours. Alice's hair was released from its torture while Ann Marie's was pinned into submission. "I have two pairs of stockings for each of you," Mama told us. "Run one, you've got a back-up.

Run both and it's the fingernail polish for you, young ladies," she said, waving a clear bottle.

Finally she draped a pale peach scarf loosely around my hair and face. "I haven't done all this work to have anything smeared at the last moment," she said. She slid the dress over my head, keeping the fabric from touching my face or hair, then whisked off the scarf, buttoned up the tiny satin-covered buttons at the back, fastened my new pearls around my neck, and turned me to face the mirror.

"That's my girl," she breathed.

She repeated the process with Lynnette.

"Ready?" she asked.

"Ready," we told her, though I wasn't entirely sure.

We followed Mrs. Sampson from the bowels of the school to the parking lot. I wished I didn't remember Roman history quite so vividly, particularly the Christians being led into the Colosseum to be torn to shreds by lions. Behind me, I heard nervous giggling, until Mrs. Sampson opened the door to the glare of sunlight, where the kudzu-covered float awaited us.

Mercifully, no one was there to see us climb awkwardly up the stepladder that Mr. Sykes, the school janitor, had placed beside the float. Mrs. Sampson directed us to our places: Mabel at the front, flanked just behind by Lynnette and me, then Glynis and Ann Marie, and Alice at the back. Lifting the hem of my dress, I picked my way through the kudzu—Joey's and my kudzu, I suspected—careful not to snag a heel. Mama seemed far away, though she was just below with the other misty-eyed mothers. Even Mrs. Carpentier ransacked her monstrous purse for a hankie, which she handed to Alice's mother after dabbing the corners of her own eyes. Mama wiped her cheek with the back of her hand.

Mrs. Sampson surveyed us, probably trying to figure out if there was anything else she could do before launching us. Her bosom rose and fell in a deep breath. "You're on your own until this evening, young ladies," she said. "But I'll be watching you."

"Out of the eyes in the back of her head," Glynis muttered.

When Mr. Sykes started the tractor with a rumble and a gurgle of smoke, we grabbed one another to keep from falling. As soon as the float stabilized, Ann Marie and Glynis jerked their hands away from one another's shoulders. Lynnette stared at her feet. I gave her a squeeze before I let go.

Mama blew us kisses and followed the rest of the mothers to Main Street, where Daddy was saving seats on the viewing stand. "Look for us when you pass!" she called, holding out her hands for Aggie and Catherine.

As we drove toward the beginning of the parade route, I concentrated on my posture, trying to push my shoulders back without thrusting my bosom too far forward. Mabel glanced back at Lynnette and me with her sweet, uncomplicated smile.

The other parade vehicles awaited us at the town limits. Mr. and Mrs. Sampson sat in the open convertible, but while the bed of Mr. Cullowee's truck was full of kudzu, the cab was empty. Float committee members, the town council, and the entire Consolidated marching band milled about, but I didn't see Danny or Mr. Cullowee anywhere. The mayor peered at his watch. Mrs. Sampson placed her handbag in her lap, reconsidered, and moved it beside her on the seat.

No Mr. Cullowee. No Danny.

Finally, Mr. Cullowee appeared between two houses, his head tucked down. He leaned over the passenger door of the convertible and spoke to Mrs. Sampson. Her shoulders jerked in a startled twitch, but she snapped open the latch on her handbag, extracted something and handed it to him. Mr. Cullowee, still bent over, thanked her and went back between the houses. When he returned, his face looked blotchy in the sunlight, and gray around the left eye.

"Do you think he's all right?" Lynnette whispered.

"Don't know," I said.

"Isn't Danny supposed to drive him?" she asked.

"Supposed to."

Without any more fuss, things seemed to settle into place. Mr.

Cullowee vaulted over the side rail of his truck to stand atop the mound of kudzu. One of the town council members climbed into the driver's seat and started the engine.

The mayor began waving as he started up Main Street. Mrs. Sampson pasted a stiff smile on her face. I wondered what Mr. Cullowee had said to her. Mr. Cullowee himself smiled quite naturally at the crowd. The marching band fell in behind the Kudzu King truck, playing "You're a Grand Ol' Flag" followed by "Yankee Doodle Dandy." With our perfect faces and magnificent dresses we stood atop swells of kudzu as if we were mermaids rising from a green sea.

On the edge of town, people sat in kitchen chairs in their front yards, sipping sweet tea or lemonade. Behind us, town council members waved from their cars and the fire truck blasted its siren to cheers from the spectators. Mr. Aronson, who had to be about a hundred years old, brought up the tail end of the parade in his antique Chevrolet roadster. No public event was complete without the founder of Aronson's grocery.

I scanned the growing crowd for Danny. By the time we neared downtown, the sidewalks were packed. I bestowed my queen wave on the populace to my left, while Lynnette waved to those on our right. I found myself wondering if I'd been mistaken about Danny driving the Kudzu King truck when I was distracted by people jumping to their feet. They pushed forward, reaching for the kudzu candy Mr. Cullowee flung from his truck. On the sidewalk in front of Aronson's stood Carl and his dad, the store's employees gathered in a knot behind them. The right side of Carl's mouth lifted in a smile of pure appreciation that made the blush start at my neck and shoot straight to my hairline. It didn't help when he stuck two fingers in his mouth and whistled.

"I think he likes you," Lynnette said, without moving her lips.

"What gives you that idea?" I wished Mama had sewn pockets in my dress, so I'd have something to shove my hands into.

At the hardware store next door, the rest of the baseball team sat on the railing, swinging their legs, but Danny wasn't with them. On the feed store porch, old men rocked and spat. In the shadows at the backs of store awnings and the alleys between businesses quietly stood the colored housekeepers and cooks, gardeners and tenant farm families I'd grown up alongside—not drawing attention to themselves.

As they stood on tiptoe, so did I, looking for Rose.

The mayor's car stopped in front of the viewing stand, bringing the parade to a halt. Mama and Daddy rose to their feet and waved wildly, with smiles so big it looked like their ears might get pushed off the sides of their heads. They lifted up Catherine and Aggie, two oddly serious children amidst the joyous pandemonium. Joey leapt up, shouting something I couldn't hear.

"What?" I yelled, glancing ahead to see if Mrs. Sampson had heard my breach of ladylike etiquette. Fortunately the Kudzu King truck and entire marching band were between us.

Joey cupped his hands around his mouth. "We've got the stuff!" he shouted as Mr. Sykes cut off the tractor in a cloud of smoke.

The mayor stood to address the crowd. "Ladies and gentlemen, welcome to the first annual Cooper County Kudzu Festival Parade. We're so enthusiastic about kudzu here we're considering a motion to rename ourselves 'Kudzu County.'" I wasn't entirely sure he was joking.

Then, as if the power of my thoughts had made her materialize, I saw Rose slip through the crowd into the street. She bent down next to Mrs. Sampson and whispered in her ear.

Mrs. Sampson's shoulders stiffened. The mayor went on, "I'd like to express the appreciation of the entire county to the Kudzu Festival committees for doing such a marvelous job. We're grateful to Mr. Rigoli for bringing out the Cooper County Consolidated High School Band and especially to our benefactor, Mr. James T. Cullowee, for the economic advantages he has brought us here in Cooper County. And now Mr. Cullowee will say a few words."

Mrs. Sampson nodded at Rose, who slipped back into the lee of Aronson's grocery.

In the sunlight, I could see that Mr. Cullowee definitely had a shiner, covered up by Mrs. Sampson's make-up.

"Ladies and gentlemen of Cooper County," he proclaimed, "no other county has been such a friend to kudzu as you have been. You have welcomed me into your homes and your hearts. You have planted kudzu in your fields and watched it grow. As I tour the county, I see families that will soon reap the harvest of this miracle vine, as you are transformed into a county others will emulate. You are indeed the great Kudzu County of the United States of America."

After the cheers settled, he went on, "Be sure to join us tonight in the auditorium of the Cooper County Consolidated High School, to be amazed by the most beautiful and talented girls in the county at our first annual Kudzu Queen Pageant." He gestured toward us, Rose and the girls in her pageant already yesterday's invisible news. "We've scoured town and country to bring you these young ladies, one of whom will be crowned your Kudzu Queen. I hope to see you all tonight, cheering on your favorite."

Mr. Sykes started the tractor, and we proceeded onward down the street at about two miles per hour. We passed the drug store, the dress shop, the cinema with its marquee that read "Cooper County Kudzu Festival," Ginger's BBQ, and the library where Miss Perkins stood on the steps, smiling and waving. Big businesses gave way to smaller ones: the shoe repair shop, the stationary store, the secondhand shop. Those gave way to big houses and smaller ones. Our waves faded into lackluster swings, until with relief we reached the eastern edge of town. There the parade took a right, hooked around on Eighth Street, headed back and halted in the school parking lot.

I crouched to loosen my stiff knees and shake out my tortured hands. "After tonight, we won't ever have to be ladylike again for the rest of our lives," I told Lynnette.

Mr. Sykes leaned the stepladder against the float. At the bottom I found myself facing Mrs. Sampson, who laid her hands on my shoulders. She looked as if she wanted to tell me something, but instead pressed her lips shut, then dropped her hands and turned abruptly away.

"Mrs. Sampson?" I called after her, but she shook her head.

Mama rushed up, trailed by the rest of the mothers. She'd always had a good swift stride when she had a purpose.

"Where's Danny?" I asked.

Like Mrs. Sampson, she shook her head.

"Did he see me?"

She held me at arm's length. "I surely hope so. It would break my heart if he missed seeing you like this." She reached for Lynnette. "I'm so proud of you, both of you."

Daddy strode into the parking lot, with Joey scurrying beside him. "There's my girl," he said. "The Queen of Kudzu."

"Shh!" I covered his mouth with my hand. "Don't jinx it!"

"It's not luck, baby girl, it's natural beauty and talent, which you get from me. Well, the talent, anyway. The beauty comes from your mother." He tucked her arm in his. "We're pretty pleased with you, but you probably know that."

"Where's Danny?" I asked him.

"I haven't seen him since this morning," Daddy said, "and I'm not happy about it."

"You look good," Joey told me. "You look like a girl."

I punched him in the shoulder. "I always look like a girl."

Families, neighbors, and friends gathered around girls they knew, oohing and aahing over their dresses. The popular town girls split unevenly, a few of them sucking up to Glynis while the rest crowded around Mabel. Behind the crowds, Rose stood by a dogwood tree.

*Can you come here?* I mouthed silently to her.

She shook her head. *Later*, she mouthed back.

Lynnette swept up her sisters, one in each arm, staggering in her heels. "Did I do all right?" They nodded solemnly.

"Pretty Lynnie." My mother smiled, reaching for Catherine.

Lynnette handed her over, so she could squeeze Aggie in a hug. When she put her sister down, I noticed a smudge on Aggie's bare arm that she hadn't washed off in her morning bath. I licked my thumb to wipe it off, but when I rubbed Aggie's arm, she winced and the smudge stayed. Not a smudge, a bruise.

"Aggie, what happened to—" I started to ask, but Mrs. Sampson held her hand above the crowd and tapped her gold wristwatch.

"It's time, girls."

I'd once seen a picture of Secret Service agents swarming around President Roosevelt as they bundled him out of danger. The pageant mothers were more effective than any Secret Service, hustling us into the school and down to the locker room. "I don't see why we couldn't have stayed longer," I complained to Mama.

"Longer?" Mama asked. "I've barely got time to redo your faces for the competition."

"But the competition doesn't start until six," I objected. "And it's only 4:35."

She counted the list on her fingers: "Undressing. Supper. Outfits. Make-up. Hair. That's two hours' worth and we've got less than an hour and a half."

"How long does it take to put on fresh lipstick?" I asked.

Mama raised her eyebrows in her "have-I-raised-a-fool?" expression and pointed at my dress. "Out. Immediately. And into your bathrobe."

Supper was a brief reprieve: pulled pork, coleslaw, and Jell-O salad, provided by Ginger's BBQ. As soon as we wiped the barbecue sauce from our mouths and washed our hands, Mama grabbed a jar of Pond's and shoved it at us. "Get a big dollop and smear it all over."

The thick cold cream glued my eyelids shut. I reached out blindly for the washrag Mama offered. "Wipe it off and rub in any that's left over while I get out your interview outfits."

Mama had altered a couple of her linen Junior League dresses to fit Lynnette and me. She'd assigned the buttercup-colored one to Lynnette and the green to me. For a woman who, like her daughter, claimed an allergy to sewing needles, she was turning out to be quite handy.

Glynis had chosen a shiny red number, cut low up top and high below, with three large black buttons. It fit as if she'd been poured into it—perfect for an interview at a house of ill repute.

Alice's pink A-line dress and white pinafore were painfully young. Mabel had been invited by Hudson-Belk to choose whatever she wanted to wear, and had, as usual, selected with perfect taste: a cream-colored suit with bone buttons over an ecru silk blouse. Ann Marie's smocked lavender dress from last year rose high on her waist, raising—when I looked at her with pity—a high color in her cheeks that wasn't all blusher.

"Thirty minutes," Mrs. Sampson stuck her head in. "The auditorium is filling up." She caught sight of Ann Marie's little brothers, who were playing a raucous game of hide-and-seek with their mother as home base. "May I borrow these two young men?" Mrs. Sampson asked. "We could use some extra ushers to hand out programs." Ann Marie's mother gratefully agreed.

Mrs. Sampson glanced at the shower stall where Aggie and Catherine had resumed their earlier perch on the ledge. "Perhaps you girls might like to help too?"

Aggie curled her shoulders inward and stared at the tile floor.

"Go on, Aggie," Lynnette said. "Mrs. Sampson is a nice lady. You look after Catherine, all right?" Reluctantly, Aggie rose and held out her hand for Catherine.

"Forward, march," Mrs. Sampson told the little boys. Loving this new game, they did as directed, lifting their knees in exaggerated steps. "Hup-two-three-four," Mrs. Sampson ordered. Mama gave her a salute and mouthed, *Thank you!*

The mothers shifted into high gear: zipping, fastening hooks and eyes, buttoning, holding out jackets, straightening skirts, and redoing hairstyles and make-up. Over the chaos, I heard a knock. Mrs. Carpentier reached behind her and pulled the door open. Rose stood in the doorway. She scanned the room until she saw my mother. "May I speak to Mathilda for a moment, Mrs. Watson?" she asked. "Mrs. Sampson sent a message for her."

"Is it urgent?"

"Yes, ma'am," Rose replied, her face as blank and honest as if she were telling the truth.

Mama held up a finger. "One minute. Mattie, don't blink until that mascara dries."

"Yes, ma'am." I shut the door and leaned my back against it. Upstairs I heard hundreds of feet in the gymnasium, a sound I hadn't noticed in the echoing hubbub of the locker room. There were a million things I wanted to ask Rose, questions that might give me the edge I needed in the pageant, but what could I say without revealing my presence the night before?

She began unbuttoning her white blouse. "Rose?" I asked.

"You be quiet, Mathilda Lee. Look and listen. We only have a minute." She peeled down her white brassiere to show the top curve of one breast.

Even in the shadows of the dim hallway, I could see an ugly bruise above her folded-down brassiere.

She jerked her head at the ceiling. "Him," she said. "Do not let him get you alone."

"What happened?" I asked.

"I won," she said, "and this was my prize."

"Mr. Cullowee did that?"

"Girl," she said bitterly. "He tried worse, but this was as far as he got."

I stared at her. "We should tell...He can't—"

"Mrs. Sampson knows already. I told her. She's all who needs to know. You and her."

"She believed you?"

"She knows me," Rose answered. She took me by the shoulders. "You win this damn thing. And you find a way to make him pay. Tonight."

"But I can't—"

"You damned well can, Mathilda."

Then she whirled me around to face the door. I heard her footsteps running down the hall.

I stumbled into the locker room, dazed. "Mattie?" Mama asked. "Are you all right?"

I caught sight of myself in the mirror. My lips were set in the same tight lines I'd seen on Mrs. Sampson's face after the parade.

"Yes, ma'am, I'm fine," I said. "What do I need to do to get ready?"

# 23

At a quarter till, Mrs. Sampson returned, the little girls and boys now wearing garlands of kudzu. "Fifteen-minute countdown." She pointed to the clock hanging ominously over the sinks.

Mama smoothed our hair and made final adjustments on make-up, sticking whatever brush she wasn't using—make-up or hairbrush—handle-first into her mouth, like one of Mrs. Carpentier's cigarettes.

Mrs. Sampson made several more trips upstairs, finally returning at 5:55. "Girls, line up in platform order, starting with Mabel. Mothers, we've set up chairs for you beside the stage, where you can see everything and help your daughters between events." She bent down. "Aggie, Catherine, you've been quite helpful. Thank you for your assistance."

"Good girls," Mama said. "Give your sister a kiss and wish her luck."

Lynnette swooped Catherine into the air, flew her close to deposit a kiss and glided her to the floor. Then she squatted to look Aggie in the eye. "You're my right-hand girl. You know that, don't you?" Aggie squeezed her arms around Lynnette and clung to her until Lynnette stood.

Mrs. Sampson tapped her wristwatch. "Time."

We followed her like ducklings. From the shadow of the stage, I could see Mr. Cullowee standing behind the podium in a tuxedo. We huddled at the foot of the stairs, waiting to be called.

"Miss Mabel Moore," Mr. Cullowee announced from the stage. Mabel ascended the steps with poise and crossed to the far end of the platform. "Miss Ann Marie Walker." "Miss Alice Tomlinson." "Miss Glynis Carpentier." "Miss Lynnette Johnson." With one foot on the steps I looked back. Mrs. Sampson was seating the nervous mothers. She held a palm flat, facing upward, while she walked two fingers of the other hand across it. *Slowly*, she mouthed.

"Miss Mathilda Lee Watson."

I strode onto the stage, placing each foot directly in front of the other on my invisible tightrope, my smile locked in place.

Stepping onto the platform, I pivoted as Mrs. Sampson had taught us, "As if you're on a lazy Susan. A single axis point. Turn right. Turn left. Bend the knee in front, very slightly." I stood beside Lynnette, resisting the urge to grab her hand and squeeze it. We were finally here.

The stage lights glared so brightly that everything beyond the first row looked dark, but the gym felt packed with people, as if the whole county had decided to show up. I took a deep breath and renewed my smile.

"Ladies and gentlemen," Mr. Cullowee's voice boomed through the loudspeaker. "I'd like to welcome you to the First Annual Kudzu Queen Pageant of Cooper County. We celebrate the dawning of a new era in Cooper County, North Carolina. Never before has such an event been held in your fair county."

I wondered how many people knew that wasn't strictly true.

"Before you stands a bevy of Cooper County beauties, the loveliest North Carolina has to offer, possibly the loveliest you'll find anywhere in the world."

Had he said the same thing at the beginning of Rose's pageant?

"Each of these young ladies is exceptional in her own right, but only one will be chosen tonight to represent you as Cooper County's Kudzu Queen." He gazed at us one by one, as if leading the audience in a hymn of silent contemplation at the wonder of us. "Please give these beautiful young ladies a round of applause."

The clapping and foot stomping sounded like summer thunder.

"Before we begin," Mr. Cullowee said, "I'd like to introduce a special guest who's come all the way from Atlanta, Georgia, to join us this evening. Ladies and gentlemen, Mr. Channing Cope of the *Atlanta Constitution* and WSB-AM radio, the 'Father of Kudzu.'"

A spotlight manned by a freshman from the drama club swung unsteadily to the front row, where a portly man in a seersucker suit bowed to the crowd's applause.

"Mr. Cope has done more than any man alive to promote this amazing plant he and I call the 'Miracle Vine.' He has generously agreed to serve as one of our three judges tonight. Serving with him will be two fine ladies from our own community, Mrs. Morris Davenport, whom you all know as the wife of Reverend Davenport, minister of the First Baptist Church, and Miss Noreen DeWitt, owner of Dewitt's Elegant Ladieswear." The two women also stood, each giving a nod of acknowledgment. "I don't envy our judges," Mr. Cullowee said. "They have an impossible task ahead of them this evening."

"And now, the order of events." He held up a program. "First, the introductions. As you can tell, we've gotten ahead of ourselves, since we've already taken care of that." He paused to let the laughter subside. "And many of you know these delightful young ladies already."

"Go, Mattie!" I heard Joey yell. I blushed, hoping Danny had finally reappeared, and was currently clamping a hand over Joey's mouth, but I was pleased just the same.

"I see that you do," Mr. Cullowee said. "Now these girls are more than pretty faces. So in our interview portion, I'll ask each one a specially selected question so we can get to know them. We'll follow that with the talent competition, when the contestants will entertain us with their special skills. They've been honing their talents in secret, so I'll be as surprised as you are."

My face was starting to cramp with smiling. The back of my right knee itched as sweat trickled underneath my stocking. Thou shalt not scratch, I commanded myself.

"After the talent competition, we'll have a brief musical interlude from the Cooper County Consolidated High School Jazz Band," he gestured to the left of the stage, "to allow our young ladies to reappear, resplendent in their evening gowns, each one custom-designed by the Cooper County Kudzu Queen Sewing Circle. Ladies of the circle, could you please rise, so we can applaud your fine work?" The mothers stepped out awkwardly into the spill of stage lights. I heard a rustle in the audience as the other ladies stood. "We'll have another brief musical interlude as the judges make their final decisions. And finally, the moment we're all waiting for, the crowning of the first Kudzu Queen of Cooper County.

"And now, the interviews! Ladies and gentlemen, your first contestant, Miss Mabel Moore." She stepped down from the platform, meeting Mr. Cullowee in the center of the stage. "Mabel." He wrapped an arm around her. "It takes courage to be first, doesn't it?"

From my end of the platform, I could see the front row faces without shifting my fixed smile. I could also see the judges as they jotted on their notepads.

Mabel smiled up at him. "I don't mind, if it makes it easier for the other girls."

"You're off to a fine start, Mabel," he said, "and we haven't even gotten to your question. So, not to hold you in suspense any longer, here it is: Miss Mabel Moore, if you had the power to change one thing in the world, what would it be?"

Mabel tilted her head and looked toward the rafters, as if her answer could be found in the lower reaches of heaven, before returning her gaze to Mr. Cullowee. "Thank you, Mr. Cullowee. I appreciate you giving me the opportunity to answer such an important question."

Repeat the question in your answer, I urged Mabel silently, but she didn't need coaching.

"Mrs. Davenport, Miss DeWitt, Mr. Cope, and Mr. Cullowee, if I could change one thing in the world, I would eliminate cruelty. If everyone thought about what their unkindness felt like to another person, they wouldn't do it."

She raised her eyes above the audience she couldn't see. "I don't believe people want to be mean. They just learn bad things growing up. If those people in Germany and Japan really considered what they were doing, if they could actually see the person they were about to kill, I don't think they'd be able to do it. So, if I could change one thing in the world, I'd have people remember their natural goodness."

I was so proud of Mabel: gracious, graceful, and good, she truly was the best of us all.

"Thank you, Miss Moore," said Mr. Cullowee. "We'll all take your answer to heart."

Mabel returned to her place on the platform, looking stunned. She seemed surprised that she'd chosen to speak with such fervor in front of hundreds of people.

"Miss Ann Marie Walker," Mr. Cullowee called. "Would you care to join me?"

Ann Marie walked stiffly to the microphone. I didn't like her any more than I had, but I began to hope she'd win some sort of consolation prize.

"Ann Marie," he began, his arm around her shoulders. "Like so many girls, I'm sure you know the value of friendship. So our question for you is: What do you look for in a friend?"

Ann Marie gaped at the audience. She couldn't possibly have been stuck with a worse question. I wondered if Glynis had secretly had a hand in picking them.

"Miss Walker?" Mr. Cullowee prompted.

"A f-friend?" She crumpled in on herself, but then her gaze flicked over to Glynis and she straightened her spine. "A friend," she said again, this time as a statement. "Well, I think a friend should be loyal. She shouldn't suddenly decide to be friends with some other girl who hardly matters to anyone anyway. And she definitely shouldn't abandon you for someone who used to be yours and her worst enemy." She glared at me so viciously I rocked back on my heels.

I snuck a glance at Glynis, who smiled at the audience as if she got a bonus for every tooth she exposed.

"And finally, a real friend, if she promised to loan you a dress, would do what she said she would instead of telling you she couldn't find it."

I waited for a "So, there!" but instead she just stood, biting her lip. After a stunned silence, the audience broke into weak applause.

"I see," Mr. Cullowee said slowly. "Thank you, Ann Marie, for your heartfelt response." Breathing hard, Ann Marie fled to stand beside Mabel. "And our next lovely young lady," Mr. Cullowee announced, "Miss Alice Tomlinson."

Alice stepped down to the main part of the stage, her tap shoes echoing in the silence. Her mother, afraid Alice wouldn't have time to change shoes between the interview and talent portions of the pageant, had insisted that she wear her tap shoes the whole competition until the evening gown finale. "No one will hear you," she'd insisted as Alice reluctantly buckled on the white patent leather shoes in the locker room. "Every time you walk on stage, people will be clapping." But in her concern over Alice's costume change, she'd neglected to think about the moment Alice would be walking across the stage alone to meet Mr. Cullowee at the microphone, her face flushing like sunrise as each step sounded like a shotgun blast.

"Well, Alice, you'd best not try sneaking up on anyone in those shoes!" Mr. Cullowee might have said it to put her at ease, but she flushed so red I was afraid she might pass out. She stood at the microphone beside him, almost as tall as he was, in her tap shoes and little girl dress. The wings of her shoulder blades lurched as she attempted to get herself under control. Mr. Cullowee didn't seem to notice the fact that she was trying not to cry.

"So, Alice, your question is: If you had a magic wand, what would you wish for?"

I suspected she wished she could disappear, but she answered abruptly, "To be short."

Mr. Cullowee looked nonplussed. Clearly the interviews were not going as he'd planned.

Before he could make another joke, she spilled out with, "Everybody likes short girls. They think they're cute and pretty and sweet. They don't make fun of them, or ask if they're boys or where they got those rowboats on their feet."

My heart ached for her. From the way everyone was answering, you'd have thought some sort of truth serum had been poured into the microphone. As soon as a girl got close to it, she forgot everything Mrs. Sampson had taught her and answered with her most deeply held secrets. You'd never have known that we'd devoted an entire Kudzu Queen lesson to The Interview.

"If I was short, everybody would think I was p-p-pretty," Alice wailed and dashed off the stage past the mothers, her shoes rat-a-tat-tatting like a brigade of soldiers. By now, the judges were probably feeling the same sort of despair Alice was, redeemed only by the thin thread of light offered thus far by Mabel.

Next up was Glynis, who sauntered to the microphone, the slit in her dress parting at each step to reveal a black rayon slip. "Miss Glynis Carpentier," Mr. Cullowee said belatedly.

"Yes?" she breathed. Her husky voice, too close to the microphone, filled the room.

Mr. Cullowee kept his hands at his sides. I didn't blame him. Glynis might be contagious. One person clapped briefly. Not her mother, I figured, who was probably filing her nails or fishing in her handbag for a small flask.

"Miss Carpentier, if you are selected to be Cooper County's first Kudzu Queen tonight, how will you use your title to benefit others?" If the question had been a baseball pitch, Danny and Joey would have called it a meatball, so easy anyone could hit it out of the ballpark.

Glynis nodded modestly. "Mr. Cullowee, I'm so glad you asked me that." She held the microphone in both hands and gazed at the crowd with utter false sincerity. "If I'm lucky enough to represent Cooper County as your Kudzu Queen, I promise to devote my time to ensuring that the entire United States of America hears about the advanced kudzu farming techniques practiced right here in Cooper County." For a girl who wouldn't have recognized a kudzu vine if she tripped over one, this was saying something, but she wasn't done.

"I know," she lowered her voice, "you'll probably think it's beyond the capacities of one young woman, but if I am able to serve as your queen, I will devote every spare minute to wiping out poverty and hunger in the United States and abroad."

That's one way to gild a lily, I thought.

"Thank you," she breathed, as applause swept over her. She resumed her place, illuminated by the glow of the crowd.

"Miss Lynnette Johnson." The clapping started from where I'd heard Joey yell out, and spread through the gym, slowly at first, then faster and faster. Three weeks earlier, no one had known who Lynnette was. But since the fire and her family's tragedies, her name had traveled through the county as a good girl who deserved better than she'd gotten.

She gave me a look that said: *Do I really have to do this?*

I gave her a nod that said: *Yes, but I promise it'll be all right.* The more you know a person, the less you have to say things out loud.

Gingerly, she stepped onto the stage, testing each step for balance. As little practice as I'd had in high heels, she'd had less.

"Lynnette," Mr. Cullowee said gently. "We would all like to know—if you don't mind telling us—who is your role model?"

Good, I thought. Not, "Where would you rather be?" or "What one thing would you change if you could go back in time?"

After Glynis, the audience was primed for something earnest, breathy, and insincere, but instead Lynnette muttered, "Role model, role model," and looked at the floor.

We'd talked about this question, and agreed that if we got it, we'd say Eleanor Roosevelt. Please don't let her freeze up, I prayed.

"Could you move closer to the microphone, Lynnette?" Mr. Cullowee asked. "Everyone wants to hear you."

Startled, Lynnette looked up and took a small step forward. I glanced down to my right. In the wash of stage lights, I saw Mama at the foot of the stairs, holding Catherine and clutching Aggie's hand. Aggie seemed to be in Aggieland. I wondered if she was nervous for Lynnette.

"My role model," Lynnette muttered again. She looked up at Mr. Cullowee. "May I have two?"

He laughed, probably relieved she'd done anything besides mutter.

"Absolutely. As many as you want."

She took a long, shuddering breath and gazed into the darkness. "I'd like to say I admire someone famous like Mrs. Eleanor Roosevelt, and of course I do." Her quiet voice boomed out. "But the person I admire more than anyone else is a lady named Mrs. Lydia Watson."

I couldn't help it. I looked off the stage at my mother, who was shaking her head rapidly. This wasn't what we'd practiced.

But Lynnette went on, her hands relaxed at her sides. "I've never known anyone like her. She's funny." Lynnette smiled to herself. "She can make you laugh even when you think nothing will ever be funny or happy again. She takes care of everything: her children, her husband, her garden, the cooking, the house. Those are things you'd expect a mother and a wife to do. But when my sisters and I lost our parents—" I was proud of her for being able to say "lost" so simply when surely thinking of her mother or father must stir up a blinding dust storm inside her.

"When we lost our parents, she and her family took us in. I know you're probably thinking, what neighbor wouldn't? Well, I'll tell you, a lot of people wouldn't. But it was more than that. She made us feel like family. My sisters and I, we'd never felt like a family before. I mean, my mother, she was—" She swallowed, looked over the heads of the invisible audience.

Then she spoke again. "She was as good as she could possibly be. But Mrs. Watson, she has a way of making you feel taken care of, all the time, like you don't have to do anything—well, except your chores, and she's pretty strict about that."

We all laughed, relieved to be released from such seriousness for a moment.

"But you don't have to do anything special for her to take care of you. She doesn't fuss—well, not too much—" Lynnette smiled. "And she's a wonderful cook, though—sorry, Mrs. Watson—she's a terrible seamstress—" more laughter. I looked at Mama, who was laughing as tears ran down her face.

"But she did this dress for me." Lynnette did a twirl and everyone clapped. "And I think you'll agree she did a good job, despite a little bit of, well, I wouldn't call it cursing, but she did use some pretty strong language. But it's more than that, more than taking us in and cooking and sewing. It's even more than the way she makes everything look easy, like it doesn't cost her anything to be good and kind and keep everything going. It's the way she sees you. She's one of the most honest people I've ever met, but at the same time, she sees you as being about fifteen percent better than you see yourself. Because she's so honest, you have to believe it, and because she sees you that way, you have to become it."

She stopped, and the audience was still for a moment. Then the applause burst out of them, making their clapping for Glynis seem like a drizzle before a thunderstorm.

Mr. Cullowee wrapped his arm around Lynnette and pulled her toward him, rocking her onto one foot. "Thank you for that. That was lovely. Wasn't that lovely, everyone?"

Lynnette squared herself on both feet again. "Thank you," she said, "but I'm not finished. I need to tell you about my other role model now."

Mr. Cullowee looked disconcerted. Lynnette's speech had already been three times as long as anyone else's. Maybe he'd forgotten what she said at the beginning. Don't mess it up, I thought. That was perfect. Don't talk about Mrs. Roosevelt now. The audience began clapping again, a scattering that resolved into a steady rhythm.

With a fixed smile, Mr. Cullowee stepped aside. "Please continue, Miss Johnson."

"Thank you," she said. She spoke to the audience. "And thank you for being patient with me. I know I've gone on a bit."

Somebody called out. "Keep going, Lynnette!" I hoped it was Bobby Mason.

"Thank you. I'll try not to keep you here all night." She smoothed her skirt and took a breath so deep I imagined the air being forced into her alveoli. "My second role model—and I admire her so much it's practically a tie—is my best friend, Mattie Lee Watson."

Oh Lord, I thought. Bad idea.

"I've known Mattie since seventh grade Home Ec class, when I'd just moved here. Some of you may not know this, but girls can be mean. If you're the new girl in school, they can make you feel like you're not in the room, or like you're taking up too much air. But Mattie's not like that. She's never been. She can be bossy—" Lynnette paused. Ever a quick study, she'd learned since she'd gotten up to the microphone that she could make people laugh and it was worth waiting until they'd finished. "And stubborn—" another pause for laughter, "and she can make a chicken madder than anyone I've ever seen." This time she had to wait longer. Had she really told the entire county about me and the chickens? "But she is never, ever mean." She paused again, not for laughter, but until it sank in. "She's brave and smart and kind. She's very kind. If you need her, but you don't know you do, or if you're pushing everybody away, she'll just wait until you're ready." She had the audience with her, in a way Glynis never had.

"She is, if you haven't figured it out, Mrs. Watson's daughter. And Mattie's that honest too, at least mostly. Well, anyway, she never lies about anything important." The laughter took her off guard. She hadn't intended to be funny. She'd just succumbed to her own honesty. "So I want to say, that if I could be anyone in the world, I'd be a combination of Mattie Watson and her mother, and every day I try to be as much like them as I can." She looked at the judges. "Thank you for giving me this question and letting me answer it." She turned to Mr. Cullowee. "And thank you, Mr. Cullowee, for letting me go on so long. I kind of had to. I'm only here because Mattie and her mother wanted to distract me, so I'd have something else to think about since things have been hard lately. But I'm glad I got the chance to say what I did, and I appreciate you all listening."

When people clapped this time, it wasn't a thundering ovation. There was a gentleness to it, like a quiet stream, the kind that flows even in times of drought. I rubbed the damp from my eyes, then quickly checked my fingers to make sure I hadn't smeared my mascara.

Looking up at the microphone, I saw an empty spot where Lynnette had been standing. "Mattie, it's you now," she whispered as she stepped up beside me.

I wished I could find the right words, but anything I could say seemed too small, so I squeezed her hand.

She squeezed back and gave me a gentle push. "Go on."

The floor seemed springier than before, as if the stage bounced me up at every step, and my smile felt like one of Mama's sunflowers opening up. I squinted through the lights to the audience, praying Danny had arrived. I didn't want him to miss this.

Mr. Cullowee could have asked any of the questions we'd dreaded, like "What are your weaknesses?" or "How do you see yourself in fifty years?" and I would have answered. But instead, he asked a question that wasn't on our list. "Mattie, if I looked you up in the dictionary, what definition would I find?"

If you don't have a chance to prepare, there's nothing you can do but say what comes into your head. Fortunately, I had a lifetime of experience with that.

He started to put his arm around me, but I stepped away. His arm, thick and heavy across my shoulders, was more than I could stand right then.

He blinked, and took a step back. Sometimes you don't have to know a person for years to get a point across without words.

"Thank you, Lynnette, for saying what you did," I said into the microphone. "I'd like to believe some of those things are true, at least on my better days." I smoothed out my dress and looked straight at the invisible audience.

"I think if you looked me up in the dictionary, it would say I was 'a compass.' There's this thing called 'true north,'" I said. "No matter where you are, it stays north. It's absolute, and can't be affected by what anyone thinks or does. I don't have that.

"But a compass knows where north is and all the other directions too. It can point you where you need to go, though you have to do the walking yourself. A compass isn't perfect. Sometimes it gets stuck, and you have to shake it to get it on track again." I felt people smiling in the dark. "And if you put a strong magnet next to a compass, the needle is attracted to it, and you have no idea what direction to go. I've been like that sometimes, losing my direction because of some attraction, and I'm not always proud to remember how I acted. But when the magnet's moved away, the compass goes back to reading right, and that's probably me too." I could almost hear Mrs. Sampson's voice in my ear. *Elders and betters, Mattie.*

"Thank you, Mrs. Davenport, Miss DeWitt, and Mr. Cope," I said. I held out my hand to the Kudzu King. "And thank you, Mr. Cullowee." He looked taken aback for a moment, but he recovered quickly and shook my hand. I resisted the urge to wipe it on my dress.

The band played, "They Can't Take That Away from Me," as we left the stage to prepare for the talent portion. Mrs. Sampson met us at the foot of the steps, murmuring, "Good job!" to each of us as we passed. I thought that was nice of her, especially considering how things had gone for Alice and Ann Marie. Then Mama was sweeping Lynnette and me into her arms. She kissed the top of Lynnette's head. "Thank you."

Mrs. Sampson wrangled us into our seats, mothers whispering congratulations and advice from behind. Ann Marie's mother kept leaning forward as if to say something, thinking better of it and leaning back. Alice's mother sat primly, her face frozen in an expression that seemed to say: *I am thinking absolutely nothing*. Alice sat the same way, except for the nervous tapping of her feet, as if she were rehearsing her routine in her seat. As the music wound down, Lynnette gently laid a hand on Alice's leg and pointed to her feet.

"Thank you," Mr. Cullowee crooned. "The Cooper County Consolidated High School Jazz Band, ladies and gentlemen. Aren't they wonderful?" How did he always know the exact amount of time to wait before speaking? "And now, for your edification and delight, the talent portion of our evening. I'm sure you've been looking forward to this moment. I know I have." He gestured as Mabel climbed the stairs. "First off, we have Miss Mabel Moore, singing 'America the Beautiful,' by Miss Katherine Lee Bates, music by Mr. Samuel A. Ward. She'll be accompanied on the piano by our band director, Mr. Rigoli."

Mabel sounded like a phonograph record, every note perfect, echoing through the gym. I hadn't known there were four verses of that song, but I didn't want her to stop. The audience loved it, which made me glad for her. Things would be a lot simpler if someone else won, and it made sense for it to be Mabel.

Ann Marie recited "The Boy Stood on the Burning Deck," her face rigidly set, as if she were the boy in question.

"It Don't Mean A Thing If It Ain't Got That Swing," piped through the loudspeakers as soon as Alice got positioned in the center of the stage. Fortunately for her, tap dancing didn't require her to speak a word. I wished she could have looked more natural, though. She could have given lessons to a metronome, but her face was frozen in a grimace that appeared in danger of cracking. I hoped it looked better from the audience.

When Glynis got called to the stage, her mother handed her a basket. She opened the lid a crack and cooed inside, then slung it over her arm and pranced up the stairs to the center of the stage, swinging her basket gaily.

"My talent isn't really *my* talent," she said in a little girl voice that made my teeth grind. Her dress rose up her legs as she squatted to set the basket at her feet. "It's Mr. Bubbles' talent. Right, Mr. Bubbles?" On cue, the lid opened and out popped the head of her rat-like dog. She covered his sharp ears and confided to the audience, "Though I did help train him."

Standing up, she snapped her fingers. "Come on, Mr. Bubbles. Let's show these nice people how smart you are." The dog leapt out of the basket, all three and a half pounds of him, and pranced around the stage, looking disturbingly like his mistress. "Mr. Bubbles?"

He paused and cocked an ear.

"Sit." The dog sat. Glynis took a treat from a red satin bag hanging on her wrist, which Mr. Bubbles snapped up with his tiny sharp teeth. The audience clapped politely, but with a minimum of warmth. Who hadn't taught a dog to sit?

"Mr. Bubbles, jump!" She held up a second treat and the dog leapt for it.

"Mr. Bubbles, take a nap." He rolled over on his back, sticking all four feet straight into the air. She might call it taking a nap, but it was nothing more than playing dead. When he jumped up again, she stroked his silky hair lavishly. "Good boy, Mr. Bubbles."

"Mr. Bubbles, sing," she commanded. The dog rose on his hind legs and began a terrifying keening. All of a sudden, blessed mercy, the dog stopped, and his ears went up. He started sniffing and took a massive leap, soaring off the front of the stage and into the judges' box. Mrs. Davenport screamed, Miss DeWitt and Mr. Cope jumped up, and the floor in front of them exploded in a snarl of yapping and hissing.

"Get that mongrel out of here!" Mrs. Davenport yelled, but it was too late. Mr. Bubbles had taken care of that himself, streaking through the gym after what I was pretty sure was Mrs. Davenport's cat at a speed that left fallen chairs, screaming women, laughing children, and cursing men in their wake, and a toppled and screeching Mrs. Davenport trying to right herself while hollering words people don't expect from a preacher's wife.

"Mr. Bubbles!" Glynis wailed. She grabbed Mr. Cullowee's arm. "You have to save Mr. Bubbles!" She ran down the stairs on the far side of the stage, popping a button off her dress that she couldn't afford to lose, and toppling a trombone player and two clarinetists as she dashed through the band.

Anyone who thought that was the end of the Kudzu Queen Pageant was a poor judge of Mrs. Sampson's determination. She swooped across the stage, strode up the aisle, trapped Glynis with a tight arm around the shoulders and whispered a few words in her ear that made Glynis go white and shut up. I'd have given good money to hear what she said.

On her way back to the stage with Glynis under her arm, Mrs.

Sampson called out to two young men the size of chifferobes: the Reverend and Mrs. Davenport's grown twins, Mickey and Kenneth. They'd been holy terrors when Danny was a sophomore and they were seniors—"the preacher's terrible twos." Mrs. Sampson pointed them toward the trail of wreckage. "Find your mother's cat," she ordered.

Mr. Cullowee tapped the microphone with a soft thud. "Ladies and gentlemen."

The room quieted. Mrs. Davenport allowed Miss DeWitt to help her back into her seat, where she sat with her arms crossed over her powerful bosom.

Mr. Cullowee cleared his throat. "Well, that was quite an adventure. I suspect Noah had much the same problem on the ark." A few people chuckled. "Mrs. Davenport," he said soothingly, "we thank you for agreeing to continue. We'll make sure Fluffy is restored to you in perfect health as quickly as possible." Mrs. Davenport gave an austere nod to acknowledge she'd received the deference she was due.

"Let's just pick up where we left off, shall we?" he suggested, somewhat hopefully. "Please welcome Miss Lynnette Johnson to the stage."

When I'd asked her what she planned to do, she'd said, "It's only a little thing." Lynnette had many talents. But unless she'd brought the chickens from home, or planned to turn an ear of corn and a cup of goat milk into supper for a family of five, I was mystified.

Lynnette reached under her chair and pulled out her schoolbag. I hadn't seen it there in the shadows. She picked up her chair.

"Do you need help?" I asked.

She shook her head. "I've got it."

"Good luck," I whispered.

When she stepped onto the stage, Mr. Cullowee started toward her, reaching for the chair. "It's all right," she said. "It's not heavy."

Lynnette placed her chair in the center of the stage and hung her schoolbag on the back, then stepped to the microphone. "I don't have a lot of talents," she said. "I mean, I can't twirl a baton and I've never been much of a dancer and I can't recite any poems."

Aggie leaned against my mother, biting her thumbnail.

"But the one talent I do have is for reading my little sisters—Catherine and Aggie—to sleep. Catherine's going to turn three soon and Aggie's ten. She just finished fourth grade. If it's all right with you, I'd like to read you a story. It might calm us all down a little.

"Could you help me with the microphone?" Lynnette asked Mr. Cullowee. "I need to sit down to do this." Where had this Lynnette come from, the one who could keep secrets, and tell adults what to do? The one who thought my mother and I were the best people she'd ever known? The one who seemed to have had all the grief burned out of her? The one who now seemed exceedingly calm as she drew a familiar book from her schoolbag?

"This book isn't very big. So maybe you could all lean forward a little?" she began, resting the book in her lap. "If you're close, you'll probably be able to see the pictures, but if not, I hope I can tell the story in a way that will make the pictures for you."

Chairs scuffed as people dragged them closer. She held up the book.

"This is the story of Peter Rabbit." She rotated the cover in a wide arc from left to right. Aggie and Catherine crept from their chairs and sat on the floor, looking up at their sister.

"'Once upon a time there were four little Rabbits,'" she read, "'and their names were—Flopsy, Mopsy, Cotton-tail, and Peter.'" She put the book on her lap and confided, "Catherine's Flopsy, I'm Mopsy, and Aggie's Peter. There's only three of us, so we decided one of our goats would be Cotton-tail." I glanced at Aggie, who was nodding. Catherine leaned against Aggie's arm, her thumb in her mouth. Lynnette continued, "'They lived with their Mother in a sand-bank, underneath the root of a very big fir-tree.'"

She held the book so those closest could see the tree with the rabbits peeking out from under its roots. Mrs. Davenport leaned forward.

"'Now my dears,' said old Mrs. Rabbit one morning, 'you may go into the fields or down the lane, but don't go into Mr. McGregor's garden. Your Father had an accident there; he was put in a pie by Mrs. McGregor.'" I marveled that she was able to read it without choking after what she'd been through: a mother who'd tried to protect her babies, a father who'd had an accident. But her voice was steady as the Cooper River in autumn.

Over the course of the story, Catherine slid down until she lay curled up asleep on the floor, thumb in her mouth. Aggie sat stiffly, as if willing her spine to stay upright.

As Lynnette read, the quiet grew round and warm, like being snuggled under a pile of quilts while snow outside softened the world's usual sounds. She read the whole book, turning it around after each page to show the pictures. Miss Dewitt propped her elbows onto her knees and rested her face in her hands. Mrs. Davenport leaned back in her chair and closed her eyes. Mr. Cope looked around, as if interested in the effect Lynnette's talent had on the audience.

When Lynnette closed the book, there was a collective sigh. A few babies fussed, and there was a cough or two as people came back to themselves. It wasn't magic after all, just a fifteen-year-old girl reading a children's book to a gym full of farmers and store clerks, parents and sisters and brothers. But when the applause came, it felt like something that mattered, as warm and round as the silence Lynnette had invoked.

Lynnette stood and carried her chair, bag, and book off the stage. When Mr. Cullowee returned to the center and raised the microphone, he seemed subdued. "Thank you, Lynnette," he said. "What an unusual talent you have."

The audience applauded again, but quietly, tapping one hand against the other, as if they were afraid to wake the sleeping children in themselves. Lynnette gathered Catherine up, reaching down to pull Aggie to her feet. They slipped past me to their chairs, Aggie on the far side of Lynnette, leaning against her, while Catherine snuggled into her familiar position against Lynnette's chest, head resting on her big sister's shoulder.

I leaned over and touched her hand. "That was perfect," I whispered.

"Ladies and gentlemen," Mr. Cullowee announced, "our final contestant of the evening, Miss Mathilda Johnson."

When I climbed onto the stage with my own chair, I saw Joey and Carl carrying our kitchen table down the aisle and past the band. I appreciated Carl's help, but it was supposed to be Danny. I couldn't believe he'd let me down like that. The cardboard box and wooden crate on top slid as they climbed the stairs, but Carl caught them. Mr. Cullowee looked startled when Joey and Carl walked the table by him and plopped it in the center of the stage.

Then they were gone and I was alone with the table, the box, and the crate.

I slid the chair under the table, and walked to the microphone. The audience was still quiet after Lynnette's story. I cleared my throat, trying to settle my jumpy nerves.

"My talent," I began, "isn't exactly portable. In fact, it's about ten miles from here." This has to work, I thought. "Not many people know about this talent of mine. Even my parents are probably going to be surprised." A good surprise, I hoped. "I share this talent with my little brother Joey—you saw him a minute ago. He was the short one."

The audience laughed, which took care of some of the nerves.

"I almost asked him if he wanted to come up here instead of me, but he's the prettiest in the family and I didn't want the competition."

This brought another laugh. I wanted the audience on my side.

"You probably wonder what I have in this crate." I untwisted the wire on the crate and pried up the lid. "I'm guessing you've seen this before," I said, pulling out an armload of kudzu.

"But maybe you haven't seen it looking like this." I took in a deep breath and held it, hoping Joey had been able to get where he needed to be quickly enough and hadn't run into any technical problems. This was his cue. Sure enough, a light shone out of the darkness. I glanced at the wall behind me. Projected over my head was a view of Aunt Mary's land from the road, three feet deep in rich, rolling kudzu, climbing all the way up the porch pillars to the second story of her house.

"Joey and I planted this field of kudzu on April fifth, the day Mr. James T. Cullowee arrived in town, which may explain why our kudzu looks so good.

"You're all invited to visit my Aunt Mary's house, at 101 Parham Road, after the church picnics tomorrow, to see this magnificent kudzu with your own eyes. I've heard from several sources"—I didn't mention that two of them were my brothers—"that this is the finest crop of kudzu in Cooper County."

"Looks like your kudzu's trying to eat that house alive, miss!" a man in the front row yelled out, which brought a laugh.

"I'd like to take credit for how well our kudzu's grown." I was careful not to catch Mr. Cullowee's eye. This was neither the time to gloat nor to lose my nerve. "But the fact is, everything Mr. Cullowee told us about kudzu is true. Well, almost everything. As many of you have discovered, kudzu practically grows itself. Joey and I started with cuttings people left behind that first day Mr. Cullowee came to town. We watered and weeded it at the beginning, but we haven't done a thing in about a month and you can see how well it's grown. That's not us. That's kudzu. It's going to grow where it wants, when it wants, and how it wants. So I can't in all honesty claim that I have a talent for kudzu. Kudzu has a talent for growing itself. If I leave it on this table long enough, it's likely to take root, so I'm going to put it away, just in case."

Returning the kudzu, I braced my hands on each side of the crate—and could almost feel Mrs. Sampson wincing. "In a *dress*, Mathilda…a lady never…" I dropped them to my sides. "But since Mr. Cullowee's come to town, I've discovered that I do have a talent. For stubbornness, as you've heard. Also, I'm not as careful as I should be when it comes to taking chances. You may not think these are good qualities, and you probably don't think they add up to a talent, but let me explain." I closed the lid on the crate and twisted the wire shut.

"I'm stubborn when it comes to protecting the people I love.

I used to think, until recently, that the people I loved were my parents, and, most of the time, my brothers, Daniel Edward Watson and Joseph Jacob Watson. And my best friend, Lynnette Johnson, who spoke to you earlier. But lately I've come to realize I've got more people to protect than I thought."

I lifted the crate off the table and walked to the edge of the stage, where I bent down and handed it to the man who'd called out. "Here you go, sir. If you plant this, you should have all the kudzu you need in a few months. Just don't plant it too near your house." There was a small ripple of laughter.

I returned to the microphone. "So I think, when you add all those things together—stubbornness and trying to look out for other people and the willingness to take chances—what you get is a lawyer. And that is the talent I'd like to demonstrate for you this evening."

I lifted the microphone stand, which was heavier than I'd expected. Carefully, I carried it to the right of the table, and adjusted it to point between the chair and me. Then I said, "Mr. James T. Cullowee, may I invite you to sit down?"

He straightened behind the podium. "Me? Mathilda, this is your talent."

"Yes, it is," I agreed.

With an uneasy laugh, he walked across the stage and sat, placing his palms flat on the table. "You know, I've had some excellent pancakes at this table." He smiled.

I looked at the audience as if he hadn't spoken. Beyond the first row, everything was in darkness, but in the judges' box, Mrs. Davenport wore a sour expression. I heard her as clearly as if she'd spoken: *This evening has been a complete and utter fiasco.* Miss DeWitt tilted her head quizzically. Mr. Cope's eyebrows were raised. I had no idea what he might be thinking.

"Mr. Cullowee," I said, "if you would humor me for a moment, I'd like for us to play a game. I realize that this is not a court of law, but would you be willing to swear to tell the truth?"

He laughed again, more confidently now. "Mattie, you know I always tell the truth."

"Excellent. Then you won't mind swearing." I opened the box and pulled out our family Bible and a smaller one I'd been given in Sunday School, along with the gavel Carl had given me.

I stacked the Bibles on the table in front of him. "Could you please place your hand on these?" I asked.

Mr. Cullowee raised his eyebrows. "Two Bibles? Doesn't that seem excessive?"

"I know. It's sort of belt-and-suspenders, isn't it?" I agreed. "But I'm new at this, so I want to get it right."

I waited until he put his right hand on top of the Bibles, raising the other with a condescending smile that seemed to say to the audience: *I'll humor her if you will.*

"Mr. James T. Cullowee, do you promise to tell the truth, the whole truth and nothing but the truth?" I asked.

"I do," he said with mock solemnity.

"Thank you," I said, striking the table with the gavel for emphasis. "Mr. Cullowee, you have generously devoted your life to a noble calling: sharing your knowledge of kudzu. You've taught young men to grow it. You've created this opportunity for girls like me to better ourselves. You've traveled throughout the county helping farmers learn about this miraculous new crop."

"You're too kind, Mathilda," he protested.

"And you've done all this without charging anyone a penny," I said. "Completely out of the goodness of your heart."

He smiled out at the crowd, ready to launch into a speech. "Well, it's only possible to do this work with the help of families such as yours, the mayor and Mrs. Sampson, the Johnsons—all the families of Cooper County that have invited me into your homes and fed me. In fact—"

"In fact," I interrupted, "not only have you helped farmers plant a crop that will benefit themselves, their livestock, and their families, you've also made it possible for them to receive a government allotment of five dollars for every acre of kudzu they plant, have you not?"

I couldn't resist sneaking a look at Mr. Channing Cope, whose head had frozen in the middle of a nod.

Mr. Cullowee's eyes darted to each side of the stage. Unlike me, he managed to avoid looking at Mr. Cope. Then he smiled broadly. "Of course, that's just the start," he said. "I'm confident that once the federal government sees how well you're doing here in Cooper County, they'll want to offer an even more generous allotment per acre."

I smiled too. "Thank you, Mr. Cullowee. You are indeed a selfless man, and we're grateful to you. That will be all."

He looked confused. "You're done, then? That's your talent?"

"Oh no," I said, my face a picture of sincerity. "I mean that's all the questions I have for you, at the moment." I opened my eyes wide. "But I don't think I've shown enough of my talent yet for the judges to be able to assess me fairly, do you?"

He stood up abruptly. "Mattie, you have an interesting talent," he said firmly, "but I believe the judges are smarter than you give them credit for. I'm sure they've seen enough." He enlisted the audience. "We're anxious to get on to the next portion of the pageant, and see all these girls in their beautiful evening gowns, aren't we?"

Everyone was silent. I looked at the judges. "With your kind permission, I'd like to call the next witness."

Mrs. Davenport crossed her arms and tilted up her chin. The other two nodded slowly.

"Well, Mattie," Mr. Cullowee said. "It seems you're a hit. I'll just step off the stage until you're finished, to let you shine." He started toward the band.

"Oh no," I said, before he'd reached the stairs. "You need to stay, so you can hear the wonderful things people have to say about you. Mrs. Sampson, Carl Davis, could I prevail upon you to come up and keep Mr. Cullowee company while we sing his praises?"

Grimly, Mrs. Sampson climbed the stairs from the mothers' side. I wasn't sure whether her grimness was directed toward me for ruining her Kudzu Queen competition or toward Mr. Cullowee, but I couldn't stop to worry about that now. I needed help to keep James T. Cullowee where I wanted him, and figured between her steel will and Carl's biceps, I could just about do it.

Carl strode down the aisle and up the steps. He grinned as he took Mr. Cullowee's arm and guided him behind the podium. Either he was pleased at the task I'd set him or he found me amusing whether I intended to be or not. He and Mrs. Sampson stood on either side of the Kudzu King, who looked worried for the first time since I'd met him.

"I realize it's bit unusual to call a judge as a witness," I said, "but since all I'm doing is showing my talent in a beauty contest, I wonder if I might prevail upon Mr. Channing Cope to assist me in this endeavor. Mr. Cope, would you be willing to come to the stand—I mean the kitchen table—as my next witness?"

He stood up. Someone held the gold rope around the judges' box so he could duck under it and people edged back to let him pass. When he sat at the table, I gestured at the Bibles. "Would you mind? It's part of the whole, well, I guess you'd call it the whole performance."

"Not at all." His big voice boomed through the microphone. He placed his palm on the Bibles and repeated the familiar lines after me. Up close, he smelled of bay rum. His hair was Brillo gray and whiskers the same color prickled out of his chin. I guessed he hadn't had time to shave since taking the train up from Atlanta.

"Mr. Cope," I said, "would you say you're the world expert on kudzu?"

He smiled benevolently. "Not at all, Miss Watson. There are agricultural experts and scientists in many places who have a far greater familiarity with kudzu than I. In Japan, for instance, where they call it kuzu, they use it in many capacities with which we have yet to experiment. I'm simply what you might call a kudzu enthusiast."

I persisted. "But you will admit, will you not, that you have been a major force in promoting kudzu in this country through your newspaper columns and radio show?"

He tipped his head modestly. "I like to think I'm doing my part."

"You mentioned that kudzu has many uses. Could you share a few?" I asked.

"Well, I've seen the flowers used to make a fine jelly." Mr. Cullowee looked perceptibly more relaxed, while on either side of him Mrs. Sampson and Carl's faces were impassive. "You can make paper from it, and cloth. Of course it makes excellent fodder for livestock, full of vitamins." Mr. Cullowee nodded, comfortable now that we were back in familiar territory.

Mr. Cope continued. "And kudzu not only prevents erosion, it's even more effective at feeding nitrogen into the soil than your traditional clover or cowpea. In the future, we hope to start grinding the roots for flour, as they do in Japan, and exploring the many medicinal opportunities kudzu offers in the treatment of dysentery and fever. I'd say we're well on our way with kudzu, well on our way."

"Thank you very much, Mr. Cope." He started to stand. "If I could just ask you a few more questions?"

"Of course." He sat down again.

"Mr. Cope, you've spoken with a number of people in the government about kudzu, haven't you? People from the Department of Agriculture, for instance, which produced a pamphlet for farmers on the proper propagation of kudzu?"

"Yes, I have," he answered.

"Which would make you a reliable source, too, would it not?" I asked.

"As reliable as any," he agreed.

"In that case, could you tell us exactly what the federal government is paying farmers across the country to plant kudzu?"

I didn't have to turn to feel Mr. Cullowee stiffen up, and Carl move closer to him.

Mr. Cope gave me a measured look. "You don't really want to become the Kudzu Queen of Cooper County, do you, young lady?"

"With all my heart, sir," I said fervently, looking at him with the same steady gaze.

Years later, when Danny came back from the war, he told

me that there's a certain sound a grenade makes when the pin's pulled, before you throw it. It's so quiet that it's almost not a sound, just an innocuous click.

Mr. Cope scrutinized me a moment more, then spoke. "Eight dollars an acre."

The audience exploded.

I held up my hand, invoking the capacity I'd seen in Mr. Cullowee to still a crowd. I felt so powerful at that moment that I wasn't surprised when they quieted.

"That's eight dollars an acre from the start?" I asked. "For every acre planted? Not five dollars an acre at first, with the possibility that the amount might be increased later."

He shook his head. "Eight dollars an acre, for any acre, anywhere in the United States."

People began to jump up. The gym rumbled like a train was passing through the basement below us. Power was one thing, but inciting riot was another. Now that I'd started it, I didn't know if I could stop it. I felt a panic swell up inside me like the fire at the Johnsons' farm.

At my elbow I suddenly saw Mrs. Sampson. She stepped to the microphone.

"Sit down," she ordered. "Every one of you. This is a beauty pageant, not a lynching. I will not have it known that the people of Cooper County behaved like a mob." It was the exact tone of voice she'd used to browbeat us into behaving like young ladies. I shouldn't have been surprised that it worked, but I was relieved. "Mattie is far too responsible a girl to raise a ruckus without having a way to settle it. So sit down and listen to her. All of you. Right now."

People sat restlessly. Mrs. Sampson stepped aside, but not before giving me a glare that said: *If you don't have a way to solve this, you'd best think fast.*

"Um." I cleared my throat. "I'm sure you all know how many acres you planted with kudzu, right?"

"Nine!" someone called out. "Seventeen." "Forty-three!" "Eleven and a half."

"Good, then." I rapped my gavel on the table. "You can do the arithmetic as well as I can. I figure you should get every penny that's due to you."

"Damned right!" a man shouted.

I tapped the gavel more lightly against the table. "Except for the nickel you're going to have to put in the jar for cursing," I said, hoping for a laugh, which I got. "At least that's what my mama makes my daddy do.

"If you'll figure out how much more money you're owed before you leave this evening, I'm going to ask my brother Joey to stand by the front door and write down your names and the amounts due to you. Because I know Mr. Cullowee is going to make good on the government's promise, aren't you, Mr. Cullowee?"

"Yes, I will. Without a doubt," he said vehemently, before the dissatisfaction in the audience had a chance to swell again.

I noticed Carl wasn't beside him any more, and glanced around to find him standing at the top of the stage steps by the band, smiling and making a scooting gesture at a group of men who'd crowded halfway up. After a few moments, their rage subsided and they trudged back to their seats. Carl returned to the podium to stand by Mr. Cullowee, gripping his arm.

I looked to the right of the stage and saw Mama, with one arm wrapped around Lynnette and the other around Rose. Where had Rose come from? Had she snuck upstairs during the talent portion? Had she heard and seen everything? All three of them were watching me, along with Catherine in Lynnette's arms and Aggie who clung to her big sister like a limpet.

Mrs. Sampson was still beside me. I covered the microphone with my hand. "There's more," I whispered. "You know there's more." I looked at Rose and curled my fingers by my side in a "come here?" gesture. She shook her head and stood, wrapped in my mother's arm.

"She can't," Mrs. Sampson murmured. "It'll only turn on her."

"You?" I asked.

"You'll have to do it another way."

She touched my arm, gently, before walking down the stairs to stand by Rose.

I looked out at the crowd. Someone had brought up the gym lights, maybe to keep the crowd accountable. People will do things in the dark that they'd never dream of doing when others can see them. Every face was tilted up to see what I'd do next. I gripped the cold black metal of the microphone stand.

"Matts." From the back of the gym Danny called, striding down the aisle.

When I caught sight of Mr. Cullowee, I was surprised that he looked more uneasy, rather than less. Here was Danny, his own personal Tonto, riding to his rescue. I'd have expected him to dance a jig. Danny climbed the stage and stood beside me, ignoring Mr. Cullowee.

"Hey, Mattie." He put his hand on the Bibles. "Aren't you going to swear me in?"

I began my recitation, hoping that by the time he'd finished with "nothing but the truth," I'd have figured out what I was supposed to ask him.

It turned out Danny was taking charge of that too.

"Well," Danny drawled, his even pace at odds with the glitter in his eyes. "Anyone can make a mistake," he said, "and I'm sure that's what happened with Jim Cullowee. Not being a journalist, like Mr. Cope, maybe he didn't deal with the most reliable person in the federal government. Maybe he was working with a bureaucrat who didn't have the best interests of farmers at heart, and Jim Cullowee, being the good soul he is, trusted in that man's honesty."

This seemed to me to be stretching it, but I was willing to do whatever it took to ensure no eyes got taken for other eyes in this proceeding.

Danny went on, "But there are some mistakes you can't make."

The audience seemed unsettled, restless.

"Mattie, I'd like you to call Miss Agatha Johnson to the table."

I stared at him. "Aggie?"

He walked toward the side of the stage where Mama stood below with the girls. As he passed me, he said quietly, "This could get bad."

"Where've you been?" I whispered.

"Driving. Trying to figure out what to do."

"Lynnette?" he called softly down the stairs, "could you persuade Miss Agatha to come up here with me? I promise I'll look after her."

Hand in hand, Lynnette and Aggie walked up the stairs. At the top, Lynnette transferred Aggie's hand to Danny. All the way across the stage, Aggie stared up at him. All the way, Danny held her gaze, as if to protect her from having to look at anyone or anything that might scare her.

When they got to the table, Danny crouched beside her. I heard him, but the audience couldn't. "You know what this is about, don't you, Aggs?"

She nodded.

"Can you help me tell about it?" he asked.

She nodded again.

"I'm going to stand you up on this chair," he told her, "so people can hear you."

Mr. Cullowee twisted in Carl's grasp, his eyes darting everywhere.

Aggie put her hands on Danny's shoulders. He lifted her by the waist and swung her into the chair. Her left hand stayed on his shoulder.

I looked from one to the other. "Aggie, I think Danny believes you have something to tell us, something we should know. Is that true?"

Her bottom teeth emerged slightly as she chewed her top lip from below. She looked at Danny. He gave her a decisive nod. She touched her arm, where I'd seen the bruise earlier, and gave me a smaller, more tentative version of Danny's nod.

"Did someone do something to you, Aggie?" Danny asked.

Aggie's hand snuck up to her mouth, and she began chewing on a ragged thumbnail. She opened her mouth just wide enough for a word to slip out, but she was close enough that the microphone picked it up and bestowed it on the crowd. "Yes."

Aggie's hand curled on Danny's shoulder, gripping like a claw, but he didn't flinch. She looked past Danny to where the Kudzu King stood, with Carl's big hand wrapped around his upper arm. She removed her thumbnail from her mouth and pointed directly at Mr. Cullowee. "Him," she said. "That man."

I stared at Danny, panicked. Where would he go next? Surely he didn't want me to make Aggie stand up in front of the entire crowd and tell them whatever "that man" had done to her.

"Miss Agatha," he gave her a lopsided smile, "you did great." He swung her to the ground. "You get Lynnette to take you out to my truck in the parking lot. I'm thinking there may be a spare Hershey bar sitting in my glove box with your name on it."

Lynnette was up the stairs and halfway across the stage when Aggie ran blindly into her. Lynnette swept her into her arms, staggering as she tried to carry her offstage and smooth her hair at the same time. "You're good, Aggie," she cried. "You're good, you're fine, I've got you now." They disappeared through the side door.

The room was so quiet everyone heard the door close behind them. Danny spoke into the silence. "I found them early this morning on what used to be the Johnsons' farm." The temperature in his voice dropped. "That man," he echoed Aggie's words, "was doing things no grown man has a right to do to a little girl."

The gym rumbled with the sounds of angry voices and chairs shoved back as people rose to their feet. It felt as if the entire audience was about to close in on the stage.

"No," Danny said sharply over the noise. "Nothing happens tonight. It's enough that you know what he's done, some of what he's done." He flexed his right hand, as if it felt stiff, and looked at Mr. Cullowee, who stood hunched in on himself, staring at the floor. Carl's hands had dropped away, fists clenched, but the Kudzu King showed no signs of moving.

Danny pulled me to him, and put his arm around my shoulders. "Mattie saw who he was. She saw what he was long before

I did, though she was every bit as taken with him as the rest of us. She's raised the questions, but a jury's going to have to decide the answers."

From the audience, the preacher's burly sons emerged, as forbidding as prison guards. Mrs. Sampson must have given them the nod. They gripped the Kudzu King by the arms and escorted him up the aisle toward the back of the gym, where the sheriff waited. On the aisles, some recoiled from Mr. Cullowee, others spat at his feet. Further down the rows, people called out angry words and threw wadded-up programs in their wake, but no one, other than the Davenport twins, put a hand on him.

Just before they opened the heavy doors to take him outside, a figure dashed across the stage and stumbled up the aisle now littered with gobs of spit and balls of paper. It was Glynis.

"James!" she wailed, staggering after the group. The doors slammed behind them, as if the sea had swallowed them up.

Mrs. Sampson reappeared beside me. She tucked her arm in mine and walked me down the stairs. "You did well, Mattie," she said. "You did very well."

At the bottom of the steps Mama pulled me in tightly but said nothing. When she rested her chin on my head, I felt tears on my scalp, first warm and quickly cooling. Rose brushed her knuckles against the back of my hand. "Good enough, Mathilda," she said huskily. "That'll do."

# 24

No one had much heart for the contest after that. When the gym had cleared and most people had gone home, Mrs. Sampson quietly came over to me, sitting with my family, and handed me the tiara.

"I believe this belongs to you, Mathilda." The judges, she said, had asked her to give it to me. She placed her palm on my cheek. "You've earned it."

The next morning, Mama made pancakes with syrup, and chocolate milk for the girls, but Aggie spent most of the meal huddled by Lynnette. I thought about Rose. I wondered if he'd taken her spirit along with everything else.

After breakfast, Joey helped me tear down all the kudzu from the front of Aunt Mary's house, draping the vines in a limp heap over the rest of the field.

When I got home, Mama folded my pageant dress in mothballs and laid it in her hope chest. "When you get married," she said, "we'll add a veil."

There was some question in the days to come as to whether Lynnette and the girls should move to Aunt Mary's house. Daddy and Mama were ready to give it to them if they wanted it, but in the end, Lynnette decided they needed family, so when Danny went to college in the fall, they moved out of my room and into his. Aggie crept in from outdoors more often and began spending time with Mama in the kitchen.

Danny could have waited until he got drafted, but three weeks after Pearl Harbor, he and Carl went to the army induction station in Raleigh and enlisted. After training, they were sent first to England, later to Normandy, from where they fought their way across Europe for the next eleven months. Danny never spoke of it, but Carl told me they'd been in the second wave at Omaha. For months afterward he saw those beaches every time he closed his eyes.

Being Kudzu Queen meant I got invited to appear whenever there was a rally for the troops, sometimes as far away as Raleigh and Charlotte. But before the year was out, I abdicated my position and passed the crown to Alice, who was far more grateful to wear it than I'd ever been. It's awful hard to rally when you're holding your breath.

Danny came back whole on the outside, but prone to frequent fevers and chills. Carl came back sad, and in search of an easier kind of girl, the kind who would know how to smooth his forehead and cook him soup when he got the shakes. I wasn't surprised when he married Mabel. It seemed right.

Taylor Wagner was killed in Germany, and young Kurt Lockabee got shot down over Italy. As mean as Taylor had been, I felt bad for both their families. When you lose a son, maybe it doesn't matter how awful he was in life.

That morning after breakfast and chores, I went back to Aunt Mary's house by myself. I fished the key out from under my shirt and fit it in the door. The sitting room was a patchwork of warm sunlight and cool shadows. I ran my fingers over the entry table, leaving a trail in the dust. Upstairs, I peeked into the spare room. The furs and hats looked patchy, but regal. I picked up the sheets from the floor and laid them over the racks to protect what was left of Aunt Mary's ragged elegance. Then I went to her bedroom.

I climbed the mahogany step and sat on the side of the bed. I straightened the wrinkles on the counterpane. I waited.

"Are you here?" I asked the empty room.

When I went outside, Daddy was sitting on the top porch step. I sat beside him. "Looks like you've kept the place up pretty well," he said. "Never saw you as the sort to play house."

"Me neither," I said.

I looked over my shoulder at the front windows, which reflected the wan gold sunlight. I turned back to Daddy.

"She looked after me too," I told him.

"She could do that, sometimes," he said. "When a person really needed looking after. Always surprised me."

He surveyed the field in that way he had. He always saw exactly what was, instead of what he wanted it to be.

"Good crop," he said. The kudzu Joey and I had pulled down had nestled its way back into the field, indistinguishable from the vines beneath it. "You and Joey seem to have a knack."

"It's kudzu," I said. "It's going to grow whether you want it to or not."

"Let's keep it on this side of the woods, shall we? I don't want it getting any ideas about bullying my cotton."

The breeze picked up the top leaves of kudzu and waved them at us. "Daddy?" I asked.

"Mm-hmm?"

I pulled up my knees and leaned my chin on them. "What's going to happen to him?"

"Court, I expect. Prison probably."

"For the money or for Aggie?"

"Hard to tell. Maybe both. I'm guessing it'll be a while before they sort it all out."

"It was more than Aggie," I told him.

"I know," he said.

We looked out at the kudzu. It really was the prettiest plant.

He stood and reached for my hand. "Come on," he said. "Your mother will be wondering what's become of us."

# ACKNOWLEDGMENTS

I am grateful to all of my friends and family, who have supported me in writing this book. My deep thanks go out to Judy French and Genanne Walsh, who nurtured the book in its fledgling stages and encouraged me to keep going, and to Kate Giles and Alice Stees Mackenzie for their enthusiastic support and insights. All are brilliant readers and dear friends. I am grateful to my teachers and friends from Warren Wilson, whose voices I still hear as I write, all these years later. Thanks also to the amazing Writeaways community, for the wonderful conversations we've had about the craft of writing and the delight we've taken in each other's work. I'd like to thank my publicist Suzanne Williams for her inspired help in getting the word out about *The Kudzu Queen* and for loving this book as much as I do. And most importantly, I am deeply grateful to John Yewell, editor extraordinaire and companion of my heart. I couldn't have done this without you.